Dr. Nicklaus Hart Series

Maya Hope
The Tree of Life
The Rusted Scalpel
The Gene

Timothy Browne, MD

Please visit
AuthorTimothyBrowne.com
You can start the Dr. Nicklaus Hart Series with
Maya Hope for free by signing up to receive updates
and information on upcoming books by Tim

Follow Tim on Facebook
@authortimothybrowne

PRAISE FOR

THE GENE

"*The Gene is a masterful, thought-provoking blend of cutting-edge genetics, gut-wrenching history, and inspiring faith wrapped inside a smart thriller that will keep you turning the pages long past your bedtime.*"

Jenifer Ruff,
USA Today Best Selling Author

"*Genetic modification research is a relevant, current issue that raises serious ethical concerns, and Dr. Tim Browne deals with it in* The Gene *in an intriguing and fascinating way bringing insights into the story through his wealth of medical knowledge. What makes his thrillers stand out, though, is the very real way that his characters struggle with their humanity while wrestling with a crisis of faith, yet through their pain find peace and acceptance of God's grace which enable them to live life to the fullest. This speaks to us in a very personal way and makes this novel a thought provoking read.*"

Rev. Duane & Joan Huie,
Pastors, Livingston Montana

"*Beginning with the Nazi's monstrous human experimentation during WW2, Timothy Browne shapes historical fact into contemporary fiction. Grounded in genetic research,* The Gene *is a disturbingly believable yet irresistible page turner. Expect to hold your breath as Dr. Nicklaus Hart must try to keep an evil history from repeating itself.*"

Karen Sargent,
author *Waiting for Butterflies*, 2017 IAN Book of the Year

"The Gene *is a must read for any medical thriller fan—packed with suspense and full of fascinating current genetic medical science and in-depth historical research that is sure to make the New York Best Seller list."*

William J Brown, MD,
Brown Integrative Wellness

"The Gene, *another masterful medical thriller by Timothy Browne, MD, explores the dangers of genetic science and the oh-so human motives of those who fund it. This compelling page-turner is full of twists, turns, and ethical dilemmas that keep the reader guessing. Advances in genetics, like many other fields of science, can be used for good or evil. The Gene will haunt you. I read it non-stop."*

Joni M. Fisher,
author of the *Compass Crimes*

"Scientist and physician Tim Browne has brought us a complex story of the atrocities of World War II that includes details of unspeakable medical experiments, the science of eugenics, and nightmares of Nazi Germany. He has raised our awareness of issues that surround genetic mutation. Most of all, Dr. Browne has introduced us to the good and questionable elements of gene therapy, possibly one of the most powerful and potential slippery, controversial slopes in modern medicine. Should we mess with someone's DNA? Should we change who we were born to be? Decide for yourself in this masterful story of controversy and hope that stresses our faith, values and ethical limits of right and wrong."

Judith Lucci, PhD,
USA Today and WSJ Best selling author

TIMOTHY BROWNE

THE
GENE

A DR. NICKLAUS HART MEDICAL THRILLER

The Gene, *a medical thriller*
A Dr. Nicklaus Hart Novel, Book 4
by Timothy Browne, MD

First Edition © 2020

ISBN-13:   978-1-947545-19-9 (hb)
             978-1-947545-18-2 (pb)
             978-1-947545-17-5 (epub)

Cover Design and Art by Brett Pflugrath
Book interior, maps by Suzanne Parrott

Library of Congress Control Number: 2020935089

Printed and bound
in the United States of America.

*To: ALL who are weary, heavy laden, or oppressed.
May your tears of grief spout wisdom in our souls.*

*In Memorial: To the death camp victims and survivors.
We cannot forget. We must not forget.*

ACKNOWLEDGEMENTS

The Gene proved to be the toughest book to write because of the subject. However, it's such an important topic, I hope I've done it justice. I'm thankful for all the help I've received on this project.

While researching and writing *The Gene*, I spent many hours in conversation with other physicians, researchers, theologians, and everyday people. The common thread in all these discussions was the vibrant and deep debate of the theme of the story; should we as humans mess with DNA—the basic human code? (As Francis Collins describes in his book the *Language of God*—Dr. Collins was the head of the Human Genome Project and a leading scientist in the study of DNA.) I am thankful to all the people that contributed in ways that were invaluable.

To my story editor, Erin Healy, who helped find areas of the story that fell short. Your wisdom goes beyond words! Thank you for helping me become a better writer.

To my copy editor, Burney Garelick, who has the hardest job of all when she receives the raw manuscript. Thank you for loving my stories enough to make them readable. You always make me laugh!

To all that provided assistance, wisdom and support: Dennis, Dorcie, Joan and Duane, Joni, Karen, Bill, Jenifer, Joan, Audrey and Judith. Thank you for diving into the story and helping flush out areas that were not clear, but mostly for your encouragement to continue to write.

To Brett Pflugrath for the beautiful cover.

To Suzanne Fyhrie Parrott for the amazing artwork, design and your patience and guidance in publishing. You are a true friend and mentor.

I am so grateful to my readers. Without you, I could not continue to fuel my imagination with story. My hope is that these stories touch something deep within you.

To my family that means everything to me. To my boys, Timothy, Joshua and Jacob and their beautiful wives, Jamie, Sarah and Devlin. And to the growing number of grandchildren…my heart grows with each one! You all make the work worthwhile. To my wife, Julie…I love you—you have lived the adventure.

"For you created my inmost being;
you knit me together in my mother's womb.
I praise you because I am fearfully and wonderfully made;
your works are wonderful,
I know that full well.
My frame was not hidden from you
when I was made in the secret place,
when I was woven together in the depths of the earth.
Your eyes saw my unformed body;
all the days ordained for me were written in your book
before one of them came to be."

—Psalm 139:13-16

"There is nothing noble in being superior to your fellow man;
true nobility is being superior to your former self."

—Ernest Hemingway.

Norway
Finland
Estonia
Sweden
Latvia
Denmark
Lithuania
Baltic Sea
North Sea
Ciekocinko Palace Hotel
POLAND
Berlin
Belarus
Pozań
Warsaw
Germany
Prague
Auschwitz
Kraków
Chechia
Slovakia
Ukraine
Austria
Hungary
Romania
Italy
Serbia
Bulgaria
Tyrrhenian Sea
Greece

PROLOGUE

Yuri huddled under a woolen blanket with her sister, Eva, in the back seat of the black sedan. The windshield wipers strained against the pelting snow as frost collected in the corners of the windows, obscuring an unfamiliar landscape flashing by in the morning light. Yuri welcomed the wool's comfort, despite the pungent odor of mildew. She was warmer than she'd been in months. Three months, Yuri guessed. She could be mistaken, of course, as the trauma had numbed her mind.

Yuri closed her eyes and tried to force the terrifying images from her consciousness. Still, the visions replayed—the Nazi SS breaking down the door to their home in the dark of the night, shooting her mother and father when they protested, and dragging Yuri and Eva to the brickyards like animals.

Then the marching. The marching and the bitter cold. The bitter cold and the bone-jarring hunger. Her mind couldn't erase the shallow, vacant eyes of the dead along the road. Starvation or exposure had taken many of them, while others were executed for seemingly random and merciless reasons. Visions replayed of the elderly man with the kind eyes who'd handed them a thick wool coat, blessed them in Hebrew, and ran toward the trees only to be cut down by machine-gun fire from a nearby SS officer, and the grandmother who shared her moldy bread and a piece of sausage with them, only to collapse and die of starvation two days later.

Yuri couldn't banish the monsters haunting her nightmare—the young German soldiers who sneered and shot insults at the continuous line of her people, and the guards who laughed at their misery, as they forced the captive multitude forward with the butts of their guns and snarling dogs. Six weeks of endless trudging through the snow to Austria, stepping over the countless dead. Numb with cold and exhaustion, Yuri had no tears except when her unyielding consciousness projected images of her parents lying dead in their own blood. Only then did tears pry their way through her frozen psyche.

Papa. Mother. Their friends had tried to protect them, but someone had ratted them out.

Yuri's eyes snapped open to the harsh voices of the two Nazi SS soldiers in the front seat who argued over which road to take. The soldiers had driven all night after they'd pushed and shoved Yuri and Eva into the automobile without an explanation. Otherwise, their escorts had ignored them for the most part. The ranking soldier in the passenger seat chain-smoked, and his agitated speech slurred more and more as he took slug after slug from a silver flask.

The sisters had a rudimentary understanding of German, but through an unspoken mutual pact at the beginning of the journey, they chose to stay mute. They concluded the driver didn't appreciate heading into harm's way with two Jewish girls while the Russians advanced on the Eastern Front. Yuri had pieced together that their destination was Poland to meet a doctor in a work camp called Auschwitz. But it remained a mystery why the Germans had singled them out.

Yuri tightened her embrace around Eva's shoulder as her sister rested her head in the crook of Yuri's neck. Because they frequently sat together in this position with Eva on the left and Yuri on the right—probably the way they'd grown in utero eighteen years ago—their mother had often joked that they acted more like Siamese rather than the identical twins they were. Yuri, the protector, was younger only because their father believed she'd pushed Eva out of the birthing canal ahead of her.

Yuri winced at the pain in her groin. She had to urinate so badly; she couldn't hold it much longer—afraid to speak up, afraid to soil the car. It had been eight hours since the Nazis had stopped the sedan and forced the girls to squat and pee like dogs while they stood over them.

A train clattered on the tracks alongside the road. Yuri distracted herself by counting the cars—fifty, all identical, similar to the livestock trains that had passed near their home in Budapest. *It must be headed to a slaughterhouse.*

Through the veil of the snowstorm, she could make out a massive complex looming in front of them. The driver shot a glance at the girls in the rearview mirror as they approached an iron gate, and he slowed the sedan. Yuri ducked her head to read the inscription. ARBEIT MACHT FREI.

The drunken ranking soldier caught her gaze and read the sign aloud, *"Arbeit macht frei,"* he sneered and motioned as if working the ground with a hoe.

Work makes you free? Yuri had heard rumors of the work camps but still didn't understand why she and Eva had received such special treatment—placed into a warm automobile while soldiers crammed the rest of the Hungarian Jews into railcars.

The Nazis forced many Jewish women to make German uniforms, and although Yuri and Eva could sew, this effort made little sense to her.

The driver stopped at the gate and rolled down the window. A snow-covered guard leveled a machine gun at them. Icicles hung from his nostrils, and his breath froze in the wind as he demanded to see their papers.

The ranking soldier leaned toward the open window, voiced his displeasure at the delay, then motioned to the girls in the backseat. The guard ducked his head through the window, showering the driver with snow, then shined a flashlight in their faces, first Eva, then Yuri, and back again.

The guard's smile surprised Yuri as he ordered the gate arm raised, then barked instructions and the go-ahead. The driver rolled up his window, and Yuri adjusted the blanket around Eva's neck. A loud whistle cut through the blustery air as the train that paralleled the road pulled into the same complex—adding to the mystery Yuri was at a loss to solve.

Like a city, the camp expanded for miles in all directions, and the driver navigated around an endless number of two-story brick buildings along with a series of checkpoints. But unlike any other city, razor wire surrounded this one.

Men in blue-striped canvas clothes wandered in groups around the yards, straining under loads of lumber or pushing wheelbarrows full of bricks. *Yes, this must be a work camp.*

In another section of the complex, women in filthy gray dresses tied at the waist marched in formation—four abreast with hundreds in each line. The stomp of their wooden clogs resounded through the closed automobile windows even as they plodded through the snow that rapidly accumulated. The desperation draped across their faces sent a shiver up Yuri's spine, but their shaved heads were the strangest sight.

The sedan rounded a corner, and a terrible stench filled the car, assaulting Yuri's senses and making her gag. It reminded her of when she had accidentally caught Eva's hair on fire with a candle, but this smelled much more foul. Even the Nazis winced. When the ranking soldier reached to click off the heater, he turned, smiled, and nodded at her. Yuri looked away.

Up ahead, a brick building with a massive stack bellowed the putrid smoke that changed falling snow to a dirty gray. Yuri almost said something in German but caught herself and faked a cough. Eva's head burrowed deeper into her neck, and Yuri tightened her protective grip around her shoulder.

At the next checkpoint, the driver turned through an entry in the middle of an elongated structure. A watchtower sat over the entrance with two large machine guns pointed outward. The train had pulled perpendicular to the building, and to Yuri's horror, the guards unloaded people, not livestock. Their escorts also seemed surprised to see hundreds, if not thousands of human beings, get off the train. Yuri had many questions, but no one to ask. The guards were in an animated discussion.

She listened and understood their debate centered on how they would get past the mob to the German soldiers gathered at the far end of the rail yard. With train tracks on both sides of the road, they would have to walk through the crowd.

The driver placed the sedan in park, opened his door, and jumped from his seat. He flung open the rear door. "*Schnell, schnell*," he waved for them to exit the automobile. As they stepped outside, the man pulled the blanket off their shoulders and tossed it into the back seat. The frigid air was as shocking as the silent mass of people. Curt orders from the German guards, the incessant bark of ferocious dogs, and the raspy caw of three crows sitting on the top of the watchtower echoed off the buildings. Yuri looked up at the birds that tucked and bobbed in excitement over the arriving trains.

The ranking soldier stepped out of the car, lit a cigarette, and pulled the collar of his heavy overcoat around his neck. He surveyed the crowd and shrugged. Then, like the parting of the Red Sea, the mass of people split in two, men on the left, women and children on the right.

Their escorts shoved Yuri and Eva forward through the open pathway. But after they'd taken a few steps, a guard dog with fierce dripping fangs jumped in front of them, stopping them in their tracks with its bark and growl. Yuri turned Eva away as the shepherd snapped ferociously at her chest. A guard with a machine gun in one hand held the dog back with the other and ordered them to stop. Warmth ran down Yuri's legs as her bladder emptied.

The guard restrained the dog when the ranking soldier stepped forward and spoke. Since they'd arrived in the camp, Yuri had heard a name repeatedly throughout the checkpoints, Mengele. *Hauptsturmführer Mengele. Doktor Mengele.*

The guard pointed to the head of the line and restrained the dog to let them pass, but the animal continued to snarl and bite at the air, inches from Yuri. Even their escorts seemed intimidated, but this time they took the lead and motioned for the girls to follow them to the front of the line.

Yuri looked from side to side. She was shocked to see so many people, garbed in their everyday clothes, men in suits, women in dresses: grandfathers, grandmothers, fathers, mothers, and children of all ages. Some shot Yuri and her sister scornful glances as though they had cut in line at the movies. She couldn't help but notice that they all had one thing in common—a Star of David pinned to their chests. They were all Jews. Jews whose pride, along with their clothes, hung dejectedly on their hollow frames.

A gunshot rang out to her left, and she jumped. A soldier pointed the smoking end of a pistol at a man who'd tumbled into the snow. Crimson blood instantly pooled by the victim's head as two men in striped suits ran to the body, picked it up, and carried the corpse away. Yuri wondered what crime he had committed.

As their escorts arrived at the front of the line, they stopped where SS guards huddled in groups of twos and threes, smoking—waiting anxiously. Not one guard acknowledged the girls or their escorts.

Men in the canvas outfits instructed the Jews to straighten their lines and reminded them to remain silent. "If you cooperate, you will soon be warm and well-fed!" one man shouted in Hungarian.

Are all these people Hungarian, like me? Yuri wanted to ask the woman standing next to her, but before she found the courage to speak, a large automobile pulled up. The SS guards tossed their cigarettes into the snow and stood at attention. The chauffeur quickly exited, opened the back door of the sedan, and snapped a salute. Out stepped an immaculately dressed man in his *Schutzstaffel* uniform. He wore no overcoat and seemed unfazed by the frigid temperature and falling snow. He placed his officer's hat over slicked-back dark hair, threw his cigarette to the ground and crushed it with the toe of his shiny black boot—slow and methodical, in no hurry, as though enjoying a Sunday stroll.

The guards remained at attention as a hush fell over the frightened crowd. The intimidating officer took his time as he walked to the head of the multitude, periodically striking the side of his boot with a leather riding crop.

If Yuri's bladder hadn't emptied earlier, it would have now. But the man did something entirely unexpected. As he approached, he whistled—softly at first and then louder. *Schumann or Strauss, perhaps.* The soldiers stood rigid, but he ignored their formality. Instead of a salute, he stretched his neck, surveyed the crowd of soldiers and Jews, and nodded in acknowledgment.

This officer frightened and fascinated Yuri. His eyes scanned the organized chaos, not missing one element. *He has done this before.* With meticulous attention to every detail, he focused on the girls' escorts in the space between the men and women. The officer pursed his lips in question, then moved his head from side to side to get a look at them. His crop smacked hard against the top of his boot.

He squinted as he walked directly toward Yuri's now sobering guard, who stood erect and saluted with the rest of the soldiers. The guard's legs flexed nervously as the man in charge approached with his jaw set and fury in his eyes. The officer unleashed a litany of verbal abuse at Yuri's escorts, but paused when one motioned to Yuri and Eva.

The ranking guard stuttered—something about Hungary, something about twins, and something about their eyes. As fast as the officer's rage had manifested, it departed. He took a step back and slid the riding crop through his black leather belt.

When he approached Eva, her knees buckled, and Yuri supported her entire weight. As gently as a father, the officer removed Eva's headscarf and ran his fingers through her silken blond hair. Then he pried her eyelids open to look into her eyes. He turned to Yuri and examined her in the same manner. His whistling had been unexpected, but he surprised Yuri when his face softened, and his mouth broke into a wide smile. Yuri didn't know why he seemed pleased, but noticed the large gap between his front teeth. She thought it an odd anomaly for such an impeccable man.

"*Wie alt bist du?*" he asked.

Yuri understood he asked their age but feigned ignorance and shrugged, wary of any trouble once their escorts discovered they spoke German.

The officer called the other guards over, displaying Yuri and her sister like prized animals. The guards inspected their eyes and touched their blond hair.

The lengthy discussion the officer had with their escorts confused Yuri. Finally, the officer patted their driver on the shoulder, reached into his pocket, pulled out a velvet pouch, and handed it to the ranking escort who opened it and poured the contents into his palm: diamonds, rubies, and emeralds.

At that moment Yuri understood this was their final destination. The name at all the checkpoints led to this man. *Mengele. Doktor Mengele just bought us.* But it made no sense. *Why us, out of all these people?* Yuri tried to understand. The doctor then ordered his men to escort the girls to his sedan.

Once inside the warm car, Yuri and Eva shed their coats. The driver handed them each a piece of sausage and cheese, followed by a rare treat, even at home—chocolate.

As they watched from the automobile, Mengele separated the people in the line, waving them in one direction or the other: old men and women, and women with children to the left, healthy men and women to the right.

What a kind man, Yuri thought.

* * *

Yuri shivered and slipped her bare feet into the examination stirrups, wishing she had something to cover her nakedness. Her body quaked. It was not the cold that ignited her uncontrollable shaking, but fear.

Others had not been as kind as the doctor. After Mengele sorted the large crowd, he had taken Yuri and Eva to a two-story brick building marked with a small placard, BLOCK 10. Yuri's frozen feet had barely carried her up the five steps. As soon as she entered, terrifying sights and sounds enveloped her. But she didn't have time to dwell on them as a snarling woman wearing a Star of David grabbed her and Eva, brutally stripped off their clothes, and covered them with a caustic spray that burned their eyes. She teased them with terrible stories of what happened in this place. *Where has this woman's humanity gone?* In one breath, she informed the girls that they would never leave Block 10, and in the next, she whispered a rumor that the Russians would soon liberate the camp.

When a guard escorted Yuri and Eva to the second-floor ward, Yuri understood that the awful woman was not making up stories. Two women arrived on stretchers and writhed in pain from injections in their private parts—their groans and cries reverberated throughout the room.

The cruel woman woke Yuri at dawn with a strike on the top of her head from a riding crop. She led her by the arm to an exam room, then ordered her to undress and lie on this cold metallic table.

Now, a merciless woman in a German uniform tossed supplies on a stainless-steel tray with a clatter—dreadful-looking items that Yuri had never seen—a metal instrument that reminded her of a large duck's bill and other tools, more appropriate for a carpenter's shop. The Nazi woman arranged a variety of syringes and colorful solutions on the back table. Yuri had rarely been sick in her life and only remembered a doctor visit twice, but never for a female examination. As she was still a virgin, there had been no need.

"You'd better behave, *mein Jüdin*," the woman warned. "You smell your fellow Jews roasting in the ovens today? You will be next if you don't open your legs to the good doctor." She forced Yuri's knees apart and stood between them, daring her to resist.

Yuri had learned in the last few months not to look directly at a German, but she stole a glance at this woman who acted with such cruelty. Yuri had to see if life existed behind the cold, dark eyes, but her daring glance did not go unnoticed. The woman drew her pistol from its holster and brought the gun barrel down on Yuri's forehead, followed by two lashes with the riding crop to the side of her head. Yuri whimpered, eliciting two more strikes from the whip.

"If you ever look at me again, you won't make it to the ovens," she hissed between her teeth and cocked the hammer on the gun.

"Maria!" a man's voice shouted, sharp and authoritative. The woman quickly holstered the pistol and returned the whip to her belt.

Yuri recognized the tall man in the doorway. *Mengele.* Modesty and fear made Yuri close her legs and cover her chest with her arms, then recoil when the awful woman cocked her riding crop.

"Maria, you're excused," Mengele ordered. "This one is very precious to me. You may not strike her again."

The woman clenched her teeth. "*Ja,* Herr Mengele," she said and snapped her crop. "Just another dirty Jew slut."

"Oh, but that is where you are wrong, Maria." The doctor took two more steps into the room. He had shed his military jacket for a white coat, and a stethoscope hung around his neck. "Have you seen her with her sister? They are identical," he said.

"We have many twins." Maria shrugged.

"Look at those eyes!" he said, emphasizing the point with his hands.

Yuri looked away when the woman frowned at her. The doctor had already made a big deal out of them at the selections when he saw that both Yuri and Eva had one blue eye and one brown.

The doctor grabbed Maria by the arm and spun her toward him. "This particular anomaly, heterochromia iridum, occurs in six out of a thousand births, and identical twins occur in only three out of one thousand births." He rubbed his chin, calculated, and then smiled. "Together, this combination is scarce—eighteen out of a million children! The condition fascinated even the great philosopher, Aristotle." He squeezed her arm harder. "The *Deutsche Forschungsgemeinschaft* will rejoice when they receive the specimens. They may promote me to *Sturmbannführer.*"

The woman ignored his excitement, but his eyes darkened, and his knuckles turned white as he continued to tighten his grip on her arm. She first looked at his hand and then to the floor.

"Yes, Maria, you will take special care, won't you?"

The woman snapped to attention and glared at Yuri one last time before walking out of the room.

Like the passing of storm clouds, the overcast darkness dissipated from the doctor's face, and he turned to Yuri with a smile. "How is my Hungarian dove this morning? Well, I hope. Did you sleep soundly and get plenty to eat?" He stepped to the table and placed a warm hand on Yuri's knee and smiled.

It was true. She'd eaten a portion of meaty soup with a piece of bread that filled her more than her shrunken stomach could hold. With a mattress and warm blanket, she'd slept a deep, dreamless sleep even among the cacophony of moans in the room.

Yuri didn't know if the doctor wanted an answer or not.

His gaze lingered on her body, and he licked his cracked lips. "Exquisite, my dear. Where have you been hiding all this time?"

Yuri understood he didn't expect her to reply, but courage rose inside of her. She spoke without thinking, "My sister, where is my sister?"

Any kindness in his eyes vanished, and darkness overshadowed his face once again. He squeezed her knee to the point of pain.

Yuri's body trembled.

"She is well cared for, of course. Do not worry your pretty head."

"*Doktor* Mengele, could you come here please?" a voice called from beyond the doorway. "It's urgent."

The doctor hesitated but released her knee and left the room.

The door clicked closed, and Yuri's eyes searched the room. Her body shuddered with fear and uncertainty. If she could only cover her nakedness. *Is there no way to escape? Why am I ensnared in this madness?* She lay back and closed her eyes.

Yuri shook her head to clear the memory of the night before the SS broke down the front door to their home. Yuri and Eva were celebrating the first night of Hanukkah with their parents. Papa carefully covered the first-floor windows before lighting the Shamash, the first candle of the menorah. All their other relatives—grandparents, uncles and aunts, and cousins—had either fled or were captured in the dragnet that forced all Jews into designated buildings, marked with the Star of David.

Despite the visible signs of persecution of the Jews, Yuri's German-born mother and Hungarian father couldn't help their nationalistic squabbling on this night of the Festival of Lights and the memorial of freedom for the Jewish people. Instead of keeping the celebration joyful, her mother vehemently defended her German heritage: "My people could do no such thing," she insisted when her father relayed the rumors swirling of death camps and Jews herded into abhorrent ghettos. Her mother would not accept the news of German families then inhabiting abandoned Jewish homes.

Papa, dear Papa. His anxiety was not overblown. He tried to stay calm and rational. Their hometown of Budapest continued as somewhat of a safe haven, but rumors swirled of persecution of Jews in other parts of Hungary, where the

Germans had invaded from the west. Through Papa's position at the bank, he'd secured false papers and went so far as to buy crucifix necklaces for Yuri and Eva. He taught them how to cross themselves properly and recite the Christian prayers.

"Our Father, who art in heaven, Hallowed be thy name," Yuri recited under her breath. She felt for the necklace but remembered she had traded it for a piece of stale bread.

She recalled their arrival in Austria and now understood why a kind, young doctor with blond hair had drawn Yuri and Eva out of the line of people boarding trains. He gave them bread, cheese, and a blanket, and put them in the sedan to Poland with the two SS guards.

She realized that it revolved around the random way they were born: twins, blond hair, and the anomaly their classmates had pestered them unmercifully about in school—their eyes of different colors. Even Papa had teased Yuri that she had stolen one of Eva's eyes in utero because one of them should have brown eyes and the other blue instead of having one of each. That seemed to fascinate Doctor Mengele.

Yuri looked with shock at her naked body to see her pelvic bone so prominent, and her ribs protruding. She was not large-breasted to begin with, but since she had lost so much weight, her breasts had all but disappeared.

She pushed on her rumbling stomach when the doctor returned.

His face flashed anger, and his breathing came sharp and fast. He said nothing more to her, any compassion had evaporated. His hands trembled as he slid a glove over each one.

Then he forced Yuri's legs open with his elbows and sat down on a stool with his face eye level to her groin. She jumped when he touched her and scooted away. He forcefully gripped her buttocks, pulled her to the edge of the exam table, and pushed her knees apart again.

Yuri's heart raced. *Why is this man doing this to me?*

The doctor grabbed the duck-billed instrument from the tray. Yuri prepared for the worst and clenched her eyes closed. When nothing happened, she squinted and discovered the doctor staring at her. His kindness returned, and he said, "*Mein yunges Fräulein*, you are still a virgin?"

Yuri slowly nodded her head. She wondered why it mattered.

The doctor sighed, placed the instrument on the tray, and removed his gloves. "We should take care of that." He stood, went to the open door of the exam room, then closed and locked it.

As he walked to Yuri, he removed his stethoscope and white coat and laid them over the instruments. Yuri closed her knees, but he put a hand on each and pried them apart. To look at him directly may get her killed, but she didn't care. If he intended to violate her, he would have to look into her eyes— to remind him of her humanity. A girl from Hungary. A Jew. But his dark eyes filled with hatred and lust as he unbuckled his belt.

Yuri instinctively understood what was about to happen to her, but froze to the table. She pleaded with her eyes and tried to protest, but only a slight whimper escaped her throat.

"This is my gift to you, my dove."

Yuri bit her lip hard, and the metallic taste of blood coated her tongue as the monster leaned over her.

He gripped the sides of the table, and her hands found his

wrists, begging for him to stop. She tore at his sleeves to push him away.

His face turned red, and his breath deepened.

Yuri's mind numbed. She had seen so much death and evil in the last seven months, her psyche wobbled on the edge of insanity.

Mengele pushed himself up and patted her on the head like a dog and smiled, showing the gap in his teeth. "Now, we can continue," he said.

"*Achtung, Achtung!*" a male voice yelled from behind the door.

The doctor twisted toward the chaos erupting in the hallway and fastened his pants and belt.

A fist banged on the door. *"Doktor Mengele. Die Russen kommen!"* A man screamed. *"Schnell! Schnell! Wir müssen evakuieren!"*

The doctor turned to Yuri and slicked his dark hair back with his hand. His eyes widened, and he started to say something. He looked from Yuri to the door, then to her again. His shoulders drooped, and he slowly shook his head. *"Mein Gott."*

He walked to the door, and with his hand on the knob, turned to take one more look at Yuri.

He opened the door to soldiers yelling and running in both directions. He nodded to her, walked out, and slammed the door behind him.

Yuri sat up and, with one hand, grabbed for the doctor's coat to cover herself. In her other hand, she realized she clenched onto a small item and brought it to her face. She fingered a gold cufflink. She turned it over to see two initials engraved in the gold: JM.

CHAPTER 1

GOD IS MY JUDGE
NOVEMBER, PRESENT DAY
POZNAŃ, POLAND

Dr. Emmanuelle Christianson's pager displayed "URGENT", but her stride remained slow and steady. She'd dreaded this day for months, and she had to will her feet forward. This was the second page imploring her to come to her son's hospital room, but she bore no urgency in her step or in her heart.

Her husband, Keith, would meet her in the room, and that only heightened her anxiety. By Keith's emotional absence from her, he'd made it abundantly clear he blamed her—she'd done this to their son, and no amount of reasoning would convince him otherwise, even though the cystic fibrosis was the real villain.

The universe's cruel stroke of fate for one of the world's leading geneticists struck when Danek's doctor diagnosed him with the disease at the age of three. The unexpected pregnancy had surprised her and Keith, especially with an IUD in place, but they grew thrilled at the idea of a son after having two daughters. Danek's rapid deterioration became a cruel harbinger to the course of their lives. Keith started to wander to escape the stress of a child with a chronic illness. Emmanuelle threw herself into work and the company as her coping method.

She'd enrolled Danek as one of the earliest patients in BioGenics's cystic fibrosis trial. Unfortunately, he would become one of their latest statistics. No wonder she walked so slowly to the urgent summons—she hated to fail, and they needed to make the agonizing decision on whether to continue his palliative care.

The sound of footsteps crescendoed behind Emmanuelle as she made her way down the long corridor connecting the clinic to the hospital.

"Dr. Christianson."

Emmanuelle turned to the woman calling from behind her. She forced a smile, trying to hide her impatience at the American doctor who'd recently joined BioGenics. Similar to Emmanuelle and other physicians on staff, the woman trained both as a medical doctor and a PhD in genetics.

"Dr. Nielsen, I hope you find the facility to your liking." Emmanuelle raised her hands, indicating the year-old, eight-hundred-million-euro BioGenics facility.

"Yes, absolutely, thank you for inviting me to work with you," Nielsen said.

"We are thrilled to have you join us," Emmanuelle said. "How are your grapes growing? Do we have a BioGenics wine yet?" She grinned at the banter going around the facility. But the new half-million-euro greenhouses constructed for Dr. Nielsen's team were no joke, nor were the chemicals Dr. Nielson would harvest from the grapes. Adding the compound to stem cells caused them to let down their natural defenses against viruses, allowing for access to their DNA for genetic modification.

"It will be some expensive wine," Nielsen said, laughed, then turned serious. "Thank you for believing in me and investing in this research. But I want to ask you about my allotted operating room time—"

Emmanuelle looked down at the emblem on Nielsen's white coat, frowned, and interrupted her. "Dr. Nielsen, I prefer you wear a BioGenics lab coat." She tried to soften her irritation of the intrusion and dress code violation with a smile. The doctor displayed her heritage from the Howard Hughes Medical Institute with pride, but the woman now worked for her.

Emmanuelle patted the embroidery on her own jacket to emphasize the point. "You are part of the team now," she said, hoping the doctor clearly read the message:

Emmanuelle Christianson, MD

Obstetrics and Gynecology

CEO BioGenics.

She smiled again at the doctor. "You are welcome to make an appointment to discuss this further. Concerning your OR time, I have competent administrators for both the hospital and clinic to handle these issues. For now, please excuse me, I have an urgent matter to attend to."

Emmanuelle turned on her heels and proceeded down the corridor. As the CEO of BioGenics, she retained ultimate responsibility but had hired excellent leadership for the different aspects of the facility. They answered to her and could solve all conflicts that arose by putting ego-driven physicians together in the same building. She had hired the best researchers from all over the globe, including Dr. Nielsen. The clinical staff of doctors, nurses, ancillary personnel, and researchers employed at BioGenics totaled over six hundred and was a sense of great pride for Emmanuelle, but that also required her to let the administrators handle many of the mundane issues.

The E-shaped medical complex included a world-renowned research facility, outpatient clinic, and hospital, specializing in the care and treatment of genetic and reproductive health, all separated by secure entryways. At the entrance to the inpatient ward, Emmanuelle brought her face to the retinal scanner. The electronic lock clicked, and she pushed the door open.

Emmanuelle nodded at the three young nurses cheerfully strolling down the hallway. *Oh, to be young and full of blissful enthusiasm. Then life happens.* She spent less and less time in the hospital as her responsibilities in research and as CEO demanded the greatest share of her time. Her clinical practice had dwindled to one day a week, but continuing her skills as a physician gave her credibility with her colleagues. Unfortunately, as a medical doctor trained in OB/GYN, a fellowship in reproductive and genetic health, and a PhD in medical genetics, her training and degrees were helpless against Danek's disease. She'd done everything she knew possible for her son.

Danek had recently turned seven. As Emmanuelle entered the elevator and pushed the button to the fourth floor, she thought back to the day when she enrolled him in BioGenics's first trial. *What parent of a child with a terrifying disease wouldn't do the same?* Danek's diagnosis came before she'd perfected the gene therapy technology. But if the research continued, she remained confident they'd find a cure for many of the genetic diseases in the next ten years. It angered her when people who hadn't seen the devastation of cystic fibrosis firsthand argued that messing with the basic human code carried too much danger.

Emmanuelle exited the elevator and walked down the hallway. At the end of the corridor, she noticed Keith sitting on the floor outside Danek's room with his forehead resting in his hands. Keith had picked the name Danek for their son. She liked it, too, but had forgotten who told her it meant "God is my judge." By his expression, God would not be her only judge.

He wore the protective gown and head covering required to visit a patient in isolation. Keith had peeled off the mask, revealing his pale complexion. He shook his head and murmured.

As she stood over him, he slowly looked up with hatred. "Have you seen your son?" he said through a clenched jaw.

She said nothing. *Yes, I see him weekly.* Keith had not visited for months.

"You said everything would be okay. You said the treatment would do no harm." His bottom lip quivered. "You said he wouldn't suffer." Keith coughed and gagged on his words. "You shouldn't do this to people."

CHAPTER 2

HONEYMOON
KONA

Nick dabbed a bead of sweat from Maggie's temple with his fingertip, and she collapsed into his arms. Her breathing came labored and deep. She snuggled her face into his neck and kissed it ever so gently. Her body radiated heat.

"You okay?" he asked and stroked her hair. The pounding of his heart throbbed in his ears.

Her body relaxed and pressed against his chest. Nick squirmed beneath her.

Maggie squeezed his frame between her legs and arms and laughed while Nick feigned suffocation. She released the pressure, sat up, and put her hands on his bare chest. Then she wiped her upper lip with the back of one hand and fanned her face with the other. "Whew!"

"Good thing we have the corner room." He laughed.

Maggie's cheeks flushed. "You're embarrassing me, Nicklaus Hart." She tucked her face into the crook of his neck again and wrapped her arms and legs around him.

Despite her petite frame, Maggie resisted Nick's attempt to pry her off his body. She had grown up bucking hay bales on her family's ranch on the Blackfeet Reservation in Montana. She locked him in her embrace, constricting his breath.

"Mag…"

She laughed again and released her death grip. "We could stop anytime if you like," she teased.

Nick flipped her onto her back and pressed his full weight against her, pinning her hands above her head. "I'll give you some of your own medicine."

She scissored her legs around his waist and pulled him down. "It's about time."

Nick howled. "You're impossible," he said, then lightly kissed her neck.

"Well, at forty-six, I am in my prime."

"That you are, Maggie, that you are." His kisses danced down her shoulder. A soft moan escaped her lips.

Their passion reignited until a knock on their door caught their attention.

Nick looked toward the door and groaned. "Knockus interruptus," he said and laughed. He pushed himself off Maggie.

"Noooo," Maggie complained and tried to pull him back down. "Don't answer it."

He resisted her, got off the bed, and slipped on a pair of swim trunks. Not the most modest way to open a door, but for Hawaii, it seemed appropriate. Maggie quickly found the bed sheet and covered herself.

A second knock came as Nick reached the door and swung it open.

Without an invitation, the owner of the inn, an elderly man with short bowed legs and a bushy mustache, pushed a cart into their room. "Rise and shine, you newlyweds," he said, as the cart bounced over the threshold, spilling some liquid from the glasses. He wheeled it to the end of the bed where, seeing Maggie, he blushed. "Please forgive my intrusion, Mrs. Hart."

Nick couldn't tell who was more embarrassed, the innkeeper or Maggie. The old man averted his eyes, looked Nick up and down, and grinned. Stretching his short arms over the food, he shrugged. "The missus made me bring you breakfast to keep up your strength," he said with a prominent accent Nick couldn't place. The innkeeper's smile matched the twinkle in his eyes, and what he lacked in height, he made up for in enthusiasm. He smoothed his thick white mustache that covered his mouth. "I'm supposed to ask if you need anything and if you want your room serviced. More towels, perhaps?"

Nick looked at Maggie and back to the innkeeper, who arranged the breakfast tray and wiped the spilled liquid.

Two days earlier, when they first arrived in Kona, they met this man and his wife, an elderly couple in their late eighties who owned the condominium. They were excited to host honeymooners. The man was a dwarf, his wife was not. His dwarfism presented as the classic genetic disorder, achondroplasia—a large head with arms disproportionately shorter than his trunk. In Nick's training at the children's hospital, he'd helped with several cases to correct severely bowed legs on the short-statured kids. A mutation on chromosome four caused the dwarfism.

The innkeeper removed the cloches covering the food, revealing a smorgasbord of fresh tropical fruits: pineapple, bananas, mango, and papaya. He peeled cling wrap off the top of a pitcher of juice. "This is homemade *liliko'i* nectar, passion fruit juice," he said and stole a glance at Maggie, who pulled the sheet tight around her neck. "It is good for…" He stopped the sentence short, but his cheeks blushed crimson.

"I meant to ask you the other day, where you are originally from?" Nick changed the subject. "I love your accent."

The man looked down, then back to Nick. "I always tell everyone that I'm from Greece. I'm not sure why I tell you the truth, but I am from Poland…I am a Jew."

The wheels turned in Nick's mind to figure the man's age when he caught a glare from Maggie, a look that said: Can't we have this discussion some other time…like when I have clothes on?

Nick picked up his crumpled pants from the floor, fished for his wallet, and pulled out some bills to tip the man.

The innkeeper quickly sidestepped toward the door and waved off the money. "No need, Dr. Hart. It is my pleasure," he said and patted his chest.

"Thank you so much for breakfast," Nick said. "We may finally leave the room today." He squeezed the man's shoulder and winked at him. "We would like to do some snorkeling. Where do you recommend?"

The man's eyes brightened again. "Oh, you have two good choices close by. You go north on *Ali'i* to *Kahalu'u* Beach Park or south to *Pu'uhonua o Hōnaunau*, what they call Two Step. Both are beautiful." The man pulled the door closed mid-sentence—saying something about having fun.

Nick turned to Maggie, who still had the sheet clenched at her neck. He smiled and shrugged.

"Well, that was awkward," she said and pulled the bedding over her head.

"Hey, at least we have some breakfast." Then he changed into the owner's accent. "You must regain your strength," he said, emphasizing the words with his hands. Nick went to the side of the bed, gently pulled the sheet back, and kissed her forehead. "Could I pour you *liliko'i* nectar, some passion juice?" He traced his finger down her sternum in lazy circles.

"Oh, I think you've had too much *liliko'i* already." She laughed.

Maggie's phone buzzed on the nightstand, and she glanced at it. "It's The Hope Center." She looked at him with pouty eyes. "You mind if I answer it?"

They had agreed to stay off their phones, but if the orphanage called, it was important.

"You take the call. I'll build up my strength," he said, and took some pineapple off the tray and bit it in two. Juice dripped down his chin. "Oh my gosh, that's good."

Maggie put the phone to her ear and answered in Spanish. *"Hola."*

Her expression turned serious. She hopped out of bed and stood in front of the wall of windows overlooking the garden that led to the ocean. *"Digame, digame!"*

Nick admired the view. With striking Blackfeet features, Maggie's long black hair tumbled down her back to above her shapely buttocks.

Maggie and her first husband, John, had built The Hope Center in Guatemala. It had been four years since his death, and Nick and Maggie talked openly about her first marriage. After all, John had been Nick's best friend. Nick still had nightmares about the terrible way the North Korean terrorists murdered John.

For years, Nick had wondered if Maggie would ever be ready to open her heart again. When she recently indicated a willingness, Nick didn't hesitate. By marrying Maggie six weeks earlier in Glacier Park, Nick promised to care and watch over her with his whole being, through good times and bad. Right now, it was all good.

He picked up a fork, stabbed a slice of papaya, and bit off a piece. It had an unusual taste, and he smelled the fruit that remained on the utensil. Its aroma reminded him of his surgical shoes after a long day. He winced, put it back on the plate, and speared another chunk of pineapple.

Maggie's Spanish enlivened and quickened. Something exciting happened at the center. *I hope it's good news.* A call from the mission hospital and orphanage could go either way. The local staff had agreed to run the place with support from Nick's previous hospital in Memphis until Nick and Maggie decided what they would do with the next chapter of their lives. But Maggie's heart remained tied to the place, and she wanted to hear both good and bad news.

In the middle of a big bite of fruit, he caught her looking at him with a sparkle in her eyes. She wiggled her bottom and raised her eyebrows, and he relaxed. Only Maggie could flirt with him and carry on a serious conversation in Spanish. She mouthed the words: "Enjoying the view?"

Absolutely—her native skin glowed against the backdrop of the lush gardens and turquoise ocean. After Nick stepped away from surgery because of injuries incurred during a mission trip to Turkey, and with their finances tight, he didn't think a honeymoon would happen. But after the wedding ceremony, his parents surprised them with plane tickets and arrangements in Kona. Spectacular arrangements. The owners built the small condominium complex into a hillside overlooking the ocean.

A bamboo-lined pathway led them through thick foliage and exotic flowers to the front door. Nick's favorite, a secluded porch protected by old teak wood decking, opened off their bedroom. A two-person cedar hot tub placed at a break in the banana trees and ferns made the perfect vantage point to watch the ocean and an occasional surfacing humpback whale. No wonder they hadn't left the room for two days. *Well, not the only reason.*

Although married the end of September, they'd delayed their honeymoon until a week before Thanksgiving. Montana got dusted with snow the day they left, and now they relaxed in a wonderland of warmth and soft ocean air. It made their vacation to the tropics that much sweeter.

Maggie's initial bashfulness had worn off, much to Nick's relief. She'd insisted they wait until after the ceremony to consummate their relationship, but even on their wedding night, the lights stayed off, and she came to bed in pajamas. With their hectic schedule after the wedding and before their honeymoon, the last six weeks were not exactly passion filled.

Hawaii's warm climate and soft ocean air sparked a great desire in her. *I guess I shouldn't be surprised. Her zeal for life comes in all forms.* Here she stood before him talking on the telephone, naked and unashamed.

She turned to look at him, and he flapped his fingers, mimicking a chatty marionette. She smiled and raised a finger to be patient.

"*Bueno, bueno,*" Maggie kept repeating. Then she said, "*Dios te bendiga,*" and ended the call.

Maggie broke into a happy dance and jumped with joy. "Juanita had her baby! It was breach, so we've all been worried."

"That's good news." Nick nodded. He'd experienced the difficulties and complications of delivering a baby feet first. He blew out a sigh of relief, with the director of The Hope Center safe. Maggie regarded every life as precious, and he adored her for it.

"It's a boy. I'm so happy for her!" Maggie swung her hips from side to side.

Nick stopped mid-chew and reached for her.

She continued to dance up to Nick with desire in her eyes. This talk of babies seemingly impassioned her. "Care to join me in the hot tub?" She pulled him up by his hand.

Nick did not resist.

CHAPTER 3

PAPA

Emmanuelle fidgeted in her seat to avoid touching elbows with the strangers on either side. First-class tickets on the train from Poznań to Berlin had sold out. Only a middle seat remained in an eight-passenger compartment that resembled a sardine can.

The constant roar of the train and the clacking of the wheels against the tracks gave her a headache. She closed and opened her jaw to release the pressure in her ears and rubbed her temples.

Keith was right—she'd failed as a mother and physician. Outside Danek's room, he scolded her with a litany of rants about her work as a geneticist, and the science she'd pioneered at BioGenics. "You're experimenting on people," he'd screamed at her in the hallway, then stormed away. With that, they made no decision on Danek's end-of-life directive.

He did not understand the progress her teams were making toward curing some of the worst afflictions of humankind. There are sacrifices in early research, and she didn't like it any more than Keith that their son had become one of them.

The manipulation of Danek's genes had initially shown promise, but the disease had won and left him in a rotting vegetative state. Keith's anger and helplessness had to turn somewhere. She only wished they could grieve the loss together.

Perhaps she deserved her lot in life. What terrible person wished their son would die? It should have happened years ago and now remained as the only humane avenue left. They could only stand by helplessly watching him decay.

As the countryside flashed by, sulfurous odor filled the tight cubicle, and she thought her olfactory glands were reliving the terrible smell of infection that surrounded her son. The businesswoman across from Emmanuelle frowned and held her fist under her nose. It was not a figment of her imagination.

She surmised the culprit involved either the obese man to her right, whose waistline partially spilled over into her seat or one of the young Canadians to her left. The couple had stored their backpacks in the luggage closet, took their seats, and examined maps and travel brochures. Emmanuelle put her money on the young man as the offender. She caught him looking around for a reaction from the other passengers while the corners of his lips curled in a concealed smile. *He probably thinks it's hilarious to fill the compartment with his stench.*

Emmanuelle hated riding the train and leaving home with her son's life in the balance. She'd traveled to Berlin recently and knew this day would come soon when she'd have to go back. Papa's caregiver called and urged her to come.

Emmanuelle gazed out the window. Low clouds hovered above the freshly plowed fields, and fall colors gave way to the dreary browns and grays of winter—*perhaps a fitting time for Papa to pass.* But somehow, even when expected, it took her by surprise. As a scientist, Emmanuelle understood the brain's ability to compartmentalize, and her father's impending death forced her mind to do that. She wasn't ready for him to go, especially since they had put her mother in the ground less than a year ago.

But other urgent news made her squirm. As she boarded the train in Poznań, her cell phone dinged, and she saw that she had a message from her graduate student in the lab. The student had completed the DNA sequencing. Curiosity got the best of Emmanuelle, and she reached between her legs and pulled her laptop from the briefcase underneath her seat.

Emmanuelle rested the computer on her lap without opening it. Instead, she turned to watch the fields of Poland flash by. She'd already predicted the contents of the email, but with the likelihood of her father's death, she wasn't prepared to face the cold truth in print or any of her new reality.

Uncovering the painful truth in front of these strangers didn't seem like the right thing to do. *Okay, if not now, when?* She gripped her laptop, deciding whether to slide it back into her briefcase. Her mind battled between intellect and will, and against her better judgment, she opened the computer. She glanced from side to side. The man to her right read a newspaper and ate a sugar donut, and the young tourists on the left remained enthralled with their maps. As she pushed the power button, the computer chimed.

Soon, a photograph of her two smiling daughters appeared on the screen. She loved this photo of them, taken after they'd finished feeding the ducks at the pond near their house. Happy days, but six years and many sorrows ago. This email could change the trajectory of all their lives forever.

Anger pushed her to open the email browser and click on the note from Izzi, her grad student. The subject line read: "The

DNA sequencing you requested." Emmanuelle had asked her to analyze the DNA discreetly. The email read:

> Dr. Christianson…
>
> I have run the STR analysis sample according to CODIS 20. Attached is the DNA electropherogram.
>
> I'm sorry…Izzi
>
> PS: You didn't ask me, but I will compare it with the national databases, then run a full genome sequencing.

Izzi's note ended with a crying-face emoji.

I should have never gotten Izzi involved. What was I thinking, handing the young grad student a pair of my husband's boxers? Maybe her brain had compartmentalized this as well, comprehending the truth but denying it all at the same time.

Emmanuelle clicked on the attachment, and as it opened, the man beside her shifted and looked at the screen. *Go ahead, take a nice long look, you jerk. This is what betrayal looks like.*

Izzi had made it all too apparent, marking Emmanuelle's twenty gene loci in green, Keith's in blue, and the mystery person in red. She recognized her own DNA immediately. A colorful mural that covered one wall of her office displayed part of her genetic code. She knew Keith's as well from the genetic testing for their son.

Emmanuelle stared at the last box of the electropherogram, surprised at her relief. The third person in their marriage was female. Over the previous six months, she'd wondered if Keith had found comfort with a man. He had charm that compelled both sexes, but the thought of losing her husband to another man short-circuited her brain. She had discounted her religious upbringing years ago, and the root of her fear had to do more with how it might complicate things for the girls.

But factually, another woman shattered their marriage. Not a surprise to Emmanuelle, as evidenced by Keith's late nights out with friends, his quickly closed laptop, the locked phone, and now the DNA. While she built her career, Keith found companionship in another's arms. *Could it be love? Stupid slut.*

Three years into their nineteen-year marriage, she'd had an affair—a one-night stand with her graduate school professor. She regretted the affair and begged for Keith's forgiveness. He never brought it up again or asked questions; she would have wanted to hear every detail. She thought his indifference strange. Perhaps this was his revenge or god's form of punishment. *If you're stupid enough to believe in god.*

Her hands shook as she closed her laptop.

She quickly wiped away a tear.

* * *

"Papa, I'm here." Emmanuelle held her father's hand. "Papa, it's me…Emy."

She glanced at the woman in the corner whose downcast eyes and drooping shoulders told the story. Maria had been her father's faithful caretaker since her mother's death last year. Older than Emy's parents by ten years, she spoke only German. Emy looked back at her father. Maybe she was too late.

With a moan, his eyes fluttered open. He stared at her, trying to clear his vision when a weary smile formed. "Emmanuelle, my dear Emmanuelle," he rasped a whisper.

"Papa, are you in pain?"

He shook his head slowly. "Not since you are here." He squeezed her hand.

"I came as fast as I could, Papa."

"*Ja, ja*, I know dear, I know."

Emy watched his chest rise and fall. Soon it would stop, she imagined. Purple blotches tinted his paper-thin skin that barely covered the tendons on the back of his hands. She lightly stroked them, afraid that she would rip open his flesh.

"Could you give your old man a sip of water?" he whispered.

Emy reached for the crystal glass on the side table and smiled: Papa would never drink from anything less, not even on his deathbed. She propped up his head and held the glass to his lips. He took two swallows but resisted more and relaxed his head back.

Emy's mind raced. The silence tormented her. *Where is Lukas?* Her brother should be here, dammit! The anger from earlier on the train boiled to the surface. *Moronic men.* Maybe that's her problem, she hates them all.

Papa began to speak, but then stopped and tried to capture his thoughts or gain his strength.

Here lay the one man she truly loved. And he loved her—unconditionally.

"Papa? What do you need, Papa?"

He opened his eyes and met her gaze. His corneas were grayed and clouded with cataracts. He shifted his head to focus on her and raised his feeble hand to her cheek. "My beloved, Emmanuelle. How I love you so. I have always been the most worried for you." He used his hand to cover a raspy cough. "You came into our lives with us on our knees." His boney finger pointed to the floor. "I would get down there again for you if I could." A smile crossed his face before he closed his eyes to conserve his strength.

She had long ago disavowed her parents' staunch Catholicism. They had given up appealing to her, understanding it drove her further away from their faith. Emy took her father's hand, bowed her head, and closed her eyes. Science. That's all she believed.

"I have to tell you," her father said.

It surprised her when she opened her eyes to find him staring at her.

"You have to tell me what, Papa?"

"Your mother tried to tell you before she died last year. She couldn't get the words out."

Emy searched his tired, dark eyes as he seemed to fade away.

"Papa?" Her voice sparked life back in her father.

"You are my child," he began and let his gaze wander beyond her, "but not from the beginning." He coughed. "Emy, please forgive your mother and me," he started again. "We always wanted the best for you...from the moment they brought you to us."

Emy smiled at her father. How she loved him. Here, with his last breath, he tried to tell her something she already knew. She was not their biological child. Ever since her first genetics class in high school, she understood why she looked so distinctively different from the rest of the family. She'd come from an entirely different gene pool. Her mean older brother never teased her about it, and she had to wonder if her parents had told him. But the truth never mattered to her, she couldn't change the past. A few times, out of curiosity, she'd wanted to ask, but the issue could unsettle the tentative stability of the family.

"It's okay, Papa. You don't have to—"

"Your mother did not want to adopt a child," he interrupted. "But I loved you the moment I saw you."

There it was—the secret.

The room suddenly turned hot and smelled of decay.

"I'm sorry that your mother treated you unkindly." He tried to reach for her cheek, but his arm collapsed to his chest. Emy grabbed it, kissed the back of it, and put it to her face. Troubled thoughts rushed through her mind. *Thank goodness for Papa. Nothing I did seemed to please Mother.* Her brother Lukas could do no wrong.

She hadn't wanted to bring up this subject, but here it was.

"Why did Lukas always get a pass?" she asked.

She regretted the question. It made her sound childish and like a jealous sibling. *The problem is, it's true.* Lukas always got a pass. He'd abandoned their father on his deathbed.

The most difficult pill for Emy to swallow came in the form of her parents promising Lukas some of their most precious belongings—items that held a special place in her heart, ones she had hoped to receive.

Painful memories from her youth assaulted her mind, and tears tumbled down her cheeks. The recollection of cleaning the entire house and not receiving one morsel of praise from her mother haunted Emy. One of many times her mother failed to show her love. Lukas, on the other hand, would pick a dandelion or weed from the yard, and their mother responded with praise and gratitude.

Her father touched her arm and brought her out of the childhood trauma. "I understand my child, I had to live with her, as well."

This brought a smile to Emy's face. *Papa, always the peacemaker.* "Thank you for adopting me, Papa. Thank you for always loving me."

"You are easy to love, Emmanuelle."

More tears tumbled down her cheeks. The image of the DNA analysis flashed through her mind. She didn't feel lovable at the moment. But an immediate thought took its place. "Do you know anything about my biological parents?"

Her father closed his eyes as he let go. His body went limp, and his breath quickened.

She wanted to shake him until he answered, but stopped herself. Did it truly matter? The answer wouldn't change her life.

It surprised her when her father raised his hand and pointed it to the bookcase next to his bed.

"I wanted to protect..." he said with his voice weakened and raspy. "You will have to do this one on your own, my child." He gasped for air.

Emy searched the titles on the spines of the books but didn't understand his directive. "Do what, Papa?" Desperation filled her voice.

"Papa?"

Her father's caregiver stood and went to the bookshelf. She took a manila envelope off the ledge and handed it to Emy, who thought she saw her name scrawled across the front. She looked at the old woman who averted her eyes and shuffled from the room. This moment seemed premeditated. Perhaps the caretaker knew more about her family secrets than she'd let on.

The envelope, her father, and the caretaker confused Emy. She turned the sealed envelope over. Her father had scribbled her name but misspelled it. He'd written "Immanuel." *How strange.*

She looked at her father, then back at the envelope. "Papa, I don't understand what you are trying to tell me, but I love you. You are my father."

This brought a slight nod, and he whispered something that Emy could not understand. She bent low to put her ear to his lips and waited for him to repeat it.

She heard him say, "You are a Jew."

CHAPTER 4

KONA

Nick and Maggie stepped off the edge of the parking lot onto *Kahalu'u* Beach Park, mesmerized by its beauty. Nick slipped off his flip-flops and let his feet sink into the warm sand. He pulled his sunglasses to his forehead and then back over his eyes. The brilliant cyan blues and greens of the ocean glowed, with or without the polarization. The white break of waves, where a barrier reef protected the bay, separated the water from the dazzling cobalt sky. Snorkelers frolicked in the clear, calm bay while others on the beach soaked up the Hawaiian sun.

"Almost worth leaving the room for," Nick said to Maggie and chuckled.

"Almost," Maggie teased back.

Nick inhaled deeply. The breeze gently swayed the palm trees lining one side of the beach. The roar of the distant waves pounding the break mixed with joyous squeals of small children playing in the shallow water along the shore. A Hawaiian family filled the pavilion next to the beach, saturating the air with the smell of barbecued fish and the soft strum of a ukulele.

"I saw the weather report from Montana today, thirty-two degrees," Nick said. "Kind of hard to believe we're on the beach half-naked in our swimsuits."

"It's magnificent," Maggie agreed, as she set down her load from the car. "I may never leave."

"How's your knee?" Nick asked, examining the cherry-red scrape over her patella, still feeling bad that she'd fallen getting out of the car.

"Did you trip over something?"

"I don't know. Just clumsy, I guess."

"I worried you'd passed out. Sure you're okay?"

"Oh, it's fine," she said and gave him a look to indicate that he should quit fussing over her. "Nothing that a little sunshine won't heal."

Nick pointed to a family of four preparing to vacate. "You mind asking if we could take their spot? I'll bring over all our stuff."

"You bet," Maggie gladly accepted. She'd grumbled about appearing too much like tourists after the innkeeper loaded them down with beach chairs, an umbrella, mats, snorkeling gear, a cooler full of drinks and sandwiches, and various flotation devices.

By the time Nick hauled their beach accessories over, Maggie had struck up a conversation with the family. From Minnesota and now headed back to frigid temperatures, they grieved over their last day in paradise. Nick agreed Hawaii provided a perfect place to wait out old man winter.

"How was the snorkeling?" Nick asked their son.

"Awesome." The young man's eyes lit up. "I saw a bunch of turtles and all kinds of fish. I even saw an octopus."

The mother handed Maggie a tube of sunscreen. "We made the mistake of not using enough of this the first day." She looked at Nick's crystal white legs. "We northerners need to slather it on pretty thick." She laughed.

Nick and Maggie thanked them, wished them safe travels, then spread out their mats and towels. Like so much of the Big Island, lava rock surrounded the beach, and the black sand absorbed the hot sun. Nick screwed the base of the umbrella into the ground and set up two chairs while Maggie peeled off her swimsuit cover, revealing a red-hot bikini. It accentuated her dark native skin, and she caught Nick staring and blushed.

"This okay?" she said and fidgeted with her stomach and thighs. "I look fat, don't I?"

"Oh, Mags, you look great!" he said and kissed her on the cheek. "Sure you don't want to go back to the condo?"

She pushed him away with a laugh. "It's been a while since I've been in a bikini. Sure it's not too much…or too little?"

Nick tilted his head at the young girls in thong bottoms lined up in a row by the edge of the water. "I think you're better covered than those." He smiled.

"Yeah, but I'm old and fat." Maggie insisted.

"Well, you're neither, and you look stunning," Nick said. "While in Rome," he added. "Speaking of that, you mind if I take a dip? I'm dying to see the marine life." Nick pulled off his shirt.

This time, Nick caught Maggie's stare and flexed a pose. He sucked in his stomach and puffed out his chest.

When she laughed, he pouted with his bottom lip. "Well, that's not exactly the response I hoped for."

"Oh my gosh, Nicklaus Hart. You are so white; you might scare the fish." She picked up the tube of sunscreen. "That mom was right, you definitely need some of this."

* * *

Nick adjusted his facemask and snorkel to stop choking on seawater and laid on his chest across the foam noodle. Born and raised in Montana, he had spent little time around the ocean, and today he made a fool of himself as he attempted to walk into the water wearing his flippers. He'd fallen a few times and a local boy instructed him to walk backward until he could float. Once he got the attention of the kids near the shore, Nick had hammed it up, pretending to be a penguin, trying to maneuver the current and hang on to his gear. The kids had howled with laughter and helped him adjust the mask and pushed him out further into the deep.

Trying to relax in the water reminded Nick of pool therapy with his friend and therapist, Chang. Nick had found the treatment essential after returning from serving in Turkey following a massive earthquake. He'd treated many physically broken people, but was then captured by ISIS fighters, and nearly lost his life. No wonder he came home with post-traumatic stress. The encounter with the terrorists had left him temporarily blind, forcing him to hang up his surgical scalpel. But with his sight restored, he had to eventually decide what to do with the rest of his life. *Step number one, marry Maggie.*

Nick took a few deep breaths through the snorkel and tried to relax.

He was a planner, while Maggie lived in the moment, a match made in heaven.

He attempted to enjoy the present, but it wasn't always easy. He'd spent his whole life looking to the future. He'd worked hard to get good grades in college, so he could get into medical school—pressed on to an orthopaedic surgery residency, next to a fellowship in trauma, and then to a successful practice at the MED in Memphis.

Nick had been out of the OR for over a year and unsure if he wanted to go back. He loved taking care of people, but medicine had become something else—all about production and the bottom line, and he hated that. Trying to figure out his life brought anxiety, something he and Chang had worked hard to overcome.

He gently kicked his flippers and breast-stroked his arms to pull through the crystal-clear water, the sun warming his back in the ocean's coolness. It was a good thing Maggie insisted on slathering him with sunscreen.

He heard his raspy breaths through the snorkel and the distant chatter of people playing on the beach. Sometimes his life seemed like floating in this ocean—pushed and directed by the unseen currents. "Trust God," both Maggie and Chang had told Nick. *Easier said than done.*

The sand and lava rocks of the ocean floor quickly gave way to mounds of colorful coral, dotted with long-spined, black sea urchins. The young boys had warned him not to step on them as the spines would break off and leave a terrible wound.

With a few more pulls of his arms, marine wildlife surrounded him. A grouping of yellow tang swam by, and two rainbow-colored parrotfish pecked at the coral. The closer he looked, the more he saw. The ocean came alive—a beautiful living aquarium. A giant sea turtle floated by like an eagle soaring on thermals. It swam close enough to grab, but Nick resisted, having seen warning signs along the beach to not touch the turtles. It gave Nick a languid glance and propelled away. Moorish idols, with their black and white striped bodies and long trailing fin, chased each other through the coral and rock formations.

Nick popped his head out of the water and beckoned to Maggie. She appeared content in the sun with her floppy hat and a romance novel in hand. She waved with the book. He didn't think he'd ever get her into the water. She'd told him the first *Jaws* movie premiered in 1975 when she turned two, and the sequel hit the theaters three years later. Her parents wouldn't let her see either of them, but she watched the movies in horror at a friend's house as a teenager. She swore then and there she would never swim in the ocean, not a hard promise to keep while living on the reservation.

She wouldn't listen to Nick's argument that the grizzly bears in Montana presented more danger than sharks. "That's what bear spray and a 44 magnum are for," she'd said. "I don't see you carrying either of those. I'm happy as a clam to stay on the beach."

Nick put his face back in the water. He had to admit, the vastness of the ocean intimidated him—as the depth increased, so did his imagination. The turquoise sea and abundant ocean life kept beckoning him further. Other tourists floating by reassured Nick that a hungry shark would eat them first. It reminded Nick of an old joke he told his pals when hiking in Glacier Park—he didn't need to outrun a grizzly bear, he only had to run faster than the slowest person in the group.

Another turtle swam under Nick, propelling itself with its front flippers. It rose to the surface, gulped air, and gracefully dove back down. A menacing eel's head appeared out of a crack in a rock and eyed Nick. It's powerful-looking jaw slowly opening and closing. No sign was needed—don't touch the eels.

* * *

Time held no meaning in the vastness of the ocean and Nick decided he'd abandoned his bride long enough. His confidence had grown, and each time he decided to head back to her something new caught his eye. The sense of adventure and wildness pulled on his soul, but as the ocean floor continued to drop off, images of a great white swam through Nick's mind. Out far enough, he decided to turn toward shore. He glided for the beach and peered above the waterline. The young Hawaiian boys splashed along the sand.

He kicked hard against the currents with his flippers, caught a small wave, and body surfed onto the beach. To the delight of the boys, he almost knocked them over. Taking a mouthful of water, he blew it out the top of his snorkel, like a spouting whale. The boys squealed at the ocean shower and helped Nick right himself on the sand.

He spit out the snorkel, pulled off the mask, and pushed his blond hair back. "Thank you, my fine sirs. What an amazing place you live in."

A four- or five-year-old boy handed him a seashell and smiled. The child reminded Nick so much of Ibrahim that he did a double-take—floppy dark hair, big ears, disproportionately large front teeth, and the same sweet innocence. Nick had fixed Ibrahim's leg after the earthquake in Turkey, and in turn, Ibrahim had ushered in Nick's restored vision miracle.

Nick turned the shell over in his hand, a colorful brown and white plaid pattern in the twisted tulip shape. "That's beautiful," he said and held it out to give back to the boy.

"That's okay, mister, you keep it," the boy said.

"That is so nice of you. Are you sure?"

"Yeah, I find them all the time. They're God's treasures."

Nick smiled at him, impressed with the boy's assurance and purity. "Well, thank you."

The boy returned to the water to search for more shells. His skinny butt barely held up his swim trunks. Nick turned to Maggie and gestured with the shell in hand. She waved back, but then reached into her bag, pulled out her phone, and answered it.

Probably an update to the new addition of The Hope Center. He smiled, watching her from a distance. *How in the world did I get so blessed?* Through all the ups and downs of his life, he never imagined he would feel this content and loved. God's message rang clearly in the last five years—through Guatemala, North Korea, Turkey, and Singapore—"*Trust Me.*"

Sitting on the warm tropical beach with the stunning, infinite ocean stretched out before him, it was certainly easier. "Father, help me trust you in all things," Nick prayed under his breath.

He looked back at the children as one splashed another, and a water fight erupted. He laughed. He and Maggie had never talked about having children of their own. When she directed the orphanage at The Hope Center, she'd joked about him becoming the father of 127 kids. She'd also confided in him that she and John concluded they would never have children after an unfortunate ectopic pregnancy early in Maggie's life.

Nick recently turned forty-seven and Maggie forty-six, not exactly the prime child-bearing age. Through the busy years of his training and trauma practice, he had never given it much thought. Maggie's love inspired this new desire to procreate. *Love needs to be shared.* "Father, I trust you in that as well."

Perhaps Maggie was right. They could live in Hawaii—get jobs to pay the rent and lead a quiet and modest life on the island. Nick looked at Maggie for a smile but realized she continued to talk on the phone. He looked again and saw her crying. *I hope nothing happened to the baby or mother?* His heart sank as he pushed himself up off the sand and quickly walked over to her.

Maggie wiped at her tears when he got to her, but she conversed in English, not Spanish. The familiar rush of adrenaline sped his heart and flooded his brain with anxiety. "Everything okay?" he whispered.

Maggie ignored him and continued her conversation. The voice of Maggie's father reverberated through the phone.

Nick considered Cliff and Mary Black Elk, Maggie's parents, as two of the kindest and most loving people on the planet. They'd raised four children in Browning, Montana—not an easy task. Impoverished, desolate, and depressed were some of the ways to describe the seat of the Blackfeet Nation, and with one of the county's highest unemployment stats, alcohol and drug problems, and suicide rates, it was no wonder. However, all four of their kids had survived and prospered. Even Maggie's two brothers, who'd seen their share of problems, had successful careers and families of their own.

Cliff rarely called Maggie, which heightened Nick's concern that something had happened to her mother.

"Yes, Daddy, I will. You know we will. I love you too." Maggie disconnected the call. She let the phone drop onto the towel, covered her face with her hands, and wept.

Nick sat down beside her and pulled her close, her weight dissolving into his arms while her tears dripped onto his chest.

"Maggie, what's happened?" he finally asked, not being able to stand it any longer.

"It's Joe," Maggie said between tears.

Nick's mind raced to all the terrible things that could happen to Maggie's younger brother. The tallest and funniest of the siblings, Joe had also seen his fair share of trouble, one short stint in jail and a longer one in rehab. But ten years had passed, and now he helped their father run the family cattle ranch. Unfortunately, car accidents on Montana's slippery roads and farming accidents all inflicted their yearly toll.

But six weeks earlier at the wedding, Cliff had pulled Nick aside and confided his concern for Joe. He didn't think it involved alcohol again, but Joe acted more and more out of character to those around him—some agitation and increased aggression. Nick recommended Joe see a physician and suggested that he could be depressed, something that went hand-in-hand with brutal winters and no sunshine. Nick hoped the despair hadn't pushed Joe to suicide; another major problem for the reservation.

"Joe's been diagnosed with a neurological disease," Maggie finally said while wiping her tears. She pulled away to explain.

"At your suggestion, Dad took him to a doctor, and they ran all sorts of tests. It is most likely Huntington's disease."

Tears continued to spill out of Maggie's deep, dark eyes, and he pulled her close again. *Huntington's disease.* Nick racked his brain to remember the symptoms and the cause of the illness. It did not affect the bones, so he didn't think he'd ever seen a patient with Huntington's, even as a medical student or intern. He recalled that it was a genetic disorder—rare and horrible. No wonder Maggie cried.

CHAPTER 5

HUNTINGTON'S

Nick leaned against the bed pillows beside Maggie. The cool breeze blowing off the ocean rattled the slats of the blinds covering the windows and patio door. He'd pulled them closed. It no longer felt like paradise. As soon as Maggie had finished the phone call, they'd left the beach and headed straight for their room to research Huntington's disease. Information precedes knowledge, and wisdom would help direct their next steps.

Nick stared at the article on his phone, afraid to share. The disease debilitated and devastated patients and their families, affecting the brain but not the bones. Since it had not been his discipline, he'd long forgotten the symptoms and etiology, and he hated to have to learn about them again. It was a horrible disease.

"What do you think?" Maggie asked, with puffy eyes and a red nose. Family meant everything to her, and what he'd learned would be difficult for her to hear.

"Hmmm…" he hesitated. He had to share the truth; she'd know soon enough. "I'm afraid it's not good."

Their eyes met, and she nodded for him to continue. He didn't know where to start, as every aspect of the disease was disturbing.

"This is the Huntington's Disease Society of America website." He flashed the phone screen toward her and then read the top line, "The symptoms of HD are described as like having ALS, Parkinson's and Alzheimer's—simultaneously."

She grimaced. "Isn't ALS Lou Gehrig's disease, the one where people grow weaker and weaker until their bodies give out?"

Nick nodded. Maggie gasped then asked, "So in Huntington's, their body gives out and their mind disintegrates?"

"I'm sorry, Maggie," Nick said. He wrapped his arm around her, and she dissolved into tears on his chest.

"Oh my God, poor Joe," she sputtered.

"It's a terrible disease, Mags. Now that I'm reading about it, I remember how devastating it is. It's pretty rare, and there is no treatment."

"Nothing?" she asked. "What happens to them?"

Nick put down his phone, sighed, and shook his head.

"Nick, tell me. I need to know. It's the only way we can fight this."

"How old is Joe?" Nick asked.

"He's forty-four, two years younger than me."

Nick looked Maggie in the eyes, "I'm afraid he'll most likely die in his fifties."

Maggie's chest heaved. "I didn't realize any of this was going on. Dad said that in the last few weeks, Joe had a tremor and difficulty working. Apparently, the doctor believes his recent anti-social behavior and depression are part of the symptoms. What will happen to him next?"

"All those symptoms progress—significant personality changes, impaired judgment, slurred speech, difficulty swallowing, then an unsteady gait and chorea."

Maggie furrowed her brow.

"Chorea is a movement disorder where the body moves involuntarily," Nick explained. "The word means dance, but there's nothing graceful about it…it's painful to watch."

"And then?"

"It's a cruel and inhumane death."

Nick immediately regretted his choice of words when tears dripped from Maggie's eyes.

"I'm sorry, Mags, I—"

"Nick, it's all right. I need to know."

She leaned into Nick, contemplated, then finally said, "What causes this terrible thing?"

Nick held her close and kissed the top of her head. He didn't want the conversation to get to this topic so soon, and he stalled. He got off the bed, went to the fridge, and pulled out a large bottle of water. He unscrewed the top and handed it to Maggie and sat back down on the bed. "Well, it's complicated and simple, all at the same time. When is the last time you've thought about the human genome?"

"You mean our genetic makeup?" Maggie asked. "You remember, my degree is in Social Work, right? We weren't required to take much science and math, thank God." She reflected for a moment. "I suppose I had a brief exposure in high school."

"You remember that all that we are—what we look like, how our bodies function—is coded in our DNA?"

"Yes, of course."

"In every one of our forty trillion cells, there is a nucleus packed with strands of DNA."

"How long are these DNA strands?" Maggie asked.

"Hmm, I've never really thought about that." Nick picked up his phone and searched.

He found an article and finally said, "Holy cow! This website says that each strand is over six feet long. If you put the DNA in all your cells end-to-end, they would wrap around our solar system twice."

"I would say, Holy God," Maggie smiled for the first time since hearing the news about her brother. "How in the world did God pack all that information into every cell?"

"The DNA is a microscopic molecule and is tightly twisted and folded inside the nuclei. We all carry ninety-two strands in each cell. Two strands of DNA make up a chromosome. So we have forty-six chromosomes. These exist in matching pairs, one from our father and the other from our mother. So, there are twenty-three pairs."

"This is giving me a headache, but I'm beginning to remember. What does all this DNA do?"

Nick drank a long swig of water and wiped his mouth with the back of his hand. "The DNA is like the master code for every system in our body. Along these strands are genes. It's wild, but the DNA is made up of only four building-block molecules called nucleotides: adenine, thymine, cytosine, and guanine."

"Only four?"

"Yes, and a series of these nucleotides along the strand of DNA creates the gene or code for the body to make proteins," Nick continued. "In turn, these proteins create our lives and run each of our delicate systems. The body's language is created when three of the nucleotides are read together, like cytosine-adenine-guanine, CAG. This codes for one particular building block of protein."

"Oh, I see, it's kind of like Morse code. Dot-dash-dot is one letter, and you start making words out of all the letters, and pretty soon you have a whole message."

"Exactly," Nick said.

"So what does this have to do with Huntington's disease?"

"These are some things I've long forgotten since my medical school days," Nick said and picked up his phone again. "So all pairs of chromosomes are numbered, one through twenty-three. On the fourth chromosome is a gene that codes for making the protein *huntingtin*, spelled with an '*i*,' I guess. The geneticists call these locations of the gene, *loci*." Nick shrugged and looked back at the article. "What's crazy is the function of huntingtin protein is not fully under-stood, but it's involved in many of the processes throughout the body. Without it, life would not exist. When there is a mutation of the gene, causing abnormal huntingtin protein, people develop Huntington's disease." Nick summarized. "At the end of the gene is a sequence of three of the DNA bases, cytosine-adenine-guanine, CAG, that is repeated several times. Huntington's disease is caused by an excessive amount of these repeats. In people without the disease, we possess fewer than thirty-five CAG repeats. Then there's a gray zone, but people with over forty CAG repeats develop Huntington's."

"Develop?" Maggie asked.

"Well, this abnormal huntingtin protein becomes toxic to the brain. Some scientists reason the aberrant molecule is sticky and clogs up the brain. That's why people don't develop symptoms until later in life."

"So do people develop this mutant gene, like from toxins in the environment?"

"No, it's…" The realization of what Nick needed to say next hit him square in the chest. He had been in his scientific mind, but the reality of the disease finally hit his heart. His words tumbled out. "It is a hereditary disease. You inherit the gene from one of your parents, and it only takes one of them."

Maggie looked at him, not understanding the implication.

"Remember how we get one of each chromosome from our mother and father? Only one parent is needed to pass on this disease; that's called autosomal dominant." His heart raced.

"But—" As the words left her mouth, Maggie's phone rang. Her father called again. She answered it straight away and placed it on speaker.

"Hi, Daddy. Nick and I are back at the condo, and I have you on speaker."

"Nicklaus…Maggie," Cliff's tired voice came through the phone. "I apologize for ruining your honeymoon with all this. We should have waited until you got home."

"Oh, Daddy, we would want to know, no matter how bad the news."

"Joe and Mom's doctor just called."

Nick's heart sank. There it was. The rest of the information that hit him like an earthquake. He sensed Maggie staring at him.

"They received your mom's genetic test. She carries the gene for Huntington's." His voice cracked.

"But she doesn't have any symptoms…does she?" Maggie demanded.

After a long silence, Nick thought they had disconnected the call.

"Are you there, Daddy?" Maggie asked.

"Yes, princess. The doctor assumes your mom's depression has been due to Huntington's all along. And she's had a few falls this year, but she didn't tell anyone."

Maggie turned to Nick. "Can this be true?"

Nick nodded. "These genetic diseases are tricky. They allow different expressions for people and create distinct symptoms, which may start at atypical times in their lives and be more or less severe."

"The doctor told me this disease is passed down through generations," Cliff said. "He also indicated that Mom's symptoms aren't as bad because she has fewer base pairs… whatever that means."

"Well, wouldn't one of our grandmas or grandpas suffer from it as well?" Maggie asked.

Nick watched Maggie process the information. Many of her grandparents and great-grandparents had short life spans, something always attributed to their Native American heritage and to the chronic conditions of life on the reservation. But Nick saw the realization in her eyes as the gravity of the news became a reality.

Maggie verbalized his thoughts, "If this is autosomal dominant, and Mom has it, then I have a fifty-fifty chance of having it as well, don't I?"

She looked into Nick's eyes for confirmation.

He nodded.

"Yes, princess…yes," her dad agreed.

"Oh, Daddy, I am so sorry. We will figure this out. We're coming home."

"Nick, I asked our doctor about treatment options, and he didn't know of any," Cliff said. "What do you think we should do?"

"I was reading about that when you called, Cliff. I'm afraid I'll need to do more research, but there may be new treatments on the horizon, especially coming out of Poland. I saw some articles on gene therapy…manipulating a person's genome, but I don't know enough about it yet."

"I wish you would stay and finish your honeymoon, but if you must come home, I understand," Cliff said. "This is turning our world upside down."

"I love you, Daddy. We'll call you when we get home," Maggie said and hung up the phone.

Nick and Maggie stared at each other in disbelief. When he reached out for her and pulled her close, Maggie melted into tears. He'd never seen her this distraught except after John's death. Typically, she lived full of faith and optimism, even through the worst news. But he also understood her quality of life hung in the balance of a coin toss, a fifty-fifty shot of having this devastating disease.

Her body quaked in his arms.

"Maggie, we'll deal with this as it comes. You have to put your faith in the fact that you have an equal chance of not having it. That's what I'm going to believe until told otherwise." He tried to say it with as much confidence as he could muster.

His attempts to comfort her were ineffective—the more he talked, the more she cried. With her firm foundation in the promises of God, Maggie had never feared death. She always faced adversity head-on with her shield of faith and the sword of the Spirit protecting and arming her. Her tower of strength had become a puddle of doubt. The transformation confused Nick.

"Maggie, everything is going to be okay. You don't have one sign of the disease, so I don't think you have it." His frustration clouded his affirmation.

She pulled away, sat up straight, and wiped at her tears. Now she scared him. Her face reflected a mixture of fear and anger, and when she stood up and walked into the bathroom, he thought he had failed her.

But she didn't lock herself inside. She returned right away with an object clutched in her fist.

"I am so angry at the devil, trying to steal the joy of this moment," Maggie said. "I wanted to share this with you at dinner tonight."

She opened her hand, and Nick took the small white stick she held out to him. He turned it over and understood immediately what upset Maggie.

The plus mark said it all, but Maggie confirmed the result out loud. "I'm pregnant, Nick."

CHAPTER 6

DOUBLE-MINDED

Emy stood at her bathroom mirror and examined her reflection. Empty eyes gazed back at her. She scarcely recognized herself and found it strange to stare into her own eyes and see nothing, feel nothing. She patted her pale cheeks as if to bring herself to life.

Her father's last words had dropped an unwelcome dilemma in her lap. Then he was gone. The funeral home picked up his body, and she paid Maria her final wages—so anticlimactic. *Is this all there is to life?* Lukas had finally answered his phone, and they agreed to have a small memorial service in the next few weeks, at *his* convenience.

Returning on the train earlier that evening, she couldn't shake the feeling that the universe, the stars, or whatever false deity people worshiped, conspired against her. Even with her parents gone, her son's life in the balance, and her husband entangled in an affair, she could think of people that had it worse off. *I guess this is life.* The thought ushered in more discouragement.

Having an innate hatred of conflict, she doubted if she'd confront Keith tonight. Perhaps it didn't matter. If he wanted to screw some brainless bimbo, *have at it*. But what if the woman was someone she knew or a good friend? *That would hurt.* But strangely, the physical act of him copulating with some other woman didn't bother her. The sweaty, body fluid-filled business of intercourse fulfilled a simple biological act. The betrayal and loss of trust stung. She always thought Keith would have her back. Loneliness poured in like a great depression.

She'd always been a deep thinker and erred on the side of melancholy. Having both her MD and PhD positioned her on the genius spectrum, but she understood the placement also increased her propensity toward mental illness. Antidepressants never seemed to work and only heightened her sense of failure in social and academic circles. During the deepest valleys of life, she occasionally entertained the notion that suicide could be a way out of her pain.

Emy frowned at her reflection, then pinched the puffy, dark circles under her eyes. No wonder she'd become depressed. Both her parents had died within the year, and her husband sought comfort in an affair. Emy scowled. *Oh yeah, and now I'm Jewish…Christ. I don't know what that even means.* Not a safe confession seventy-five years ago in Europe, but now it didn't matter to anyone around her and especially to her.

How she detested all religions. The world fought every war over gold, oil, or some absurd god. The most hypocritical people she knew were religious zealots, including her PhD professor. He was a devout Jew, and she'd slept with him, for who knows what reason. He wasn't even sexy. She grimaced at the memory of the coarse black hair that covered his body.

She coated her toothbrush with Colgate, turned on the water, and applied the brush with vigor and determination. A quick glance in the mirror confirmed the closed door. Keith told her she brushed her teeth with such vengeance she needed to keep it shut.

She scrubbed harder and harder until her gums bled and ached. *Maybe he is right.* She spat, bent to rinse her mouth with water, and spat again. Looking at her reflection, she peered from one eye to the other: the right eye was blue and the left, hazel. She was unique—something that made her proud, and another reason she'd suspected, early in high school biology, that her parents had adopted her.

Her teacher explained the amount of melanin in the specialized cells in the eye called melanocytes controlled eye color. Her further study confirmed this truth. But he taught that a single gene influenced eye color, a misconception. Now, as a geneticist, she understood that, yes, the OCA2 gene on chromosome 15 had a heavy hand in determining eye color, but researchers have identified eight genes that impact eye color—and there could be more. Her teacher communicated correctly that brown eyes dominated over blue. Everyone in her family had dark eyes, and that made it highly unlikely that she would have anything different.

Her biology teacher didn't understand that heterochromia iridum, two different colored eyes, was rarer still. This trait, autosomal dominant, required that a parent or grandparent had the same. None of them did. Besides her eyes, her appearance differed from the rest of the family.

Emy flexed her lips into the mirror to check her teeth. Stupid gap. Most days, the space between her front teeth didn't bug her. She'd stopped obsessing about it. Although in grade school, the other girls teased her unmercifully. Her parents never put her in braces to correct it, maybe because her mother didn't like her.

The bathroom door creaked open. "Mama, I'm headed to bed."

Emy wiped a tear from the corner of her eye as her daughter, Cecylia, appeared in the mirror.

Cecylia, wearing silky pants and a simple white tank top, stepped into the bathroom and hugged her from behind. "Goodnight, Mama," she said.

Emy turned and held her. "Goodnight, Ceci. I hope you sleep well."

Her daughter hugged her tight. "I'm sorry about Grandpa."

"Me too, Ceci, me too." She patted her back. Cecylia's breasts pushed into hers. At seventeen, she had grown into a woman.

Emy released the embrace and held her daughter by the shoulders. "Are you getting enough to eat these days? You seem a bit thin." She examined Ceci up and down.

"Oh, Mama, you know I am. We've been working out extra hard for the championships."

Emy had forgotten that Ceci's school team vied for the national volleyball title next week and hoped she'd marked time off on her calendar. She stroked a strand of her daughter's hair behind her ear that had fallen out of her ponytail. Truth be told, Ceci had become the spitting image of herself at that age—tall, athletic, thick black hair. Ceci's sister, Hanna, was shorter and squarer in the face, but when they were all together, they were often mistaken as sisters—especially when Emy remembered to cover the speckling of gray in her hair. *Children reflecting their parents' image—that's genetics, the way it should be.* Although, neither daughter inherited her heterochromia iridum, as both had beautiful crystalline-blue eyes.

One song Emy shared with her girls came to mind, and she sang the first line:

"You blue-eyed brunette baby," she crooned to move the conversation to happier ground.

Ceci joined in and rapped the verse:

"So make it quick, candle lit. It's the way you move. Snap your fingers, move your legs, and shake your hips. You amaze me." She wiggled her bottom with her arms overhead as she sang.

They finished the chorus together:

"You blue-eyed brunette baby."

Emy pulled her close and didn't let go. *How does time slip away?* Ceci had spring semester to finish, followed by a quick summer, then she'd join her sister at the University of Kraków in the fall. *I better carve out some time with her.*

It made her feel old that she'd soon have two college students. The university emphasized sciences, something both girls excelled in. At least the school produced quality citizens. One of the Jagiellonian University's famous alumni was Karol Wojtyla, who became Pope John Paul II. When Emy and Keith moved from Germany to Poland four years after the pope had died, the country still mourned the beloved man. And although she wanted nothing to do with her family's faith, she celebrated with the locals about having the legacy of a Polish Pope. It brought a great sense of pride for the people. Besides, he was a decent man and that, in Emy's mind, was scarce these days.

"Sure I can't talk you into attending the University of Poznań? You could stay at home and save money."

"Oh, Mama, we've been through this," she said, sounding irritated.

"I know, I know, Ceci. It's a mother's prerogative to try," she hugged her tight.

Emy had tried to convince both Hanna and Ceci to stay closer to home, but the girls wanted some distance from their parents, an unspoken truth. *Probably a good thing right now.* BioGenics, a privately funded institution, remained separate from the local university, but she knew all the professors in medicine on a first-name basis. The girls would have had an easy path into medical school, but they wanted to make their own way. They'd inherited their strong will and interest in medicine from her. Keith's head spun at the mere mention of blood and was better suited as a musician.

Emy had become the first physician in her family. *Well, her adopted family.* She knew nothing about her biological relatives but assumed they came from impoverished Polish immigrants, Gypsies even. She hoped Hanna and Ceci became the second and third doctors in the family.

"I'm very proud of you, Ceci."

"I know, Mama," she said. "I'm sorry again about Grandpa."

"In Papa's last moments, he told me to tell you he loves you and is so proud of you," Emy said. It was untrue, but she felt she had to say something to comfort her daughter. A little white lie to encourage her and make her feel special. It seemed to have the effect, and Ceci released her embrace and wandered off to bed.

Emy returned to the sink and looked in the mirror. She twisted the handle of the cold-water spigot and splashed her face. Once Ceci left for school, she'd be alone.

She toweled off the moisture and forced down her anger to face Keith in the bedroom.

She clicked off the bathroom light, walked to her dresser in the bedroom, and grabbed a hair tie to put her hair up for the night. Keith reclined in bed; the glow of his phone lit his face as it did most nights. Now she understood why.

He'd hardly acknowledged the death of her father, saying something pacifying when she got home. That was it. Heat rose in her neck.

She looked down at the unopened manila envelope on the dresser. *Immanuel. How could Papa misspell my name?* She couldn't deal with it right now. Emy took a deep breath, sucking in courage. "I'm Jewish," she said.

He acted like he hadn't heard her, as his attention stayed on the screen. He continued typing. A love note, no doubt. Or sexting.

She turned to him and put her hands on her hips. "I'm a Jew," she said again, loud enough to be heard.

It broke the trance, and he glanced up at her for a moment, then resumed typing.

"Christ, Keith, did you hear me?" she shouted.

He looked at her over his phone with suspicion. "Uh… what?"

She rarely erupted in anger. She was more the passive-aggressive personality—a burn-your-toast-type of fighter.

The heat shot from her neck to her face, and her hands tremored.

"I'm Jewish," she said, trying not to let her voice betray her emotions.

His face contorted into a ludicrous surprised look. "Jewish?" he repeated.

Years ago, they had discussed her adoption suspicions but decided it didn't matter, so they had rarely spoken about it.

"Uh, not sure what that means for you?" Keith said. "You're not exactly the religious type."

Emy resisted the urge to run from the room, and when he returned his attention back to the phone, she squared herself to fight.

"Put down the damn phone, Keith!" she screamed.

The outburst had the desired effect. He dropped the phone to his side and stared at her. It broke the dam of emotions that bubbled under the surface, and she covered her face with her hands.

"Do you love her?" The question escaped her lips as the tears brimmed her eyelids.

She spied between her fingers. He looked away. She could see his wheels spinning to whirl a lie.

"What?" he asked.

She recognized he was stalling for time to fabricate a story. She knew him all too well.

"Don't even try that crap with me, Keith," she yelled and dropped her hands to her hips. Rage displaced her tears. "You've already betrayed me, so don't you dare lie to me."

He reached for his phone, turned it off, and sat up. He couldn't look her in the eye. A frown covered his face, and his body swayed back and forth.

"Is she pretty?"

He sat in silence.

When Izzi tested the woman's DNA, Emy would learn everything about her—down to each base sequence of her genome, but she wanted to hear it from him. Seething fury sickened her as bile filled the back of her throat.

"Is she young?" Her voice cracked under the weight of his infidelity.

Nothing.

"Say something, damn it!"

Keith released a long exhale. "How did you find out?"

"It's pretty obvious, don't you think?" She pointed to the phone.

He shrugged and put a hand on the phone.

His nonchalant attitude threatened to send her into violence. She was a pacifist, but at the moment, she pictured herself gouging out his eyeballs.

"I didn't think—" he began.

"Oh, screw you. I had a pair of your shorts DNA tested."

His face instantly flushed, and he cleared his throat. "You what?"

She heard shock and anger and sarcasm. "That's what I do, remember? I'm a geneticist, for Christ's sake."

"You took a pair of my underwear?" he said with indignation and laid back on the pillows.

Emy's head swirled, and she reached for the bedpost to steady herself.

"Our relationship has turned to this?" he said defiantly. "I'm not sure you have much room to talk," he accused her and sat back up, glowering at her.

Ah, always the victim. A role Keith had perfected.

Emy collapsed to the floor on her knees and held her forehead with her hand.

There it is, after all these years. She assumed it would come. Like the thousands of DNA samples that she'd tested for mutations of genes that signaled a person's cancer risk. *It was only a matter of time.*

Her mind and body went numb. *What am I going to do? Leave him? Stay with someone who stabbed me in the heart?* She picked herself up and clung to the bedpost.

"Why?" she said through tears.

"Jesus, Emy, you really want me to answer that?" he said with resentment. "It's like there are two of you. One minute you are kind and loving, and the next, you're a cold fish. I never know who I'm coming home to." He sighed with desperation. "We've talked about this for years. You are so stinking… double-minded," he yelled. "It's making me crazy."

He was right, but this was the last thing she needed to hear.

"Is it one of our friends?" she finally asked.

He slowly shook his head.

She nodded. *One small victory*—if she dared call it that. At least it wasn't another betrayal.

"How long?"

"Long?"

"Christ, Keith, how long has this one been going on?" Her anger rose again.

"Only a few months," he said, as if that was supposed to make her feel better.

"Where did you meet her?"

He shrugged and shook his head. "At a club."

She knew the danger. Every girl wanted to bed the drummer.

"Is she pretty?" she asked again.

He shrugged, but a slight smile betrayed the truth.

"How old is she?"

"Emy, do you really want to hear these things?" Beads of sweat glistened on his forehead.

"Do you love her?"

Emy expected him to lie, but Keith nodded. "Maybe."

CHAPTER 7

OCEAN ANGELS

Maggie waited to sit up until she saw daylight around the edges of the blinds. Nick stirred and sighed. It had been a fretful night between the elation of Maggie's pregnancy and the possibility of Maggie or their baby having Huntington's disease. They'd hardly slept. The more they researched, the deeper their fear penetrated until Maggie became angry. "I refuse to let discouragement tear away our joy!" she'd said and then prayed. Her strength lifted the heavy quilt of oppression from them both, and they slept off and on the rest of the night. However, when Maggie had stepped out of the shower, she'd noticed Nick on his phone, further investigating the disease.

Now at breakfast in the dining room, Maggie saw fear in Nick's eyes as worry of the disease crept back into his brain. Plain and simple, Huntington's was a terrible diagnosis. It struck people in the prime of their lives with debilitating symptoms that ended in a horrific death. The truth that no treatment or cure existed created hopelessness and anxiety in Maggie and Nick.

Maggie watched her husband as he munched on the fresh fruit and homemade sweet rolls that the innkeeper's wife had prepared. He sat quietly, and his pupils seemed to focus somewhere in the distance—the ever so subtle signal that his mind raced a million miles an hour. Nick was a rescuer, and the traumatic news percolated in his brain. This produced an unsolvable puzzle, impossible to relinquish.

She finally leaned across the table and stroked his chin with her fingertips. He hadn't shaved for a few days and sported a dark five o'clock shadow. The sun had bleached his wavy blond hair and highlighted the laugh lines around his eyes, and his Oakley sunglasses were suspended by a colorful lanyard around his neck. He looked ready for the cover of Surfer magazine. When she'd met him a decade ago, she recognized him as ruggedly handsome. A long line of women had hoped to become Mrs. Nicklaus Hart, but he chose her.

"You okay?" she asked.

He startled from his trance, sighed deeply, and nodded.

"Look, Nick, I've lived trusting God. That means trusting Him with everything, my life, and my death. Number one, we don't know if I have the disease until we get the lab test. Number two…well, let's wait for number one."

Nick took her hand and brought it to his lips. He tenderly kissed the spaces between her knuckles. "I love you so much, Maggie. You are my everything…I don't know what I would do—" he stammered and stared out the window to the ocean below. Maggie followed his gaze.

The gentle rollers of the ocean swelled with a rising tide. Offshore, a humpback whale breached the surface and came down with an enormous splash like a cement truck dropped from the sky. Other diners at the tables along the windows saw the performance as well and erupted with a unanimous cheer. Soon, people at the inside tables left their chairs to stand next to the windows in hopes of another splashdown. They weren't disappointed as the whale breached two more times to applause from the group. More whales from the pod spouted water into the air in clouds of mist. The sightings tapered off until one of the mature adults flashed its tail, and the pod dove deep and disappeared.

"They put on quite a show for the honeymooners, I see."

Nick and Maggie turned to see the innkeeper standing beside their table, smiling ear to ear. Suddenly his face turned serious, and he lowered his voice while the standing guests returned to their seats. "The missus told me of the news about your brother and mother. I am so sorry, and we want to know if there is anything we can do for you two? We are sorry that you have to leave us so soon."

Maggie considered the man's eyes and saw genuine sincerity. "Thank you for your concern for my family. It means a lot to me. We appreciate all your care and hospitality."

"I'm disappointed you have to leave this paradise so early." The man stretched his short arms over the expanse of the ocean.

"We tried to get a plane out today, but the first available seats are tomorrow," Nick said.

"*Co ma wisieć, nie utonie,*" the man said in a strong accent.

Maggie and Nick looked at him for understanding.

"Old Polish habits die hard." He chuckled. "We have lots of crazy sayings. It translates to: 'what is meant to hang, won't drown.'"

Maggie gave him another confused look.

The man laughed. "Yes, that is the problem with Polish sayings, sometimes they don't translate well. Polish people understand the meaning, but for others, it is confusing." He rubbed his chin. "It means, 'what is meant to be, will be.'"

He shrugged. "And what it means is that we must make the most of this day!" the man declared. His enthusiasm returned, "Tonight, I will make you the most special Polish dinner and serve it to you on your private veranda overlooking this gorgeous sea." He clapped his hands together and brought them to his heart.

"You are a true romantic," Maggie said, encouraging him.

"Yes, tonight you will feast on *kotlet schabowy and pierogi*, Polish pork schnitzel and dumplings."

"Sounds great, but do you mind if we eat early?" Nick asked. "We decided to swim with the manta rays tonight."

The man drummed his fingers together. "Yes, by all means. You must dance with the ghosts of the ocean. It is an out-of-this-world experience."

He turned to go when Nick stopped him. "Do you mind if I ask you a question about Poland?"

Maggie raised her eyebrows and tilted her head, but quickly understood that Nick still worked to solve their dilemma.

"I have been reading about the disease that Maggie's mother and brother are diagnosed with, and I understand that there is a considerable amount of research coming out of Poland on Huntington's. Can you tell me about your country?"

The innkeeper came back to the table, swaying from one foot to the other with excitement. "You want me to tell you about my beloved Poland?" His eyes danced. "It is one of the most beautiful places, filled with some of the smartest people on earth." He jabbed his thumb at his chest as if to say, *including yours truly*. "We are known for our humor as well." He laughed. "Poland has a highly advanced education system. With all the political arguments happening in America, you must know that it has state-funded social security and a universal health care system for all citizens. Honestly, if you get a chance to go, you will not be disappointed." He smiled at them. "But tonight, you will get a taste of Poland." He threw a kiss with his fingertips. "It makes me hungry thinking about going back."

"Do you get to go home often?" Maggie asked.

"After we left, I have only visited a handful of times, as most of my family is scattered around the world." His jubilation dissolved to sorrow. "I'm afraid, Mrs. Hart, my home changed forever after World War II. In my mind, I go back to the early days and relish the stories woven by my family and friends."

"May I ask how old you are?" Nick asked.

The man's eyes narrowed. "Yes, Dr. Hart, you are a smart man, and you understand why I live in Hawaii. Maybe you, too, have Polish blood running through your veins." A faint smile appeared, but then vanished. "I am eighty-five. I turned five years old when the Nazis invaded. Their intentions for us Jews became more and more clear and sinister, so my family escaped to Greece. That was a godsend, in hindsight. I most likely would have ended up in the hands of the 'Angel of Death,' Mengele, that monster. He murdered dwarfs." The innkeeper flashed with anger but instantly turned it off. "But enough of that because now I host these most wonderful people—Dr. and Mrs. Hart." His smile returned. "Please excuse me, I must start on my mouth-watering dumplings," he said and turned to the kitchen.

* * *

Nick and Maggie almost missed their nighttime excursion after eating the feast and resting. The taste of Poland did not disappoint. The innkeeper hadn't exaggerated his ability to prepare the cuisine. A romantic table set in white linen and fine china, with rose petals scattered on the table and floor, transformed their private patio. Over the main course, they'd agreed to live fully and not walk in fear.

At the dock, the crew had fitted all the passengers for wetsuits, masks, and snorkels. Maggie pulled at the neoprene around her belly. The swells of the ocean rocked the large boat off the shore of Kona, giving Maggie the thrill of being alive but threatening to exacerbate her morning sickness.

Mild nausea had started a few days earlier, just enough to make her suspect she might be pregnant. She bought a test kit and the result surprised her. She never thought, in her wildest imagination, that she'd get pregnant on their wedding night, or anytime, for that matter. She adored children and always wanted one of her own—flesh of her flesh—but it'd never happened for her and John.

This reality of the baby remained a miracle and a mystery too immense for her to absorb. As a tiny speck on an endless ocean in the pitch dark with distant scattered lights as her only bearings, the fact that a living soul grew in her belly jumbled her emotions.

"How are you doing?" Nick held her hand.

"Uh…I kind of forgot that I don't go into the water. And here I am about to jump into an ocean in the middle of the night."

"I would never make you do anything you didn't want to do. You really don't have to go in."

"We made a pledge to live life to the fullest and not walk in fear, right?" She gripped his hand hard. "I should have vowed not to swim in fear," she said nervously, "but I'm gonna go for it!"

As the words left her mouth, the ship's captain cut the motor, and complete silence enveloped them. A hush fell over the other ten tourists on the boat as their eyes adjusted to the darkness, and the stars shined in brilliance. Nick and Maggie had witnessed the celestial display from on top of the Mission Mountains in Montana, but this was even more splendid. The Milky Way dazzled, and for the first time, Maggie perceived the subtle colors floating through its center. Never had she seen this many stars so bright and intense.

One of the other passengers said it all for them, "Wow."

Chills flowed through Maggie's body. It was as if she were looking directly at the Divine. It was all she could do to keep from breaking into one of her favorite songs, *The Heavens Declare*.

"Isn't it something?" The captain had made his way to the center of the group. "I never tire of seeing this. But we better get you all in the water." He flicked on a headlamp, and the stars instantly diminished. "The crew is putting the light ring in the water, and we'll help each one of you out of the boat. Once in the water, please remember your instructions: grab onto the ring, let yourself float on the surface, and hold on. Let's hope the manta rays are hungry tonight."

"Yeah, and the sharks are not," said another tourist, verbalizing Maggie's thoughts.

"You ready?" Nick asked and put his arm around her as they stood in line, holding their equipment.

"You really want me to jump off this perfectly good boat into that black ocean?" She peered over the side. "How do we know there aren't any sharks?"

A young boy in front of them turned to her and said, "Actually, manta rays are in the shark family. But they only feed on plankton." The boy had the classic features of Down syndrome, upward slanted eyes and a flattened facial profile.

Maggie smiled but wasn't convinced. "Don't they have a barb on their tails?"

"Those are stingrays," he said, "the mantas have a similar tail, but no barb. They're harmless."

Maggie's wetsuit squeaked as she squatted down to his eye level. "You are very smart. How do you know all this?"

"I swam with the mantas two times before. I can help you not be afraid," he said and reached for her hand.

She smiled at him and then up at Nick and shrugged. "Ha! I have an escort."

The boy's parents jumped into the water, and the crew helped Maggie and the boy with their flippers, masks, and snorkels. They eased into the water with Nick right behind them. The boy's innocence and bravery melted Maggie's fear as they kicked out the few yards in the dark to a large floating ring.

The crew swam behind them and placed foam noodles under their feet, so they floated motionless on top of the water. The high-intensity lights along the ring cast pillars of light into the bottomless ocean. A rope disappeared into the deep that tethered them to the ocean floor. For a moment, Maggie imagined herself leashed to the space station, floating in the vast cosmic emptiness.

Tiny flashes of light quickly invaded the beams of light, like fireflies dancing on a summer night. Before the voyagers had submerged, the captain told them as soon as the lights came on, the plankton would follow and then hopefully the mantas. Maggie searched all around but only saw a few smaller fish darting in and out of the edges of illumination. She looked toward the boy on her left, and he gave her a thumbs up. She returned it and then flashed Nick the same.

Maggie shivered. She was cold, even with the wetsuit, and wasn't sure how long she'd last in the chilly water. But before she retreated, a massive shadow floated into view from the depths of the sea—then another, and another. The manta rays had come. Their massive fins flapped gracefully as they circled and swirled underneath. Maggie had never seen such creatures up close: their bulgy eyes were set on the sides of their heads, they had long needled tails and shark-like dorsal fins. Large cephalic loops protruded off the edges of their enormous gaping mouths, scooping up plankton like cruising alien ships. Their black topsides blended into the dark water, but as they loop-de-looped, they revealed their bellies, and Maggie saw the unique markings of white and black speckling. Enormous lever-like gills on their undersurface filtered planktonic food from the water.

The mantas circled closer and closer as the plankton concentrated under the bright lights. A massive ray headed straight for Maggie, but before she could scream, it turned and glided inches from her chest; the gigantic beast stirred up a current that rippled along her body. It was the most terrifying and peaceful moment Maggie had ever experienced in her life. Another massive manta swam toward her, but she let her body go limp, and again, it somersaulted under her body. The control of these magnificent creatures with wingspans over twelve feet in width astonished her.

It was mesmerizing to watch in silence as the peaceful and elegant creatures flapped and danced a slow-motion ballet all around them. The innkeeper was right: the mantas were sea angels.

In the majesty of the moment, Maggie's worries and fears of pregnancy and the horrors of Huntington's vanished—she forgot how scary life could be.

CHAPTER 8

EUTHANASIA

DECEMBER

Emy and Keith's days of argument over his infidelity ended in her exhaustion. She'd slept in Hanna's bed for the last two weeks, and her psyche edged on overload with Papa's death and Danek's rapid deterioration.

Walking down the corridor of the hospital, Emy whispered under her breath, "Thank god I can get some rest with the upcoming holiday slowdown." Her body ached from the train ride after her father's funeral.

The ceremony to bury him was quick and straightforward. She hadn't planned to invite the local priest, but he came anyway and babbled with religious jargon. Lukas came late. Papa was dead. That was it.

All she could manage was to shelf the grief of Keith's betrayal and coexist in emotional isolation. Izzi would soon have his girlfriend's DNA analysis completed, and Emy would have a complete picture of every aspect of the woman—down to each individual base pair. Until then, she tried, unsuccessfully, to not think about it.

She still bristled at his question: "What would you think of an open marriage?"

Yeah. You get laid as much as you want, and I provide for our family. It made her angry, and she couldn't dismiss the statement any easier than his comment about her double-mindedness. He was right, and that was the problem. She was of two distinct minds—one that was endearing and gentle and the other, aggressive and demeaning. She'd learned from her DNA analysis that antidepressants didn't work for her and wouldn't bother to try them again.

As she pushed the elevator's button for the fourth floor of the hospital, her father's final words echoed in her mind. "You are a Jew."

The coincidence that the origin of the name Danek was Hebrew seemed so appropriate now, and probably the reason she bore the mutant gene. One in twenty-nine Ashkenazi Jews is a carrier.

After having two healthy children, the disease wasn't on Emy's radar. She'd ignored the fact that her genome testing had shown the cystic fibrosis transmembrane conductance regulator, CFTR, gene mutation on chromosome seven. She hadn't considered having Keith's genome tested. But after Danek was born, they ran Keith's DNA—he, too, carried the mutation. Cystic fibrosis, an autosomal recessive disease, required both parents to pass on the mutant gene. This gave them a one in four chance of having a child with the syndrome.

Emy and Keith had passed on the faulty gene that produces an abnormal CFTR protein responsible for regulating the flow of salt and fluids in and out of Danek's cells. They'd witnessed the results when the mucus in Danek's body was so thick and sticky it quickly choked his lungs, pancreas, and bowels, sentencing him to an early suffocating death. *No wonder Keith had checked out.*

Currently, in some afflicted children, advances in medical care increased the life expectancy into their twenties and thirties. Still, the real victory would come when Emy and her colleagues around the world used their tools to cut out the defective gene and replace it with a healthy one.

Danek's decline showed that editing the mutant gene was not so easy, but with more recent advances in gene therapy, Emy still had hope for the future.

However, she didn't feel like much of a competent physician since Danek got sick. He had displayed all the early signs: frequent respiratory infections, stunted growth, greasy stools, and salty-tasting skin. Her brain had shut them all out. The day she and Keith sat with Danek in the pediatrician's office, and the doctor revealed the genetic test results, a stabbing pain pierced her under the ribs. Her own mind had betrayed her. *How could I have missed the diagnosis?* In her darkest moments, she imagined her colleagues chuckling at her behind her back.

Emy exited the elevator and walked down the hallway to where a nurse outside of Danek's room peeled off the protective gear required for entering a room with a patient in isolation. As Emy walked up to the door, the nurse acknowledged her with a curt nod. When the nurse wouldn't look Emy in the eyes, a wave of guilt and shame washed over Emy. Not only had she passed the gene to her son, but she'd also failed him in her treatment.

Emy examined the personal protective gear, all neatly stacked on the cart. Her own regulations required all personnel going into a contaminated room to don a gown, surgical cap, mask, and gloves. She hadn't had skin-to-skin contact with her son for a year. She glanced at the departing nurse and over her shoulder to the deserted hallway.

The nurses on the ward performed all the necessary medical care to keep Danek alive. Still, it was her son's full-time caregiver, Frieda, who faithfully watched over every other aspect of his moment-to-moment concerns. Emy handpicked the no-nonsense German nurse from Berlin who her father had recommended. Frieda's husband had died in a tragic auto accident three years ago and they had no children, so she was a perfect choice. If Emy hadn't been the CEO of BioGenics, there was no way that she and Keith could have afforded this level of attention.

She hesitated before reaching for the handle and pushing open the door. The sickeningly sweet, grape-like smell of pseudomonas hit her nose. Frieda, who stood over Danek, stared at her with horror.

"Dr. Christianson…you mustn't—" Frieda started, but Emy cut her off.

"Not today, Frieda. Not today."

"But you put yourself and others at risk," Frieda shot back in her German frankness.

Emy put her hand up for her to stop.

"Today, I am his mother."

Emy took two steps into the room, but without a mask, the smell threatened to make her vomit. Either that or it was the sight of her emaciated son, curled into a fetal position, naked except for a diaper. Fans blew cold air over him to keep his fever down, but diffused the awful stench throughout the room.

She had done this to him. She'd manipulated his genes four years ago using the early CRISPR technique. For the first year, he'd shown rapid improvement in his lungs and gastrointestinal system. They all celebrated the victory of restoring her son to good health.

The second year after treatment, he demonstrated significant behavior problems, including social withdrawal and the inability to be comforted. At three years, they recognized the gene therapy had knocked out his pain receptors.

Who would have considered that the CFTR gene was similar to the genes involved in pain regulation? The absence of pain sounds idyllic, but pain is a necessary motivator. Pain forces a human to stop doing something harmful, to move from an uncomfortable position, or to change from something destructive in their life. It took the medical team two years before they realized that Danek had no sensory feedback, which caused his severe behavioral issues. He was floating free, untethered to what it means to be human.

Soon after, he developed pressure ulcers. His body's regulatory and protective systems that told him to move reflexively off an elbow or a sore backside turned off. A sacral ulcer grew to the size of a cantaloupe, and the skin covering his heels and elbows wore off to the bone. Even under the watchful eye of Frieda, the ulcers grew and became infected. On and off antibiotics for the last two years, the bacteria won. The pseudomonas, with a classic sweet smell, underwent DNA mutations of its own and became resistant to every antibiotic.

In the last year, he'd finally stopped his constant screaming—a haunting howl as if he were trapped in a continuous night terror. For the previous twelve months, Danek had been locked in a fetal position in this vegetative state. What was left was an unrecognizable creature.

Emy swallowed down her bile and stepped to his bedside,

aware of Frieda's watchful glare. Emy sensed the caregiver stiffen as she reached for her son and touched his forehead. The child was burning hot and did not react to her touch.

She looked up at Frieda, whose eyes bore into her from above her mask.

"Dr. Christianson, you must. It is time."

Emy's eyes traced back to her son: his head balding except for patches of wispy tufts of hair, his eye sockets sunken and closed, his skin an eerie blue from the translucent nature of his skin—probably because of another gene that had inadvertently changed. She swallowed hard and forced herself to not vomit.

"I think we should give it more time," Emy said. "Nature will take its course."

Frieda scoffed loudly. "That ship has already left the port," she said in a strong German accent. Her accusing glare pierced Emy's conscience.

"This child…your child is suffering. You must end his misery."

"I am a physician," Emy snapped back. Frieda's forwardness forced rage to surge from deep in her belly. "I took an oath to preserve life, not take it."

Frieda spread her gloved hands over the boy. "This is no longer life. You are blind if you do not see that. Ja, he will be dead soon enough, but don't prolong his agony."

"I don't believe he is in any pain."

"How do you know that? You don't know what is going through his mind. You must put a stop to this. You must put an end to his suffering."

Emy's anger brought words to her mind, and they spilled out her mouth. "Ja, we Germans comprehend how best to do this." She regretted them as soon as they came out. She saw the mask tighten over Frieda's face as she clenched her jaws. "I'm sorry, I didn't mean—" Her tears prevented her from saying more.

Frieda nodded. Her eyes filled with compassion and forgiveness. She unzipped her protective body cover, brought out a syringe of clear fluid, and held it out to Emy.

Emy's hand shook as she took the pentobarbital. In Poland, the right to die laws were unambiguous; the authorities could charge her with murder in medically assisted euthanasia. But since no one would ever know, it wasn't that knowledge that made her body tremble. It was the fact that she was about to kill her son—she'd done that long ago when she'd signed him up for the trial, but this became the final act.

She bent down to kiss her son, the boy who'd grown inside of her, but the smell of bacteria and rotten flesh snapped her head back. Her legs threatened to give way, and she held herself upright beside the bed.

Frieda was right. She had to do it. She unsheathed the needle and aimed it to the port that went directly into his internal jugular vein. The medicine would go directly to the heart. Emy plunged the needle into the receptacle and pushed the pentobarbital without pause.

There was no response, and Emy worried it wasn't enough. Her mind raced as she feared she'd made the wrong decision. She cursed she'd taken him off the heart monitor months ago.

She watched and waited.

His chest rose and fell with each breath.

One minute passed. Still no response to the medicine.

At two minutes, she started to swear at Frieda, but before words came out, Danek took a long deep breath. She remembered he used to breathe like that right before he'd fall asleep in her arms.

His fragile body relaxed and uncurled. Emy pulled a sheet up to the boy's neck and laid her head on his chest. There was no breath. There was no heartbeat.

Her body shook with sadness and relief.

"My dear Danek. Please forgive your mommy." Tears fell freely onto his chest. "My Danek. My sweet, sweet Danek."

She would call Herr Bauer and inform him they had failed.

God is my judge.

CHAPTER 9

Maggie and Nick stepped off the elevator on the fifth floor of the Regional Medical Center in Memphis, affectionately called the MED by the staff. The three weeks had flown by as Maggie and Nick had spent two of them in Montana with her family.

They'd grieved leaving the bliss of Hawaii and stepping into this new reality, but the sooner they got answers, the better. The day they'd arrived back in the US, Maggie had her blood drawn for DNA testing for the Huntington's mutation. The lab told her it would take a few weeks for the test results. They could have received the news anywhere, but Nick insisted they return to Memphis and Dr. Chiranjeev Brahmbhatt, one of the leading geneticists in the country. For obvious reasons, she simply went by Dr. B.

Maggie had tried to talk Nick into staying in Montana, but she understood that returning to Memphis, where he'd been a respected trauma surgeon, was his safe zone. Fifteen years ago, and fresh out of an orthopaedic trauma fellowship, he started his medical career as a junior partner. Since he'd temporarily lost his vision on a mission trip to Turkey a year ago, he had not been back into the operating room. Now, Nick told her he was both relieved and unnerved to be back in the hallowed halls where Elvis Presley had died. He told her it seemed like a hundred years had passed.

"Kind of miss that smell," Nick said.

"What is *that?*" Maggie crinkled her nose at the pungent odor.

"It's the smell of old building, disinfectant, and over a hundred years of death and dying." Nick smiled at her.

Maggie stuck out her tongue.

"For fifteen years, this was my life: call every third or fourth night, long days on the wards, and countless hours in the operating room."

"Well, I hope you like your current life," Maggie said and put her arm through his.

"I have to admit, I kind of miss taking care of people, but I wouldn't change a thing. I love you, Mrs. Hart." He squeezed her arm. "How are you feeling?"

"I'm good…just have to pee again. I'm not sure if that's the baby or the nerves."

Besides the blood draw for the genetic screen, Nick had ordered a hCG pregnancy test. It showed that Maggie was, indeed, pregnant. She looked forward to getting the appointment with Dr. B behind them so she could settle her heart and mind and prepare herself for becoming a mother. Nick had arranged for an OB appointment in the afternoon with a well-respected obstetrician friend.

Maggie had convinced Nick not to tell either set of parents about the pregnancy until she passed the twelve-week mark. At forty-six, her chance of having a miscarriage was close to 80%. She also didn't want to think about the reality that her odds of delivering a child with a chromosomal disorder increased as well. She wasn't afraid of that. Her love was big enough to care for any child—with or without a disability. But a child with Huntington's was a different story altogether. She would never want her child to suffer.

A cold shiver tingled up Maggie's spine as they stepped across the threshold from the old hospital to a newly completed office building.

Dr. B's office was midway down the corridor, and Nick held the door for Maggie. The subdued lighting, easy listening music, and soft leather couches were no comfort for their anxiety. Two other families sat quietly—an expectant young couple and another couple with a child afflicted with a genetic syndrome strapped into an elaborate wheelchair. Both women looked nearly full term. The couples appeared exhausted and nodded to Maggie and Nick as if to say: "Welcome to our world."

Maggie's first instinct was to turn and leave, but she took a deep breath and prayed silently, *Oh Father, help me.* Nick tightened his hold of her arm and went to the receptionist window.

"Hi, we're the Harts. We have an appointment with Dr. B," Nick said.

The receptionist met them with a warm smile. "Welcome, Dr. and Mrs. Hart. Do you mind filling out our forms? We'll get you back shortly."

Maggie and Nick made themselves comfortable in the corner chairs, and Maggie worked to fill out the stack of paperwork, including a detailed medical history, family history, legal documents for treatment, and the HIPPA privacy policies.

By the time she had completed the forms, the staff had called the other families back to the exam rooms.

Maggie and Nick did not have to wait long and soon found themselves in Dr. B's office. It was as comfortable and well decorated as the reception area. Medical textbooks, along with wooden carvings of Hindu gods, filled the bookcases. The receptionist asked them to make themselves comfortable in the chairs facing the desk and offered them bottles of water.

When the receptionist left, Maggie looked at Nick and raised her eyebrows. He responded by taking her hand.

Dr. B walked in behind them and apologized that they had to wait for her.

"Oh gosh…if that was a wait, I'll take it any day," Nick said to ease the tension. He stood to shake her hand. Maggie rose as well and didn't know what to make of it when the doctor hugged her. The woman was more beautiful than her picture revealed with dark olive skin and long black hair that matched Maggie's. She had a red dot, *bindi,* on the center of her forehead, and smelled of a delightful, soothing fragrance—a mix of fruity and floral with a hint of amber or sandalwood. Her bubbly smile and flawless skin gave her a youthful air.

"Dr. and Mrs. Hart, please, please make yourselves comfortable," she said and motioned to the chairs.

She walked behind her desk and sat in a large leather office chair that swallowed her petite frame. But she scooted forward onto the edge of her seat and opened a file. "I hear we are both Indian." She smiled at Maggie.

"Yes, cousins from a different mother," Maggie said.

Dr. B laughed. "You never know, right? I suppose we're all related somehow if we looked at our genes far enough back."

Humor. Maybe that's a good sign, Maggie thought. But when Dr. B slumped back into her chair and sighed, she knew it was bad news.

"I will get straight to it, as I realize you have been waiting for the results of your genetic testing. I do not have good news."

Maggie's mind raced, and pain stabbed her side as if a knife had been slowly inserted into her kidney and twisted. It was difficult to concentrate and harder to breathe.

"I'm sorry, Mrs. Hart, but you carry the gene for Huntington's."

Dr. B sat forward and rested her chin in her hands, allowing Maggie and Nick to absorb the news.

Maggie tried to take a deep breath and pushed on the painful place where her psyche had driven the stake into her side. *Thank God, Nick is here.* Maggie worried she'd dissolve onto the floor.

"I am sorry, Dr. and Mrs. Hart. I imagine you understand what this means, but I am here to answer any questions you have. I know this is difficult."

"How many CAG repeats does Maggie have?" Nick asked.

"Yes, good, you have been doing your research. The physician in Montana has sent me the test results of your mother and brother. Your mother has thirty-nine CAG repeats, just under the forty threshold, and probably why her symptoms are late in onset. Your brother, on the other hand, has fifty-five and why his symptoms appeared earlier and more severe. This variation in expression is prevalent in the disease; the size of the CAG trinucleotide repeat often increases in size from one generation to the next. Maggie, you have forty-two repeats."

Maggie was having a difficult time hearing and comprehending. "What does that mean? Do I have it?" She looked at Nick and back at the doctor.

Dr. B slowly nodded. "I'm afraid so, Maggie. The threshold

is forty to fifty. In that range, patients will develop the disease. Above sixty, the disease forms in childhood."

"But I have no symptoms," Maggie argued.

Dr. B nodded and pursed her lips together and said, "This is true, Maggie, but I would not be doing my job if I didn't tell you the truth. You will eventually develop the symptoms. I'm sorry."

"All of them?"

"Yes, all of them."

"What about treatment?" Nick asked with tension in his voice.

"Dr. Hart, you must understand that there is no treatment that can alter the course of Huntington's disease. There are medications and modalities that can lessen some of the movement abnormalities and psychiatric disorders."

"Like what?" Nick asked.

"We usually use Tetrabenazine to suppress the involuntary jerking and writhing movements, Haldol for antipsychotic effects, and antidepressants and other mood-stabilizing drugs. Typically, well into the disease, we get speech, physical and occupational therapists involved to cope with activities of daily living."

Dr. B stood and came from behind her desk to take Maggie's shoulders. Maggie wept and hugged the woman.

They held their embrace, and Maggie felt herself dissolve.

The doctor gently pushed Maggie back and held her arms. "I understand this is terrible news. We come from very different cultures and backgrounds, but I have heard of your and Dr. Hart's good works and your faith. I would tell you to hold on to that. Hold on to hope. There are some very promising and exciting therapies coming. Possibly even before you develop symptoms."

"Are there any current clinical trials in the US?" Nick asked.

She shook her head, frowned, and sat on the edge of her desk. "I'm afraid the FDA has severely limited our ability to proceed with gene therapy modalities. Most advances are being made outside the US." She picked up a folder on her desk. "Before your appointment, I looked for possible options for you. The leader in gene therapy for Huntington's is a company called BioGenics. It's in Poland and operated by a woman that I have met many times at our conferences, Dr. Emmanuelle Christianson." She handed Nick a piece of paper. "I have taken the liberty of calling her, and she is willing to consult with you. Only you two can decide what is best for you. Dr. Christianson is world-renowned, plus she is dually trained in both genetics and obstetrics."

"And my baby?" Maggie asked between sniffles.

Dr. B stood, took Maggie's hands to comfort her, and sighed. "Yes, this is a challenging circumstance. Because you carry the gene, your child will have a 50% chance of carrying it as well."

"When can we know? Can't you just test my blood?"

Dr. B shook her head. "It is pretty complicated. I understand you have an appointment with the OB doctor this afternoon. You are around nine weeks pregnant?"

"Yes, but we're hoping to get more solid dates at the appointment," Nick said.

"There are two choices you will have to consider. First, does going ahead with this pregnancy put you at an increased risk? No one knows for sure, but the stress of pregnancy and labor may hasten the symptoms of Huntington's. And second, should testing be done on the baby in utero?"

"When can that be done?" Nick asked.

"At this time, your baby is too immature." She leaned back against the desk, folded her arms over her chest, and explained. "There are two methods to test the fetus for Huntington's. At ten to thirteen weeks, we remove a piece of the placenta—either through the cervix or abdomen, depending on the placement of the placenta. The second method is done at fifteen to twenty weeks of pregnancy when an amniocentesis can be performed safely. Either of these methods should be done at a highly qualified center to mitigate the risk to you and the baby." Dr. B looked at the floor, then back to Maggie. "Also, this kind of testing is typically done when the couple would consider aborting the pregnancy if the genetic analysis is positive."

* * *

Maggie hugged the toilet bowl, while Nick held a wet folded paper towel on her forehead. She couldn't stop retching. Never in her life had so much fear and doubt flooded her mind and body. Never did she think she would face the abortion dilemma again.

The reservation where she grew up was full of social landmines. Maggie had two teenage pregnancies. One ended with an abortion and the other in an ectopic pregnancy. She had long forgiven herself for her choices, but the memory bore a deep wound covered by a thin scab. The abortion debate carried out in the media typically missed one crucial point entirely, the lifelong psychological effect that abortion had on a woman.

Maggie wished she'd never had the abortion. She wished she'd had the courage to keep the baby, but she was very young and didn't think she had any other option. Would she have decided differently if she knew what she knows now? Here she was, faced with the possibility of an impossible choice. If the baby carried the gene for Huntington's, how could she sentence her child to such a terrible demise? On the other hand, she'd sworn never again to abort her baby—under any circumstances.

With nothing left in her stomach to vomit, she sat and pressed her back against the cold tile on the wall. "I'm so sorry, Nick. I would have never put you through this if I had known."

Nick smiled and wiped the bile from the corner of her mouth. "Through sickness and in health, remember?"

He bent down and kissed her forehead. "It's all going to be okay. I realize this news is hitting you hard, but we'll take it one step at a time. Nothing is impossible with God."

She looked into his eyes and smiled. She had always encouraged Nick with God's promises, but now he turned the tables. Here he was, quoting scripture to comfort her. How she loved this man.

Nick looked at his watch. "You think I could help you up, and we could go see our baby?"

The OB's office told them they would perform an ultrasound on their baby, so Maggie had to arrive with a full bladder. *Our baby. What a crazy thought.* Maggie had the side effects of pregnancy; tender and swollen breasts, constant fatigue, and a sour stomach over strong smells. But until this very moment, everything else had taken priority, and she'd barely let herself get excited over this miracle.

She wiped her eyes and held out her hand for Nick to pull her up. "Yes, let's go see our baby."

* * *

Maggie settled onto the heated exam table, complete with warmed lamb's wool stirrup covers. It seemed absurd to her that Dr. McCoy and her husband caught up on old times while the doctor gently performed a pelvic exam. The obstetrician was kind and confident—a rotund, jovial man who bragged about his five grandchildren.

The exam was quick and painless, and then Dr. McCoy covered her legs with the sheet. After he snapped off his exam gloves into the trash can, he stood opposite Nick with Maggie between them. He held Maggie's hand, and his joviality became serious. "Maggie, everything looks fine. Your exam is normal, and your pregnancy is advancing like it should. At nine weeks, your baby is an inch long and about the size of a martini olive." He smiled. "Its liver and kidneys are forming, the baby's bowels have moved from the umbilical cord into the abdomen, and it's starting to look like a little person." He wrapped both his hands around Maggie's.

"I'm sorry about the news you received today," he continued. "I honestly don't know what I would do in your position. I always side on getting as much information as possible. It might be a good idea to do the genetic testing on your little nipper. Then you know." He sighed deeply. "Look, one of my grandkids is disabled. It's not easy on his parents, but we love him every bit as much as all the others. No one can tell you what to do." He stopped and rubbed his chin. "I'm in the baby business, and I think every life is precious. For me, life begins at conception…period. I think the arguments opposite *that* truth are silly. I can't even claim to begin to understand it, but there is a new life growing inside of you, from day one through nine months. Part of you and part of Nick have come together…and forgive me…in that mystery, God is woven into our DNA."

Dr. McCoy had practiced OB for almost forty years. What he said revealed a very tender part of his heart.

His smile returned, and he squeezed Maggie's hand with joy. "At nine weeks, your baby has a beating heart. You want to see it?"

"Please," Maggie and Nick said simultaneously.

McCoy turned to the ultrasound machine and grabbed the handpiece. He uncovered Maggie's belly and shook a tube of lube until it dripped, then squirted a large mound above her pubis. Maggie flinched, expecting the chill of the gel, but, like the rest of the room and the instruments, it had been warmed.

Dr. McCoy flicked a switch, and the TV screen on the wall came to life with blurry waves of black and white lines. The images moved with the probe as he rolled the transducer across her abdomen.

"Sorry, Maggie, I'm going to push on your full bladder for a moment. At this stage of your pregnancy, we can see better through the liquid. Bear with me."

Maggie squeezed hard not to pee, trying to comprehend what the picture on the screen showed.

"Aw, here's the little guy."

"Guy?" Nick gasped.

McCoy laughed. "Oh, sorry, I always do that—guy, gal. It's way too early to know."

"Wow," Nick said and squeezed Maggie's hand hard.

"What, what? I don't understand what you guys see," Maggie complained. All she could make out was a sea of abstract lines and shapes.

The doctor adjusted some dials and increased the magnification on the machine.

"Oh, my Lord!" Maggie covered her mouth with her hand. This time tears of happiness flowed.

What she saw was a baby—head, body, arms, legs, even the umbilical cord was easily seen extending from its belly. A flicker rhythmically moved in its chest.

The doctor turned a dial. The sweet rhythmic sound of their baby's heartbeat filled the room. "Swoosh, swoosh, swoosh, swoosh, swoosh…"

CHAPTER 10

HERR BAUER

Emy wept the day they cremated and buried Danek, and she cried for three weeks, stopping only when she knew she had to make this call. She mustered her defenses to keep her emotions at bay. Perhaps Herr Bauer reminded her of her father, and to call him with bad news smacked of disappointing them both. She felt the old and familiar sense of failure instilled in her by her mother.

Danek had been removed from the family for years, and Emy wasn't sure if she and Keith should involve Hanna and Ceci in his final arrangements. But she decided that somewhere deep in their psyches, they hadn't forgotten their brother. It would be beneficial to all of them to put closure to this chapter, so she allowed them the opportunity to say their goodbyes. Keith treated her unusually kind and attentive since Danek's death, and she couldn't decide if his behavior was genuine, or if he was sucking up because of his infidelity.

As Emy dialed Herr Bauer's number in Germany, a muscle memory calmed her pounding heart; the smell of pipe tobacco that both he and her father smoked.

James M. Bauer was the godfather of a patient when Emy first met him. His friend's daughter was afflicted with cystic fibrosis. The child died before the early clinical trials of gene manipulation; otherwise, she may have ended up like Danek and the rest of the children in the trial. Bauer understood the personal stakes involved in the research.

Strangely, Emy had met face-to-face with Herr Bauer only a handful of times. He was a private man who preferred to communicate over the phone, and even that was rare. His German telecommunication, computer, and security company in Berlin was shrouded in secrecy and rumors of political ties, but his net worth was estimated in the billions, although no publication could exactly say how much.

"*Guten Tag*, Herr Bauer's residence. How may I assist you?" a feminine male voice answered.

"Hello, Kenny, it's Emmanuelle Christianson. May I speak to Herr Bauer?"

"Certainly, Dr. Christianson. Herr Bauer is tending his roses in the garden today. Do you mind holding while I collect him?"

"Of course not, Kenny. Thank you." She couldn't remember a time when she hadn't waited for BioGenics's primary benefactor to take her call—keeping callers waiting was part of his mystique.

Emy heard the phone click on hold, and she leaned back in her office chair. She'd only met Kenny once. The young man was tall and thin, always formal, and very gay. She heard rumors that Herr Bauer was homosexual as well, and imagined that Kenny was more than his assistant. It didn't matter to her; she respected the man, just as long as he kept paying her bills.

It reminded Emy of the paper MIT scientists presented last year at the International Society of Human Genetics on the *PgmNr 278* gene. The discovery wasn't necessarily the gay gene that everyone had been searching for, but it went a long way to show homosexuality was partially genetically influenced, but not genetically determined. This variant was strictly related to men. Other articles showed that the biological understanding of homosexuality in women lagged far behind. Some researchers suggested that this was partially due to the tendency for women who have sex with women to be more fluid in their sexual orientation.

Either way, she would not judge Herr Bauer. He'd shouldered much of the start-up costs for her company. In BioGenics's twelve years of existence, they only recently approached any kind of profit. Bauer was the majority stockholder and willingly paid his share of the half-a-billion euro annual budget burden. He had also built, and therefore owned, the facility. He'd told her in one of their few face-to-face meetings he was in it for the long haul. He was convinced his outlay would be well worth the investment once they moved into therapeutic treatments.

At seventy-four, born September 2, 1945, Bauer loved to tell people that he was birthed on the last day of World War II. He was a formal man who lived in a provincial estate outside of Berlin with sprawling gardens. In every photograph Emy saw of him, and the few times they had met, he wore a black suit and gray vest with a polka-dot blue ascot tie. He was a German aristocrat with a bald head, bushy sideburn chops, and full eyebrows. His hefty frame resulted from his love for schnitzel, and his yellow teeth were due to a fondness for his pipe.

Ten years earlier, when Bauer offered to invest in her dreams, Emy thought the man had mistaken her for another geneticist with a similar name, Emmanuelle Charpentier. This confusion was constant—something Emy detested. She was forced to explain that she was the *other* Emmanuelle, the lesser one. Dr. Charpentier, along with the American Jennifer Doudna, had advanced the DNA editing tool of CRISPR/Cas9 and were rumored to be candidates to receive the Nobel Prize. In a moment of rare vulnerability, Emy had asked Herr Bauer directly why he hadn't picked the other team to support. He'd replied, "I believe the person in the number two spot always works harder."

With a superior academic environment and the favorable political and financial climate of Poland, Herr Bauer suggested BioGenics establish a presence in Eastern Europe. Emy and her family didn't relish moving to Poland ten years ago, but now it was home, and they loved it like their own country.

Bauer was a hands-off type of investor and rarely reached out to Emy. It surprised her when she'd received his note of condolences over Danek and a message to call him, ASAP. She suspected that he used covert methods to keep track of the company, fiduciary and technically. It was likely that someone in the institute reported directly to Bauer. For all she knew, Danek's caretaker could have been his spy. Emy decided that a man who had built a multi-billion euro computer and security firm would somehow gain direct access to BioGenics's systems. She kept that in mind every time she used the computer system.

The phone clicked, and Bauer answered in a friendly and upbeat voice.

"Dr. Christianson, it is so good of you to call me," he said.

"Herr Bauer, uh…yes…I had a message to call you." Emy stumbled over her words. He always had a way of unbalancing her. *Wasn't it you who asked me to call?*

"First of all, Emmanuelle, I am truly sorry about Danek."

Herr Bauer was one of the few, besides her father, who used her full name. She knew he would not explain how he found out.

"Yes, Herr Bauer, I meant to call you—"

"You've had a lot on your mind, Emmanuelle," he said, interrupting her with his brand of kindness that held the tension of a reprimand. *Perhaps the reason he built such a successful communications empire.*

"I'm sorry I failed," Emy blurted out, unable to hold back her emotions.

There was a long uncomfortable pause as Bauer sucked on his pipe.

"Emmanuelle, you must not blame yourself," he began in the voice of a kind father. "These early trials were bound to have challenges. Look how much we have advanced the technology because of issues encountered in the early research. You must remember that every medical advancement known to man has cost something. There are always sacrifices."

Emy choked down her thoughts. *Yes, like my son and my marriage.* She would have responded harshly if he wasn't so correct. She put her emotions in check. "Thank you, Herr Bauer." She swallowed and said, "The latest trials are showing great promise, especially with Huntington's."

"Yes indeed," he said, as though he knew the recent results that Emy had reviewed a few days earlier.

He paused, and Emy expected he was finished with his condolences and encouragement. Typically, his thoughts ran miles ahead of whatever was being discussed. This was no exception.

"You are aware of the Chinese researcher, Chen Wangwei," Bauer said and paused to let the statement dangle.

"I understand Chen is under house arrest by the Chinese authorities," Emy said. The researcher had caused an uproar in the genetic world when he announced that his team had engineered mutations into the DNA of two human embryos that produced baby girls. He claimed to have disabled the CCR5 gene that produces a protein that allows HIV to enter cells, giving them protection against the virus. The scientist had set off heated arguments on what type of genetic research should be permitted, and who would monitor and enforce policies. "Chen has certainly stirred the pot," Emy finally added.

"Yes, indeed," Bauer agreed. "But you have to admire the man for having the courage to advance the science."

"I suppose," Emy said diplomatically. She and Herr Bauer had already discussed this topic, and it was clear that he leaned not only toward fighting diseases with gene therapy but improving the genome and, therefore, the human race.

"I am told that other research on the CCR5 gene shows that deleting this gene increases memory and cognition," Bauer said.

"Well, much of that research is on mice, but yes, there are indications that it does the same for people," Emy said, adding, "but we have no idea of the other consequences."

"Do you think that is what Chen was after, increasing the children's IQ?"

"Well, there is speculation of that possibility. It's hard to guess the man's motivation, but cutting out the gene may also shorten the girls' life span."

"Can you remove the CCR5 gene?" Herr Bauer asked, ignoring her warning.

It was a rhetorical question, and Emy chose her words carefully. Bauer knew she was capable. "If we use it to eliminate disease, by all means," she answered.

"I had to laugh at the news reports of the silly Americans who paid millions of dollars to place their children in what they considered good schools or to pay scholars to sit for their child's college entrance exams." He scoffed. "We send our children to better schools for free."

Bauer didn't have to spell it out for her. She understood the potential that gene therapy unlocked for the human race along with the financial benefit to those invested. She decided it was best to say nothing.

"It's food for thought," he said. "I have a responsibility, after all, to my estate to invest my finances wisely. Don't you agree, Emmanuelle?"

"Yes, Herr Bauer. All of us at BioGenics appreciate what you have done for us."

"Ja, ja. *Guten Tag*, Emmanuelle."

The phone clicked off, and she let the phone dangle by the cord in her hand. "What the hell? Was that a threat to pull our funding?" she said under her breath. *Thank god he hung up before I started to grovel.*

CHAPTER 11

ABORTION

Izzi looked over Emy's shoulder at the report on the desk. A piercing shrill and blinding LED lights triggered above the office door. Wavy flashes of visual distortion danced across Emy's eyes, instantly escorting in a swell of nausea and a throbbing headache. She wasn't sure whether the migraine was from the report or the alarm.

Emy glanced at the colorful mural of her genome on the wall in an attempt to clear the scotomata blinding her vision, but the orb grew larger. This visual distortion would increase in diameter until it disappeared, typically interrupting her sight for thirty minutes and leaving her with a terrible headache. Emy's migraines always followed this course. Her genome testing was similar to other sufferers, revealing forty-four variants in thirty-eight genes that regulated vascular and soft muscle tissue tone inside blood vessels. This gave her and other migraine sufferers a higher risk of stroke and cardiovascular disease. She understood every last variant or mutation of each one of her genes—some giving rise to increased odds of several diseases. Like the rest of the population, she was a living time bomb.

"Why do they have to test that stupid system every week?" Emy asked Izzi as she massaged her temples with her fingertips. It was a rhetorical question, of course. As CEO, she was the person who gave the order. At eight-hundred-million euros to build, she would do everything she could to protect the BioGenics facility, including high-tech security. Her small army of armed guards prepared for any event, including fire, security breaches, and terrorist attacks. Genetic testing was a twenty-two billion euro industry. As the race to unlock the secrets of the human genome intensified and genetic treatments increased, investors hoped to add a couple zeros to the end of that number.

"Could I get you some Advil?" Izzi asked.

"No, Izzi, it will pass, eventually." Emy smiled at her student. Due to Emy's genome makeup, some medications worked, and others made her symptoms worse. Her body could not metabolize ibuprofen, so it was toxic to her. She'd have to review pharmacogenetics with her grad student one day soon.

Emy tried to focus on the report, but to read it, she had to look around the twinkling lights in her visual field.

"I'm sure sorry about all this," Izzi said, stepping anxiously from one foot to another.

Emy reached over and touched her arm. "It's really okay, Izzi. You're the messenger." She wanted to reassure her and hopefully stop the woman's shuffling feet that aggravated her migraine headache.

"However," Emy said, "I trust you to keep this absolutely confidential."

"Oh, definitely, Dr. Christianson," Izzi said and stopped her mindless dance. "I wouldn't think of—"

"It's okay, Izzi, I trust you," Emy interrupted and squeezed Izzi's arm. She examined the young woman from head to toe.

Izzi was short and square-shaped, with cropped bleach blond hair and a pleasant smile. Her pierced tongue gave her a slight lisp. She wore tattered army boots over black leggings. *I hope I can trust her.*

She could make or break Izzi's career. Within the walls of this facility, Emy ruled. People tread lightly around her, and she liked that.

Izzi responded to Emy's scrutinizing with a smile, and Emy turned back to the report. Izzi had completed the sequencing of the girlfriend's DNA in record time, and she was excited at her achievement. A multi-national team completed the Human Genome Project in 2013. It had taken thirteen years and two point seven billion dollars to finish generating the three billion base pairs in one person's DNA. Nowadays, companies sequenced DNA in a few weeks for under a thousand dollars. Izzi had turned that into days.

"Did you sleep?" Emy asked her.

She smiled and shrugged, shifting from leg to leg on caffeine-fueled energy.

"Well, thank you for working so hard on this."

"The bitch is Chinese," Izzi blurted out.

Unperturbed at her effusion, Emy nodded and looked at the report: 100% Han Chinese.

"We don't have access to China's genetic database," Izzi said. "But I've done favors for one scientist in Beijing, and he ran it for me. Strange, but this is what I got back from him." She handed Emy a printed email that only read: "Genome matched, but identity blocked."

"I wonder what that means," Emy said and handed the paper back to Izzi.

"You know China, always a bit of mystery." Izzi shrugged.

Emy nodded. China was eons ahead of any other nation in the genome testing of its citizens. They not only collected, analyzed, and stored the DNA of vast numbers of their own people, but they did the same with many other people from all over the world—including millions of Americans. Emy recently read a report detailing China's "Physicals for All" policy, where the government forced DNA testing on all twenty-five million occupants of Xinjiang province. If people refused, the police paid them an unfriendly visit. The World Health Organization estimated that China's database exceeded one hundred million and grew daily.

"You want me to pay a visit to this skank?"

Izzi's question broke Emy's trance. "Uh…what?"

"I know people," Izzi wrung her hands together.

The thought made Emy grin. The tough dyke defending her boss. "Don't send the hit squad out yet." She laughed. "We still don't know who the girl is." She looked at Izzi. "Besides… it's complicated."

Emy stood to usher Izzi out of her office, putting her hand on her shoulder. "You did good, Izzi, but leave the kneecapping to me." She laughed again.

"You and your husband going to be okay?" Izzi asked as they walked to the door.

Emy bobbed her head indecisively. "You've met Keith, you think he's handsome?"

Izzi shot her a strange look. "Well, I uh…I suppose most find him attractive. I tend to swing the other way." She blushed. Izzi said it like the revelation might surprise Emy.

Emy waved off the confession. "Each to their own."

Emy shut the door behind her assistant and went back to her desk. She picked up the report and paced the floor, scanning through the pages. *Bitch is right.* Typically, Keith went for the blond Dutch type. This was not his first infidelity, but it was the first time he'd used the word love. Her stomach rumbled as she flipped through the report to the woman's estimated age. They used a technique developed in Belgium. DNA has a process of gene expression that gradually changes over a lifetime as select genes turn on or off—like looking at the rings of a tree— with an accuracy within three to four years. Keith's mistress was somewhere between twenty-five and twenty-nine. *Figures.* He tired of her near fifty-year-old body with its love handles and cellulite. Even she wished for her nulligravida body.

She scanned different sections of the woman's profile. She had black hair and brown eyes. She certainly didn't need to be a geneticist to guess that. But the girl would most likely die from breast cancer because of her mutations on both the BRAC 1 and 2 genes, on chromosomes seventeen and thirteen, respectively. That is, if she didn't die of lung cancer first, having a high nicotine dependence.

The woman had over thirty-thousand variants of her genes, an average number for a typical person, making every individual unique. The genes showed everything: the woman was unlikely to have dimples, and she shouldn't drink because of a low tolerance to the effects of alcohol and an increased propensity for gout. She probably had terrible flatulence after pizza from her lactose intolerance and would develop macular degeneration as an old woman.

Stupid girl. She threw the report on her desk. It landed beside the unopened envelope from her father. She'd brought it from home as she didn't want Keith or the girls to snoop through it.

She caressed the top of the envelope. *Maybe this will give me some answers.* She looked at her watch and saw that she had twenty minutes before her next procedure. She sat in her desk chair and moved the computer mouse to wake it up. She typed in the twenty-digit code. Everyone at BioGenics had a unique password and leadership immediately terminated them if it was lost, written down, or shared. Such a termination had only happened twice in BioGenics's twelve years of incorporation. If an employee misplaced their log-in, they rebooted the whole system, and all personnel had to learn a new code. They couldn't be too careful. Even with the tight security of the new building, one lost password could take down the entire company. Herr Bauer gave BioGenics access to the most sophisticated computing in the world. It was also the reason Izzi could code the entire three billion base pairs in days instead of weeks.

Emy opened Google and stared at the blinking cursor. She typed in *Jew*, paused, and then added *ish*. But then deleted it all. Did she really want to start down this road? She didn't even understand what it meant to be Jewish. She stared at the keyboard again. *What does it mean to be Jewish?* She typed.

It surprised her when multiple links populated the screen. Obviously, she was not the first person to ask this question. She double-clicked on the first link, which was a YouTube video. She skipped the ad, and soon, people from all over the world told short snippets of what it meant to them to be a Jew:

"As a Jew, I think we have universal values that we can gift to the world. One of those being, if you have a dream that is two thousand years old, don't give up on it."

"To me, Judaism really feels like peoplehood. To be Jewish is to take my story and weave it with the story of other Jews living today and the older tapestry of Jewish history."

"There are many people that identify as Jewish but are not the least bit religious and express that identification in various ways."

"It's very personal to me. It means a profound attachment to Jewish culture and Jewish history."

"Being Jewish affects every decision of my life, whether it's how I parent or what I buy at the store."

"Being Jewish is being part of a very ancient religion. Our Torah and our religion say that we have a special mission in the world. To preserve it in terms of people and the environment, with a high degree of morality."

Emy hit the pause button. It was shocking—no religious pitch or proselytizing—no one had even mentioned God. She continued to let it play. It was clear there were many ways to practice Judaism, but it was the last statement that brought a tear to her eye.

"It's my history. It's my family. It's my basic identity."

All of Emy's life, she had hoped for a sense of belonging.

Her pager interrupted her reflections. She wiped away a tear and looked at the message: "We are ready for you in procedure room three."

* * *

Emy changed her clothes in her office. Wearing royal blue scrubs, she walked from the research arm of the facility to the outpatient clinic. The third arm of the facility was for inpatients. She glanced out the window and then at her watch: 3:33. The sun was already setting. Like so much of Poland, grasslands stretched for miles. The golden hour cast gilded hues over the wheat and barley fields, already harvested for the winter. The fading light turned the wafting clouds to shades of pink and purple as the sun quickly dropped below the horizon.

She hadn't left their location to chance. A military installation bordered BioGenics on one side and open meadows on the others. The terrain was ideal for the high-tech motion detection security system that could distinguish an animal from a human.

She stopped for a moment to admire the view as the countryside would fade into darkness soon enough. She hated the short winter days. They gave her life a sense of urgency that brought on prickly anxiety. Part of the torment she battled was the decision she'd made about Danek.

The nurses impatiently chimed her pager again as Emy turned down the corridor. She made her way to a procedure room in the clinic that smelled of extra strength industrial cleaners.

The nurses, busy setting up instruments and bustling around the room, paid no attention to a frightened woman on the stainless-steel exam table with her feet placed in padded stirrups. Emy went directly to the patient and took her hand. "I'm sorry, Martha. You okay?" Emy then gently placed her hand on the woman's sweaty forehead and smoothed her hair back. "Do you have any questions?"

The woman's bottom lip quivered, and Emy bent to hug her. "Everything will be okay. You're making the right decision."

Emy forced the images of Danek's diseased body from her mind. A morsel of solace was that she was saving Martha from a similar nightmare.

"I don't know, Dr. Christianson. How did this happen?"

Emy stood and took both of Martha's hands. "I'm afraid it's one of the flukes of the universe, Martha."

"Did my husband and I do something wrong? I still don't understand."

Emy hid her frustration. She'd explained the genetic disorder to Martha and her husband numerous times, but she understood the woman's doubt. From the outside, Martha's belly bump indicated a healthy pregnancy with all the excitement and expectations of a new life. Martha's doctor had ordered a genetic test because she was in her forties, the age of a high-risk pregnancy. That's when they discovered the fetus was a boy who carried one of the most unfortunate genetic abnormalities.

"This is not your fault," Emy insisted. "When either your egg or your husband's sperm formed, instead of all the chromosomes splitting, chromosome 18 stayed together. The fetus ended up with three strands of that DNA instead of two. Remember, this genetic abnormality is called Trisomy 18?"

Martha nodded. "I was reading last night that Down syndrome is like the same thing except chromosome 21. I don't mind a child with that. Why does the number make such a difference?"

"It's all in the genes of that particular chromosome. With Trisomy 18, there is a significant possibility that the fetus will die before it's full term, putting your life at risk. If it's delivered at forty weeks, it is unlikely that it would survive past a few months. If the baby lived longer, its quality of life would be meager—heart defects, neurological issues, retardation, joint contractures, cleft lip, hearing loss, and the list goes on. You're doing the right thing, Martha," Emy said with as much patience as she could find.

"Will he feel anything?" the woman asked.

"I'll be quick," Emy said, not directly answering the question. She hoped that Martha hadn't seen actual footage of fetuses trying to move away from the surgical instruments.

"How big is my baby?"

"The fetus is about the size of an artichoke."

The woman looked from Emy to the nurse who was standing at the ready to inject anesthesia into the IV. Compassion emanated from the nurse's eyes, and her head nodded, both giving her support to the patient and the doctor, and in agreement to proceed.

Martha sighed, pursed her lips together, and gathered her courage. "Okay," she whispered.

CHAPTER 12

Nick and Maggie pulled their rental car along the curb in front of Buck and Katy's house in Memphis. They hadn't seen Nick's best friend and his wife for three months, ever since the wedding. Nick had reminded Maggie, "Sometimes when you can't pray or gain understanding because you can't see through the fog of pain, you need your friends." They'd planned on seeing the Hansons anyway, but after Maggie's doctor appointments yesterday, the visit was essential.

Nick smiled as he looked at the house through the side window. Buck and Katy had decorated their home with bright Christmas lights around the eaves and windows, and a giant blow-up Santa with one arm raised in a permanent wave swayed in the breeze on the front lawn. Through three tours in Afghanistan and a horrific life-changing injury, Buck had found peace.

Nick pushed the car door open, ran around to open Maggie's, gave her a hand, and they walked arm-in-arm up the sidewalk.

Nick and Buck had been through so much together, they shared an unbreakable bond. They'd met seven years ago when Buck's life shattered from an explosion of a roadside IED in Afghanistan. He lost both legs and sustained multiple other injuries. After life-saving surgery at the in-country MASH unit, the military shipped him to the trauma center in Memphis, where Nick was in charge of his multiple operations and rehabilitation. Buck loved to harass Nick that he had barely survived the care at the MED.

In turn, Nick teased Buck that they'd only become best friends because he couldn't get rid of him. Not only had Buck saved Nick's life in Guatemala, but he'd kept him alive throughout their captivity in Turkey. The mutual respect fostered their deep friendship.

Nick smiled at Maggie, then rang the doorbell. He'd told Buck they came to Memphis for Maggie to have some tests—a partial truth. Nick hated to dump this burden on them, but if anyone understood trials and tribulations, it was the Hansons.

The front door sprung open.

"HO, HO, HO!" Buck yelled. He was dressed in a rich burgundy velvet Santa outfit, complete with fluffy white trim, a large black leather belt with an etched buckle, pom-pom hat, and a full beard and mustache. Floral board shorts and red and green metal leg prostheses replaced the pants and black boots of an authentic Santa suit. "Merry Christmas! Have you been a good little boy and girl?" Radiant green eyes twinkled above his fake beard and mustache.

Nick looked at Maggie and then back to Buck. "We've only been married three months." Nick snorted.

"Okay, okay…TMI," Buck said and laughed, making Maggie blush. "God, it's good to see you guys. What a sight for sore eyes."

Buck, famous for his bear hugs, stepped forward and wrapped his massive arms around them, lifting them onto their tiptoes. With his six-foot-four, two-hundred-and-twenty-pound frame, he could have effortlessly boosted them off the floor.

Buck was a former drill sergeant, and Nick loved to hear his stories about giving his men the same affection. Buck explained it with a laugh, saying, "Most of these boys never got much lovin' from their fathers." Buck intimidated the men as he towered over them; if he set his square jaw and piercing eyes, they'd practically wet themselves. When Buck saw their fear, he'd grab them, hoist them up, and give them a mammoth bear hug. This made him beloved by his men. Many had followed him into battle, and some had made the ultimate sacrifice for their country.

Buck set Nick and Maggie down and laughed. "Whad'ya think? Do I make a decent Santa, or what?"

Nick poked Buck's belly, "In the off-season, you can play the Pillsbury Doughboy."

In an Aikido-like move, Buck pulled Nick toward him, whirled him around, and, before Nick could react, placed him in a headlock. "Hey, don't mess with my waistline," Buck argued, "I like it just the way it is; besides, I'm forty-two, you know."

With his neck locked in Buck's muscular arms, Nick was totally helpless.

"See, I can still whup your butt," Buck said and flexed his rock-hard abs. Then he applied enough pressure on Nick's neck that required him to tap out or be choked out.

"Okay, Buck, don't harm the guests!" Katy said, as she came around the corner and laughed. Buck instantly let go and pulled Nick upright. Both men snapped to attention.

She huffed and waved them off. "Oh, go on, you two." She went right for Maggie and embraced her tightly. "This is who I really want to see anyway."

Nick smiled. If there was anything tougher than a Marine drill sergeant, it was a Marine drill sergeant's wife. Katy was every bit of that. She wasn't but an inch or two taller than Maggie's five-foot-one frame, but the only person who could stand Buck down with a glower. From East Texas, she was as sweet as they came, with gracious manners and cropped blond hair.

"Ain't he the goofiest looking Santa you've ever laid eyes on?" She thumbed over her shoulder at Buck.

"Hey, the kids at St. Jude's love me." Buck faked offense. "The Corps asked if I'd represent them during the holiday week at the children's hospital."

Buck was no longer on active duty, but he represented the Marines or the Wounded Warrior Project for special events.

"It's a blast," Buck continued. "But I gotta take this beard off. It's hotter than heck," he said and peeled it from his face. The heat inflamed a jagged scar down his left cheek.

"I bet the kids didn't know that Santa was a double amputee," Nick said.

"It's funny. Not one kid asked me about my prostheses," Buck said. "So many of them have their own. They accepted me as I am."

Buck's eyes watered, and Nick understood that as big and robust as Buck was on the outside, he had a tender and loving heart on the inside.

"Let's go, tough guy." Katy patted Buck's rear. "Get out of that ridiculous suit and go fire up the grill. I bet our friends are famished."

"Okay, but first, I'm gonna show these guys my new legs." Buck turned to Nick and Maggie. "These are new prototypes. I asked them to make them in Christmas colors for the kids." He hiked up his shorts and showed off his limbs. Nick had amputated both of Buck's legs above the knee. He'd tried to save them, but after five operations on the left and ten on the right, with the injuries to the vascular systems and the effects of severe infections, it was impossible to preserve the limbs—a remorseful outcome for them both.

Buck took several steps forward and then back. "I impressed my physical therapist since so many bilateral above-the-knee amputees don't regain adequate ambulation," he said and laughed. "Good thing I was nimble and athletic before I lost them 'cause it helps me to overcome some of the usual obstacles."

Nick shrugged, "So what's new?"

"What's new? You ready?" Buck held his arms out in front of his body and bent his knees. Nick flinched and reached to support him, but Buck pushed him away and performed a full squat. Then he miraculously pushed himself up to stand.

"That's awesome!" Nick said. "That's usually an impossible move for most double amputees."

"I got them to incorporate microprocessors in the knees and ankles with micro-hydraulics. They're a little heavier than my last ones, but pretty remarkable, don't you think? The onboard sensors detect movement and timing, so it makes impossible motions feasible."

"Incredible," Maggie added.

"Okay now for the real coup de grâce," Buck said, pulling his smartphone out of his pocket, and standing up straight. He pushed on the screen and spoke into the microphone. "Go-go gadget, lengthen."

Nick howled when a mechanical hum emanated from the prostheses, and they started to slowly elongate.

At almost seven feet, Buck stretched out his arms and puffed out his chest. "I'm a giant." His usual baritone, John Wayne-like voice deepened, and Nick and Maggie laughed so hard, Nick thought he might collapse. "I see why you're such a hit with the kids."

"The techs let me program in the commands," Buck said and then addressed the microphone. "Go-go gadget, shorten." The hydraulics droned, and as if on an elevator, Buck's height shortened to below Nick's six-foot-two frame.

"They have included this option in the legs so the leg lengths can accommodate for activities of daily living, which is one of the biggest struggles for amputees. Besides, it makes for a great party trick, don't you think?"

"Okay, Inspector Gadget, enough show and tell," Katy interrupted. "The rest of the dinner will ruin if you don't get cooking soon."

* * *

The Christmas candles on the table had burned low when Nick took his last bite of pumpkin roll. He was stuffed and content. The fellowship with Buck and Katy was the medicine he'd hoped for—true communion and the breaking of bread with friends. Katy had put on a big spread—grilled filets, her special Texas cheesy potatoes, grits and, of course, southern fried okra.

Between bites, they'd reminisced about their work in Guatemala and Turkey, and the joy of the wedding, but the highlight of the evening was when Buck prayed before their meal. A blanket of peace and joy enveloped Nick that he hadn't experienced since Hawaii. Maggie had shared about their honeymoon and the news about her mother and brother's diagnosis of Huntington's disease, but nothing more. Nick sensed she didn't want to spoil the jovial mood.

When the conversation lulled, Buck leaned back in his chair, looked at Nick, and crossed his arms. Buck read him well and waited patiently to hear the rest of the story. They knew Maggie had taken some tests, so it wasn't difficult to connect the dots.

Nick looked at Maggie and asked with his eyes if she wanted him to share. She nodded and tightened her lips. Nick hit it head-on.

"Huntington's disease is autosomal dominant. Each of Cliff and Mary's kids has a fifty-fifty chance of having it. Joe has it…" Nick paused, still in shock, "…so does Maggie."

"Oh dear," Katy said and put her hand on Maggie's arm.

Buck stretched his neck and straightened his back. The muscles in his forearms and jaw tightened as if preparing for battle. "Hmm," was all that came out, but his thoughts seemed to disappear into another world.

They sat in silence as the candles flickered. Nick explained the awful symptoms of the disease, how it robbed the mind and the body and destroyed the will to live; how the disease killed unmercifully.

Maggie held her face in her hands and wept. Katy wrapped her arms around her.

Nick glanced at Buck, who prayed, rocking slowly back and forth with his eyes open but glazed over. Nick had seen it many times before—Buck's spirit communicating directly with the Divine. Nick waited.

When the trance broke, Buck looked at Nick "We've heard what the specialists say…I'm trying to listen to what God says. I think it will take more time in prayer." Then he fired questions at them, "What do you guys hear when you pray? What do you think you should do? What options are out there?"

Nick looked at Maggie, who wiped her tears as Katy released her embrace.

"It's even more complicated," Maggie said. "I'm pregnant."

"What?" Buck exclaimed. "That's awesome!" He reached out and slugged Nick on the arm. "You dog, you. How exciting…" It took a moment for him to realize the ramifications of her news. When it hit him, his joy turned to anger. "Oh, that low-lying scum devil."

Buck couldn't take the news sitting down any longer. He stood and paced. "Have they tested the baby yet?"

Nick shook his head. "It's a few weeks too early."

"What treatment options are there for you? And if the baby is positive?" Katy asked.

"The doctors want me to consider…" Maggie couldn't verbalize the rest of the words. She took a deep breath. "But I could never do that."

"A significant concern is what they call 'anticipation of the Huntington's gene', where the symptoms worsen in the next generation," Nick said sadly. "The baby could have a more severe form of the disease complex." He shook his head. "The only treatments are on the cutting edge of medicine. There are reports that they could cut out the bad gene." He turned his palms up and raised his arms. "But there are so many unknowns. No one in the US even has the capability."

"Where are the leading doctors?" Katy asked.

"China, Germany, and Poland are what we can find so far," Nick said.

"Who seems to be the best in the world?" Buck asked.

"The doctor we saw here in Memphis recommended a physician in Poland. But that brings up another whole issue. I can't even imagine how expensive something like this is. Just the travel might break the bank."

Buck stopped pacing and shot a glance at Katy, and Nick saw her nod.

Buck left the dining room for a short time. When he returned, he carried a small stack of one hundred dollar bills.

"Here's a little over two thousand dollars. It's our rainy-day fund. But you need it more than us. Go see this doctor. Knowledge brings understanding." He held the money out to Nick.

Nick raised his hands in surrender. "Oh, you guys, thank you, but there is no way we can take that."

Buck grabbed Nick's hand, put the bills in his palm, and closed his fingers around them. "You can, and you will. And we'll find a way to get more. It sounds like the first thing you need to do is to explore all the options."

Nick tried to give back the money.

"Hey, don't make me use my leg lengtheners and grow into a giant," Buck smiled. His humor broke the tension.

Katy hugged Maggie, and Nick stood to hug Buck.

Buck laid one hand on Nick's shoulder and his other on Maggie's. "Look, you guys, we'll *walk through this valley of the shadow of death* with you. When I close my eyes, I see a mountain of doubt standing before you. The only way to defeat it is with faith and a symphony of prayers. Remember Jesus telling his disciples, 'Have faith in God. Truly I tell you, if anyone says to this mountain, "Go throw yourself into the sea," and does not doubt in their heart but believes that what they say will happen, it will be done for them.'"

CHAPTER 13

ALLIGATOR CLUB

After work, Emy ran home to check on Ceci, showered, and drove downtown. The dilation and evacuation, D&E procedure, had taken Emy fifteen minutes. It would have taken less time if the woman's uterus hadn't been retroverted—the backward curve presented a challenge to remove all the fetal tissue from the far end. Martha's genetic makeup determined the shape of her uterus. "Change the gene, change the person," resonated in Emy's mind, a mantra from an early professor. Her own beliefs and the BioGenics Mission Statement, *Advancing the Human Genome,* echoed this. Until they eradicated genetic disorders, abortions would continue.

As Emy pulled her car into a parking spot in front of the Poznań's District Government Office, *Inwestycje Wielkopolski,* anger throbbed in her chest from the cause that she was most passionate about, a woman's rights over her reproductive system.

A few years earlier, Polish lawmakers tried to impose a full ban on abortions, threatening to imprison women and the doctors involved in the procedure for a sentence up to five years. The thought still infuriated Emy, but thankfully, enraged thousands took to the streets and forced the lawmakers to abandon their plans. The government permitted abortions strictly when the pregnancy threatened the mother's life, a fetal abnormality, or in the case of rape or incest.

Unless you own your own hospital. It was a benefit of running a multi-million euro facility and having favor with local authorities. Emy and her carefully chosen staff eagerly offered abortions for any reason to any woman to save her from seeking the procedure in back alley chop-shops.

The clinic and Emy had received death threats from religious fanatics—a significant motivation to install such an elaborate security system. The secure facility provided crucial anonymity for multi-national patients who came seeking care for various genetic abnormalities. Some of the wealthiest and well-known clients required ultimate privacy.

Emy pushed the engine shut off button on the console of her Bentley Bentayga SUV then slid her hands around the smooth leather steering wheel. Only a year old, she loved how it still smelled new. She and Keith could afford the quarter-million euro automobile only because of her position at BioGenics, but they wouldn't be able to make the payments if Herr Bauer pulled funding from the company. She still ruminated about their conversation. She'd given the appearance of acquiescing to what he wanted because there was too much at stake to disagree.

She took in a deep breath and slowly blew it out between her lips, understanding her pent-up anger had more to do with Keith's adultery than the government's attempts at control over women, and what compelled her on this ridiculous mission.

Emy had driven around the *Stare Miasto*, Poznań Old Town, several times to look for Keith's car and a place to park. Keith drove a red Fiat Panda, a square Mr. Bean-looking automobile. She hated the car, but Keith thought it made him look hip, and besides, he could fit his entire drum kit into the back if he packed it right.

She intended to leave before he finished the gig and didn't want to take a chance of being discovered coming or going. She glanced out the back window and saw nothing unusual under the dim lighting. She couldn't be too careful. Poznań, with over a half-million people, was still small enough that she could easily run into a friend or someone from BioGenics, and she wanted to meet neither.

She flicked on the overhead lamp, smacked her lips together in the mirror to smooth her red lipstick, and adjusted the baseball cap over her forehead. The whole idea seemed foolish: the hat, the jealousy, and the sneaking around to spy on Keith. But some unknown power pulled her out of the car and down the street to the nightclub. She glanced at her watch—a quarter past midnight. Late enough that Keith's band played their final set, and with the club sufficiently packed for her to go unnoticed. She pulled up her coat collar against the cold December air.

The unknown power fought her urge to return to the car and dump the scheme and the hat. She worried the hat would make her stand out; she hoped she'd be mistaken for a tourist with the navy Yankee's cap. She'd purchased it at a genetics meeting in New York City last year on a whim and had never worn it until tonight. Polish women were much too stylish for an American ball cap. She pulled her ponytail through the hole in back and fidgeted with her ears, uncertain whether to fold them in or leave them out.

Emy tucked her chin into her coat as two men came around the corner. One man supported the other, who stumbled with each step and slurred loud curses. The newspaper warned men to avoid the Ukrainian strip clubs that edged closer to the square. As their modus operandi, they enticed men with a free shot of vodka included in the entrance fee. But the clubs tainted the alcohol, and soon the clienteles' bank cards yielded to the mercy of the women.

Emy passed the men, glancing at them over her shoulder and then back to the square. Its lights glowed into the darkened side street. The Old Market Square always buzzed with activity. On this Thursday night, with Christmas only five days away, it dazzled. Entering the square felt like a visit to Santa's workshop at the North Pole. The town adorned every building with strands of lights. A forty-foot Christmas tree, surrounded with enormous boxed gifts, filled the area in front of the historic Poznań Town Hall. Throughout time, fire, lightning, and a tornado had destroyed the iconic clock tower with mechanical goats that butted heads at noon. But they rebuilt it each time, a triumph of the Poles' resilience to the tragedies that had befallen them over the centuries. Emy hoped that she could gather a smidgen of that resilience.

The thought that Hanna would arrive home on Monday for her Christmas break, and they would all be together, brought joy to Emy's heart. She had always laughed at herself for her hypocrisy—she hated religion and loved Christmas. She tried to not think about the fact the holiday celebrated one of the holiest days for Christians and instead, enjoyed family, friends, goodwill, and gift-giving. How she loved showering the girls with presents and couldn't wait for them to open the clothes she'd ordered for them from Paris. Her fashion sense always helped keep her "cool" in the eyes of her daughters.

Emy slowed her steps as she approached the Alligator Club at one corner of the square. The owners had added a red light to the metal eye emblem above the door. Loud rock music spilled into the square, along with patrons coming and going to and from the popular nightspot. Windows on each side of the door vibrated with the frivolity of evening fun.

At one window, moist and frosty from the heat of the packed crowd, she gasped when she realized that only the glass prevented her from touching her husband. *Crap.* She'd forgotten that the stage in the Alligator sat upfront in one corner. Fortunately, Keith faced away from her with his head bobbing in rhythm to the music as he played the drums. He wore the white T-shirt full of holes she'd washed yesterday. She'd tried to throw it out many times, but he always rescued it from the trash.

Emy turned away and walked to the back of the building to the rear fire escape exit. She considered abandoning her plan, but the unknown power got the best of her. *Perhaps the woman is here.* Emy longed for the old days when she followed the band, adoringly swooning over her love beating the drums. She hadn't seen him perform in years. She'd stopped going when the pressing crowd, loud music, cigarette smoke and stench of stale beer nauseated her.

People smoking and partying packed the back entrance. The pungent skunk aroma of weed intoxicated Emy with nostalgia for the college days when she and Keith dated. They would smoke a joint and make love in her dorm room to the sounds of Phil Collins and Joan Jett.

Emy squeezed through the crowd and got past the bouncer without resistance, something the second X chromosome still made possible. She and Keith came to the Alligator after they'd first moved to Poznań—when the girls were young and before Danek's birth—back when they took time for dates and before life hadn't overwhelmed them. *Rest in peace, my dear child.*

As she searched for a place to sit, she'd forgotten the enjoyable atmosphere of the dive with its rough-hewn brick walls appearing through mosaic patches of plaster. Subtle lighting of reds and greens cast colorful shadows around the patrons, all trying to converse over the blaring music. Emy pushed her way through the party until she reached the end of the bar as two girls in miniskirts vacated their seats.

"You mind if I take your chair?" Emy shouted to one girl who gave her a disapproving scan up and down but nodded.

Emy removed her jacket and placed it over the barstool as she pulled it out to sit. She watched the band through the mob, certain that Keith couldn't see her. *He won't even be looking for me.* His group, the Fire Dragons, bellowed out "Sweet Home Alabama," and the crowd sang along. It surprised Emy that the band sounded decent. She had to laugh about the catchy tune; she figured that most of the patrons couldn't point Alabama out on a map. Keith sang and played the drums, and the fantastic new guitarist fingered the nimble riff.

Keith, at forty-seven, two years younger than Emy, looked hot tonight, in spite of all they had gone through. He oozed charm—part of what had won Emy over when they'd met. Perspiration glistened off his forehead and curled his jet-black locks. He didn't have one gray hair. Yes, every girl wanted to bed the drummer...including Emy. Desire welled up for the first time in a long while as his musical talent revved her engine—he could play the drums, guitar, and piano equally well. *So much talent, so much misdirection in his life.*

The bartender motioned to her for a drink. *What the hell.* "I'll have a Krupnik and Zywiec," she yelled. He nodded and poured her a shot of the sweet honey liqueur and a beer. He slid the beverages in front of her, and she handed him a Polish twenty *zloty* and refused the change.

She sipped at the Krupnik. Its sweet burn coated her throat, and for old times' sake, she tossed the rest down in one gulp. She held the shot glass out to the bartender, who refilled it. She toasted the man and swallowed that one as well. He offered to pour another, but she covered the glass with her hand and waved him off.

Emy fidgeted with the shot glass and examined the tattoo on the inside of her left forearm, a memento from her college days. She tightened and relaxed her hand to flex the muscle and move the two Chinese characters. After cheating on a difficult math test and feeling guilty over it, she'd decided on the tattoo—success with honor. At least, that's what she hoped the symbols meant. Who knows? The young tattooist could have inked "dumb, gullible girl." But it reminded her that when she took future tests, she would have success under her own merits. She ran her hand over the characters. She hoped the same held true today.

Unaccustomed as she was to alcohol, the potent liquor mainlined to her head and filled her with a pleasant warmth. She sipped the Zywiec to cool her throat when she sensed a presence standing next to her.

"Hey, that's pretty good for an American," a man said with a strong Russian accent.

Emy thought he mistook her for someone else, then remembered the NY on her hat and turned to smile at him. His handsome appearance surprised her. She laughed out loud at the absurdity of being hit on by the twenty-year-old. As a tease, she took the shot glass still in her hand, slowly ran her tongue around the rim, and sensually stuck it inside for the last drop.

He licked his lips and focused on her breasts. It felt nice to be the center of someone's desire for a change, so she flexed her chest and let him look.

"Hey, you want to dance, pretty lady?" the man said into her ear, pressing his lips close.

But the rage of Keith's betrayal crept in with the stranger's advances.

She turned, ran her hand down his chest, stopping to play with a button, and then pulled him close to whisper in his ear. "*Ivan, krieche zurück in das loch, aus dem du gekommen bist,*" she said with as much venom in her voice as she could manage through her alcohol fogged brain—telling him to crawl back into the hole he'd come from. She used the old World War II slang for the hated Russians.

He shrugged and tried to move closer to her. It appalled her the younger generation didn't get it, or maybe they didn't care about the old animosities caused by the war between the Germans and the Russians. Emy's father hadn't let her forget.

The young man tried to put his arm around her. She pushed him away, only to have him force himself upon her. Emy's heart pounded with fear until she heard a loud slap on the bar behind her. Immediately, the Russian backed off. Emy turned to see the bartender glaring at the young man who raised his hands in surrender, then walked away. Emy nodded a thank you to the barkeep.

What the hell am I doing here? She stood and picked up her jacket, trying to decide if she should slink away out the back or walk past the band and surprise Keith. Maybe if he saw her there, their passion could burn once again tonight.

The band played one of Emy's favorites, "Desperado," a song that Keith sang so beautifully when he had won her over so many years ago. He had changed from the drums to the keyboard, which pulled her forward like a magnet. The revelers spilled onto the dance floor and blocked the path to her man.

She stood at the edge of the crowd, swaying to the music as a swarm of people pressed in. From her vantage point, she saw Keith's closed eyes. He sang with such passion that she felt sorry for him. He had his pain as well. So much could be forgiven.

As the song ended, she wanted to force her way through the mob, hold him, kiss him. But as she took a step forward, a young Asian girl bounded onto the stage and wrapped herself around Emy's husband. She kissed his neck, then Keith reciprocated with a passionate kiss on her mouth. The girl adjusted her body to sit on his lap, wrapped her legs around him, and kissed him again, as the partiers erupted in jubilation. Keith and the girl moved their bodies in sensual rhythm in front of everyone.

Emy took two steps back and almost vomited, but found the bar with one hand and steadied herself. The Asian girl in Keith's lap lifted both arms in celebration, then ran her fingers through his hair. *It's her—bitch is right!*

The adulteress's genome couldn't tell Emy of her stunning beauty. Even in this moment of wrath, Emy admired the woman. Long black hair that feathered back like a L'Oréal model. One bleached platinum ringlet heralded a wild streak. Her superior genetic makeup resulted in flawless skin, thick eyebrows, perfectly proportioned features, and perky breasts. Her delicate blue-laced blouse opened in the back to show off her smooth, spotless skin and defined musculature.

If she hadn't been grinding on Keith's lap, Emy thought she might find the woman irresistible too.

Keith stood with the rest of the band and bowed to great cheers and accolades. He hugged his girlfriend sideways and stepped off the stage to his adoring crowd—shaking hands and receiving praise. He waved to the rest of the crowd and walked out the front door with the woman.

Emy stood frozen in shock and indecision until someone bumped her from behind. The momentum carried her forward, and she made her way with the rest of the mob out the front door. The freezing temperature hit her neck and cleared her mind. She pulled on her jacket and zipped it up, hiding part of her face. She thought she'd lost sight of Keith and the woman, but as the crowd dispersed, she saw them walking toward the Mars Fountain in the corner of the square. She made her way to the darkened side street and watched them from a distance.

Keith reached into his front pants pocket, pulled out a blunt, and lit it. Emy had noticed the scent of marijuana on him recently. Her warnings of psychosis with too much weed use had only inflamed a fight.

As they passed the joint back and forth, the woman clung to Emy's husband and rubbed his crotch—*in public, no less.* The couple seemed oblivious to the people around them or the statue of the god Mars squatting behind them. The god of war held a large spear over them. "Yeah…this is war, all right," Emy said under her breath.

When the couple finished their smoke, the woman pulled Keith upright, and they walked toward one of the apartment buildings that lined the square. They disappeared through the front door.

"Huh, wonder if they'll have sex?" Emy scoffed.

She waited for a few minutes when rage boosted her boldness. She walked straight to the front door of the apartment building, peered through the glass, and pulled the door open. With an empty lobby, she walked down the hallway to the post boxes. Maybe she'd get lucky.

She ran her finger over the labels of each row, finally coming to the only Chinese name she could find, Ping Wusu (Lilly).

* * *

In the middle of the night, Emy didn't know where else to go to clear her head, so she drove to BioGenics to regain her balance. At the side entrance of the building, the security palm reader and retinal scanner confirmed her identity, and she entered the six-digit security code into the finger pad. Emy and the head of security were the only two people with authorization codes, always the last to leave at night and the first to arrive in the morning. She insisted on the tight control. The staff had access to the hospital wing twenty-four-seven, but security locked the clinic and research arms of the building every night.

Emy recalled her father's advice that she'd heard often throughout her high school years: nothing good happens after midnight. She believed it as truth and wanted BioGenics to set an example for other corporations. She directed her staff to go home to their families in the evening.

The code automatically disarmed the security system and turned on the entrance lights, so she could walk freely throughout the facility. Secure corridors connected the separate hospital, clinic, and research wings of the E-shaped building. Her office on the fourth floor occupied one corner in the research section.

She flicked on the lights to her office. She loved this space. It belonged to her, and she reigned. The bulky German furnishings reminded her of a Bavarian castle. Her dark wooden desk seemed too small for the room, but it had been her father's, and she would use nothing else. She reached for the switch to turn on the lighting of the large curio cabinet next to the door where she stored the cherished souvenirs of her international travels.

Then she draped her jacket over one of the large leather chairs, walked to her desk, and sat. She stared at the neatly piled files on each side. *What in the world am I going to do?* The girls adored their father. It would break their hearts if they divorced, or she told them about his infidelity. *Maybe he'll come to his senses.* Lilly was beautiful. Even her name evoked images of a lovely mythical fairy.

Emy moved the mouse of her computer, and it came to life with a blinking cursor waiting for the twenty-digit code. She rapidly typed it in, and the BioGenics's homepage image popped onto the screen. She went to the Google search bar and typed in the woman's name, *Ping Wusu.* Several doctors from around the world topped the list: neuroscientists, addiction researchers, and Chinese medicine physicians. *I can't imagine the woman is any of those.* Google listed two Chinese American actors, but when she clicked on the links, they were not Lilly. The further she scrolled into the pages, the more the search took her into nonsense. Out of curiosity, she clicked on images, and hundreds of photos loaded. It, too, resulted in a dead end. In the search bar, she added the word *naked* after the woman's name. *Maybe she's a porn star.* After scanning the first few pages, she realized the absurdity of her actions.

She pushed the power button to force the computer into sleep mode, leaned back in her chair, and sighed. When she brought her arms up over her head, she looked again at the Chinese characters on her forearm. "Great, just stinking great."

Emy needed something to ground her and take her out of this emotional, out-of-control free fall.

She looked at her bookcase and noticed the envelope that her father had given her teetering on a shelf. She reached for it, laid it on her desk, and spun it around so her misspelled name faced her. The thinness surprised Emy, but she noticed for the first time that it also contained a small object.

Maybe whatever is in here would help distract me. She sure wouldn't get any sleep tonight thinking of that woman making love to her husband.

She reached for a letter opener but stopped. She needed a drink and glanced at the small mini bar in the corner. She never drank at work but had the bar installed for the hospitality of visitors.

She pushed herself up from her chair and walked to the locked cabinet enclosing the minibar. She pulled her keys from her pocket and opened it. The cabinet contained a bottle of liqueur that Herr Bauer had given her when she had presented her latest breakthroughs on Huntington's at the meeting in New York.

She removed the fancy silver box and pulled the lid open. Because she didn't drink cognac, she thought he had gifted her with a simple bottle of the bitter liqueur, and she had tried to give it to her roommate at the meeting. Her roommate researched the beverage, which turned out to be a good thing. The company made the Hennessy Ellipse Cognac's decanter from Baccarat Crystal, a collector's item in its own right. The small bottle of liqueur cost slightly under ten thousand euros.

Emy chuckled at the set of two-euro tumblers next to the valuable bottle. "You're probably not worthy of holding this gold," she said to the glass, "but what the hell." She smiled as she clunked ice cubes from the freezer into the tumbler. Then she broke the seal of the Hennessy and poured.

Emy walked back to her desk, sat, and raised a toast. "Here's to you, Herr Bauer."

She picked up the envelope and letter opener and sliced open the top.

CHAPTER 14

MOTHER

Emy startled when the head of security opened her office door and stridently cleared his throat. Her foggy mind made it difficult to orient to time and space. She lifted her head off her dead-asleep arm that draped awkwardly over the contents of her desktop.

"Dr. Christianson, you okay?" the man said so loud her hungover head buzzed.

Emy pushed herself back and wiped the drool from the corner of her mouth. Her eyes tried to focus on the man, then her office. The neurons in her brain fired, and flashbacks from the previous night played over in her mind—her husband, the Chinese woman, her office…the envelope and cognac.

"Dr. Christianson?"

Emy recognized Bruno, the head of security, and loyal to a fault. He and the rest of the staff loved and respected her, as well as feared her. She tried to speak and reassure him so he would leave, but at the moment, her stomach churned.

"What happened?"

Emy raised her hand in defeat to quiet the man.

He ignored her direction. "I received a text at 0130 last night that you entered the building. The security camera confirmed that it was you, so I didn't investigate further. I'm so sorry, Dr. Christianson. I drifted back to sleep and didn't realize you hadn't left the building until I got here this morning. Are you okay?"

Emy pumped her hand to quell the chatter. She didn't need sympathy. She didn't need an apology. She needed silence.

The room spun.

Emy gripped the edge of the desk to steady her body and mind and opened her mouth to speak, only to vomit. The regurgitated bile and cognac burned her throat.

Only when she looked up in embarrassment was she aware that Izzi stood behind Bruno.

Her research assistant raced into the room and supported her from slipping off the chair and collapsing onto the floor.

Izzi usurped Bruno's authority and told him to leave, which set off a heated exchange.

Emy tried to find her voice to beg them to stop, but Izzi stood her ground. Bruno slammed the door behind him, and Izzi dragged Emy to the sofa, put a pillow under her head, and placed cushions under her legs.

"By the looks of it, you've had quite the bender, Dr. Christianson," Izzi said and walked into the private bathroom. She grabbed a hand towel, ran it under some water, returned to the office, and laid it on Emy's forehead.

Emy used the corner to wipe the vomit from her mouth as the coolness jelled her thoughts. "Coffee, can I please get some coffee?"

* * *

After three cups of cappuccino, Emy's strength returned, and she sat upright. The bread and cheese that Izzi found in the mini-fridge had stayed down.

Izzi sat in the leather chair opposite the sofa and examined the documents from the envelope. Emy's grad student was the closest thing she had to a confidant—tattoos, abrasive personality, and all.

As she watched the girl inspect the contents, she noticed a new tattoo etched into her forearm—a screaming skull with lacy flowers growing out of all its orifices was inked onto her skin. Perhaps it represented some memory trying to burst out of her psyche. To Emy, the image portrayed precisely how she felt at the moment.

Emy had read and reread her father's note so many times last night she could almost recite it word for word as Izzi read it back to her:

"Dear Emmanuelle,

I knew this day would eventually come when you would want to know of your heritage. Please understand that you are and forever will be my child. Nothing can take that away.

I'm afraid my memory is fading. All I can remember is your beautiful smile and the fond memories of you growing into an amazingly strong woman. But you had a rough start in life. I thank God for His lovingkindness to us all.

Shortly after your birth, a friend from social services called me and asked if we wanted to adopt a child. Apparently, the authorities found you and your mother in a flophouse and took you both to the hospital. Your mother was a heroin addict, and so you were born addicted as well. The doctors told me it surprised them you survived at all. I am sorry to say that your mother abandoned you in the hospital.

The police helped track her down, but she was back to her drugs. I want you to know that I tried to do all I could to help your mother. She begged me to take you. I asked her to write this letter, which is included here. She also gave me the few items she possessed of your family.

I am sorry to inform you she died from an overdose three weeks after your birth.

Emmanuelle, I love you. None of these things ever mattered to me. Please forgive me where I failed as a father...Papa"

Izzi grimaced, put the letter down, and picked up the others. "This is all that's left of your family?" Izzi asked, holding up the letters, a birth certificate, and a few photos. "That's messed up."

Emy shrugged.

"I never knew you were adopted," Izzi said.

Emy picked up a glass of ice water Izzi had poured for her and took a long drink. "I'd always suspected, but it never mattered to me. I didn't know for sure until my father handed me the envelope."

"Your adopted father," Izzi said, a statement rather than a question.

"Yes." Emy took another sip.

Izzi squinted to read the name on top of the faded, hand-written birth certificate, then held it toward Emy. "Who is this Immanuel Frankel?"

Emy cleared her throat. "Me…I'm Immanuel Frankel."

Izzi dumped out a small object from the envelope into her hand. "And what's this?"

"It's a cufflink," Emy said with irritation. Her head throbbed.

"You read the letters?" Izzi asked, ignoring Emy's agitation.

"I read the one from my father and…uh, Bella…my mother." It was the first time she'd said the name out loud. "The other one is written in Hungarian, I think." Emy remembered trying to decipher it when the cognac swirled through her brain and body. Now that she had sobered up, her mind whirled with emotion more than alcohol.

Izzi inspected the letter from Emy's birth mother. "What's it say?" she asked, emboldened by the intimacy with her boss.

"You don't read German?"

Izzi smiled, *"Ich verstehe nicht,"* she lisped through her pierced tongue. "I've drunk pints of German beer, ate some mighty excellent schnitzel, and even enjoyed some pretty German girls." She laughed loudly. "I mean, dated some Krauts, but I can't read the language." She handed the letter to Emy.

Emy picked up her reading glasses from the coffee table and put them on. The letter was handwritten on a filthy and tattered piece of plain motel stationery paper. The shaky script contained several misspelled words. It took her hours to decipher the note.

Emy translated:

> "*Mein liebstes kind.* My dearest child. I'm afraid I have nothing to give you. Like my mother, I leave you now with only this letter. When you read my mother's letter, you may understand better the *dämonen,* the demons…"

"It took me the longest time to figure out that word. Her writing is difficult," Emy said and continued reading:

> "…the demons I have fought. I was born Bella Frankel on Halloween, October 31, 1945, to Yuri Frankel. All I know about my parents is written in my mother's letter. My mother died at my *Geburt*, childbirth."

Emy held the letter out to Izzi. "I think that's what this word is."

Izzi shrugged. "It's such terrible handwriting, I don't see how you can read any of it."

Emy continued:

> "As far as I know, I was born in a displaced persons camp outside of Berlin. My mother was Jewish. I am Jewish, and that makes you Jewish as well."

"You're Jewish?" Izzi asked, then laughed. "*Mazel tov.* Isn't that something you people say?"

Emy looked at her assistant, trying not to take offense, and went back to the letter.

> "I remember nothing of my childhood. My first memories come from being moved from one *Pflegekinderheim*, foster home, to another. I did what I needed to survive.
>
> I do not remember your *Vater.*
>
> I'm sorry."

Emy stared at the page and wished for more words. She envisioned her adoptive father as he stood by and encouraged her to write. This letter was all she had of her birth mother, that and twenty-three of her chromosomes. She figured the father Bella mentioned was her biological father and the other half of her genome. *Probably someone who traded sex for drugs. How in the world did I become one of the world's leading geneticists from this union?* Nature versus nurture…the great debate, but Emy believed an individual was mostly a function of the genetic pool rather than upbringing.

The weight of the words hung in the room, and she looked at Izzi.

"Dude, that's messed up," Izzi said and wiped a tear from her cheek. "I thought my life sucked. I'm sorry." Izzi handed Emy an old black-and-white photograph. "Who do you think this is?"

Emy studied the face of the young woman in the photo. If the hairstyle had been more modern and the hair darker, she would be the spitting image of Hanna. Emy covered the woman's hair with her fingers. *Definitely, Hanna.* The woman was turned sideways and looked back at the camera. Her skin glowed, she had a slight dimple in her left cheek, and a black cashmere sweater and pearl necklace hinted at wealth. Her thoughtful eyes captivated Emy's heart.

When she turned the photo over, the scripted name *Yuri Frankel*—Bella's mother and Emy's grandmother, surprised her. She'd always pictured her heritage as an impoverished immigrant family, but this photo shocked her. *How did Bella come from this genetic stock?*

"This is my grandmother, Yuri Frankel, as a young woman," Emy said and gave the photo back to Izzi, who handed Emy another.

Damaged at the corners, the photograph appeared yanked from a photo album. The family of four sat straight and proper; the man on the right wore a dark suit, vest, and fedora. The short stout woman was nicely bedecked in a silk dress and French beret. A young girl stood beside each adult. The girls looked between eight and nine years old and wore matching woolen dresses and oversized bows in their blond hair. Their bows tilted outward, framing the symmetrical family unit.

Emy adjusted her glasses and looked closer at the girls.

"They're identical twins," she said.

She turned the photo over. In cursive writing, it said: Yosel and Chava Frankel. Underneath, the children had written their own names: Yuri and Eva.

Emy traced her finger over the penmanship like she was retracing time. Her grandmother, Yuri, her great-aunt, Eva, and her great-grandparents, Yosel and Chava.

Next, Izzi handed her an old brown and faded photo of a somber man and woman. The woman, clothed in a floor-length dress of heavy fabric, held the dress in place with a large sash around her waist. The man wore a long coat, black puff tie, and a Jewish kippah or yarmulke head covering. A proud Jew. Not marked on the back of the photo with names or a date, Emy assumed they were her great-great-grandparents.

She dropped her hands to her lap. Here was, at least in part, her true gene pool. She knew nothing about these people, yet felt a deep longing—a connection to her heritage.

"Any other pictures?" Izzi asked.

Emy shook her head. A sense of panic and a great longing to see a picture of her mother rose in her. Even though she'd deduced she was adopted, she'd had no desire to hear more, until now. Seeing the photos and letters opened a flood of emotion and yearning. She looked at the colorful genome pictograph on her wall that previously had no anchor—now it had meaning.

"What are you going to do with this?" Izzi held up the other letter written on fragile parchment paper.

"Do you know anyone in BioGenics who reads Hungarian?" Emy asked.

"No, but I'd be happy to run it through Google translator for you," Izzi said. Her body subconsciously bounced as if she heard hip-hop through imaginary headphones. The intrigue of Emy's heritage had opened a vault of curiosity in them both.

"Look, Christmas is in two days, this can all wait until you get back from the break. You need to go home to celebrate with your family," Emy said.

Izzi jumped to her feet.

Emy had a feeling Izzi would translate the Hungarian as soon as possible, but before she dismissed her student, Emy blurted out in a rare moment of extreme vulnerability, "I saw the Chinese girl last night."

Izzi sat back down and stared with inquisitive eyes at the confession.

"I went to the club where Keith performed, and she was there."

"Oh, that little—"

Emy cut her off before she swore and sighed. "She's beautiful."

Izzi sat up straight and crossed her arms. Her biceps flexed.

"I watched them go into her apartment building."

"You know where she lives?" Izzi's face turned red, and the veins in her neck bulged.

Emy nodded.

"Tell me where and some of my girls and I will mess her up. Let her know that she shouldn't mess around with a married man." She smacked the back of her hand into the palm of the other.

For a moment, that thought actually appealed to Emy. Instead, she stood and reached for Izzi, who jumped up and hugged her.

"You are sweet, Izzi, but violence won't help my situation."

It was the first time she had hugged the girl. It felt strange, but as they held each other, the closeness brought Emy comfort.

CHAPTER 15

Maggie collapsed onto the bed in their hotel room overlooking the Old Market Square in Poznań, Poland. Booking a flight a few days before Christmas proved difficult and expensive. Because of some last-minute cancellations and Buck and Katy's invaluable gift, Nick and Maggie arrived on Christmas Eve. They'd left Memphis midafternoon, and with the seven-hour time difference, had reached the Hotel Brovaria almost the same hour the next day.

Nick flung open the curtains that overlooked the square. "What a guy I am, bringing you to Poland for Christmas."

Maggie huffed.

"What? You don't like Poland?" he asked.

"Oh stop," Maggie said. "You're giving me an even worse headache. What I don't like is that my back is killing me from sitting for nineteen hours, and my feet are like turnips." She stretched her body over the king-size bed. "What I do love is this bed."

"Well, I'm glad we're here. If it's as nice as our innkeeper in Kona said, I think we are in for a real treat. There's so much history and culture here."

"When do we see Dr. Christianson?" Maggie asked, ignoring his optimism.

"We've got a few days to sightsee, then we see her on Thursday. It was awful nice of her to see us at all during this week between Christmas and New Year's."

"Tell me again why you like her, and that we're doing the right thing." Maggie lifted her head off the bed and looked at Nick. "It feels weird to travel all this way for medical care."

Nick sat on the bed beside Maggie and rubbed her back. "I understand this is frightening, but BioGenics has the best reputation in the world for genetic disorders and especially the advanced treatment of Huntington's. They also have the fastest turnaround time for genetic testing of the baby. We'll find out in days rather than weeks or months if it affects our little one."

"It won't give me a lot of comfort when they stick a giant needle up my cervix or through my abdomen to do the biopsy."

"Remember, we're mostly here for information. We don't have to do anything more if you don't want." Nick sighed, knowing it would not be the last time he reassured her. "Even if we decide not to have the baby tested, we still have to understand what options are available for you. I'm not going through this without a fight. I felt much better after talking directly with Dr. Christianson. You'll like her."

Maggie curled around Nick's legs. He rubbed at the frown lines on her forehead and smoothed back her hair. "It's all going to be okay," Nick said.

He didn't believe his own words; what he said was as close to a lie as he hoped he'd ever tell Maggie. She would like Dr. Christianson, because Maggie connected with everyone. But he didn't feel better at all after talking with the doctor. Although pleasant and kind enough, the diagnosis remained dire. The doctor agreed to see them this week after she'd initially said that they would have to wait several weeks for her next available appointment. He wondered why she relented to his plea, perhaps as a favor to Dr. B or because he was also a physician. She seemed distant, if not distracted, consumed by responsibility, much like Nick remembered from his practice.

He stopped rubbing Maggie's back.

She looked up at him and asked, "You okay?"

"Yeah, just praying for you." *God, another lie.* Although it was true, he'd prayed more these past weeks than ever in his life. "I'll let you rest, and then we should get you and our baby something to eat."

* * *

The friendly and gregarious waiter in the Brovaria's restaurant reminded Nick of a taller and younger version of the innkeeper in Kona.

"I'm sorry for the delay," he said in near-perfect English. "The owner is quite traditional, and we can't break the Christmas Eve fast. We don't have our usual menu but are serving the traditional *Wigilia,* vigil supper. I'm afraid there is no red meat, but I hope you will enjoy our traditions."

"Oh, we're good," Nick said and smiled at Maggie, who'd complained of her hunger and resisted any celebration. "Simply a bit groggy from our siesta." Nick looked the young man up and down—thin and dressed nicely in black pants and vest over a white shirt. "Your English is great."

The man shrugged. "You will find many people in Poland are multilingual: Polish, English, German and often others," he said and smoothed his mustache.

"I thought you might have studied in the US," Nick said.

"No, I graduated from Warsaw in history, but I quickly learned I can make more money as a waiter," he said and puffed out his chest. "But I can tell you all about Polish history if you'd like."

"I want to hear about Poland," Maggie said. "First, tell us what we are waiting for?" she asked with palpable hunger.

Before the waiter could answer, a young boy and girl burst through the door.

"It's here. It's here. The star has come!" they yelled throughout the dining room and into the kitchen.

"Oh, good. Thank God it's a clear night," the waiter said and looked at his watch. "We, Poles, fast on Christmas Eve until the first star appears. It represents the Star of Bethlehem. Our legends say that what happens on *Wigilia* affects the incoming year." He shrugged profoundly and raised his hands.

Nick checked his watch. It read five-thirty, but it was already dark outside. Evening came early in Poland because of winter solstice and the country's northern proximity.

"What time did the sun set?" Nick asked.

"I believe three-thirty today," the waiter said.

A man, woman, and the two children came from the kitchen in great cheer.

"Aww, our owner will present the blessing and break the *opłatek*, Christmas wafer," the waiter said. "It is a time to forgive each other for any hurtful things over the last year and to wish each other happiness in the coming year."

The owner spoke in Polish, with his family and waitstaff, gathered around him. When he finished with a prayer, everyone said, "Amen," and crossed themselves.

The owner took a large white rectangular wafer decorated with the icon of Mary and baby Jesus from the tray his wife carried and held it up. "May God grant you peace and prosperity for the coming year," he said in English for the guests and then snapped it in half.

Nick and Maggie sat closest to the owner and his family and received the first pieces of wafer and the blessing. The owner broke off a corner for each of them and pressed it into their hands. The owner's children smiled and said in unison, "*Wesołych Świąt.*"

Maggie looked at their waiter.

"Merry Christmas," he interpreted.

"Merry Christmas to you as well," Maggie said and reached to touch the cheek of the young girl, who blushed when Maggie tickled it.

"Merry Christmas," Nick said to the couple. "Thank you. We needed a blessing." He smiled at Maggie.

"Okay, I can bring you the first course of twelve," the waiter said when the owners went to the next table.

"Twelve?" Maggie asked.

"Yes, I hope you're hungry. It is a good thing that Christ had only twelve apostles." He laughed and hurried into the kitchen.

Nick raised his water glass to Maggie. "Merry Christmas Eve," he said. "Peace be with you."

"Yes, peace be with you," Maggie touched her glass to Nick's.

The waiter returned with bowls of red soup and a loaf of braided bread. He held his hand toward Maggie's bowl. "This is our traditional clear borsch, beetroot bouillon with *uszka*, mushroom-filled dumplings." He waved his hand over the bread. "This is the special challah bread." He put his hand to the side of his mouth. "We borrowed this from our Jewish brothers who eat it on their Sabbath."

Maggie sipped a spoonful of soup. She tilted her head from side to side and then took another bite.

"What do you think?" Nick said after he tasted the soup.

Maggie raised her eyebrows and nodded. "It's good, a bit sour, but anything tastes good after potato chips and airplane food."

"Mmmm, try the dumplings. They remind me of what our friend in Kona made for us." He swallowed and tore a chunk of bread off the loaf.

Maybe it was the food or the blessing, but Nick's shoulders relaxed as he munched on the bread. He sat back comfortably in the chair and looked around the room. Only half-filled with tourists, the dining room had a modern elegance with warm ivory walls and dark wood accents. The website boasted of the Brovaria's own brewery and beer selection. On check-in, the front desk clerk apologized over and over that the brewery dining room, bar, and basement club were closed for a few days for the Christmas holiday. That didn't bother Nick; he preferred the intimacy of this smaller dining space. After all, they hadn't come for the libations.

Nick savored the international flavor of the dining room, with couples speaking different languages. He wondered how many countries were represented by the people in the room.

Maggie seemed to read his thoughts. "Isn't it amazing how God made us all different? How many people are in the world?"

"Something like seven point five billion, or something like that," Nick said.

Maggie shook her head. "And look at how every one of us is different. I mean, sometimes you see a person who kind of looks like someone else, but with over seven billion completely distinctive people—it's amazing. How can that be?"

"It's all about the DNA, I guess."

"How are all these unique babies made?" Maggie asked.

"Well…" Nick feigned sincerity. "When a mommy and daddy love each other very much, they lie very close to each other, and—"

"Oh stop it, Nicklaus Hart. You know what I mean."

"Tsk, tsk, tsk," the waiter scolded Maggie from behind. "No quarreling on *Wigilia*, or else it foretells of a troublesome year." He laughed and placed a small plate in front of them from the serving tray he carried.

"Oh, he was just teasing me," Maggie said. "The soup is wonderful, by the way."

"I can get you more of anything. Merely give me the word." He pointed to the odd-looking rolls on the new plate. "These are Polish rollmops—pickled herring rolled around onion and pickles."

Maggie crinkled her nose.

The waiter looked around for the owner and then whispered. "Yes, not my favorite, either. My mother would make me eat the whole thing before I could open my Christmas Eve present. I won't be so cruel, but at least try one bite."

The waiter turned to the next table and gave the guests a similar warning.

Nick picked up the plate of rollmops and waved them in front of Maggie's nose. The scaly blue skin on the herring resembled an eel and smelled like vinegary mustard.

She recoiled. "You realize I'm pregnant, right?"

"I thought the pickles might be right up your alley." Nick laughed.

"Only if they're wrapped in chocolate." Maggie laughed and pushed the plate away.

Nick brought the plate to his nose and inhaled deeply. He coughed at the odor.

"See? You're not even with child."

Nick held a fish roll gingerly with his fingers and bit off the end. He tilted his head back and forth with indecision, but finally nodded that he liked it.

"Back to our discussion about what makes us all different," Nick said between bites. "We share some DNA with even this poor little herring. DNA is what makes all things. I think I read one time that we have 60% identical DNA with a banana, fruit fly, or chicken. All living matter comes with an instruction manual, the genome. It tells each cell what to do and how to function."

Maggie thrust out her lower lip. "I'm feeling like a chicken."

"A chicken with an egg," Nick smiled, but he understood her fear, took her hand, and recited a prayer they said over and over to each other. "Lord, help us."

"Yes, Lord, help us," Maggie agreed.

The waiter stood at their table with another large tray of food. Nick looked up at him, smiled, and let go of Maggie's hand so the waiter could put down two more courses.

"I think you'll like these better than the rollmops," he said and presented plates with a different type of roll and a grilled fillet of white fish. "This is our delicious traditional *gołąbki*, or cabbage rolls and carp dish."

Nick and Maggie took a serving of each on their plates, sampled the food, and nodded with approval.

"What's crazy about our DNA, especially when you look around at the diversity of humans in even this room, is that we all share 99.9% of the exact same genetic information. It is only that last 0.1% that accounts for our differences," Nick said.

"Makes all the distinctions of race and classes seem fairly petty," she said.

"Exactly," he said. "We're so much more alike than some want to admit."

"So how, exactly, do we pass on this genetic information?" Maggie asked.

"Well remember, each cell has a nucleus packed with the ninety-two strands of DNA that pair up to form the forty-six chromosomes. Because there are two of each type of chromosome, that makes twenty-three pairs. When a cell divides, mitosis, each chromosome duplicates, and the new cell receives the exact copy of all the chromosomes."

"But at the moment of conception, don't we get genetic information from both our father and mother?" Maggie asked.

"Yeah, that's true. But that's called meiosis. It occurs when a female ovum or male sperm is made. During that process, the chromosomes split so each egg and sperm consists of only twenty-three *single* chromosomes."

"It seems like somewhere in school, I learned that a woman is born with all the eggs she will ever have."

"Correct."

"Isn't that crazy? So, in my mother's womb, I had the egg for this baby inside of me already." She rubbed her belly.

"Blows your mind, doesn't it?" Nick nodded.

"So, if our baby is a girl, she has the eggs for her babies already inside of her?" Maggie asked.

"If I recall correctly, her body started making ova at nine weeks in utero, and she'd be well on her way to making all she'll carry for the rest of her life. If he is a boy, he'll make sperm throughout his lifetime. Both the egg and the sperm contain only one copy of the chromosomes. Our genetic information gets scrambled a bit during reproduction. We don't simply pass on exact copies of our genes in our egg and sperm. During meiosis, before they split apart, each chromosome exchanges segments of itself with the other, helping increase genetic variability. The process creates virtually limitless combinations of genes from parents to their children."

"So we're echoes of our parents and grandparents and great-grandparents. It's truly a miracle," Maggie said.

"For sure. Like I said, Mommy and Daddy love each other very much and…"

"You better eat your dinner before I throw something at you."

CHAPTER 16

It surprised Emy to find Izzi at the front door of her home. Izzi's speech was rapid, and she shifted from one foot to the other. Emy worried that drugs caused her mania.

"Dr. C, I translated your letter over the weekend and thought you'd want to see it," she lisped, lashing her words together.

"Izzi, it's Christmas Eve. You should be home with your family," Emy scolded.

"Nah, the old man and woman split, and I'm not exactly welcome since I came out."

Emy felt a little guilty as she looked at the young woman. She recalled that Izzi studied in Warsaw, where she'd gotten her degree in genetic biology. Typically, Emy's graduate students rotated with her for a year, so she didn't make it a priority to get to know their personal lives. She justified her disinterest by their temporary status—it was challenging to keep track of everyone. Emy kept a professional distance from her staff, but she'd already crossed that line with Izzi and saw no choice but to invite the girl in for Christmas Eve.

Even though a backward baseball cap partially covered Izzi's hair, Emy saw that it had gone from platinum blond to emerald green.

"You like it?" Izzi asked as Emy lingered on her hair. She whipped the cap off and ran her hand over her short hair. "It's my Christmas doo." Her laugh came sharp and staccato.

She wore no coat and had rolled her plaid shirt sleeves past her toned biceps, revealing an oversized watch and multiple tattoos on her arms.

"Izzi, aren't you freezing? It's below zero this evening."

"Oh, I'm cool. Just thought you'd want to see this ASAP." She held up the envelope marked "Immanuel."

Emy looked past Izzi at the clear evening sky. Hanna and Cecylia had declared the appearance of the first star, and they were just sitting down to eat. Forecasters had predicted several inches of snow to fall tonight, making for a white Christmas.

"We've gathered around the table for *Wigilia*. Please join us."

"No, thank you, Dr. C. I'm supposed to meet up with my mates later." She continued to sway back and forth.

Emy doubted that Izzi had anywhere to go. She saw no indication of illicit drugs: Izzi's pupils were neither abnormally dilated nor pinpoint. BioGenics strictly prohibited drug use and frequently tested employees, so Izzi's mania was unlikely due to that. *Perhaps she's bipolar.* She speculated Izzi had run her own genome, and they could check to see if she carried the specific marker for bipolar disease. As an undergraduate, Emy had researched this mutation on the gene that plays a critical role in neurotransmission and other processes in the brain.

Emy's professor had discovered this particular SNP, single nucleotide polymorphism, or "snip" for short. It was early in genetics when the scientific world had first discovered snips. They determined that when a cell replicates, it can make a mistake in one nucleotide during the copying process—kind of like a typo. These SNPs generate biological variations between people that are passed on from parent to child. This phenomenon is how all the ancestry investigation works—the more SNPs you have in common with a person, the more likely you are related to them.

"Mom, do we have a guest?" Hanna startled Emy and pushed passed her to Izzi. She extended her hand. "I'm Hanna."

"Izzi." The young women shook hands.

"Merry Christmas. You look cold. Would you please come in?"

"I really shouldn't…" Izzi said and glanced at her boss.

"Oh, nonsense. Absolutely, you should," Hanna said, took her hand, and led her across the threshold and closed the door behind them.

"Holy crap, it smells good in here."

Emy cringed as Cecylia came around the corner, wiping her hands on a towel. "We have a guest?" She clapped her hands together.

Emy sighed with pride seeing her girls extend hospitality to a complete stranger, but embarrassed that she had not done the same. She grabbed Izzi's shoulder and gave her a sideways hug. Izzi shivered from either the warm reception or the lingering cold.

"Izzi, these are my daughters, Hanna and Cecylia. Hanna got home today from the University of Kraków, where she studies pre-med," she said proudly. "Ceci is a senior in high school and will follow in her sister's footsteps in the fall."

As Ceci hugged Izzi, Emy realized that the delicious aroma permeated the house. She had become immune to the smells since she and the girls had cooked all day and recently finished baking the Christmas *piernik*, gingerbread cookies. Keith had set up the Christmas tree in the morning, and after lunch, they'd all decorated it. Emy loved the beautifully handcrafted glass ornaments with lace details, a spectacular Polish craft.

Keith appeared in the entry hall to check out the commotion.

"Izzi, this is my husband, Keith. I think you may have already met."

"Sup," Izzi raised her chin without extending a hand and eyed Emy.

Emy gave her a slight nod and smile to indicate she'd buried the hatchet for the day for the sake of the girls.

Keith didn't seem to notice or care and waved the *opłatek*. "Who's ready for Christmas Eve?"

Hanna and Ceci cheered like youngsters. They were nine and seven when they'd moved to Poland ten years earlier from Germany. Even though they weren't Polish, the girls had quickly acclimated to the culture through their friends. This became a good thing; otherwise, Christmas was just another day for her and Keith.

Keith held up the wafer. "May this next year fill us with love and joy." He snapped it in half.

Izzi huffed, and Emy struggled to swallow her own anger. Keith broke off corners of the wafer and handed a piece to each woman. As her daughters hugged Emy, she wondered if Izzi put the cracker in her mouth or in her pocket. The girls had taught Emy that by taking the *opłatek* she needed to forgive others—for now, not committing murder would suffice.

"Let's eat!" Hanna announced.

As they turned to the dining room, Emy put her arm around Izzi. "I'm delighted you came."

Izzi shook the manila envelope. Emy had almost forgotten the reason she'd come. She took the envelope from her hand. "Thank you, Izzi. Maybe we could look at it after dinner." Izzi looked at the floor in disappointment as Emy guided her through the house. But her face gleamed with delight as they entered the dining room.

The girls had set a delightful table and lit the candles. Her brother, Lukas, had gotten the silver and the family china she'd really wanted, but no matter—the gold-rimmed white dishes and crystal glasses Keith had given her for their fifth anniversary accented the table beautifully. In the Polish tradition, the girls had set an extra place setting for baby Jesus or for a lonely wanderer who may be in need of food—possibly part of their excitement to find Izzi at the door. They'd even placed a handful of hay under the tablecloth to symbolize Jesus's birth in the manger. Emy suspected that the girls' friends had encouraged them to explore their spirituality. Religion made no difference to Emy; the truth was the truth.

Emy offered the extra chair to Izzi, and the family joined her around the table.

First thing, Keith slurped at the Borscht soup.

"Mom and Dad, do you mind if I say grace?" Hanna asked.

Emy looked at Keith, who shrugged and put down his spoon.

"By all means, Hanna," Emy said, "if that would make you feel better, please do."

"It would," Hanna said and reached for her father's hand on her right and Izzi's on her left. The others fell in line, and all hands joined the circle.

Emy had been forced to say grace when sharing a meal with her parents, but this was the first time grace had been said in her own family. While she thought it peculiar, it gave her a strange sense of comfort.

"I am thankful for my family and friends, and this food," Hanna prayed. "I hope Danek is there with You and has no more suffering. Amen."

* * *

Emy had sat stunned and in tears after Hanna's prayer as the girls talked so naturally of their brother. The room filled with joy and peace after the initial shock wore off. Emy was proud that her girls had become kind and compassionate women.

With the candles melted into puddles of red wax, the girls and Izzi nibbled on gingerbread men cookies. After a slice of poppy seed cake, Emy couldn't manage another bite. Everyone had settled into a comfortable food coma. Even Izzi relaxed, and Emy's fear of drugs or mental illness had abated.

"Can we open Herr Bauer's gifts?" Ceci asked.

For the last ten years since Bauer had invested into BioGenics, he had always gone all out with Christmas gifts to Emy and her family—sometimes strange or exotic presents and occasionally money, but always extravagant. In the beginning, Emy felt uncomfortable with his generosity, but like her girls, she'd grown to anticipate it. She and Keith had used some of the financial gifts to help buy an apartment in Kraków for the girls. When she thought about it, Emy figured Bauer had a Scrooge complex, but she would not complain.

Hanna and Ceci ran to gather Bauer's present from under the Christmas tree before Emy could say no. She worried about opening presents when there were none for Izzi. The girls brought the large box back to the table, tore the tape, and opened it. Emy had no idea what to expect. Eight years ago, a delivery man had arrived on Christmas day with an aerated box that contained a kitten. The cat grew to the size of a domestic house cat but sported the coloring and unusual markings of a Bengal tiger. Later they realized that the breed sells for up to five thousand euros.

The girls pulled wrapped presents from the Styrofoam popcorn packaging. To Emy's relief it contained no puppy or other animal to care for, as another mouth to feed would bring more chaos.

Ceci pulled out a card and handed it to her father. Typically, it contained a check. The girls each had two gifts, a small ring box and a slightly larger one. The biggest package, at the bottom of the box, rattled as the girls maneuvered it from the container. Marked for Emy, they set it down in front of her.

Emy glanced at Izzi, who'd folded her arms and tilted her chair on its hind legs, taking a posture of indifference. Ceci held her gifts out to Izzi. "I want to share one of my gifts with you. Pick one."

Izzi raised her hands in surrender. "Dude, I can't do that."

"No, really," Ceci said. "I'm good. I have everything I need; I want you to pick."

"Here, I'll make it easy," Hanna joined in. "Typically, Herr Bauer gives us the same thing." She took her smaller box and Ceci's larger box and set them both in front of Izzi.

Izzi's chair screeched as it landed back on all fours, and she looked at Emy for help.

"I don't think you can reject a gift on *Wigilia*," Emy said.

Izzi exhaled and swayed back and forth. Emy thought a tear might break through Izzi's roughened façade.

"You girls open your presents," Keith said.

Simultaneously, all three girls tore open the wrap and found that Herr Bauer had sent matching sapphire rings and necklaces.

"Wow, these look expensive," Ceci said.

"Like family heirlooms," Hanna added and helped Izzi arrange the jewelry around her neck.

Izzi tried on the ring, which looked too small and horribly out of place on her masculine finger. She guffawed. "I guess this girly ring doesn't fit this Cinderella."

Everyone laughed.

"I've got a reputation to uphold. If you won't think poorly of me, I'd like you to have this back." Izzi handed the ring to Hanna. "But if you don't mind, I would like to keep this." She put her hand over the glimmering blue stone dangling from her neck. "Thank you. I've never received such a nice gift before."

The girls cheered and turned to Emy and encouraged her to open her present.

Emy untied the elegant ribbon and carefully unwrapped the package. She loved to reuse the ornate paper, and this looked especially expensive. Underneath, she discovered an antique wooden box delicately carved with a crest. She ran her fingers over it. "I wonder if this is Herr Bauer's family crest?"

She picked up the box and gave it a jiggle. It sounded broken when the girls had taken it out. She set it down, clicked open the small latch on the front, and lifted the lid. To her surprise, it contained an ornate set of antique silverware.

"Oh my," she said.

The girls gathered behind her as Emy pulled a spoon out of the stack. The silver handle was delicately carved in roses. She put her hand to her mouth and slowly shook her head, trying to quell her emotions.

"You think that's his family's silver?" Hanna asked.

"I don't know." Emy closed the lid to look for clues on the outside of the box. "He doesn't have any other family," she said, raising the lid again and running her fingers over the stacks of silver.

"Well, he has us," Ceci said, her cheeks turning red.

Emy smiled at her. *How nice of her to think of Herr Bauer as an adopted grandfather.*

"Speaking of family, can we look at the letter from your grandma?" Hanna asked.

Earlier in the day, Emy broke the news to the girls about her adoption. Throughout dinner, the girls pleaded with her to share the letters that Izzi had brought. After all, this became their heritage as well.

Izzi had given Emy a look of warning every time the subject had come up. When Hanna jumped up from the table and retrieved the envelope, Izzi grimaced and raised her brows. Before Emy could stop Hanna, she had removed the contents.

"Hey, this is me," Hanna said and held up the picture of her great-grandmother, Yuri. She showed it to her father and Ceci, who nodded in agreement.

Emy reached for the letters and snatched them from Hanna's hand. "I don't know girls, sometimes graves are best left unopened." She held the letters to her chest.

"I think the girls have a right to learn about their ancestry," Keith said.

"Yeah, Mom," both girls chimed in.

Heat rose up Emy's neck. She didn't like the pressure, but she also realized that she'd have to share eventually. Maybe it was good to air it all out on *Wigilia.*

She summarized the letters from her adopted father and biological mother instead of reading them out loud. "Your grandfather seemed to think that what these letters contain will be hard to hear. All I know of my mother, Bella, was she lived an unfortunate and short life." Emy pulled the letter from her grandmother, written in Hungarian from the stack and opened it. The cursive writing was clear and precise. She looked up to see everyone stare at her in anticipation—except Hanna, who had fished out the cufflink from the envelope and examined it between her fingers.

"Okay, here goes. This is the letter from my grandmother, Yuri Frankel…your great-grandmother," she said to the girls and turned to Izzi, who paled. "Thank you for translating this for us." Izzi had paper-clipped the translation to the letter, and Emy put her glasses on to read:

"My dearest Bella,

We will all be surprised if you turn out to be a boy, as the old ladies think I am carrying you high like a girl. I am going to name you Bella, as beauty rises out of ashes.

The weather has turned cold, and fall has arrived. Soon, you too, will come into the world and thank God that it is changing for the better, and the Nazis have been defeated.

If anything the last years have taught me, your life can be over in the blink of an eye. So, while I am able, I wanted you to know about your family. My strength is gone, I'm afraid, but know I have done all I can to protect your precious life. While you were tucked safely inside of me, the world had gone mad.

I write you this letter from the Jewish displaced persons camp that is being run by the Russians. Sachsenhausen is north of Berlin from what I understand, but we have been moved so often, I have a hard time keeping track of all the places. I'm afraid the living conditions here are one small step better than the Nazi camps, but at least we don't fear for our lives from one hour to the next. Many of us are suffering from disease and discouragement. We long for any news of our families and our homes. Rumors swirl that the Germans deny what they did to us, so while the memories are fresh in my mind, I wanted to tell you my story, which is your story as well.

My sister Eva and I were born December 25, 1927. It was the seventh day of Hanukkah, in which candles are usually given as gifts. Father said that God brought two bright lights into the world. Eva and I are identical twins, and I thank God for her as she is the only reason I survived this last year.

My parents, Yosel and Chava Frankel, were kind and loving. Father's heritage is Hungarian, and he worked at the local bank in Budapest, the city where we were born and raised. Mother was a strict German but loved Eva and me with her whole heart. Born in 1902, her family fled Germany to Hungary during the first war when she was twelve."

Emy paused and looked up. The girls were entranced. "I imagine that this old picture is Chava's parents from Germany." Hanna held it up for everyone to see.

"So, this is a picture of Yosel and Chava holding Yuri and Eva?" Ceci held up the other photo.

"Yes," Emy said and then went back to the letter:

"When the second war started, we all thought we were safe in Budapest, but the Nazis closed in from the west and the Russians from the east. Even though the Nazis moved Jews out of their homes into ghettos, Father tried to protect us. On the night of the lighting of the Shamash, the first night of Hanukkah in 1945, the SS broke down our door, and Mother and Father were brutally shot and killed in front of us.

The ten months that followed are a blur and nightmare, so forgive me if I do not remember every detail.

The Nazis took us from our home to the brickyard, and we were forced to march through the snow for six weeks into Austria. There, a guard fed Eva and me and put us on a transport to Auschwitz. Eva and I were to learn later that the Nazi doctors performed experiments on twins. They were especially interested in us because of our two different colored eyes and our blond hair."

Emy stopped reading, unsure she could continue. Electricity shot up her spine and forced her to shift in her chair. "Can I see the picture of Yuri?"

Hanna held it out to her, and Emy took it and brought it close to her eyes. The black-and-white photograph didn't reveal the heterochromia iridium. But there it was—her DNA, passed on from her grandmother.

"You want me to finish reading?" Hanna asked and reached to take the letter, but Emy resisted and started to read again:

"Please, never let anyone tell you anything different about the horrors of the extermination camp of Auschwitz. It was worse than a nightmare. I do not know an exact count, but from what I witnessed and heard, the Nazis murdered thousands upon thousands of people in Auschwitz. One man told me it was over a million, but my mind cannot even comprehend this. They were cruel and inhumane people, seeing us Jews as subhuman.

> Eva and I were the lucky ones. We arrived at Auschwitz on January 16, 1945, the day before the camp was evacuated ahead of the Russian liberation. However, our misery did not stop there. We were forced to join the death march to Loslau. I do not know how we survived as tens of thousands fell on each side of us from starvation, the cold, or from the Nazis' guns. From Loslau, we were loaded onto unheated freight trains and deported to the concentration camp in Sachsenhausen. On April 22nd, units from the 1st and 47th Polish Army along with the Russians liberated the camp. We remained in the encampment as I was three months pregnant with you.
>
> We are so desperate to go home but remain here until we can find a way."

"Wait a minute, Mom," Hanna said. Emy looked at Hanna, counting on her fingers, the cufflink still in her other hand. "If she was three months pregnant when the Russians liberated the second camp, she had to have gotten pregnant..." she recounted to be sure, "in January."

Emy looked at Izzi, who shook her head. Emy didn't heed her warning and continued reading:

> "My eyes are full of tears as I tell you the rest, and I fear for your heart. God above holds every life precious—you, so much more. But

you must know the truth, so the rest of the world won't forget.

The day Eva and I arrived in Auschwitz, they took us to Block 10. That monster, Dr. Josef Mengele, raped me in his clinic. I have his cufflink to prove it.

My prayer is this—although you were a product of this evil, you know that you are my greatest gift. My womb protected you from the horror of it all. I love you, my precious daughter. I have found peace within the midst of the darkness, and you will too."

Emy looked up as tears rolled down her cheeks. Ceci whimpered. Hanna dropped the gold cufflink on the table, and Keith glared at Emy with shock and disdain.

Izzi mouthed the words, *I'm so sorry.*

CHAPTER 17

AVE MARIA

The *Wigilia* dinner—topped off with a piece of delicious *babka*-sweet cake, *makowiec*-poppy seed roll, and chocolate Christmas ornaments—lasted most of the evening for Maggie and Nick. A chilly stroll around the Old Market Square helped quicken their digestion and cleared their heads. Snow lightly fell as Maggie turned up her collar and tucked her arm through Nick's.

"Isn't it beautiful?" Maggie asked.

"Magnificent," Nick said.

They had circled the square twice, not surprised at the number of people who were likewise celebrating Christmas Eve. Their waiter had suggested this holiday stroll. The Old Market Square glowed with Christmas lights and cheer. A four-story tree, as tall as the pastel-colored buildings lining the square, stood in front of the Poznań Town Hall, decorated with lacey lights and ornaments. They surrounded the tree with eight-foot-tall faux presents and candy canes. Hand-carved *Kraków szopka*, Poland's own version of the nativity scene, stood at each corner of Town Hall—painstakingly painted and decorated as replicas of ornate historical buildings of Kraków.

Maggie and Nick had stopped at the four fountains in each corner of the square. The waiter had provided the names of each: Proserpina, Apollo, Neptune, and Mars. They exchanged pleasantries with the locals gathered around the fountains to socialize, smoke, and return hardy holiday greetings.

Eventually, Maggie and Nick made their way back to the front of the Brovaria. The soft lighting of the hotel showed off the Renaissance style laid out in the thirteenth century.

"I can't wait to explore this city in the daylight," Nick said.

"It looks like there are plenty of museums," Maggie said and grabbed her abdomen. She'd just entered the end of her first trimester and a flutter quickened deep within her belly.

Nick stopped and turned to her. "You okay?"

"Probably a little bubbling from that rich dinner." Maggie snuggled closer into his chest. "Sometimes, I can hardly believe I have a baby growing inside of me."

Nick wrapped his arms around her.

"I don't know if it is the excitement of Christmas or anticipation of this baby, but I feel so grateful," Maggie said. "I love you, Nicklaus Hart. And no matter what the outcome, this baby is part of us. It's hard to fathom the miracle of conception."

"Having my baby, what a lovely way of sayin' how much you love me," Nick sang.

Maggie hugged him tightly. "That's such a schmaltzy song."

"Hey, you don't like my singing?" Nick gasped from her grip and laughed.

She released her hold and stood on her tiptoes to peck him on the lips.

Nick returned a passionate kiss.

Under normal circumstances, public displays of affection embarrassed Maggie, but as she'd observed many young couples cuddling around the square, she didn't object. The romance proved contagious in this picture-perfect setting.

Nick relaxed his embrace and rubbed her arms. "You still want to go to the midnight mass…or do you want to go back to the room?" He arched his eyebrows.

She punched his chest. "Oh, that's an easy one." She teased him. "I'd choose Christmas Eve mass any day."

They both laughed.

"You know I love you, but I could sure use a touch from God. Besides, I'm so excited to see what the Polish service is like."

Nick smiled at her and then pointed to the street sign of the lane that split the tenement houses. "Our waiter said we should walk up *Franciszkańska*, Franciscan Street, for a block to get to the *Kościół rzymskokatolicki*. He said it is a beautiful Franciscan Catholic church that he and his family attend."

As they rounded the corner, the lights of the square faded.

"Do you think it's safe?" Maggie asked.

"Yes, our waiter said it's okay to walk around Poznań, especially on *Wigilia*. Remember, what happens on *Wigilia* sets the tone for the rest of the year, and everyone is on their best behavior." He smiled at her and pulled her arm in close.

The dark, narrow street only extended one block, and to Maggie's relief, they entered another area with lights and festivities. A massive castle-like structure towered to the right, and on the left stood a yellow baroque-style building with groups of people walking up an old marble staircase.

"Oh, wow. That must be the Royal Castle of Poznań." Nick said. "The waiter said it housed one of the first rulers of Poland in the tenth century. Meko or something like that."

"Mieszko I," Maggie corrected him. "He brought Christianity to Poland. I think you had gone to the bathroom when the waiter told me the rest of the story. Legend has it that when the church baptized Mieszko I, it so angered Satan that he decided to flood Poznań. He and his demons took a hill from nearby and tried to block the flow of the river. But when the evil forces celebrated too early, their ruckus woke the local roosters. Their crowing scared off the demons, and they left the hill on the bank of the river. This is where the castle resides." She spread out her hands.

"That's crazy," Nick said. "Talk about spiritual warfare."

"The rest of the legend is that Mieszko I developed blindness during his first seven years of life and had a miraculous healing." She looked at Nick and smiled. "Sounds kind of familiar, huh?"

Nick nodded.

"I guess when they asked the elders what it meant, they called it a prophesy—Poland was blind and now could see."

Nick sighed. "I guess I understand that. When I received my miraculous healing, the eyes of my heart opened wide to the truth of *who* I am and *whose* I am. But I have to say, your diagnosis has shaken my faith. I'm fighting the thought that the attack on you and our baby is punishment somehow for things I've done and left undone."

Maggie slowed her pace and shook her head. "With such a battle raging around us, I can't find peace."

"It's terrible, but typically when I'm weak, you're strong and vice versa," Nick said. "And you're usually the strong one—it's hard when we're both struggling."

They looked at each other and said in unison, "Lord, help us."

They merged with the rest of the churchgoers celebrating *Pasterka*, the Shepherds' mass, memorializing the announcement of Christ's birth. The accumulated snow made the granite stairs of the old Franciscan cathedral slippery, and Maggie held tight onto Nick's arm.

As they entered the vestibule through the heavy wooden doors, Maggie savored the pungent odor of burning wax candles and the airy sound of organ music that reverberated off the ancient walls. Maggie and Nick bypassed the holy water font that the locals dipped a finger into and crossed themselves. They accepted small candles and doilies from an usher. The arched foyer covered in murals was stunning, but when they entered the Baroque-style nave, Maggie gasped, "Oh my, it's breathtaking."

The vaulted ceiling showcased a magnificent series of interlaced arches. The architects filled each geometric space with more murals inspired by Jesus's life and ministry. The empty spaces painted in pastel pinks and yellows reflected the colorful buildings that surrounded the square. Heavy, dark wooden pews already filled with worshipers stretched over the checkerboard gray and brown granite that graced the floor. The walls gave the illusion of motion, generously adorned with carved scrolls and volutes, statues of angelic figurines, saints, and martyrs of the faith. Halfway up the nave, large alcoves extended to each side and glowed with Christmas trees lit with white lights. At the front of the sanctuary, arched balconies, similar to an elegant opera house, opened over the altar. The effect was complex and stunning, but the altar captured Maggie's full attention. "This has to be one of the most beautiful churches I have ever seen."

Nick nodded and whispered, "No room in the inn. We may have to stand."

Nick pulled her to the left, toward the wall where some parishioners stood. After a few moments, a man with a name-tag approached them and reached for Nick's hand.

"*Wesołych Świąt,*" he said and then repeated in English, "Merry Christmas. You must be guests. Please, there are a couple seats in front." He led them to the first pew.

Strangers smiled and gave them holiday greetings as they walked to the front. Maggie thanked a young couple at the designated pew, who happily made room for them by holding their two children on their laps.

As Maggie and Nick squeezed into place, a man escorted a group of young boys dressed in black trousers and red sweaters to the chancel. They formed a line, and the entire congregation fell silent.

The choir director waved his arms. Like wispy clouds of incense, angelic voices rose from the boys' mouths and echoed off the ornate walls of the Franciscan cathedral. Their melody expanded, saturating the sanctuary. Maggie thought it seemed impossible for only fifteen voices to fill such a vast space, and she imagined angels harmonizing as the choir crescendoed with Alleluias.

As the director guided them into another beautiful hymn, Maggie examined the Rococo-style altar wall. At first glance, it looked like organized chaos, integrated reddish-brown marble held up by massive green marble pillars. The wall appeared more jeweled and elaborate than a queen's crown. Cherubim adorned the top and hovered over an iconic picture of Mother Mary holding baby Jesus. Massive pearly white marble statues of archangels surrounded them. Maggie guessed the central painting represented a Franciscan monk or John the Baptist attended to by angels. A massive golden eagle with wings stretched over the enclave of the cross surprised Maggie. It reminded her of the Nazi symbol. Then she remembered that for Catholics, the eagle symbolized the belief that the bird could gaze into the sun. Likewise, Christians must contemplate, with equal focus, the inspiration of the gospels.

Maggie wanted to spend hours examining every ornate detail, but the boys' choir finished, and the processional hymn began, accompanied by the pipe organ in the second story alcove. Everyone stood as the priest, various deacons, and acolytes walked down the aisle with the cross and altar candles.

Her spirit stirred during the entire service. She didn't understand a word but recognized the liturgy. She had attended Catholic services with friends in Guatemala and the similar Anglican rite with Nick. She and Nick stood or sat at the appropriate times with the rest of the congregation.

Throughout her life, Maggie had visited many worship services—from large cathedrals to small protestant churches to people congregating under a tree—each sacred and holy, but the majesty and piousness of this Polish service made it special. The joy, enthusiasm, and reverence were palpable.

The deep baritone voice of the priest resonated throughout the nave, as he spoke and sung the service. His prayers and those of the worshipers rose like the incense burning in the thurible.

The priest gave no sermon, perhaps to shorten the service on behalf of all the excited children waiting for Christmas to arrive. A communal prayer began, and by the cadence, it sounded like the Nicene Creed. Near the end, Maggie repeated a line under her breath, "I believe in one holy, catholic, and apostolic church." Knowing the collective church had worshiped and prayed together as Jesus taught his disciples brought comfort.

As Holy Communion started, Maggie prayed for the answer to their dilemma. A twinge of guilt burned in her chest that she hadn't stopped to listen to what the heavenly Father might tell her in the chaos and rush of the diagnosis, pregnancy, travel, and fear of the unknown.

She understood the diagnosis from the perspective of modern medicine—from her experiences as CEO of the hospital in Guatemala, watching John as a general surgeon and Nick as an orthopaedic surgeon—she understood the western paradigm. The doctors treated diseases and did everything possible to preserve and improve the health of their patients. But she deemed her current condition different from diabetes, diseased gallbladders, and broken bones. The diagnosis of a genetic problem, and the possibility of gene therapy to correct the disorder was anathema to her faith. Although not Catholic, Maggie agreed with the Church's adherence to clear doctrine—don't interfere with a person's genetic code. The church followed an unequivocal and rigid stance against any manipulation of human reproduction: birth control, abortion, artificial insemination, or any other form that altered the course of procreation.

For the first time in a long time, Maggie felt broken. Through the years, her faith had made her whole, but this ticking time bomb in her genetic code shook her to the very core.

"For you created my inmost being; you knit me together in my mother's womb. I praise you because I am fearfully and wonderfully made; your works are wonderful, I know that full well,"

she whispered to the heavenlies. "Father, how can that be true when I'm defective?"

Maggie brushed a tear from her cheek as the priest lifted the holy sacraments to the congregation. How could she find peace within the midst of this darkness? She'd witnessed many miracles, including when Nick had his sight restored, but this seemed different, and she struggled with her faith. This disease towered like an immovable mountain or some other impossibility.

"Lord, help us," she repeated their mantra as the congregation filed forward to take communion.

Nick leaned in to whisper to her, "How are you doing?"

She nodded. "I wish we could take communion…I realize we can't because we aren't Catholic."

"That's okay, we can take our own sacraments together in the morning." Nick put his arm around Maggie and pulled her close.

To Maggie's surprise, the line of people taking communion passed quickly, and soon the priest went to the front of the sanctuary and offered a blessing over the congregation. With that, the artificial lights in the cathedral turned off, but the flickering candles on the altar and the glow from the Christmas trees around the nave and alcoves remained.

The priest walked to the advent wreath and lit the white center candle, which represented the birth of the Christ child. He turned and lit the handheld candles of the assistant priests, nuns, and acolytes who spread out among the congregation to share the flame.

A petite, elderly nun in a full, black tunic stopped at Maggie and Nick. She held her candle first to Nick and then to Maggie.

Her crippled spine hunched her at an uncomfortable forty-five degrees, and arthritis gnarled and deformed her hands, but she smiled benevolently as she lit their candles. She attended the next person, then turned back to Maggie and took her arm.

She said something in Polish that Maggie couldn't understand, but it sounded like a prayer. The nun's grip loosened and tightened as she spoke.

Finally, she finished and looked up into Maggie's eyes as best as her deformity allowed. "Ave Maria, Ave Maria," she said and placed her palm on Maggie's forehead. Maggie bowed her head to receive the blessing.

The nun took Maggie's hands into hers and shook them, "Ave Maria," she said again and moved on to light candles for others.

Maggie looked up at Nick, who smiled. He started to whisper to her when a young woman in a red and green Christmas dress appeared at the front, and the congregation fell silent. The glow emanating from all the individual candles danced off the vaulted ceiling and walls. The woman stood with her eyes closed, waiting.

Then, softly at first, her soprano voice rose in an *a cappella* Polish version of "Silent Night."

Her voice, the incense, the flicker of the candles, the reverence and joy of the service, the nun's blessing—the whole experience was magical…and just what Maggie needed.

CHAPTER 18

MENGELE

Emy sat at the dining room table. The holiday dishes were cleaned and put away. The tree in the living room remained as the only remnant of the celebration, and she decided she'd tackle that project with the girls before Hanna returned to school in a few days.

She opened her laptop and cursed Izzi. *Damn it, why didn't she stop me from reading the letter from my grandmother? The girls need not wrestle with this news yet, if ever. I don't know if I would have ever told them.* Emy surmised that more than likely, Izzi would already be back in the lab on the day after Christmas. Despite all her quirks, Izzi excelled as a graduate student. Still, the news angered Emy, and she considered letting her go. Definitely, a reprimand was in order. *But it's my fault to let her get so close.*

"Maybe she tried to stop me, and I missed the warning signs," she murmured under her breath.

She pushed the power button and waited for her computer to boot up. Josef Mengele's gold cufflink lay where Hanna had dropped it; no one had dared touch it, as if infected with hatred.

Last night, Keith wouldn't discuss this new revelation. It added fuel to his anger and justification for his infidelity. He'd left the house early and probably stayed with that woman.

Emy clicked on the Google search bar and typed in *Josef Mengele*. It showed no shortage of information: Wikipedia, books, lectures, articles, and even three publications penned by the doctor in the early 1900s. A bubble rumbled her queasy stomach.

Emy's German heritage ran through her veins. She'd grown up in Berlin and attended high school and college in the late eighties and early nineties. In classes they discussed World War II nonchalantly, as if it had happened on foreign soil to foreign people. When the Berlin wall came down her sophomore year in college, and the dust had settled, the German citizens took a collective sigh of relief—thankful to have that era behind them. Her family didn't belong to the Nazi party and most definitely didn't adhere to any of the old Socialist National fundamentals. Forty years later, the whole society had changed and encouraged people to forgive their past and move on—this generation held no responsibility for the sins of their fathers.

Obviously, she'd heard about Mengele, the "Angel of Death," but the information meant no more to her than any of the other criminals of the Third Reich. Maybe she'd seen a picture of him; all those monsters looked alike. But when she opened Wikipedia, she gasped at the photo of Mengele, her grandfather, that accompanied the article. Sharply dressed in his SS uniform, he smiled as if strolling through a park. The picture showed a gap between his two front teeth. *My gap.* Reflexively, she covered her mouth. She recognized her dark hair and complexion had come from him as well.

Emy flicked the touchpad to get rid of the image. The cursor landed on Mengele's early years. Born as the second son of a wealthy Bavarian industrialist and considered *nouveau riche*, his family adhered to strict Catholicism. He studied physical anthropology and genetics under Otmar von Verschuer at the Frankfurt University Institute of Hereditary Biology and Racial Hygiene. A footnote mentioned that Mengele shipped many of his specimens from Auschwitz to Dr. Verschuer, who the courts never indicted on war crimes.

Further down the page, the website outlined Mengele's military service. He joined the Nazi party in 1937 and, in 1941, while stationed in the Ukraine, he earned the Iron Cross, the Wound Badge, and the Medal of Care of the German People. After being wounded and deemed unfit for service, he was assigned to Auschwitz.

Mengele married Irene Schönbein in 1939 and had one son, Rolf, born in 1944. Emy scrolled back to the top of the page that showed the bullet points of Mengele's life. Heat flushed her cheeks as she realized that he raised a family during the height of his crimes against humanity in Auschwitz.

Emy flicked the touchpad again, skipped over Mengele's role in World War II, and to the end of his life. The man had escaped justice, and although much urban legend speculated about his whereabouts after the war, he died in Brazil in 1979 after suffering a stroke while swimming. A chill ran up Emy's spine—the man existed in her lifetime. The authorities exhumed his body in 1985, and forensic examination produced a high probability that the body was that of Josef Mengele. They confirmed his identity through DNA testing in 1992.

Emy inhaled a deep breath and slowly exhaled. Like the rest of the world, she'd seen the horrific pictures of Auschwitz and heard the victims recount the terror. The infamous extermination camp was located only three and a half hours away by train, but Emy and her family had never visited.

She clicked the back button and found an article titled, "In Their Own Words," written by people who had survived Auschwitz:

> "As an inmate helper on the intake dock, I knew the doctor as a prominent feature of the selection ramp—handsome, well dressed, and confident. With a riding crop in one hand, he made split-second life and death decisions… right to live, left to die. The man seemed to enjoy the process, often whistling or singing, even joking with the other SS officers. But never forget he was a monster, beating or shooting anyone that stepped out of line. In one heartbreaking scene, after he shot a mother and son for their disobedience, he sent the entire group to the gas chambers in retaliation."

Emy had heard of the selection process. Those who could work were spared for the time being. The Nazis marched the sick, old, feeble, and children under the age of sixteen to the gas chambers. Her grandfather played this role as judge:

> "I ran ahead to see what was happening at the front of the lines. I quickly came back and told my wife to hand our baby to her mother

and to say to the officer that she worked as a nurse. When her mother and child were taken off in the opposite direction, Dr. Mengele told her not to worry. Later, when they frantically asked the doctor where their baby was, they were told to look at the camp's smokestacks. My wife never forgave herself."

And another note from a prisoner who worked the hospital wards:

"One never knew which Mengele was going to show up. Like the random winds of change, he could be kind and sweet, especially to the children, but then in the next moment, he could send those very children to die in the crematoria. In the camp, he was the lord of life and death—sending someone to die for a skin blemish or small scar and saving the lives of women he found extraordinarily beautiful. The doctor hated bad smells and ordered the doors and windows to be opened before he arrived. He wore a clean, white coat over his uniform, but don't let the immaculate dress or cologne fool you. I saw him injecting phenol into patients to kill them as if he were giving them a shot of vitamins. If patients provoked him, he would shoot them on the spot."

Her will begged her to stop, but Emy continued to scroll, unable to look away from the reports.

A prisoner doctor, a Jew forced to act against his own people, wrote the next article:

> "Mengele was a collector of humans and had a keen eye on heredity and genetics. His strongest passion was for the research he performed on twins and eye color. One experiment he performed was to inject methylene blue into children's eyes to see if they would change color. Perhaps he wished for his eyes to be blue instead of brown. He had a particular fascination with heterochromia iridum. He found a Gypsy family with seven members that had one blue and one brown eye each. After serendipitous deaths, their eyes were dissected out, placed in preservatives, and stored with his many specimens."

In the reflection of her computer screen, Emy's eyes stared back—a Jew with heterochromia iridum. She, too, would have been part of the research and extermination. Emy scrolled and saw hundreds of these testimonies. As she continued to read, bile rose into her throat. This man…this monster had raped her grandmother and so, too, violated Emy and her girls—entering their lives unexpectedly and unwelcomed, much like how a cancer cell invades the body. But here in part, the story revealed her own genetic code—the torment that Bella, her mother, couldn't live with and had numbed the pain with drugs and finally death.

Emy clicked on the website with his photo and stared at it. She didn't understand how he could have become this monster…this enigma of a man who seemed driven by evil yet exhibited compassion and caring—this man who acted as healer and killer. "He was so…" Emy searched for the word, and when it came to her, she pounded her fist on the table. "Double-minded." Keith's accusation of her.

Emy sensed a presence behind her.

"Is that him?" Hanna asked.

Emy slammed the laptop closed and turned to see Hanna and Ceci peering over her shoulders. Anger fueled her heart.

Hanna put her hand on Emy's sweaty back.

"It's okay, Mom, we can figure this out together," Ceci added.

The girls sat down on each side of her. Hanna picked up the cufflink. "So that awful man was our great-grandfather?"

Emy wanted to snatch the object from her hand and throw it out the window. Burn it. But destroying it would not undo the past or their connection to this man.

"I'm so sorry, girls…" Emy's lower lip quivered. "If I had known ahead of time, I would never have told you. This is a burden you need not live with." Tears rolled down her cheeks.

Hanna and Ceci threw their arms around Emy.

"It's okay, Mama. This is not your fault. It is what it is," Hanna said.

"I think it's kind of cool," Ceci said.

Emy broke from their embrace and jumped to her feet. The statement filled her with rage. "No, Ceci, this is not cool. That man was horrible! You must not speak of this outside of our home. Do you hear me?" She grabbed Ceci by the shoulders. She saw fear in Ceci's eyes and wanted to slap her.

Instead, Emy brought her hands to her head. "Oh my God!" she yelled, covered her face, and collapsed to the floor in tears. "My God…" If the outside world learned about her connection to the Angel of Death, it could destroy everything she had worked for, building her reputation and business. It could ruin the girls' lives as well. Here lies their inherited disease, their cancer, their sickness. "What if Herr Bauer found out?" she murmured.

The girls sat on the floor beside her.

"It's okay, Mama, I won't tell anyone," Ceci cried.

Emy's heart instantly softened as Ceci's shoulders slumped, and she spun the sapphire ring that Herr Bauer had given to her for Christmas.

"Ceci, my dear child, I am so sorry. I didn't mean to—"

Ceci's tears enhanced her bright blue eyes as she stared into her mother's. She started to say something but retreated.

"What is it, Ceci?"

"Well…" she stopped and then started again. "Isn't Herr Bauer related to us, anyway?"

Emy's mind raced. "What are you talking about?" Her anger returned.

"Mama, please don't be mad at me."

Emy wanted to grab her by the shoulders again and shake the words out of her.

"At the beginning of the year, our biology class did an ancestry DNA test for fun. I got a list of distant relatives." She paused.

"And?" Emy demanded. She was angry the school would do this without her permission. Her own daughter's DNA had probably ended up in the Chinese database. News reports revealed that China quietly purchased many of these ancestry companies.

"Herr Bauer popped up on my list." Ceci looked at Emy with more fear in her eyes. "So, I emailed him."

Emy's mind spun and threatened to unravel. "Herr Bauer?"

"Yeah, he told me he is my great-uncle."

"He knew?" Emy sputtered out the words. "That can't be." Emy's mind sorted through the family tree. *If that is true, Bauer is Bella's brother and my uncle.* She'd read that Mengele had only one son, but many of the articles also made it clear he hailed as quite the ladies' man and entertained more than one mistress. Like her mother, there could be more offspring.

"Why didn't you tell me?" Emy demanded.

"He told me it was our secret."

Emy covered her eyes with her hands, and an unexpected image came to mind—Herr Bauer's gate to his estate with the gold-colored monogram in the center of the woven wrought iron: *JMB.*

CHAPTER 19

FORT VII

Nick and Maggie held hands and strolled through the doors of the picturesque Town Hall into the Old Market Square. Luminous clouds streaked the brilliant blue sky. A blanket of fluffy snow scrunched under their feet in the subfreezing temperature as Nick squinted against the sun's reflection.

"Wow, that's bright," he said, bringing his sunglasses down over his eyes. The sunlight bounced off the crystalline flakes showcasing the snow as if it was inlaid with diamonds.

"Sure glad you suggested that we bring our winter coats and snow boots," Maggie said and exhaled a frozen fog of breath. "It feels good to get out and stretch our legs. The food has been great, but I needed some exercise to wear it off."

So far, they'd spent the day relaxing and rejuvenating. They'd slept in, took time for intimacy, and ate a hearty breakfast. Maggie hinted she'd rather rest and finish her book, but Nick suggested that for a distraction from their upcoming meeting with the doctor, they should wander outside and take in the tourist highlights. The friendly waiter from Christmas Eve armed them with tidbits of Polish history and various sights to visit.

"I'm still mad at you," Maggie said.

"Yes, and I love it. The gift is small, it's nothing."

"We promised not to give each other anything for Christmas except this trip," she said and pulled her arm out of her jacket sleeve to admire the moonstone bracelet. The sun illuminated the pearly-blue stones set in gold. "This is not nothing."

"I thought you'd like it." Nick squeezed her hand. Maggie had worn it ever since he'd given it to her on Christmas morning, and he often caught her admiring it. She rolled her wrist as the stones glittered with a blue opalescent luster.

"I love it," Maggie said.

Nick grinned, proud of himself for hitting the mark with the gift, and guided her to the complex of buildings in the middle of the square. "Well, you *are* highly favored," he said, referring to the nun's Christmas Eve blessing. When they'd returned to the hotel, they looked up "Ave Maria" and found the Catholic prayer to the Virgin Mary from the book of Luke: *And the angel came in unto her, and said, Hail, thou art highly favored, the Lord is with thee: blessed art thou among women.*

"That was the sweetest blessing I think I've ever received. I wonder if she knew that I'm pregnant. I am truly blessed," Maggie said and cuddled closer to Nick.

Besides Town Hall, they had sauntered through the museums displaying the history of Poznań: the Municipal Weighhouse, the Greater Poland Military, and the Wielkopolska Uprising.

"It's amazing how the world has fought over this land," Nick said.

"Wonder what it is about certain places in the world where so much bloodshed has occurred. I wish I could see into the spiritual world to understand the battles," Maggie said.

"Speaking of battles, I enjoyed the museum showing all the weapons throughout history: crossbows, swords, and all the wild guns," Nick said.

"So many ways to kill each other." Maggie shook her head in disgust. "What I truly found interesting was to learn about the history of Poland."

"I think I've always looked at Poland through the lens of World War II," Nick said. "But there is so much more to it. It's crazy that Poland has been independent only three times in their history with the third Polish Republic established only thirty years ago. They're resilient people."

"The Poles have definitely been persecuted," Maggie said. "Don't you wonder what principalities lie behind wars and the need to conquer?"

"Power, I guess," Nick said. Nick found the Polish people engaging, smart, and typically full of humor. But after their visit to the museums, he learned the Poles had clearly been a tyrannized people, conquered and reconquered many times throughout history—most likely due to their geographical location rather than antipathy toward them.

"I used to watch *A Streetcar Named Desire* with my folks," Nick said. "You remember the movie? Marlon Brando played a blue-collar worker—the caricatured image of the son of a Polish refugee who came to America after World War II. Quite possibly, that's how many immigrants are judged to this day."

"I don't understand where people get their prejudices." Maggie shook her head. "When I left the reservation for Stanford, the stereotypes that students had made up about my people shocked me. I suppose at the heart of it all is ignorance or fear."

"Yeah, we don't want those…fill in the blank…people mixing with our chosen race," Nick said in disgust. "Did you know the root of eugenics is in the UK and US?"

"Eugenics…is that race selection?" Maggie asked.

"The term means well-born or good genes. We talked about it a bunch in medical school ethics class. Eugenics has probably occurred since the early history of mankind, but Charles Darwin's cousin, Francis Galton, popularized the term in the late nineteenth century. Even in the early 1900s, eugenics had a considerable following in the US."

"Seriously?"

"Where do you think the Nazis got the blueprints for their final solution?" Nick hesitated, then added, "The Indian reservation system and how the US government persecuted the Native Americans fascinated Hitler." He looked at her and grimaced.

Maggie shook her head.

"And you wouldn't believe some of the institutions and people who got involved—the Carnegie Institution, the Rockefeller Foundation, and other large organizations dedicated to the promotion of the idea. The American Breeders' Association started as one of the first."

"What? I thought they concerned themselves with cows!"

"Those and anyone they thought of as inferior," Nick said. "Margaret Sanger worked as an early female champion of eugenics."

"That name sounds familiar."

"She founded Planned Parenthood. She started the organization to provide birth control to blacks…let that one sink in."

Maggie pursed her lips.

"But that's the tip of the iceberg. At the heart of the US eugenics movement was 'protecting and building a better America.'" Nick put air quotes around the statement. "But the early immigration laws were grounded in eugenics—to keep what some considered inferior races from immigrating into the US and diluting what they thought as the superior American racial stock. They worried that mixing these supposed less-civilized races posed a biological threat."

Maggie stopped walking and turned to Nick, trying to absorb the information.

"But wait, it only gets crazier," he said. "The US enacted laws to keep people from marrying those deemed as substandard—the epileptic, imbecile, or feeble-minded. Then they took it a step further, and many states enacted compulsory sterilization laws—criminals, handicapped people, and the institutionalized. They targeted poor women to control their sexuality. This immorality crept into performing involuntary sterilization on minorities: Blacks, Hispanics, and even…" Nick grimaced, "…Native Americans. In the early 1900s, it's estimated that over sixty thousand people were victimized. This sound familiar?"

"Hitler," Maggie said with disgust.

"Exactly. It's awful, and the worst part was many doctors played significant roles in the eugenics philosophy. Our professors taught us that the California eugenics program had a direct hand in spreading the idea to the medical professionals in Germany. The Rockefeller Foundation funded some of Germany's programs, including one run by Josef Mengele before the war. The Nazis took it to a whole different level, but still." Nick crossed his arms. "In medical school, we discussed how these doctors crossed the line. The sick thing is, I think they all thought they did the world a favor. Most people don't understand that the abortion issue is also grounded in the eugenics movement. The world adopted it as a new technique of birth control for the poor."

"This all makes me sick," Maggie said.

"Right!" Nick agreed.

He waved his arm as a taxi approached. The driver slowed, stopped, and rolled down his window.

"Can you take us to Fort VII?" Nick asked.

"With pleasure," the driver said in English with a strong accent.

Nick opened the back door, and they slid into the seat. The warmth of the cab elicited a shiver from Maggie.

"Oh man, that heat feels good," she said to the driver.

"Da, welcome to Poland in winter," he said. "You Americans?"

"Yes," Nick said tentatively, not sure if that was good or bad.

"Me, I'm Russian. Used to be engineer in Moscow and now drive taxi in Poland. Go figure," he examined them in the rearview mirror.

"How long does it take to get us to Fort VII?" Maggie asked and then mouthed to Nick, "I have to use the bathroom."

"Oh, only a very short time," he said. "I like America." He smiled at them in the mirror. "But I don't know about your president. He should visit us here in Poland, but I guess he has other things to do."

Nick didn't want to talk politics with the driver and changed the subject. "Our waiter at the hotel said that Fort

VII was an old fortress that the Germans took over in the war. He encouraged us to see for ourselves the shocking result of pure wickedness."

The driver grimaced and nodded. "Da, Prussians built these forts in the nineteenth century to protect city. But in 1939, the Hitlerites captured fort and turned it into one of their first death camps. That is until we Russians kicked their *zhopas* in the Battle of Poznań," he said. "It resulted in terrible skirmish. Many lives lost. But it broke the back of the Germans in Poland. One of the many victories of the glorious Red Army."

"Why did you move to Poland?" Maggie asked, ready to change the subject again.

"Oh, I love tropical weather," he said and laughed, smiling at her in the mirror. Then he turned somber and said, "No work for me in Russia…I had to support my family somehow."

"That's a noble thing to do," Maggie said. "So do you have family here?"

"Yes, my dear Sasha, and our daughter." He pointed to a faded picture clipped to his visor. "Aw, here we are. I told you I would get you here quickly."

Nick peered out the window at the nondescript entrance and wondered if they'd come to the right place. With the rolling hills, the only manmade structure visible was the menacing front gate—chipped and worn brick, topped with a wrought-iron spiked fence.

The driver turned to them. "Your fare is sixteen z's," he said, referring to the Polish zloty, worth twenty-five cents to the dollar.

Nick handed the driver a hundred-zloty bill and waved off change.

"Thank you, my American friend." The driver looked at the bill with pleasure. "For that, I wait to take you back if you would like."

"That's kind of you," Nick said.

Nick and Maggie walked through the gate marked with a small sign, MUZEUM MARTYROLOGII WIELKOPOLAN. They entered the small museum and quickly found the restroom.

As they exited the building, Nick understood why they couldn't see anything from the front gate. The architects designed Fort VII to fit into the landscape. Historians reclaimed one-half of the historical site, and the surrounding forest overgrew the other side.

The main entrance into the ominous-looking structure stood across a walkway that resembled a drawbridge over a moat. The sign to the massive fortress read: KONZENTRATIONSLAGER POSEN with the Nazi SS lightning bolt symbol displayed below it.

Halfway across the bridge, Nick stopped and turned to Maggie. "You okay?"

"I think so, just cold. Why?"

"You have a bit of a limp."

Maggie looked away. Nick's physician sense alerted his mind. "Maggie?"

She wouldn't look him in the eye. "My legs feel heavy is all. I think I'm a bit tired from traveling."

Nick held her arms. "How long has this been going on?"

Maggie grimaced, bobbed her head side to side, and hesitated. "Hmm, about six months. I'm sorry I didn't tell you, Nick. I kept thinking it would go away."

"We should go back to the hotel."

"Nick…I refuse to let this define me. It could be nothing. Besides, I think everyone needs to see one of these heartbreaking camps."

* * *

Nick looked back at the entrance to Fort VII as their taxi pulled away. He couldn't help the anger and revulsion that roiled in his belly and filled his eyes with tears. He couldn't imagine what it must have been like for a person escorted through that gate. *Did they comprehend the terrors awaiting them? Did they know that few would live to tell their stories?*

He looked at Maggie, who had barely removed her hand from her mouth during the entire tour. She had been right. Everyone needed to experience the shock of the past, but he worried it had been too much for her. *Why didn't she tell me about her symptoms?* Denial was strong medicine.

They sat in silence as the taxi driver steered back to the city.

Nick scanned the brochure he'd picked up at the fort and wished the facts weren't true—both the atrocities of the past and the actuality of his present. He wanted the whole blasted reality to go away. *Why isn't life more like a bountiful buffet where I could choose what I want and reject the rest?* He would refuse Maggie's illness and the possibility that their baby carried the same destiny. *Oh, Lord, help us.*

It remained a challenge to not let discouragement and fear overtake him. He felt conflicted in this place between his own suffering and those who endured such horrors—where the cold dark chambers held men and women sleeping on rotten straw—many of them dying of starvation or disease;

most killed in executions: tortured, hung, or shot. His anguish seemed minuscule compared to the agony inflicted at Fort VII, where thousands of Poles imprisoned as political and military activists died at the hands of the brutal SS. Fort VII served as the impetus and inspiration for other larger camps like Dachau and Auschwitz.

Nick tried to shake the images out of his head of the guillotine and the blood-stained wooden block. Or the stairway of death, where guards required prisoners to carry massive stones up the stairs, only to kick them back down to their death. And Bunker 17, the underground experimental gas chamber where the chemists and doctors had honed their craft of mass murder. They started their experiments with psychiatric patients from a nearby hospital—men, women, and children deemed defective. Once they emptied the hospital, the perpetrators developed specially adapted death vans, where they euthanized patients from other facilities. They then moved on to the next people group they considered *Untermensch*, subhuman.

Eugenics at the extreme. Worse, this was the beginning of unfathomable crimes against humanity during World War II and a glimmer of things to come.

Finally, Maggie looked at Nick, her voice quaking, "How could they have done that?"

CHAPTER 20

Emy's headlights illuminated the deserted road through the fog that lifted off the Bogdanka River. Thick this time of year, she kept a wary eye out for deer attempting to cross the road. This morning she found it difficult to concentrate as her emotions flashed by like the patches of mist. She'd hardly slept, a combination of the unwelcome revelations of her heritage, her kinship to Herr Bauer, and the fact that Keith hadn't had the decency to come home last night. The girls would notice and were smart enough to understand the disarray of their marriage. *They will have lots of questions tonight.*

Being alone with her thoughts intensified her loneliness. One thing she decided, nothing would derail the company she'd built. She took a deep breath and focused on the Mozart that softly emanated from the speakers—the science showed the frequency that the composer elicited from the piano connected with the brain for concentration and relaxation. *How did he inherently know that in the eighteenth century?*

Emy needed harmony today more than ever before. The appointment with the Americans didn't worry her; it was her time away from work. Whenever she took a few days off from BioGenics, it always seemed to put her weeks behind. In such a hurry to return this morning, she hadn't taken time to shower;

she'd only run a comb through her hair and brushed her teeth before she left. She'd put her makeup on in the car.

The automobile's clock read: 5:42 a.m., two hours before sunrise. Emy expected to find empty parking lots at the research building, as well as at the clinic arm of the complex. At the opposite end of the facility, they kept the hospital open around the clock. Because they focused on treatment of genetic disorders and reproductive health, they didn't take trauma patients. But like all hospitals, BioGenics had beds full of sick and recovering patients—mostly from the multiple clinical trials. Her role as CEO necessitated that she allowed her capable medical staff to oversee the care of the inpatients. More and more of her attention centered on the administrative duties of the multimillion-euro organization. She'd resigned herself to the fact, but she missed the constant, intimate patient care. She accepted the reality that she had become more of a paper pusher and less of a doctor.

As she turned into the parking lot, her tires laid down the first tracks across the sheen deposited by the morning fog. She steered to the side of the building to her reserved parking spot and pulled in. She allowed herself one more minute in her warm car and one last gulp from her coffee tumbler.

As she exited her car, the sub-freezing temperature burned her nostrils, and she hurried to the side entrance of the building, her Uggs gripping the slippery walkway. She kept her dress shoes in her office during the Polish winters. When she reached the security box, she placed her palm on the reader and bent so the retinal scanner could scrutinize her eye. The screen cleared her for entry. As she punched in a six-digit security code to open the door lock, a movement out of the corner of her eye startled her. When a figure moved from the shadows, Emy yelped, her legs almost collapsing.

A short woman with green hair in a black leather jacket stepped into the light.

"Holy crap, Izzi, you scared me to death. What are you doing here?"

"Hey, Dr. C. I didn't mean to frighten you. You said you'd be in early, so I thought I would get a prompt start as well."

Emy glanced over one shoulder and then the other. The lot remained empty. "How did you get here?"

"I ride my bike every day," Izzi said and pointed to the mountain bike with oversized tires leaning against the building in the shadows.

"Even in this weather? You must be frozen, Izzi," Emy said with less empathy than anger. She remembered how furious she was at her student for letting her read the letter from her grandmother in front of the girls and Keith.

Izzi's shoulders drooped, and she looked down.

Compassion struck Emy for her pathetic student. Izzi's unexpected early morning appearance undoubtedly attempted to make up for her error.

"I'm really sorry for the other night," Izzi pleaded. "I didn't realize…I mean, I tried to stop you before you read it."

Emy sighed and nodded as concern rose for the battered girl. She didn't have to travel far in her imagination to envision Izzi's probable back story. "Well, let's get out of the cold and get to work," Emy said and pulled open the steel door.

Instantly, Izzi returned to her optimistic and eager-to-please self. "I have all the information on Dr. and Mrs. Hart that you asked me to gather."

"Let me get settled first, and then we can review it," Emy said. "The Americans are supposed to be here at eight this morning?"

"Yeah. I'll go make us some coffee," Izzi said and bounded up the stairs.

* * *

Emy relaxed in her leather desk chair, sipped her coffee, and reviewed the end-of-the-year reports. Her adrenals had stopped pumping out cortisol, the stress hormone, and the muscles in her back had relaxed. *Compartmentalize.* That is what she did best, and here at the office, she commanded the environment.

The financials showed a surprisingly significant increase in revenue for BioGenics for the year. Poland levied only the CIT corporate tax. At 19%, she'd happily pay it, and besides, she carefully buried most of their income in research expenses. The Polish government had given BioGenics generous incentives to open the multi-national corporation in the country.

A sound came from the hallway, and Emy looked up from her desk. She glanced at the clock: 6:43 a.m. Bruno, the head of security, typically arrived around this time and often stopped by to say good morning. But when the office door opened, her body flooded with adrenaline again.

Izzi followed on the heels of a man whose appearance surprised Emy. Her emotional horror from Christmas Eve returned.

"Herr Bauer…how?" Words escaped her, and she swallowed hard. "What a surprise to see you…"

He smiled warmly and stopped abruptly, forcing Izzi to pull up short. He glanced back and said to Emy, "I have met

Ms. Izzi, your charming assistant." When Emy did not respond, he said, "Forgive me for letting myself in. I am on my way to Beijing this morning, and I thought I would stop by to see you."

"How did…?" Emy asked, trying to wrap her mind around the fact that he stood in her office. She made a mental note that she and Bruno were not the only people with access to the research building.

"It is the benefit of having my own plane and pilots," he smiled, ignoring her question about how he had entered the facility.

"Please come in. Can I get you some coffee?" Emy found her voice and motioned for Izzi to fetch another cup as she recovered her composure. She smoothed her hair with a stroke of her hand and wished she'd taken the time to shower. Her emotions fought to send her mind into a panic. *Why is he here?* Herr Bauer, who typically held a hands-off approach to BioGenics, stood before her in her office unannounced and uninvited. *Besides this intrusion, he knows we are related through that monster, Mengele, and told Ceci before he talked to me.* Emy's heart pounded in her chest, and she had a hard time catching her breath.

"Black," he said and looked down at Emy's hands.

She thought the slight tremor betrayed her anxiety and put her hands in her lap.

"I would like my coffee black," he said, glancing at Izzi, who stood frozen.

Emy directed the man to the area opposite her desk and held out her hand to offer him one of the leather armchairs. "Please, Herr Bauer. I am delighted to see you," she said, regaining her equilibrium. She sat in the chair across from him. "It's just that I would prefer you to visit when the team is in full swing. It is Christmas break, you understand. Everyone will be hard at work after the first, next Wednesday." She tried to control her breath, angry that she'd behaved like a blabbering schoolgirl.

Comfortably seated, Bauer waved off Emy's comment, took the coffee cup from Izzi, and thanked her. Izzi looked from him to Emy, absorbed their silence, backed out of the room, and closed the door. He sipped the coffee and waited for Izzi to leave. "I came on an off day on purpose," Bauer said. "I understand you have a patient to see this morning, but I need to talk with you before my meeting in Beijing."

Herr Bauer always seemed to be a few steps ahead of her. *How does he know my schedule? What is so crucial for this rare face-to-face?* The man hadn't changed in the past eleven years. His appearance—bald head, bushy eyebrows, gray sideburn chops, and Germanic nose and jowls—remained the same no matter his age. He wore the same aristocratic black suit, gray vest, and polka-dotted blue necktie, but his dark piercing eyes reminded her that here stood Josef Mengele's son. Her adrenals pumped out adrenaline that increased her nervous quake.

"*Meine Nichte*, I am meeting with some very influential people today, and I need to hear your thoughts on my desire to move BioGenics into enhancement of the human genome."

Emy stared at him, ignoring his statement on the company, but fighting back her shock. *My niece. So, it is true.*

He smiled and nonchalantly sipped his coffee. "So now you appreciate our little secret," he said.

Emy struggled to swallow the inflamed words on her tongue. He never should have involved Ceci. *Did Ceci tell him?*

"Please don't look so shocked, Emmanuelle."

"How long have you known this?"

"We share the same, well-bred, Aryan bloodline," he ignored her question. "Although my mother and your grandmother were not the same."

Emy leaned back in her chair. *Has he seen the letter? Does he know my grandmother was a Hungarian Jew?*

"We are family, and that is what is important."

"I don't think the rest of the world would feel the same," she said with anger.

"Aww, but that is where you are wrong. Few know my full name, James Mengele Bauer. But those who do, appreciate my legacy." He placed the coffee cup on the table between them, sat back, and crossed his legs. He raised his hands, palms up. "I think you have experienced the benefit of our heritage."

Emy's stomach rumbled. She did not choose to share Mengele's flesh.

"There are many important people who appreciate our bloodline, some of whom I am meeting today. Faces you would recognize in an instant—even a past American president." He folded his hands in front of him, his elbows rested on the arms of the chair, while Emy absorbed the news. "I don't know your grandmother, but it does not matter to me."

Emy maintained direct eye contact with the man, afraid to reveal her secret.

"For me," Bauer continued, "my mother was *mein Abstammungsnachweis,* my proof of pedigree. My mother is none other than *Reichsführer* Himmler's daughter, Gudrun.

My father, your grandfather, *Hauptsturmführer* Mengele, enjoyed many affairs," Bauer shrugged. "He was thirty-four and my mother sixteen," he smiled in amusement. "He intended to increase the Aryan nation with his superior genes. I assume your grandmother has a similar story."

Emy tried not to blink.

"I believe your grandfather would be proud of the work you…we…do here."

Emy ignored the comment. "Why are you telling me this?" She could barely control her anger.

Bauer stared at her as if probing her soul. He adjusted himself in the chair and finally said, "There are those of us who believe the world is at a crossroads. It is a matter of survival of humankind—what future are we leaving for the children?" He tightened his jaw. "Have you walked down the streets of any major city these days? The homeless…the sick, the mentally ill are overrunning our society. The disabled ruin the world's economy. Our group has hired a firm to calculate the enormity of the cost of caring for the handicapped. The problem is so massive, they cannot put a figure to it."

"What does all this have to do with BioGenics?"

His face flushed. "It has everything to do with BioGenics," he said and cleared his throat. "It is why I have put my fortune into the company…into you." He softened his tone.

When Emy didn't respond, he continued. "We have a chance to complete the work that my father and the Third Reich started. Their biological vision fostered national and racial healing. They understood the crisis and started the project with good intentions. Unfortunately, he and the rest of the Nazis got distracted by the Jewish problem."

Heat shot up Emy's neck and face. "They murdered millions under the auspices of healing!" She scoffed.

Bauer paused and pumped his hands at her to slow down. "Emmanuelle…please hear me out. In no way do I suggest that we return to those barbaric days. One of the doctors in our group said it eloquently: 'Certainly, as a physician, I want to preserve life. And to save a life, I would remove a gangrenous leg from a diseased body.'"

Emy crossed her arms in front of her chest.

"The Reich understood the need to look at the whole rather than the parts. The concept of *Volk*. Have you heard of this?"

Emy shook her head.

"Our people were advanced thinkers. They did not look strictly at their own short lives. Their concern revolved around the Thousand Year Reich. People do not understand they wanted to build a better world—for humanity as a whole…its collective essence."

"They were monsters."

Bauer ignored her comment and continued. "Do you understand the cost to care for the sick and disabled?"

"Herr Bauer, how dare you! I had to relieve the suffering of my own child."

"*Lebensunwertes Leben,*" he said and continued before she could interrupt. "Life unworthy of life. A harsh saying during the war, I know, but it is still true to this day. Emmanuelle, what I say is true. The world is dying, humanity is failing. If something is not done soon, life as we know it will perish."

"Are you suggesting we get rid of the Jews, the Blacks…the homosexuals?" she stuttered.

Bauer waved his hand and sighed. "You are not perceiving what I am saying. I am not talking about mercy killing or sterilization, or any other of the cruel methods." He reached into his jacket pocket, pulled out a small card, browned with age and faded. He held it out to her.

Emy hesitated but took it and read:

> "The völkisch state must see to it that only the healthy beget children…Here the state must act as the guardian of a millennial future…It must put the most modern medical means in the service of this knowledge. It must declare unfit for propagation all who are in any way visibly sick or who have inherited a disease and therefore pass it on…Adolf Hitler"

"Unlike the Führer," Bauer continued, "our group does not care if people are white, black, or purple. It does not matter if they are Jew or Asian or any other race or nationality. The group's only concern is the health of the human race. That is all."

Emy released the card that burned in her hand, and it fell to the table—it had the same power as her grandfather's cufflink.

"Emmanuelle…BioGenics holds the keys to this prosperity. You…you, Emmanuelle, can change the world for the better."

"Herr Bauer, this talk makes me highly uncomfortable. BioGenics is already making a difference in people's lives. We can heal a handful of diseases that no one could have imagined a cure for ten years ago. Soon we will double or triple that number."

"See Emmanuelle? You still don't get it. We have the chance to improve the human race so that these diseases are a thing of the past and then go beyond to improve the entire genetic pool. We can make permanent modifications to human germlines."

"Herr Bauer, you are talking about eugenics, and that is morally wrong. The world would not allow it." She could not stand the discussion any longer and rose to her feet.

Bauer did not move. "The world already accepts eugenics and allows it in many ways: abortion, prenatal tests for diseases, and in vitro fertilization. My collective group desires to take it to the next logical step. I think we recognize what is best for mankind."

"You and your *group* of men? You sound like good Nazis. Are you going to choose what changes to the human genome must be made?" Emy scolded. "The Nazis tried to eliminate schizophrenia, but studies show that nothing changed after World War II."

"It is a myth that we are all created equal…this is simply not true. And we have a chance to level the field for everyone." Bauer raised his voice and finally stood.

"You cannot disrupt millions of years of evolution in an attempt to create a genetically clean population," Emy rebutted. "No one can predict the long-term effects. Humans don't have a good track record when interfering with nature. It may lead to a loss of genetic diversity and ultimately result in permanent inbreeding."

Herr Bauer reached for the card on the table and took a few steps toward the door. He stopped and turned to face Emy.

"Emmanuelle, you are foolish to think that I have invested millions into helping diseased people...the *Untermenschen*. These subhumans should be eliminated. It is the strong that we must strengthen."

Emy started to speak, but Bauer held up his finger. "You will have to decide if you are working with us. No one is irreplaceable."

"Are you threatening me?" Emy yelled. "I am BioGenics. My attorneys wrote my contract just for this reason."

"Yes, and contracts are made to be broken," Bauer said and walked to the door. "Because you are *meine Nichte*, I will give you a short amount of time to think this through." He opened the door, started to walk out, but turned and said, "Oh, and one other thing, Emmanuelle. I understand your marriage is in trouble."

CHAPTER 21

CRISPR/CAS9

Dr. Christianson had instructed Maggie and Nick to meet her in her office. She'd explained that once they parked, they should enter the right side of the large E-shaped BioGenics's complex. Most of the staff were still on holiday break, so she would have her assistant, Izzi, meet them in the foyer. Izzi would escort them up to her fourth-floor office. The doctor also encouraged them not to be put off by Izzi's appearance and assured them that she shined as an exceptional researcher.

After the taxi driver exited central Poznań, Maggie noted the contrast of the modest countryside. But as they pulled into the sprawling BioGenics's complex, the building stood starkly juxtaposed to the ancient city. The rising sun bounced off the blue-tinted windows of the contemporary building, dusted with a layer of snow, which seemed more appropriate for Seattle or Portland. Overall, the design gave BioGenics a cutting-edge flare, and the country locale felt safe and inviting.

Maggie took a deep breath and exhaled slowly to relax her shoulders as Nick directed the driver to the appropriate side of the campus. They paid the fare and exited the cab, then walked to the door. As they approached, a door swung open. Maggie appreciated Dr. Christianson's warning when a young woman in black leggings, boots, Metallica T-shirt, and bright green hair motioned for them to enter.

"Hi, Dr. and Mrs. Hart, I'm Izzi," the chipper young woman said. "I'm Dr. C's graduate student."

"Thanks, Izzi," they both said, and Nick added, "You don't have Christmas break?"

"Oh, I'd rather be productive," Izzi said. "The doc wants me to sequence your DNA pronto like." She looked Maggie up and down.

Maggie's face flushed. "Uh, I don't—"

"Oh, it's okay," Izzi interrupted. "I don't mind."

Maggie glanced at Nick, who clasped her hand, and reassured her that she controlled the next steps. She didn't have to take part in any of it if she elected.

"First thing, we better get you inside," Izzi said and led them to the elevator and up to the fourth floor. The doors opened to a modestly furnished but comfortable waiting area.

"Dr. C asked that I offer you water or coffee and inform you she had an unexpected meeting this morning. She shouldn't be too long."

"We've had breakfast," Maggie said. "I'm good."

"Same," Nick added.

"Okay, but if you change your mind, I'll be through those double doors and down the hall. Just give a shout out," Izzi said and left them alone.

Nick gave Maggie a reassuring smile, in spite of the wait and the nervous, energized girl with green hair.

They settled in to wait. Nick picked up a BioGenics's brochure from the coffee table, and Maggie opened the small Bible she carried. It surprised her how unbalanced and broken she felt. The visit to Fort VII didn't help, nor did one placard

She'd read there concerning the German's T4 program initiated before the war even started. The T4 euthanasia agenda strove to eliminate diseases such as schizophrenia, epilepsy, senile disorders, paralysis, syphilitic disease, feeblemindedness, encephalitis, and the one that brought tears to her eyes, Huntington's chorea. It had shocked her to see her diagnosis in writing. A few months ago, she'd never heard of the condition. Now she realized that she and her family would have been sent to the gas chamber because of it.

Maggie couldn't erase the images of emaciated men, women, and children who survived unimaginable hardships—starvation, bone piercing cold, torture, the knowledge of their impending death, and the sound of the daily firing squads.

She'd left Fort VII with one piece of solace. A message etched into a board on one of the wooden tombs the Nazis called *Betten,* beds where the sardined inmates awaited their death. She would have easily overlooked the symbol, but a tourist from Israel pointed it out—a small, faint scratching in the wood, probably ignored by the Germans eighty years earlier. The tourist translated the faint squiggly lines: היעשי *41,* Isaiah 41.

Maggie turned to the passage and reread it for the hundredth time. She focused on the thirteenth verse:

For I am the Lord your God
Who takes hold of your right hand
And says to you, Do not fear:
I will help you.

The scripture reverberated through her soul. Here, someone who faced certain death had found strength and knew that regardless of what happened next, God was with them. It had to come from the deepest of faith and a knowing that the current anguish was merely temporary. Within the midst of total darkness and misery, that brave person had laid down an anchor to hold on to against the raging storm. *Perfect peace.* Maggie knew her grief and fear couldn't compare, but in this collective suffering, she sensed harmony.

Maggie thought she heard a raised voice and looked up as the door to Dr. Christianson's office opened, and a well-dressed, elderly man came out and shut the door abruptly behind him.

* * *

Emy entered her bathroom to take a few minutes to gather her composure after her quarrel with Herr Bauer. She wanted to look presentable for the Harts, who had traveled a great distance to see her. She found it difficult to stop thinking about Bauer. How does the mind wrap around the fact that the man she'd respected and trusted for all these years held deep-seated secrets set to unbalance the equilibrium? She couldn't help but imagine that monster, Mengele, standing in her office to argue the rationale of the medical experiments he'd performed to advance the health of the German individual and society. No wonder she seemed double-minded—part victim, part perpetrator. She'd always believed humans held two parts in balance, good and evil. But here the line in her own genome was drawn more acutely, and she couldn't erase the image of her own son Danek, his body riddled with ulcers from her own form of research. The thought forced dry heaves of emotion.

She stared at her image in the mirror. She'd helped hundreds, if not thousands, regain their health. *Medical advances always cost something.* Herr Bauer's voice echoed in her head.

She splashed cool water on her face. *No, I am a healer. Different time, different situation.*

She dried her face and reapplied her makeup. In part, she understood the beliefs and vision that Bauer held. On occasion, she'd embraced the same prejudices and racism and joked with friends that one day, she hoped to find and eliminate the *stupid* gene. Especially when a moron cut her off in traffic, treated her rudely in a store, or when she'd read about the ludicrous antics of a criminal.

What was this mysterious group Bauer alluded to?

The leaders in genetics had decided that gene therapy, or gene manipulation to cure diseases, fell within ethical boundaries. Still, there were too many unknowns about germline changes to mess with the genes of sperm, egg, or embryo, although rogue scientists pushed the limits of conscience. It remained a considerable concern within the scientific community that enforcing international scientific recommendations proved impossible.

Why is Bauer pushing me so hard on this issue? She'd explained the pitfalls and dangers to him before. *Had he not listened and understood?* And yet, in the dark of night, she too, had wondered about the possibilities. What could it mean for her own girls and her eventual grandchildren?

How does he know about my marital problems? And what about his implied threats to remove her from BioGenics? She had discussed this with her attorney when they first drew up her contract. All too often, she had seen several entrepreneurial physicians sidelined by corporate greed. BioGenics had volumes of patents and applications pending, advances made possible by Herr Bauer's endowment. But Emy was BioGenics—her ideas, her research. She'd compartmentalized some of her own departments, and only she held the whole picture—secrets kept to herself.

She examined her makeup in the bathroom mirror before walking through her office to invite the Harts in. She took a cleansing breath. *If Bauer wants to play hardball, I'm prepared.*

Emy opened the door to her office. "Dr. and Mrs. Hart, will you please come in? Forgive me for keeping you waiting."

She shook their hands. *What a handsome couple.*

"Everything okay?" the doctor asked.

It caught Emy off guard. She shrugged nonchalantly and tried to keep her emotions in check. "Dr. Hart, I'm sure you have dealt with plenty of hospital administrators. Business matters always annoy me." She rolled her eyes, closed the door, and invited the Harts to sit in the comfortable leather chairs.

She sat across from them and picked up the chart Izzi had prepared from the coffee table. "Dr. and Mrs. Hart, you have traveled a great distance, and I'm sure you have many questions for me. But I want to start by letting you know that everything is going to be okay. Our goal at BioGenics is to cure some of these horrendous diseases." She paused, smiled, and looked at them, regaining her confidence. "And the good news is, we are."

Mrs. Hart dabbed a tear from the corner of her eye with a tissue she pulled from the box on the table.

This is why Emy loved her work. She often came to work with the sense that she was born for this job. Every individual told a different story, but the pain of genetic disorders created universal fear.

She touched the woman's hand. "Mrs. Hart, we will take excellent care of you and your baby."

"Thank you," she said, "but please call me Maggie."

"That's a deal," Emy said, squeezed Maggie's hand, and relaxed back into her chair. "I hope you don't mind, but I had my assistant do some research on you both, so in many ways, I feel that I already know you. Your work in Guatemala is admirable, and part of the reason I agreed to see you this week. I, too, have a great heart for children." She turned to the doctor. "Dr. Hart, your reputation also precedes you. My friend, Dr. B, tells me you are a talented surgeon. We do not do trauma here at our hospital, but we pride ourselves in the finest care for women and children in the world."

"Please, call me Nick, and we so appreciate you seeing us on your holiday week. Truly."

"It is my pleasure. Let me tell you my thoughts, and then I want to answer all your questions."

She waited to make sure they both agreed.

Emy picked up the iPad from the coffee table. "As you already understand, Huntington's is a progressive, autosomal dominant, neurodegenerative disease initiated by an extension of CAG repeats in the HTT Huntington gene on the short arm of the fourth chromosome." Emy pulled up the picture of the number four chromosome, represented as an asymmetric X, and turned the image to the couple. "This chromosome has one hundred and ninety-one million DNA building blocks or base pairs, representing around 6% of the total DNA in the cells, and contains approximately a thousand genes. The gene for the huntingtin protein is located here on the short arm."

She put the tablet in her lap.

"The reason we are excited for you…and I know that sounds strange…is because this disease is isolated to one location, one allele. Huntington's makes for a perfect candidate for gene therapy—to go in and snip out this defective section."

"You make it sound so easy," Maggie said.

Emy smiled. "Yes, billions of euros and years of research, easy. Here, let me show you how this works." Emy started a video on the tablet and turned it toward them again. "We use a technology that has revolutionized the treatment of many of the genetic diseases. The name is more complex than the technology, 'clustered regularly interspaced short palindromic repeats.'" She laughed. "We shorten that to CRISPR or CRISPR/Cas9, if you include the enzyme that is the molecular scalpel, so to speak, that cuts the DNA double helix. We introduce the Cas9 protein into the cell along with a short strand of messenger RNA that matches the DNA base sequence exactly. The combined molecule goes in, finds the abnormal CAG repeat segment on chromosome four, snips it out, and the body naturally repairs the sliced DNA end-to-end."

She let the couple watch the animation with her voice-over that described the process.

When the video finished, Dr. Hart nodded, "That is something. It reminds me of that old movie, *Fantastic Voyage*. They shrank the humans and a spaceship to get inside the cells to treat the patient."

Emy laughed. "Yes, they filmed that movie before we were born, but I have seen it."

"How do you get this CRISPR into the cells?" Maggie asked.

"Simple, we introduce the two molecules into the brain via a virus. This virus is otherwise harmless but carries the enzyme and the RNA to the cells. And Dr. and Mrs. Hart, forgive me if I cannot share with you all our proprietary methods, but suffice it to say, BioGenics leads the way in these techniques."

"Does it go into every cell?"

"This is a good question, Maggie." Emy did not want to lie to the woman. The truth remained that they did not know, but collective wisdom believed that if enough cells were corrected, the abnormal huntingtin protein load would decrease, and the patient would not suffer from the disease. "The answer is, we believe enough of the cells are affected to prevent you from getting the symptoms."

Nick looked at Maggie, then back at Emy. He bit his lower lip, and his eyes were full of worry.

"There's a significant update since I talked to you on the phone," Nick said. "I thought Maggie was asymptomatic, but as it turns out, she has some heaviness in her legs; some early muscular weakness."

Emy nodded and frowned. "Have you fallen?" she asked Maggie.

Maggie looked apologetically at Nick and said, "A few times. I thought I was being clumsy."

"How about any trouble swallowing, difficulty concentrating, or mood swings?"

"I'm pregnant, remember. I thought mood swings came with that." She smiled, then turned serious. "This whole thing is stressful."

"I understand, Maggie, but if you have any symptoms, you must say so. Time is of the essence. We are evaluating our patients who have undergone the procedure to see if there is a reversal of the effects of the abnormal huntingtin protein. I'm afraid the data is inconclusive at this point. To err on the side of caution, I believe your treatment should start next week. It's clear that an increased mutant protein in your brain is detrimental."

Maggie sighed deeply.

"What about off-target editing?" Nick asked.

"Yes, excellent. You have done your homework." Emy looked at Maggie. "The question is, are there other places in the miles of DNA that could have this CAG repeat? And could the CRISPR/Cas9 system inadvertently remove a section that is vital for some other function? The short answer is, we don't believe so. And this has been born out with other patients' results." She spread her arms. "One of the great advantages we have at BioGenics is our artificial intelligence computing system. BioGenics has spent billions on that alone. As you can imagine, to sequence someone's DNA, and to figure out the exact area that needs changing, and then to perform the changes, takes unfathomable amounts of computer resources. Using AI, we can figure these things out in a fraction of the time."

"This AI won't turn me into a monster?"

Emy laughed but realized Maggie's sincerity. "No, no, no…that is strictly science fiction."

"Is anyone else around the world doing this?" Nick asked.

Emy nodded but looked down at the iPad and chose her words carefully. "Gene therapy is like the new race to the moon. All the geneticists know each other and present our data at the meetings. I imagine it is the same in Orthopaedic Surgery.

BioGenics is light years ahead of anyone else in the industry. One of the benefits of having our facility hosted in Poland is that this country has the largest and most complete registry of Huntington's patients. Penn Medicine recently started clinical trials of their own," she smiled at them and waited to see if she needed to say more.

"What kind of results are you getting?" Maggie asked.

"Excellent!"

"What about our baby?" Maggie asked and grabbed for Nick's hand.

"This is what I recommend, Maggie. First, I need to take a buccal swab from your mouth. My assistant Izzi is standing by to sequence your DNA. With our AI, we will have it done by Monday. We will know you down to your every base pair." She smiled. "Next, I believe it is important to test your fetus."

"Baby," Maggie corrected.

"Yes. Because you're at twelve weeks, it is safe to take a few cells from the placenta and sequence the fetus's…uh, baby's DNA as well. That sounds scary, but because you are still early in your pregnancy, your placenta will be low in your uterus. I'll insert a tiny catheter through your cervix and take out a tiny amount of tissue. We only need one cell. We could do that this morning if you would like."

A tear rolled down Maggie's cheek. "And the risk to our baby?"

Emy looked at Nick. "With every procedure, there are risks. You have come to one of the most advanced centers in the world, and that in itself minimizes those dangers."

This brought more tears to Maggie's eyes, and Emy welled with compassion. She reached for Maggie's hand again.

Maggie blotted her tears. "And if we elect to do the gene therapy on me, how will it affect the baby?" she asked, staring into Emy's eyes.

Emy nodded and held her stare. In fact, Emy didn't know. Maggie would become their first pregnant mother to receive the CRISPR technology. It would be a clinical breakthrough if the virus crossed the placental/blood barrier. But she simply said, "We will take the best of care of you and your baby."

CHAPTER 22

THE FIFTEEN

Bauer had chosen fifteen as the number of members for the covert organization, as well as the name for the group. His choice represented both the past and the future. The digit represented a biblical symbol of restoration and healing, and The Fifteen would bring this to the new millennium. Practically speaking, fifteen members afforded perfect balance. Any more would create too much chaos, and any less would be insufficient to establish influence.

As he looked around the table, Bauer had to laugh—fifteen of the most prominent people in the world squeezed into the *hutong,* traditional Chinese residence.

"Wu, I asked for an out-of-the-way location, but you have outdone yourself." Bauer bowed slightly toward the elderly Chinese man with a wispy gray beard and mustache. Wu wore a tailored and expensive navy Tang Dynasty suit.

Wu raised his teacup to Bauer and smiled a near toothless grin. "I thought it appropriate for The Fifteen to meet in the humble surroundings of my family's home. My ancestors established this hutong a thousand years ago," he said and bowed to the four quadrants of the universe and the men and women around the table.

Among other holdings, the Chinese gentleman owned five of the most prominent buildings in downtown Beijing.

The irony that they had gathered in the back streets of ancient China didn't escape Bauer. He lifted his cup. "*Gānbēi*," he toasted. The rest of the group followed suit.

Whether they met here, the outback of Australia, or the wilderness of Montana, The Fifteen had become accustomed to convening in unique locales—away from the hustle and bustle of life, but more importantly, removed from prying eyes of the public and electronic eavesdropping devices. No one in the room flew on commercial airlines, so the location never presented an issue. Like all previous meetings, Bauer did not permit cellphones and other electronic devices. Body scans at the private airport confirmed compliance. The participants never took notes or shared written messages and communicated only via secure phone lines.

Bauer surveyed the delegates as two elderly Chinese women distributed bowls of soup and baskets of dim sum. Three members had reached the Forbes top twenty list. The others weren't the wealthiest people in the world, although if they or their empires collapsed, the world economy would have a severe decline. Wealth indicated only one measure of intelligence, and Bauer valued other attributes. After all, he had plenty of money. The network of The Fifteen extended much further into the web of society, but these individuals were the heart and soul of the organization. These people would make decisions to change the world, and each one of them committed to the goal with religious fervor.

After the women served the visitors, Wu opened his hands in welcome, "Please, be my guests. These recipes are as old as this home."

"Hopefully, the pork is fresher," Bauer smirked as he lifted off the cover to his soup bowl. His comment elicited a hearty laugh from Wu and the rest of the group.

Bauer took a bite of a fluffy dumpling, nodded in approval, then stood. The members of The Fifteen were busy. He would not waste their time and got down to business.

"The issues we discuss cannot leave this room. I trust each one of you as a confidant," he said, and waited for group members to nod as they ate. "I, like the rest of you, saw the broadcast of the British princess grieving over the birth of her daughter with genetic abnormalities. The baby died four days later. She wept as she spoke into the cameras and said, 'If the medical community has the skills and the knowledge to fix these diseases, then for heaven's sake, please do.'"

Bauer smiled and raised his hands. The members applauded.

"It is as I have told you. Ours will be a bottom-up revolution. The downfall of the well-meaning forefathers of eugenics was their top-down approach—they wanted the government to control and enact the laws that regulated reproduction. The most potent force driving our mission will be consumer demand for achieving healthy individuals and eradication of genetic diseases for the advancement and survival of future generations."

Bauer took a sip from his teacup.

"We only use the term eugenics amongst ourselves. It has become a word fraught with images of forced sterilizations, abortions, and euthanasia. Thank the stars we will never have to return to such barbaric methods to improve humankind. A nobler and well-accepted term is gene therapy. If any of you have a better term, I'd like to hear it." He paused for comments, received none, and continued. "Gene therapy conjures up images of healing and a healthy society. No legislative power will be required. We open the floodgates and watch it happen organically…and watch our investments grow exponentially. If any of you have lingering doubts, I point you to the American college scandal. Parents paid hundreds of thousands, if not millions, to promotors and colleges to gain access to privilege for their children. Others cheated the system, and hired proctors to take their child's college entrance exams. How much more will parents pay to ensure mentally and physically healthy, superior children? You have all been selected for your exceptional intelligence, which translates directly to your success in this world. The studies are clear, success begets success. Now, with the opportunities before us, my hope is that in a few short generations, the leaders will be so brilliant they will look back at us, The Fifteen, as high-grade morons."

They all burst into laughter.

"We will be long dead by then, but rest assured, our vision will live on. Ladies and gentlemen, we stand on the shoulders of the great forethinkers who came before us. We need to understand their intentions and learn from their mistakes. Our goals are the same—to build a better society through the health of the individual. But unlike our forefathers, we will not concern ourselves with race or religion. We will only involve ourselves with the health of the human race as a whole and the survival of our species. We too, understand that the world can't bear the financial burdens imposed by defective individuals. Our forefathers tried to eradicate feeblemindedness, criminality, homosexuality, poverty, promiscuity, and social dependency by eliminating what had already been conceived—lives previously set in motion. I believe each one of you agrees with me: you cannot kill or sterilize your way to produce the results we desire. These great thinkers believed that they could identify the unfit and stop them from reproducing. History has demonstrated there is not enough birth control in the world," he said and laughed. "The basic code of life must be altered. We will apply rational design to humanity and improve the human stock—healthy children equal a stronger society. This is our moral obligation." Bauer pounded his fist on the table.

A gentleman in an Israeli military uniform cleared his throat and said, "If the Jews had been allowed to populate the earth, we would not be in such a mess…after all, we are the chosen people."

The group laughed again.

Bauer pacified him with a smile. "We must intervene before it is too late," he said. "Natural selection does not work, the world is getting dumber, more violent, and corrupt. These are the people who reproduce in vast numbers. Immigration can no longer be controlled." Bauer cleared his throat. "Eventually, there will be such a mixing of the races, our species will become homogeneous…where do you want the average to be set?"

He spread his arms over The Fifteen. "We are the elite and brightest, and we understand what is best for the people. Everyone should have the ability to be like us. What the world has accepted as *normal* brings continued destruction to our planet. Some people want to support the poor, with the belief that the poor would rise to our standard. This is hogwash. Enhancement of the stock of human society solves all the broader social problems. Other people are more worried about plants and animals becoming extinct than our own species. The salvation of the human race requires socialism to make a better world to live in and eugenics to make better people to live in that world. This could be achieved in a century or two—a relatively short time to elevate the majority of the population to equal or exceed the intellectual qualities of some of history's most brilliant minds, such as yours."

The Fifteen's chief medical director from Japan spoke. "Along with my Chinese colleagues here, my researchers have sequenced the genome of highly intelligent individuals from around the world. We believe we could increase the IQ of subsequent generations by fifteen to twenty points. Envision the repercussions in those third and fourth generations from now."

Bauer took another sip of his tea to gather his thoughts when a woman from Africa raised her hand. She was the most beautiful woman Bauer knew, especially today, dressed in yellow, blue, and red traditional Africanized garb, and her pearly white smile set against her dark black skin. "Tell us about the progress of BioGenics," she said. "We are all eager to hear of your discussion with Dr. Christianson."

Bauer sighed and decided to start with the positive. "Our friends from Japan and China have demonstrated great possibilities. I will soon share with you the advances we have made at BioGenics that will propel your work by light years and improve your success. I am hopeful that Dr. Christianson will join us next month at our meeting in Brazil. Her discoveries will astound you. I have been very open with you about her rigid beliefs and her hesitation to be brought into enlightenment. I believe some of this misdirection comes from her liberal husband." He paused to measure his words carefully. "We have applied appropriate pressure to this very talented physician. But, if we are unable to persuade her, we have set other options in place." He looked at Wu, who nodded.

Bauer searched the members' faces. They seemed satisfied with his assessment.

"Science must catch up to our vision. We want to match the technology with the characteristics that our group designs, knowing that the expertise will only advance with the improved intelligence of our species. We understand that, at first, it will produce a society of two classes: the genetically sound and everybody else. Our goal is for the future superior race to take over and out-populate the *Untermenschen*. The American geneticist, HJ Muller, predicted a hundred years ago that human genes one day could be manipulated, and heredity would no longer be the prerogative of an unreachable god playing pranks on us. That day is here, and it will usher in the genuine Thousand Year Reich."

Bauer paused to let The Fifteen comment.

The gentleman from Egypt raised his hand. He wore the traditional red and white checkered *ghutra* over his head, held in place with the black-banded *iqal*. Bauer motioned for him to speak.

"Herr Bauer, I agree with everything you say. However, I must speak my mind on the matter of homosexuality. You have asked each one of us to provide you with a list of characteristics we desire in this new world. Our religion…my backers… would not tolerate a world in which men are attracted to men and women to women. This is still our number one priority."

It took all of Bauer's willpower to not blink or swallow. *This man may need to be removed from The Fifteen for his ignorance. If the Arab only knew.*

"Please, please, my friend," he said and chose his words carefully. "I beg you. I beg all of you to put away your prejudices. We must not focus on our hatred, but on our love for the human race as a whole."

Bauer crossed his arms.

"We are the new evangelists of an improved society, ushering in a perfect human race. And we will present such a sound case that the public will demand this human improvement. We will finally take charge of our own evolution," he said. "The large pharmaceutical companies caught on to this vision ten years ago when they began to market directly to the consumer." He winked at the CEO of one of the most prominent drug manufacturers in the world. "Entice the people, and they will run to their physician to demand the new drug."

Bauer reached for his computer tucked inside his briefcase. "You have been kind to allow me to break our rules on electronics, but I think you'll share my excitement in this presentation," he said and pushed the power button on the laptop. "It is premature to release this, but I show it now to spark further discussion and creativity for our eventual launch. A Hollywood producer, sympathetic to our cause, used his own money to create this. We are in the process of purchasing the rights to the song. It will cost us millions but will be well worth it."

Bauer plugged the computers HDMI cord into the large TV screen behind him and started the presentation. The video rolled with a time-lapse, seedling sprouting from fertile soil and unfurling into a lime-green plant that quickly matured. It bloomed with beautiful flowers of purple, fuchsia, and pink tones. John Lennon's version of "Imagine" played as stunning images of earth's natural wonders from every corner of the world faded in and out. The video and the music reflected some of man's greatest achievements that changed the planet into a utopian society living life in peace. The images synced with the lyrics. "*Imagine all the people,*" the song played.

Then, with the flare of movie magic, a sperm and an ovum combined and proliferated rapidly through all the stages of development until, like the seedling, a young boy emerged—grown from conception and morphing into a healthy, prosperous man. Then, a girl born with horrific genetic defects, deformed and imprisoned in a wheelchair, physically metamorphosed before their eyes to a healthy young woman. The female transfigured into a space explorer, and the camera followed her point-of-view, looking back at the earth as the video finished with the word "IMAGINE" in large bold capital letters across the screen.

Bauer shut down the computer and paused, looking at each one of the members who nodded their approval. His smile broadened, and he raised his hands in praise. "Yes, I am a dreamer." He paused. "I'm thankful I am not the only one." He raised his cup to The Fifteen.

CHAPTER 23

BIOPSY

Maggie waited patiently in the chair while Nick paced back and forth. After a tour of the facility, Dr. Christianson allowed them some time in the clinic to process all the information. They also had to wait on Maggie's blood work before proceeding.

Maggie and Nick were overwhelmed by the evidence of the disease progression in Maggie's body. Upon neurological examination, her patellar reflexes had diminished, and her quads showed signs of weakness, all early stages of Huntington's disease.

Deep lines creased Nick's brow above his tense jaw muscles.

"Are you mad at me?" Maggie asked.

"Oh, Mags, not at all," he said, going to her side and tenderly combing his fingers through her hair. "I'm frustrated for not noticing your symptoms earlier." He kissed her forehead.

Maggie wiped a tear and patted his hand. She understood that Nick took his job as her protector seriously. But in a foreign country with several unknowns, everything was out of his control.

The decision to proceed with the biopsy challenged them both, but with Maggie in the initial onset of the illness, it seemed the most advisable pathway. The doctor had reassured

Maggie that the risks of this procedure remained low—less than 1%. With Maggie and Nick involved in medicine, they both realized that anyone could be that 1%, and complications often involved doctors or their family members.

Maggie pushed her tongue against the inside of her cheek, where Dr. Christianson had taken the buccal swab, a brisk scrape with a toothbrush-like tool. Soon, they would know every detail of her genetic makeup from her Blackfeet heritage to her risk of diseases.

Nick went back to his pacing, and Maggie took a swig from a water bottle. Emy's tour of BioGenics confirmed in her mind they had come to the right place.

Overall, the facility impressed her, from the state-of-the-art research labs to the comfortable clinic and modern hospital. The doctor took Nick into one of the six operating rooms while Maggie got her blood drawn. With a two-million-dollar da Vinci Robotic System in every suite, Nick had told Maggie they had spared no expense.

When Emy took them to the third floor, it surprised them to learn that a supercomputer filled the entire level. A retinal and palm scanner ensured that only certain people had access from the elevator and again into the hyper-cooled room full of computer banks. She explained that, typically, they allowed only those with the highest clearance in BioGenics on that level, but because of the holiday and the fact that Emy was the boss, she let them see it.

She took them far enough so they could look through the thick glass at the computers flashing with lights. Emy told them that the floor and the room needed tight security for several reasons. First, with all the data breaches around the world among businesses, BioGenics had to guarantee absolute confidentiality. Who would want their genome floating around on the dark web? Someday, someone would figure out how to extort money with the information. Second, corporate espionage remained a genuine crisis, and BioGenics had to protect their proprietary scientific advances. The Chinese had already offered billions of dollars to buy out the company.

After the tour, Emy had explained to Nick and Maggie the colorful pictograph on one wall of her office. "When the sequencing is performed, we label each base molecule with a fluorescent dye, which results in the beautiful mosaic of life." She explained in detailed technical terms how a person's genome is read. Maggie understood that the DNA was built from repeating A, T, C, and G base molecules with six point four billion in each person's entire genome—enough to fill four thousand, two hundred books. She further explained that BioGenics's computer and the artificial intelligence systems allowed her team to wrestle with the miles of DNA. Scientists theorize that out of all the DNA, only 1% functioned as genes, another 9% appeared useful in other utilities, and the rest seemed to serve no purpose at all. Emy had told them geneticists debated these percentages. However, they all agreed that when they manipulated a gene, their goal was to minimize accidental changes along the rest of the DNA.

As Nick continued to pace, Maggie's anxiety increased. "Are we doing the right thing?" she asked.

Nick whirled around. "Yes, we are." He answered so fast, Maggie wondered if he debated the same question in his mind. "We need to know, Mags. It's the only way to get all the information so we can make informed decisions."

"I say we go home and forget about all this," she said.

"I'm afraid that's not an option," Nick said and then softened his tone. "I like Dr. Christianson. Sometimes as a doc, you can sense the competency of another surgeon. Maybe it's the swagger. She can be a bit abrupt and distracted, but what surgeon isn't? Look at what she has built."

"I sure like her name, Emmanuelle, *God is with us*," Maggie said, then turned somber. "Nick, I don't know about this gene-editing. I'm not sure humans should mess with the code of life, as the doctor described it. Besides, how could we ever afford it—a quarter of a million dollars?" she scoffed.

"Well, the testing is a fraction of that amount," Nick said. "If we decide to go ahead with the next steps…well…maybe we could take out a second mortgage on our home."

"You know how many kids I could feed in Guatemala with that money? It seems excessive…" Maggie held her tongue when she heard the clicking of the doctor's heels in the hallway.

Dr. Christianson appeared from around the corner. She was smiling.

"Your lab work all looks fine. A few of the important things we check are confirmation that your blood coagulation is normal, and you are not Rh-negative. Also, your blood typing, and if you are pregnant." She smiled. "You are."

Dr. Christianson walked over and sat down next to Maggie while Nick took a chair across from them.

"There are a few other things I want to discuss with you both." She put her hand on Maggie's arm.

"I hope I've explained well enough that the reason we need to sequence your DNA is so we have it for a reference," Emy said. "We especially need the exact base-pairing around the Huntington's mutation so that we can design the messenger

RNA to match the area for the Cas9 to cleave out the bad portion. Izzi is at work on that process and will have your genome finished by Monday."

Maggie nodded.

"We will do the same for the fetus's genome once I take the biopsy. We will identify how many repeats the fetus has at the HTT gene and whether it's in danger of developing Huntington's disease."

"What is the risk of doing nothing at this point?" Nick asked.

"That is both a good question and an option," the doctor said. "Unfortunately, one issue we have not discussed is amplification of the gene, meaning that the CAG repeat can get longer in the subsequent generation. If the fetus has sixty or more CAG repeats, there is a significant risk of juvenile expression—all the terrible symptoms we've discussed can happen in early childhood. The juvenile form is horrendous. If there are that many repeats, most people terminate the pregnancy."

Maggie flinched. She didn't want to upset the doctor, especially right before she did a procedure, but she had to know. "Dr. Christianson…when do you believe the life of *my baby* started?"

"Mrs. Hart…Maggie." She continued to hold her arm. "I am sorry. I do not mean to offend you with my medical terms," she sighed. "In my work, it is easier to make the distinction and draw the line at birth. I see too many things that can go wrong during pregnancy. Reading your dossiers and recognizing your Christian beliefs, I understand that you probably consider life starting at conception."

"Yes, and *termination* of my baby is out of the question," Maggie said as heat rose in her cheeks. "And what about you? What is your faith?"

The doctor looked at the floor and seemed to hesitate, but then said, "I'm Jewish."

It helped Maggie understand the doctor's perspective, as most of her Jewish friends believed that life started at birth. "It would help me if we refer to our baby as a *baby* or *he or she*," Maggie said.

"Yes, by all means," Dr. Christianson said. "Speaking of that, this was my next question. We will identify everything about your baby. Will you want to know the gender?"

Maggie looked at Nick.

"It is up to you, Mags. I'd love to, but you make the call."

"Let me think about that one," Maggie said.

"We will test the baby's DNA for other issues. Because you are over thirty-five, we consider you a high-risk pregnancy. You're at a much higher risk of having a child with Down syndrome or other congenital abnormalities."

"Why is that?" Maggie asked.

"Well, remember you're born with all your eggs. So, the ova are forty-six years old as well. We think the proteins that hold the chromosomes together decrease with age, and that increases the possibility of instability in the pairs and a higher likelihood that division will happen unevenly."

"More good news," Maggie huffed.

"Again, all the risks are low, but you need to know everything. We will have lots of information about you and the baby." The doctor paused and grimaced. "My last question is difficult, but one we have to ask everyone. In the business of genetics, there are no mysteries. Unfortunately, we occasionally rock the boat by uncovering family secrets: illegitimate children, long-lost relatives, adopted children, and maternal or paternal…uh…indiscretions. I need to know if Nick is the father."

Maggie stared horrified at the doctor and then at Nick, who looked like he'd swallowed a lemon. Her face flushed, and words failed, until her inner comedian came out to play. She put her hand to her chin and mused, "Hmm, let me think about that. There was that one night…and then that other time. Oh, and that really handsome guy." She couldn't continue the charade any longer and burst into laughter.

* * *

Maggie detested gynecological exams. Even with the comfortable setting and care that Dr. Christianson and staff took to protect her privacy, the position left her feeling vulnerable. The nurse had inserted an IV for precautionary reasons, but Maggie declined any sedation.

Dr. Christianson started with an ultrasound. The baby appeared about the size of a plum, with a heart rate of one hundred and fifty beats per minute.

"Does that mean it's a girl?" Nick held Maggie's hand and stood near the head of the exam table.

The doctor laughed. "I'm afraid that is an old wives' tale, Nick. But we'll know soon enough."

"What a change there's been in the few weeks since the last ultrasound," Maggie said. "Look at our baby!" She glanced up at Nick.

"Yes, at twelve weeks, the little one has developed all the

critical systems and parts," the doctor said. "The baby is already opening and closing its fingers and curling its toes."

Maggie was relieved the doctor finally referred to it as a baby. Emy had asked Maggie to drink lots of water as they waited and firmly pushed on her full bladder with the ultrasound transducer, moving it back and forth.

"Good," Emy said. "The placenta will be easy to access for the chorionic villus sampling." She pointed at the screen. "The placenta is low within the uterus. The chorionic villi are cells that join the placenta to the wall of the uterus—where oxygen is exchanged between you and the baby. They carry the baby's DNA."

"What if the placenta sat higher?" Maggie asked, looking at the homogeneous gray area of tissue on the ultrasound image.

"Then we would put a needle through your abdomen."

"Thank God for small blessings," Maggie said and grimaced at Nick.

"Okay, Maggie. I'm going to insert the speculum and take the sample," the doctor said and moved between her legs as she held the ultrasound probe in place.

Maggie felt certain the doctor was familiar with female parts, but still, she wanted to close her knees together and push the sheet between her legs. She shifted her feet in the stirrups as the doctor touched her perineum as she'd warned. The speculum produced pressure.

"I'm going to cleanse the cervix with antiseptic and then thread the tube into the uterus. You may feel a twinge of pain or cramping. That's normal."

Maggie closed her eyes, tightened her grip on Nick's hand, and forced herself to stay still. Just as she experienced a cramp, the doctor removed the speculum.

"Okay, all done. Easy-peasy, right?" Emy extended the footrest of the exam table and helped Maggie stretch out her legs. "I want you to relax here for a while. The nurse will give you an instruction sheet of what to look out for over the weekend. Go back to the hotel and rest. No sex, however." She looked at Nick.

Dr. Christianson came to the head of the exam table and touched Maggie's cheek.

"We'll know on Monday." She pursed her lips together, nodded, and walked out of the room.

CHAPTER 24

THE OFFER

Bauer endured the fourteen-hour flight from Beijing to New York, but wasn't put off by all that time in the sky. He believed the wait worthwhile as he finally stood on the ninety-second floor of the new Freedom Tower. He'd waited for this moment for years, and his hand shook as an attorney held out the notebook. The attorney wore white protective gloves, and Bauer thought he probably should as well. But he wanted to connect, flesh to flesh, as it were. He wanted to feel his father's writing on the pages of the spiral-bound composition notebook titled *Illustrated Zoology*.

Eight years ago, an unexpected case of pneumonia had put him in the hospital, and Bauer had missed the Alexander Autographs auction. At the time, an American corporation reportedly run by an Orthodox Jew purchased the collection for three hundred thousand dollars. Until this day, Bauer didn't know if the negotiations would go his way, but every man had his price. He'd offered a million for the thirty-five-thousand-page anthology. The end result nearly tripled the Jew's initial investment...way too much for the man to pass up. As Bauer held his father's journal, the sentimental value far exceeded the cost.

Holding the notebook, he couldn't help feeling light-headed, and the attorney invited him to sit at the mahogany table to inspect it.

"May I get you something, Herr Bauer?" his assistant, Kenny asked. "Water, perhaps?"

"No, please, nothing but privacy." He nodded at Kenny to hand the bag to the attorney.

Kenny struggled and groaned as he lifted the leather duffel onto the table with both hands. The forty pounds of gold clunked against the wood.

The attorney and Kenny said something to him as they left the room, but Bauer was already engrossed in the notebook.

At forty-nine, his father penned the diary. Bauer ran his fingers over the strange crayon drawings of animals on the cover. Experts had authenticated the work. *Father.*

He opened the one-hundred and eighty-page journal. As the attorney had noted, his father wrote the first page in pencil, the rest in blue ink—stylistic script, complete with footnotes and drawings, and an occasional word or sentence scribbled out.

Bauer glanced at the rest of the collection laid out carefully on the table. It included a green hardback journal labeled *Agenda Classica,* and two others with unusual covers. One was marked *Cultura General,* and the other depicted a mermaid and was titled *Bloco Copacabana.* Informed historians had scoured all the pages and indicated that the volumes contained the author's thoughts on a variety of issues: art, literature, religion, and, of course, the Nazi ideology of natural selection. Bauer would have plenty of time to inspect the other documents on the flight home, but he treasured his father's journal. *I've waited a long time to hold this.*

Bauer slowly flipped through the pages, written between 1960 and 1975, when his father lived incognito in Paraguay and Brazil. He had a familiarity with many of his father's quotes, but his heart pounded to see them in the man's script:

> "Everything will end in a catastrophe if natural selection is altered to the point that the gifted people are overwhelmed by billions of morons."

> "The real problem is to define when human life is worth living and when it has to be eradicated."

> "The age of technology has created new conditions...the feeble-minded person ('village idiot') was separated from farmers because of his social status and low income. This separation is no longer the case in the age of technology. He is now on the same level as the farmer's son who went into the city..."

> "We know that selection rules all nature by choosing and exterminating...those unfit had to accept the rule of more accomplished human beings, or they were pushed out or exterminated. The weaker humans excluded from reproducing. This is the only way for human beings to exist and to maintain themselves."

> "There's only one truth and one true beauty... there's no 'good' or 'bad' in nature. There's

only 'appropriate' or 'inappropriate'…both sides receive equal chances. Nevertheless, nature provides a strainer. Things that are 'inappropriate' fall through since they lose in the struggle for survival."

Bauer realized he held his breath as he read. He'd forgotten to swallow and wiped the spit from his lip before it landed on his father's musings. His excitement to share with The Fifteen at their next meeting mounted. Here, Father predicted in his own handwriting that 90% of humans would starve due to stupidity.

Bauer continued to turn the pages and smiled at his father's view on feminism. A fact to hide from the females in the syndicate:

"Biology doesn't support equal rights. Women shouldn't be working in higher positions. Women's work must depend on filling a biological quota. Birth control can be done by sterilizing those with deficient genes. Those with good genes will be sterilized after the fifth child."

Bauer turned to the last page and read:

"I see how right my plans have been all along, and I understand now that following people's advice mostly results in irreparable nonsense.

But I refuse to pass guilt onto others: I was solely responsible for my decisions."

* * *

BERLIN, GERMANY

Emy savored her first experience on a private jet. She enjoyed the comfort and convenience of the airplane and the limo that picked her up at the jetway—a lifestyle she could relish. In a matter of a few hassle-free hours, the limo had pulled through the wrought iron gate marked JMB in front of Bauer's estate.

Herr Bauer insisted she come and sent his plane. He had explained to Emy that he'd recently returned from a trip abroad and wanted to make amends to her for their disagreement.

It was not a good time for Emy as Hanna and Ceci were scheduled to depart on Sunday morning. Emy had given Ceci permission to accompany her sister to the university. With Ceci's school on break for another week, she would have time to hang out with her sister, and Emy wanted Ceci to become less dependent on her. Bauer had offered to fly them all in his private jet; the girls could get off at Kraków while Emy went on to Berlin. But Emy had told him the girls preferred to take the train, and it wouldn't be necessary to transport them.

When the car pulled into the circular drive, it surprised Emy that Herr Bauer stood at the front door instead of his assistant Kenny. *He really must be repentant for his words the other day.*

"Emmanuelle, I am so glad you could come, my dear," he said as he opened her door and offered his hand. "I hope my staff made your trip comfortable."

"Thank you for the convenient travel arrangements," she said. "You spoiled me."

"Please forgive me, Emmanuelle, for my anger and impatience in your office the other day. And thank you for the opportunity to start afresh."

As Herr Bauer escorted her up the steps and through the ten-foot doors of the mansion, she studied him. He seemed exceptionally jovial as well as repentant. *Maybe I was too judgmental.* After all, by supporting BioGenics, he had allowed her to surpass her own dreams.

"Welcome to my humble abode," he said, his baritone voice bouncing off the marble foyer.

Humble was an understatement. Bauer's abode had the feel of a museum, with priceless sculptures and vases arranged on antique tables and Renaissance paintings and beautiful tapestries hanging on the walls.

Kenny, wearing pink skinny jeans and a white cardigan, entered from a side room and smiled.

"May I take your jacket, Dr. Christianson?"

Emy unwound her scarf, removed her coat, and handed the bundle to him. "Thank you." She fought the urge to curtsy as if they'd welcomed her to Buckingham Palace.

"Kenny, we will be in the library. Could you please bring some tea?" Bauer asked, then led her to an adjacent room.

Shelves of books filled the panel-lined study, and at first glance, many appeared to be first editions. Between bookshelves, large paintings hung in gold frames. An enormous desk filled one side of the room. Bauer steered Emy to the other side and invited her to join him in plush leather chairs in front of a blazing fireplace.

Emy accepted his invitation, sat, and held her hands out to the heat emanating from the fire. "How wonderful, Herr Bauer. My parents' home also had a real fireplace, and I confess, this makes me homesick."

"*Meine Nichte*, it is so lovely to have you in my home." He reached for a pipe on the table between them and held it up to her. "I hope you don't mind an old man's nasty habit."

"Not at all. My father used to smoke."

She pondered her paternity as Bauer meticulously scraped the bowl, filled it with tobacco, and lit it with a wooden match. With the recent news of her adoption and extended family, she hadn't processed the information enough to figure out how to refer to her people. *Should I call the father who raised me, my adopted father?* The issue grew all too confusing to deal with right now.

Her uncle inhaled through the pipe and blew a cloud of smoke toward the fire. Right away, the nutty aroma of the burning tobacco relaxed her. She'd pleaded with her father to quit for years, yet his pipe smoke had grounded her childhood, and deep down, she was glad he'd never stopped.

Kenny supported a tray of elegant cups and a silver tea set as he glided across the room. He placed the tray between them and started to pour, but her uncle waved him off. "Thank you, Kenny," he said.

Bauer poured tea into both cups. Emy accepted his offer of a splash of cream and a lump of sugar.

They sipped the brew in silence. Her uncle leaned back at ease and seemed more relaxed than she'd ever seen him. She allowed herself to settle into the chair.

She studied him contemplating the flames, alternating between a sip of tea and a puff on his pipe—occasionally nodding as if coming to a decision. Emy wondered if she imagined his eyes misting over, but when he wiped a tear, she understood it touched something deeper, something that claimed his heart.

He took an exceptionally long drag from his pipe, blew out the smoke, and finally spoke. "You will have to forgive an old man's musings and my mistakes," he said, looking at her.

In the handful of encounters she'd had with Bauer, she sensed a personal connection for the first time. She felt no fear or insecurity, or any of the vagueness of business dealings, only compassion, perhaps even affection.

"Herr Bauer, please, I am sorry as well. I spoke too hastily in my response and judgment—"

He waved off her apology and said, "Let us figure all that out on another occasion. Today, I have something more important to talk with you about." He smiled at her, then his gaze went back to the fire. "I suppose everyone has regrets," he started again. "Mine is that I do not have children. I never wanted any, but now I realize children are a person's legacy. Emmanuelle, I understand the news of our connection, our shared heritage, is a shock. Perhaps keeping it from you was another misstep I've taken."

Emy tried to interject, but he cut her off and continued.

"You, Emmanuelle, are *meine Familie*. You and the girls. I regret I have kept you at arm's length."

Bauer put his pipe back in the stand and turned to her. He reached for her hand.

"*Gott*, only He knows the length of our days, and I'm sure mine are numbered. My wealth is nothing unless I pass it on to my family."

He released her hand and took a sip of his tea.

"I understand the revelation of your relationship to Mengele has shaken you. He, like so many of us, had shortcomings, but in time I hope you will see the glimmers of his brilliance. After all, you carry his genius for science and medicine. You will never have to accept everything about him, but you are a product of his genetic makeup. Now, I offer you a greater stake in your inheritance. Wealth brings power, and with that power, think of the good you can do for the world."

Emy was at a loss for words. *Mein Gott is right. Is this man telling me he wants to pass his wealth on to us?* She leaned back in her chair. This was not a simple matter of money, but unimaginable wealth rooted in history.

"I brought something for you, Uncle," Emy said and dug into her pocket. Before she left home, she'd made a split-second decision. Now, she held her closed fist toward her uncle. When he reached out, she dropped the small object into his palm.

He looked confused and held it to his eyes to examine it. When he saw the initials, a huge smile crossed his face. "*Mein Gott*, is this what I think it is?"

CHAPTER 25

THE VAULT

After Emmanuelle left, Bauer placed his hand on the palm reader and his eye to the retinal scanner next to his desk. A series of mechanical sounds emanated from behind a panel of books. The shelves hinged open and revealed an antique, carbon-black steel vault. He loved the look and feel of it, with a turnstile combination lock and handwheel. Bauer spun the dial in one direction, then the other and back again, until he heard a subtle click in the mechanism. Then he turned the handwheel and pulled the heavy steel door open. The comforting smell of antiquities hit his nostrils. He turned on the lights and stepped into the large room…his safe place, his sanctuary. Four times larger than his office, this room held most of his beloved treasures, all preserved in a carefully controlled environment. He allowed no one else in this room, not even Kenny.

After his death, he planned to share the trove with the world. His estate would build a grand museum in Berlin and display works and historical documents by some of the greatest minds including da Vinci, Michelangelo, Darwin, Galton, Himmler, Hitler, and Mengele—his brilliant father.

Since many established museums refused to carry the works, he would build his own. *My museum will be a magnificent edifice.*

Bauer wasn't sure the world would accept his vision and that of The Fifteen. He chuckled. *The imbeciles may not grasp our genius.* But when his estate built the museum and immaculately displayed his collection, the true story would be told.

He wondered whether Emmanuelle understood his dream. He hoped he could manipulate and entice her by the vastness of what she would inherit. *Would she truly ever comprehend my desire to change the world for the better?* Now was the time. He'd discussed with Emmanuelle the difference between somatic-cell and germ-line gene therapies. The first sought to eliminate or reduce genetic flaws once they were detected, and the second corrected genetic defects before life formed—transforming one generation to the next, which permanently affected society as a whole.

Well-read on the subject, Bauer understood other geneticists, who denounced the use of gene therapy for enhancement, influenced Emy—so did her freethinking husband. They drew the line between treatment and augmentation of the species, between curing the disease and improving the person or race. Bauer thought the scientists were foolish. Why limit the technology to one sick individual when you could affect humankind en masse? *Doesn't that make more sense? A much wiser use of the world's resources.* Making human beings smarter, stronger, and healthier—isn't that the goal of all parents who take their children to the doctor, enroll them in the best schools they can afford, and drag them to weekly violin lessons? *Gene therapy is no different.*

Bauer walked through his inner sanctum, lightly touching his treasures. He paused at a large desk to admire the newly acquired books and documents written by his father. He wished he could have shared them with Emmanuelle, but she was not ready. *One day soon.* She had yet to understand genuine power. It was not wealth per se. Money, along with other institutions like banking, military, social systems, and government, were mere tools for obtaining power. He didn't understand why people gave up their power so readily. *They are so naïve.* He reached into his vest pocket, took out his father's cufflink, kissed it, and placed it on Mengele's stack of journals. *What a treasure.*

Bauer hoped Emmanuelle would grasp what was at stake—this influence, this authority, and dominion; what some have called immoral. It's not that at all…*power*, that's greatness and supreme enlightenment.

He paced slowly and contemplatively along one wall. How he longed to share his artifacts with the masses. Relics and plunder that the Third Reich confiscated and were never recovered by the Art Looting Investigation Unit.

Bauer reached and straightened Renoir's painting, *Tête de jeune fille.* He smiled, knowing that this and Pissarro's *Rue de village* appeared on Interpol's twelve most wanted list. More pieces from Polish masters adorned his walls, including Raphael's *Portrait of a Young Man* and Gierymski's *Jewess with Oranges.* The experts estimated Raphael's painting to be worth in excess of one hundred million euros.

Bauer admired all the art on the walls of the vault. There was no contemporary artist represented. The *Führer* made sure of that after the Vienna Academy of Fine Arts denied his admission. Hitler later denounced all modern art as degenerate.

One painting rumored to be a favorite of his father's, as well as Bauer's, hung next to the Jewess. Perhaps his father adored it after the prisoners at Auschwitz gave him the nickname the

"Angel of Death." A winged demon hung over two naked men locked in mortal combat in the eight-by-ten-foot painting. One man bit the neck of the other, who had swindled the man's inheritance. It symbolized the struggle between good and evil, the battle for humanity—the crusade Bauer fought now.

His heart thumped hard as it skipped two beats, making his chest hurt and unbalancing his equilibrium. He pressed his fingertips into his sternum and steadied himself with the other hand against the wall. This irregular heartbeat had become more frequent, but it worsened whenever he thought of his father. He'd never met him, but attempting to live up to an imaginary standard that his brain manufactured, drove him forward. He forced down the painful emotion, acknowledging that his own father would have selected him for the gas chamber because of his sexual orientation. Justification between this realization and the love for his father proved too much for his heart and was something he'd have to push away from his consciousness.

As his heart and mind settled, he realized that his hand pressed against framed, handwritten speeches by his grandfather, Heinrich Himmler. Bauer's mother, Gudrun, had passed down the letters which hung next to the artwork.

Bauer paused at a speech titled: Poznań, 4 October 1943 and read portions of it:

> "One basic principle must be the absolute rule
> for the SS men: We must be honest, decent,
> loyal, and comradely to members of our own
> blood and to nobody else. What happens to a
> Russian, to a Czech, does not interest me in the

slightest. What other nations can offer in the way of good blood of our type, we will take, if necessary, by kidnapping their children and raising them here with us. Whether nations live in prosperity or starve to death interests me only so far as we need them as slaves for our culture; otherwise, it is of no interest to me. Whether 10,000 Russian females fall down from exhaustion while digging an anti-tank ditch interests me only insofar as the anti-tank ditch for Germany is finished."

"I am now referring to the evacuation of the Jews, the extermination of the Jewish people. It's one of those things that is easily said: 'The Jewish people are being exterminated,' says every party member, 'this is very obvious, it's in our program, elimination of the Jews, extermination, we're doing it, hah, a small matter.' And then they turn up, the upstanding 80 million Germans, and each one has his decent Jew. They say the others are all swine, but this particular one is a splendid Jew. But none has observed it, endured it. Most of you here know what it means when 100 corpses lie next to each other, when there are 500 or when there are 1,000. To have endured this and at the same time to have remained a decent person—with exceptions due to human weaknesses—has made us tough and is a glorious chapter that has not and will not be spoken of. Because we know how difficult it would be for us if we still had Jews as secret saboteurs, agitators and rabble-rousers in every city, what with the bombings, with the burden and with the hardships of the war. If the Jews were still part of the German nation, we would most likely arrive now at the state we were at in 1916 and 17."

Bauer nodded. He disagreed with his grandfather's hatred of the Jews, but understood these words were as valid today as in the Nazis' reign concerning the delinquents of the world.

His mother had also given him the original of his grandfather's speech to the SS Gruppenführer. Bauer had burned it in the fire after he read his grandfather's speech, where he described drowning homosexuals in a swamp, but the hateful words were seared into his mind. *"That wasn't a punishment, but simply the extinguishment of abnormal life. It had to be disposed of, just as we pull out weeds, throw them on a heap, and burn them."*

Bauer's heart ached and skipped another beat. His father and grandfather would have never understood his lifestyle.

He sighed and turned to admire the rest of his secret room. Everything in it's place. The gold bars stacked in the pyramid against the far wall. The shelves full of silver tea settings, wooden boxes of silverware, and cases stacked three-deep of jewelry and loose stones. He had visited Auschwitz and saw the display of shoes—thousands upon thousands. But here lay the real treasures of that time. Acknowledging this reality fueled his resolve and covered his shame.

Before he turned off the lights, he stopped at the pinnacle of his collection, the one that would probably horrify the world. This particular artwork contained the collective agony of the Jews, Poles, and Gypsies of Auschwitz. Bauer ran his fingers across the silky fibers of this unique tapestry, its muted colors of browns, blonds, and streaks of red did not please the eye. *How ugly it is.* He almost shivered. *Yet how valuable.* The tapestry made with human hair.

* * *

Nick and Maggie sat on the bed in their hotel room. Maggie hadn't bled or showed other signs of complications from the biopsy. Nick stirred with cabin fever, but Maggie didn't mind the prescription for three days of bed rest. Anxious to move, Nick had left the room to wander through the weapons museum again, and he'd purchased a plastic replica of a crossbow. Back in the room, he became accomplished at sticking the suction darts to the mirror across from the bed, much to Maggie's annoyance.

"Stop it, or I will take that toy away from you," she scolded half-heartedly.

"You better get used to this if the baby is a boy."

"I pray for good results tomorrow, so we can quit worrying," Maggie said, ignoring his comment.

"Amen to that," Nick said and looked at his watch. "We told Buck and Katy that we'd call them and keep them up to date. You feel like doing that now?"

"Sure."

Nick grabbed his cell phone, dialed the international code and Buck's number, and placed it on speakerphone.

Buck answered after the first ring. "Hey, you knucklehead.

Weren't you going to call me right away to let me know how you both are doing? We've been worried sick."

"Well, hello to you," Nick rebutted. His best friend was the only person in the world who could talk to him like that, condescending and loving at the same time.

"We went to the late service at church and just got home," Buck said. "The whole congregation is praying for you guys."

"Hey, Nick and Maggie." Katy got on the phone call.

"Oh good, I'm glad your better, nicer half is there with you," Nick teased.

Buck hooted his infectious laugh. "You have no idea."

Katy got right to the point. "How are you guys?" she asked and added, "Hi Maggie."

"Well, besides the insecurity and fear, we're falling in love with Poland. The people here have been wonderful," Maggie said. "Thanks so much for your prayers. You don't know how much that means to us. It's been pretty scary."

"I wish we were there with you," Katy said. "So how was the doctor? What did she say?"

Nick looked in Maggie's teary eyes and answered for her. "Dr. Christianson has been good. She seems very smart and competent—her company and genetics program are quite impressive. She took a biopsy of the placenta three days ago, and we are supposed to find out tomorrow about our little one." Nick looked at Maggie and shrugged to see if he should elaborate. She nodded. "So you guys know how to pray..." he hesitated. "Maggie is having symptoms of Huntington's. Maybe it's all the stress, but she has some early neurological deficits in her legs."

There was a long pause, finally broken by Maggie. "I don't understand any of this," her voice cracked. "I'm trying not to ask the *why* question, but…" she gathered her thoughts. "I know that God is good, and He is sovereign, but…"

Nick put his arm around her.

"I'm afraid we're both struggling," Nick said. "Why us? Why now? Where is God in all this?" Nick asked all of Maggie's questions. "We've seen miracles, but we've also seen plenty of times when the answer doesn't come."

Maggie found her voice again. "On top of it all, we are facing some impossible decisions. It seems like the doctor is suggesting an abortion if the baby is positive, but I could never…"

Nick held her close. "Dr. Christianson suggests that we treat Maggie right away before the symptoms get any worse."

"How do they do that?" Katy asked.

"Well, it's crazy, but they have the science to cut the bad spot from her DNA," Nick said.

"The problem is, no one can tell us what that does to me long term, and the worst part is no one can tell us what that does to the baby," Maggie added.

There was another long pause. Nick understood this was not a lack of empathy from their friends, but after enduring their own trauma when Buck lost his legs and almost his life, simple pat answers weren't enough. Nick knew they were praying. Both Buck and Katy had wise and discerning hearts, but human wisdom wouldn't suffice right now.

* * *

When Emy unlocked the front door to her home, the hair on the back of her neck stood up. Something was wrong. She'd expected a quiet house with the girls off to Kraków, but she'd noticed Keith's car in the driveway and thought he'd be watching soccer or playing his guitar. Keith lived as a night owl; after a gig and too restless to sleep, he always stayed up late. But she heard nothing. The house stood quiet and dark.

She turned on the lights, went into the kitchen, set her car keys on the counter, and took off her jacket.

She'd left her laptop on the breakfast bar. The apple icon on the front throbbed on and off. *That's weird. I thought I had shut it down.* She'd pulled out the computer to buy tickets for the girls that morning. *Probably a little distracted.* She flipped open the top, and her sign-in page appeared as usual. No one knew her password for the laptop since it connected to BioGenics's network. She was the only person allowed remote access.

Emy entered her security code, and the computer opened to her desktop, so she could shut it down. She paused and then opened the browser. She shrugged when she saw it was still on the train schedule page. She powered it off and closed the lid when she heard a loud thump from upstairs.

"Keith?" she yelled.

She walked halfway up the stairs and called out to him again.

No answer.

Poland became one of the few countries in Europe where gun ownership had increased. Keith tried to persuade her to buy a handgun for home security, but she'd refused. She didn't know why, but tonight, she wished she carried a weapon as she walked up the stairs.

"Keith?" she yelled again.

She heard a muffled moan coming from their bedroom.

She tiptoed across the landing and cracked open the door. It was pitch black. She stood still to allow time for her eyes to adjust to the dark. Her heart sank in her chest when she perceived the scent of another woman's perfume and the sub-tle, musky odor of lovemaking.

When Emy heard another moan, she fumed with anger.

She flung open the door and flicked on the lights, expecting to find Keith and his lover.

The bedsheets were rumpled, the blankets kicked off, and a used condom discarded on the floor. Keith lay naked and alone on the floor between the bed and the bathroom, rubbing his temples.

Emy was a tangle of rage and confusion. She entered the bathroom, flicked on the lights, and ruffled the shower curtain. No one. She returned to the bedroom where Keith had propped himself up on his elbows, and his mouth hung open.

"Where is she?" Emy yelled, her hands on her hips, ready for battle. "Where is the little slut?" She bent over him. "What have you done?"

She stared at his ashen face that registered no emotion as his hands reached for a blanket. She stood up straight, shook her head, and said, "Keith, you stupid, stupid man."

CHAPTER 26

EXPERIMENTATION

Emy had hardly slept, fighting hopelessness. She came into work at noon on Monday, and only then, managed to put on a pair of light-blue scrubs and pull her brunette hair into a ponytail. The research arm of BioGenics remained closed until Wednesday, so it didn't matter. Emy had scheduled to see the Harts at two. By then, Izzi would have finished all the DNA sequencing on Maggie.

Emy had a difficult time concentrating on the report on her desk. The words and numbers jumbled together in a crazy rhythm of her brain that flashed the image of Keith on the floor in a post-coitus stupor. Inviting his girlfriend into their home, to their bedroom, and to their bed was the last straw. He hadn't even tried to make excuses or justify his behavior—just that the woman had suggested taking ecstasy together at the bar. He said he'd passed out and only remembered waking up with Emy screaming at him.

She could not tolerate his wandering, even if it meant the girls would have to deal with a broken home. *It's already broken.* She loved Keith, the only reason she'd put up with his infidelity, but she couldn't cope with the heartbreak of his latest affair, especially with everything that happened at work. She'd file for divorce. *Won't he be disappointed if I take Herr Bauer's generous offer?* Maybe they'd make peace in the end.

Emy shook her head, trying to make the image disappear. Rage rumbled in her gut again, threatening to regurgitate. She thought she'd lose control like she'd done last night. It was a good thing she'd stopped Keith from buying a gun. If she'd had a gun, he'd be dead. *Now, at least he's gone.* Last night she had dragged him out of the house by his hair and hoped the naked bastard froze to death. More than likely, he'd gone to the Chinese girl. *Good riddance.*

She hated the thoughts urging her to run full steam through the large picture window in her office. But with only four floors to fall, she'd survive, breaking her legs or back. With suicide on her mind, Emy looked around the office. The only thing that resembled a weapon sat in the corner cabinet, a crossbow, a gift from Herr Bauer. He loved to send her antiquities of various shapes and sizes. She stored most of them in the large glass-paneled curio—German Hummel figurines, china pieces, and vases. Occasionally something odd, like the Han Dynasty crossbow worth sixty thousand pounds he'd sent her a year ago. She'd meant to donate the weapon to the museum in the Town Square. She had no idea if the thing worked and decided it was probably not the ideal choice to off oneself. *Come on, I need to pull myself together.*

Her attorney wouldn't be back in his office until later in the week. As soon as he returned, she'd file for divorce—if she could survive the psychological trauma of waiting. In the divorce, Keith would get half of their savings, but if she accepted Herr Bauer's offer, that money would look like a pittance.

Bauer's proposal hadn't left her frontal cortex—the only thought that kept her sane at the moment. She'd fantasized about the kind of wealth the inheritance implied. She'd jet around the world and pick up trinkets for herself and her daughters. *The fortune would change the lives of the girls.*

The girls. The consequences of infidelity and divorce would change their lives as well. When Ceci returned home next week, she'd notice first thing that her father had moved out. Emy would make Keith explain it to them. She'd make sure they understood he'd screwed up. *It's no wonder rage and suicide fight for room in my mind.*

She forced them away and tried to concentrate on the report. Over the weekend, Izzi had correlated the latest, long-term follow-up on the Huntington's patients. What had started with excellent results dissolved into several failures. Perhaps in the initial clinical trials, they hadn't introduced enough of the CRISPR/Cas9 into the patients' cells. With only three-years post-procedure in the initial ten patients, three had experienced a return of their symptoms, four had developed clinical manifestations of the disease, and one had died. *Not exactly stellar results.* The long list of strange side effects: personality changes, neuralgias in various locations, GI complaints, and many more concerned Emy. Huntingtin, as a protein, had many unknown functions throughout the body. The researchers hadn't yet discovered what the CRISPR changes actually did to the rest of the systems, and the reason that new drugs, procedures, and gene therapy needed clinical studies.

The cystic fibrosis patient trials revealed even worse results. But with each set of new patients, they continued to make strides. With the adjustments from the initial protocols, their latest outcomes showed improvement. But most new patients were less than a year out, with only a few less than two. Indeed, if Mrs. Hart chose treatment, her case became a reportable event that would fascinate geneticists around the world. It would be the first CRISPR treatment of a pregnant woman.

"There is always a cost to medical advances," Bauer's mantra echoed again. It remained true. Whether surgeons tried to mend a malfunctioning heart or broken bones, the early treatments often produced disastrous results. Now, those procedures are successful and routine—often with the patient released from the hospital the next day.

Bauer proclaimed that the Nazi doctors understood the necessity for experimentation. He'd told her that the standard of care to treat open fractures came from the Germans who broke prisoners' legs and infected them with horse dung, only to treat those wounds with sulfa drugs. The Nazis discovered and perfected colposcopy, the microscopic examination of the cervix, now used routinely to look for cancer in women. Using the prisoners, the Nazis developed treatments for hypo-thermia, high-altitude sickness, and perfected reproductive sterilization. Their methods were horrendous, but their experiments advanced medicine. Bauer wanted Emy to understand the importance of her work.

"I am no different than my grandfather," she said and looked at the report. "Perhaps the apple doesn't fall far from the tree," as her father often said.

Emy turned a page of the report. If not for Bauer's recent proposal, she wondered if she could resist the urge to end it all. These poor results destroyed companies, but his offer would allow her the opportunity to direct her own destiny and con-tinue her work. She looked at his offer as strictly a business deal. "That's how a good Jew would think of it," she said. She realized that he would demand certain advancements, but she would control the implementations of those. She would dip the company's toes into areas of enhancement without compromising her aim of treating diseases.

Izzi walked into her office without a knock and interrupted her thoughts.

"Hey, Dr. C. Happy New Year, almost."

Emy sighed with exasperation, stretched her neck side to side, and started to scold her for bursting through the door. Instead, she found some civility and inspected the girl who had gone back to bleached blond. "Izzi...yes..." she said. "*Szczęśliwego Nowego Roku* to you, too. You need something?"

"I have Mrs. Hart's genome finished. I should have the fetus's done by the time they get here."

"Okay, Izzi. Thanks for doing that." She held up the report she'd just read. "And thanks for this. I think."

"Yeah." Izzi nodded. "It's a bit of a disappointment but think of the condition of those patients without treatment. All of them might have croaked by now."

Emy nodded. "Some optimism is good to hear."

"You okay?" Izzi asked. "You sound kind of worried or something."

Emy pushed back in her chair and blew out a long exhale, not sure on how much to confide.

"Izzi, what do you think of the work we're doing?"

Izzi looked confused, but her optimism returned. "Dr. C... it's awesome. No one else in the world can do the shit we do. Don't get discouraged by one bad report. Look at the advances we've made. Uh, you've made."

Emy nodded. "You don't think we're like the Nazi doctors?"

Izzi crossed her arms. "Dude, those guys were sick. They based half their crap on torturing people. Everything you do here, Dr. C, is based on medical evidence. There's not even a comparison."

"Still, it seems like we experiment on people."

"Isn't that science…one big test? Actually, that's life."

"I suppose." Emy fought back tears. If her life was an experiment, it'd blown up in her face.

"Dr. C?"

"You'll be happy to hear that I kicked my husband out last night. He brought that girl to the house yesterday while I was gone."

"Screwed her in your own bed?" Izzi said. "That a-hole."

The images reeled through Emy's mind, and once again, her rage surged. Opening her mouth to speak would make her sick. All she could do was nod.

* * *

The graduate student with the wild hair, this time dyed platinum, met Maggie and Nick at the entrance, escorted them to Dr. Christianson's office, and offered them water. Maggie sat quietly praying, while Nick wandered around the doctor's office. Besides the colorful wall with the pictograph of the genome, diplomas and awards crowded another section. Framed certificates of BioGenics's patents filled one whole wall. It reflected an extraordinary life's work. He peered into the lit cabinet that contained all sorts of collectibles, some looking quite expensive. *I guess when you charge a quarter of a million dollars for treatments, you can afford such luxuries.*

Dr. Christianson surprised Nick from behind when she walked into the room.

"Sorry to keep you waiting. I checked with Izzi. She should have the baby's DNA done shortly."

Nick followed the doctor to the sitting area and studied her for clues while she read through Maggie's chart. The doctor displayed telltale signs of call: scrubs, pale skin, quickly applied lipstick, and dark bags under her eyes. Her blue shirt highlighted her one aqua-colored eye.

Emy looked at Maggie. "You have any problems after the biopsy?"

"No, only with sleep. The worry is sapping my energy and attention. All I can do is fight it with prayer."

"I'm sure you have more questions," the doctor said.

"If we decide on the treatment, how soon could we start, and how long does it take?" Nick asked.

"Again, because you have these physical symptoms, Maggie, I would advise that we begin gene therapy as soon as possible. Now that we have your genome, we could design and manufacture your CRISPR/Cas 9. I'm confident we could start next week. The procedure is as simple as an IV. We infect you with the virus, and CRISPR does the rest."

"What are the possible side effects?" Nick asked.

"Dr. Hart, you recognize how medicine has changed." Emy reached into the folder and pulled out a three-page disclosure and consent form. "Our attorneys make us take the patient through all the risks. The risks are listed here. One possible complication is a reaction to the infusion. But this we have rarely seen. Occasionally, a person will experience flu-like achiness, as the immune system reacts to the viral load."

"How soon would we ascertain if it's working?" Nick asked. "What about follow-up?"

"Maggie already has some buildup of the abnormal huntingtin protein in her brain, so our goal is to stop any further deposition. Our hope is that her body will replace the aberrant with the normal protein. I cannot guarantee this, but that is the goal. Dr. Hart, you can monitor her symptoms from home as well as any of us. For our clinical protocol, I need you to return in six months unless there is a decrease in her neurological status."

Maggie cleared her throat. "I still have no idea how we can pay for this treatment."

"On Wednesday, when the rest of the staff is here, I will have you meet with our financial delegate. She can go over the different options with you." The doctor paused, looked down at the chart, and shook her head. "I wish there were a better way. I'm sorry, but you need this treatment, Maggie."

Izzi came through the door and handed Dr. Christianson a sheet of paper.

Nick again looked to Izzi for clues. With her masculine exterior, the assistant was difficult to read. But when the doctor read the note and flinched, he knew the report brought bad news.

Maggie read the body language as well. She gasped and covered her mouth with her hand.

"This is not good news," Emy said. "I'm sorry." She handed the report over to Nick. "Your baby has seventy-four CAG repeats."

CHAPTER 27

GRIEF

Maggie rested her head on Nick's bare chest that was wet from tears. As soon as they'd returned to their hotel room from the appointment with Dr. Christianson, they'd undressed and crawled under the covers to grieve. They'd cried buckets of tears now that they knew their baby tested positive for Huntington's. With the number of repeats and without treatment, their child would develop the disease early in childhood and most likely succumb to its effects before puberty.

The baby had a fifty-fifty chance, and the dice hadn't rolled in their favor. Nick alternated between the most profound grief and the fiercest rage. Three months after marrying Maggie and lifted to the highest high, this news felt like falling off Mount Everest. The pain was unbearable.

How could God do this to them? Didn't He know? Didn't He care? Had their prayers fallen on deaf ears? Nick wanted to smash things, rage against everything and everyone in his way. If Maggie wasn't pressed against him, his emotions would have overtaken him. How could something so beautiful like having a child turn so dark—fear, pain, anger. Nick tried to lean on lessons from the past—where God had provided, heard their cries, and healed. But the darkness threatened to swallow him and lock him in a bottomless pit of despair.

He shifted under Maggie's weight. Her body had gone limp, both of them dehydrated from spilling a well of tears. Watching her, his compassion returned, and he stroked her face at her hairline, slowly drawing circles and pushing back her hair.

"I'm so sorry, Maggie." He'd repeated over and over.

Maggie rolled to her back, wiped her face on the sheet, and covered her body. "It's my stupid genes. I'm the one that should be sorry."

Nick turned on his side, faced her, and put his hand over her baby bump. It was no one's fault.

He leaned in and kissed her forehead. Then he pulled the sheet back, laid his head on her abdomen, and talked to their baby. "Hey, little one. We are so sorry to give you such a rough start." The few tears that remained rolled onto Maggie's belly. "We're going to make this right. We are going to do everything to fight for you. Don't give up on your ol' Mommy and Daddy."

Maggie's body quaked.

"I don't know what we should do," she cried.

Nick laid back on his side to look into her eyes.

"We fight, Maggie," he said. "We fight. I have no frickin' idea why we've been dealt this hand. But we're not going to give up and do nothing."

"Do I sentence my child to a horrific disease...to an awful life?" She wept. "Nick, I can't do what the doctor recommended."

After Dr. Christianson broke the news, Nick hardly remembered much after that, except she suggested they abort the baby. That's when Maggie stormed out of the building.

In medical school, Nick had seen an intrauterine video of an abortion. The images flashed through his mind—the baby crushed with an instrument and then sucked out, bit by bit. "No, we're not going to do that," Nick said with anger. "That's off the table."

"So, now what?" Maggie asked. "I think I just want to go home. All I can hear when I pray is, 'Do you trust me?'"

Nick sat up. "Maggie, we can't stick our heads in the sand. I understand your faith is different than mine...stronger, but *you* need treatment. Dr. Christianson told us that if we decide against terminating the pregnancy, she would talk with us more on Wednesday about doing CRISPR on both you and the baby."

"I don't think that humans should mess with DNA. It's the way God knitted me together."

"You always say, 'God doesn't give what He doesn't have.' If that's the case, He didn't give you or our baby Huntington's. Who knows what evil this came from, but should the person with diabetes go untreated because somehow that's God's will or design for them?" Nick had made up his mind and spoke with authority. "Do we withhold corrective surgery on a child with a clubfoot because of how it was born?"

Tears welled up in Maggie's eyes, and more guilt and anger rose in Nick's chest. "I'm sorry, Maggie. I didn't mean to—"

"I'm not certain that they've figured it all out yet. Dr. Christianson seems confident, but I continue to get a check in my spirit."

"Well, it's the best choice we have right now. You have symptoms, and it seems to me that the sooner we treat you, the better. It might make a difference for the baby. We have to tell Dr. Christianson our decision when we see her next."

"Nick, I'm sorry. But I don't think I want to do it. I'll take my chances."

Nick pushed himself out of bed and paced back and forth, then reached for his pants.

"What are you doing?" Maggie asked.

"Maggie, I'm not going to stand by and do nothing and watch you get sicker and sicker and then watch our baby do the same. You heard the doctor—simply carrying this baby to full term without treatment puts you at significant risk. It could totally speed up the disease process for you." Nick stared Maggie in the eyes. "This pregnancy could kill you."

He pulled on his shirt and buttoned it.

"I don't know what you're going to do," he said, "but I'm going downstairs to get a drink."

He opened the door and slammed it behind him. "Happy New Year."

* * *

On the way to the bar, Nick dialed Buck and Katy's number for the third time. He looked at his watch, three in the afternoon in Memphis. They knew about the scheduled appointment with the clinic and wanted to hear the results right away. No answer and another disappointment for the day. *I really need a drink.*

With three bars in the Brovaria, Nick headed to the basement club. Like his heart and mood, it was dark and lined with brick. Revelers packed the place for New Year's Eve, but he found an empty stool at the far end of the bar and sat down, nodding to a group of young people. A piano player in the opposite corner of the room chorded and crooned out a Billy Joel song in mostly adequate English.

Nick ordered a gin and tonic from the bartender with a pretty face and round bottom. He pulled some *Zlotys* out of his pocket and threw the money on the bar. He had enough for a few drinks.

The bartender placed his cocktail on a coaster in front of him, nodded, and smiled. Nick took a long drink and looked over his shoulder. The New Year's partygoers celebrated with joyous exuberance.

He finished the drink and waved for another. A year and a half ago, this was his life. Surgical trauma burnout had driven him to find comfort in the bottle and one-night stands. That was before he'd responded to the massive earthquake in Turkey that shook him out of his misery and into the arms of Maggie. Now, another seismic event threatened to upend his life. Was God punishing him for the miserable life choices of his past? *I thought with Maggie's help, I had resolved that and gotten beyond it.*

The bartender made him another drink and placed it in front of him. "How's your night?" she shouted over the crowd.

"Great," he said sarcastically.

"You American?"

Nick nodded. "Are we always that obvious?"

She shrugged. "Just a guess. I've never seen your handsome face in here before." She laughed.

Man, how the old lesser comforts come crashing back on me at the slightest opportunity. He needed relief, and the booze was a thousand-milligram tablet. He tossed back the second drink and held out his glass for a third.

The bartender looked beyond him, and Nick sensed a presence. He turned to see Dr. Christianson's assistant behind him.

"Hey, Dr. Hart. I thought that might be you." She looked at his drink. "I'm sure sorry for the results today. It really sucks the big one."

The effects of the alcohol had already softened his brain, and he frantically tried to remember the woman's name. "Hi… uh…"

"Izzi," she said and stuck out her hand. "No worries. You've got a lot on your mind."

Nick looked at her hand, up her tattooed arm to her plaid shirt, and then to a baseball cap turned backward over her bleached hair. She shook his hand firmly like a man.

"Sorry about your little guy," she said. "If I could have changed the results, I would have." She took a swig from her beer bottle.

Nick stared at her. "Little…guy?"

Izzi looked at the floor, and her cheeks flushed. "Uh…I didn't mean—" She took another swig from the bottle. "You guys didn't talk about that?"

Nick fought back tears. *A boy. We're having a son.*

"Please don't tell Dr. C on me. I'd get in a butt load of trouble."

Nick smiled and nodded. "I needed some good news about now."

"What are you and the missus gonna do?"

Nick slumped his shoulders and shook his head. "I don't know. I think we should go for the treatment, but Maggie's not so sure. What would you do?"

Izzi looked down again. "It's a hard decision, but what other choice do you have? I guess I'd go for it. I'd like a little upgrade on this." She spread her tattooed muscular arms and laughed.

"Can we make sure the baby gets his mother's good looks?"

"Someday soon, that will be a reality," she said seriously. "Dr. C is the best. Before long, we'll all be smarter and better looking."

"Yeah, those who can afford it," Nick quipped. He wasn't sure she heard him as she looked over the crowd, distracted. "You here to celebrate New Year's Eve?" he asked.

Something had captured her attention from across the room, and the muscles in her neck tightened.

"Yeah, something like that." Izzi pointed to a table with four girls in similar garb, smoking heavily. "My mates and I are here on a little mission." She hesitated and looked back at Nick. "You want to hear something really effed up? See the piano player over there?"

Nick stood to look over the crowd and saw the man with the long black hair. He sang Elton John's "Your Song" to an attractive Asian woman in a skimpy pink dress who sat on the bench beside him.

"That's Dr. C's no-good cheating husband. Got himself a girlfriend." She patted her bicep. "Gonna make the skank understand she's not welcome."

Nick wasn't sure what to think—about the girl, Dr. Christianson, the husband, and mostly about the less than enthusiastic endorsement of the treatment.

Izzi said something he couldn't hear and then asked, "You two staying here?"

"Yeah," he said and stood up. "You all be careful," he nodded to her friends. "I better get back to Maggie."

CHAPTER 28

SEARCH

Emy had celebrated the New Year with a sleeping pill. She welcomed the first decent night's rest in weeks. Feeling refreshed, she sat at the breakfast bar in her pajamas and looked at the screen of her laptop. The house was eerily quiet except for the coffee maker in the corner that spit and sputtered dark roast.

She'd pulled the letters from the envelope and reread them. How in the world would she find out any more information about her lost family? She typed *Bella Frankel* into the search bar and scrolled through the first three pages of hits, not expecting any answers. A few unrelated professors at US universities with the same name appeared.

Such a tragic life. She realized the only connection she'd had with her mother involved her recent suicidal ideation. This filled her heart with sadness.

Why Papa hadn't shared these things before his deathbed remained a mystery to her. He had to have read the letters, but maybe it was too sorrowful for him to discuss. She longed to find out more. He had such a kind and wise heart, and before his death, he could have given her astute advice or answered some of her questions. Instead, she drifted in a sea of chaos and confusion.

Her cell phone beside the computer buzzed. Ceci called.

"Hi, sweetheart. Happy New Year."

"Hey, Mom. To you as well," Ceci said.

"I'm so glad to hear from you. I've been a little worried about you and your New Year's Eve celebration," Emy said.

"A little?"

They both laughed. *God, how I miss the girls right now.*

"How's your time with Hanna at the university?"

"Mom, it's been so fun. Thank you for letting me come. It makes me excited for next year."

"Well, don't have too much fun. Did you drink last night?"

"Oh, Mom, you know I'm underage."

"And?"

"I only had one beer."

Emy read between the lines. "You meet any nice boys?"

"Only a whole dorm full." Ceci laughed hard.

"Please don't give your mother an ulcer."

"You sound tired, Mom. You okay?"

"Uh…just a little stressed out right now."

"Is it you and Dad? Hanna and I are worried about you."

"Well, I need to talk to you both. Your father has moved out."

With a long pause, Emy didn't know whether Ceci muted the phone to tell her sister, or if she was lost in thought.

"Hey, Mom." Hanna got on the phone. "Can you take the train down and spend a couple days with us?"

"I don't know—"

"Please, Mom."

Emy heard the phone click over to speaker. The girls ganged up on her to plead their case.

"We need some retail therapy," Ceci said. "You could use it too."

Emy smiled. At least she'd raised good kids. "I have some clients first thing in the morning, but maybe I could come for a couple days afterward."

The girls celebrated as she said her goodbyes. *God, how I miss them.*

Emy woke up the computer with a touch of the mousepad and typed *Yuri Frankel* into the search engine—another dead-end. She sighed, put her elbows on the counter, and rested her chin in her hands. How in the world would she find more information? *Maybe I'll ask Izzi to run my genome through the database.* Although that meant her DNA information became available for all to see, especially the Chinese. *I'll have to think that through.*

She had another thought and typed *finding relatives assigned to Auschwitz.* Surprisingly, a link came up: How to search for Auschwitz prisoners. She clicked on it. The website, Auschwitz.org, was the official link to the Auschwitz-Birkenau Memorial and Museum. The search bar for prisoners' names appeared disabled. A message invited searchers to visit the camp in person.

Emy's phone buzzed, and she answered without looking at the caller ID. She hoped the girls were calling again.

"*Frohes Neues Jahr, meine Nichte.*"

"Happy New Year to you, Herr Bauer." She tried to sound upbeat.

"Emmanuelle, I wanted to follow up with you on our conversation over the weekend. I hope you took some time to ponder it."

"Yes, Herr Bauer. Your offer has left me speechless. I'm not sure what else I can say but thank you."

"You could say yes, *meine Nichte.* It would make an old man happy and let me live the rest of my life in peace."

"Definitely, my head says yes, Herr Bauer. I have decided to go visit the girls in Kraków tomorrow. Before I give you my final word, do you mind if I talk about it with them? It affects the girls as much as it does me."

"Certainly, my dear. That is why I love your scientific mind—collect all the data first. I am confident they will agree."

Bauer paused, and Emy imagined him sucking on his pipe.

"Emmanuelle…are you ready to continue our discussion on the future of BioGenics? I wanted to do it in person, but I'm afraid I don't feel up to traveling today."

"Yes, Herr Bauer." Emy realized his generous offer had put her in an awkward position, forcing her to listen to what he had to say. She tried to not react as he continued.

"I understand this new and unknown frontier is daunting," he said. "How much of Francis Galton's life work have you read?"

"I'm afraid I only recognize him as the person who coined the word *eugenics*." She tried to say without judgment.

"I don't know if you saw the small plaque in my office. It is one of my favorites of Galton's sayings, and it makes me chuckle. 'Men who leave their mark on the world are very often those who, being gifted and full of nervous power, are at the same time haunted and driven by a dominant idea and are therefore within a measurable distance of insanity.'"

Emy nodded. *Probably true.*

"I'm afraid there are those who would say the same about me," Bauer said. "My ideas are a bit radical. But Galton advanced the world in so many ways: as an anthropologist, psychologist, statistician, explorer, and so much more. He produced over three-hundred and fifty papers and books. Did you realize he invented scientific meteorology and devised the first weather map?"

"I had no idea," Emy said.

"He notably advanced the field of genetics. Charles Darwin, his cousin, strongly influenced Galton. Darwin's book, *The Origin of Species*, led Galton to devote much of his life to the study of human populations. He gained much understanding of the role of heredity on human ability. Using twin studies, he concluded that the evidence favored nature rather than nurture. Hence, we are a product of our genes."

"Interesting," Emy said.

"Through his research and genius, Galton became one of the first to write about regression toward the mean. What he warned about over a hundred years ago is coming to haunt us. Our species regresses toward the mean."

Emy heard him take puffs from his pipe again.

"Emmanuelle, I know you comprehend this. It does not take a genius or a geneticist to see how the world is failing. The morals and abilities of the human race are in a rapid decline. If not stopped…" He left the statement unanswered.

Thinking of Keith, she had to agree.

"I suppose because I am German and especially because of our heritage, I am much more sympathetic to the opposition of eugenics. But you have to agree with me, we have a chance to reverse the decline of our species."

"Yes, I understand." She wanted to say more but stopped.

"Please look past the radical Nazi policies," Bauer said.

"That's difficult for me."

"I think one interesting concept of Galton's that may fascinate you is historiometry. As a research tool, he measured hereditary genius. He published his findings in his book, *English Men of Science: Their Nature and Nurture*. He recorded how an individual's interest in science was due less to the influence of the parents and environment and more to innate ability—a product of their genes. I don't recall that your adopted parents had much aptitude for science."

Emy recoiled as Bauer continued to connect her to his father, her grandfather. She understood the truth in theory, but changed the direction of the discussion. "The international community would not tolerate rapid advancements in the technology."

"I would not have it any other way, my dear. That is why I need you…to guide BioGenics and eventually direct my estate. We have to look to the long-term future. Who knows? Perhaps your talented daughters may one day lead this movement."

Emy had always thought her daughters would excel at pediatrics or geriatrics…something kinder and gentler than the cutthroat world of medical research and industry.

"Did you know the Queen knighted Galton for his scientific contributions?"

"I did not."

"Look, Emmanuelle, if we don't do it, someone else will. And perhaps someone with less experience and integrity. BioGenics has to lead the way."

"I suppose you're right," Emy acknowledged. "It will be done someday."

"Yes, and it should be you."

"Okay," she said and realized she said it with little conviction.

"Can I count on you to write up a report on BioGenics's ability to advance the human genome? I would like you to present your proposal at my next gathering of like-minded leaders."

"Who are these people?"

"You will meet them soon enough."

Emy decided to not push. She would take time over the next few days to formulate her thoughts.

Since Bauer remained her only true family, she decided to open up. "Herr Bauer," she said, falling back to her intimidation of the man. "I need to share something with you."

"Yes, certainly, *meine Nichte.*"

"I have asked my husband, Keith, to move out of the house. I am going to file for divorce."

The call went silent, and Emy worried she'd just blown everything.

Finally, Herr Bauer answered, "I am afraid that when I thought about passing my estate on to you, my only hesitation was Keith. He is a man who is easily manipulated and led astray. The divorce is probably best for you, my dear. He proves my point of the regression of society…perhaps why some enhancement of the human race is needed."

Emy couldn't decide whether to laugh or cry. "Thank you for understanding Herr Bauer."

"Please *meine Nichte*, call me *Onkel.*"

Emy hesitated. "Thank you. I will call you in a few days."

Emy started to hang up, but Bauer continued.

"Emmanuelle, as you write your proposal, I would ask that you consider something."

"Yes, Herr Bauer, what is it?"

"A few of my colleagues are quite interested in the area of athletic performance enhancement. I hesitate to bring this to your attention, but these are men with considerable resources. With the upcoming Olympics, they want to hear your thoughts on the topic."

"I will have to think about it," Emy said and wished she'd hung up. This was precisely the reason she loathed the topic of genetic enhancement. "Where are these investors from?"

"China," Bauer said. "But please don't let that frighten you off."

"I will give it some consideration, Herr Bauer. Thank you."

Emy said her goodbyes and hung up the phone.

She imagined a world in which athletes morphed into superhumans through her technology. The International Olympic Doping Committee would become obsolete. What if the games simply became a race to create superior genetic athletes?

She stared at the computer screen that still showed the Auschwitz page, then clicked the mouse on the "getting there" tab. The Nazi camps stood outside of Oświęcim. She pulled up google maps, looked for the city, and found the location on the train route to Kraków.

CHAPTER 29

CHINA

Bauer leaned back in his chair and smiled to himself as he hung up the phone from Emmanuelle. *How easily people are manipulated, whether it is by money or sex.* Like moths to a light, he'd found no one who resisted temptation. He had unbalanced the brilliant doctor; she'd become putty in his hands. He felt no remorse over the destruction of her family unit. Keith was an idiot and a weak link, and now properly removed from the picture. In Emy's vulnerable state, the offer to manage his estate was too much to pass up. Little did she understand that most of the estate would go to build and maintain his museum. Yes, she'd live in luxury, but not experience the power grab he believed she envisioned.

He picked up his phone from his desk and dialed an international number in Beijing.

"Hello, Mr. Wu. I hope you are well," Bauer said, intentionally leaving out a New Year's greeting. This year, the Chinese New Year fell the first week of February.

"Good morning, Herr Bauer. How did your discussion with the doctor go?"

"I believe it went well. But as discussed, we must prepare for the alternative if the need arises."

Bauer prided himself on contingency plans, something that had served him well as he'd built his empire. He truly cared for Emmanuelle, but she, too, was dispensable. She was brilliant, but sometimes neurotic and unpredictable—often double-minded. He'd tolerated her this long because of her genius and genuinely hoped she'd become part of the larger team.

"I understand that congratulations are in order," Bauer said.

"Thank you, Herr Bauer. News travels fast. We were surprised when the US company took our first offer, but with their financial troubles, as it turned out—we forced their hand. They grew too fast and failed without the benefit of support from their government such as ours. Due to the acquisition, we now have access to their DNA database, which contains a vast number of the American population."

"And the US government did not protest?" Bauer asked.

"Not until the deal closed." Wu chuckled. "We have one of the greatest abilities for large-scale sequencing, so we are quickly, and quietly I might add, signing numerous contracts with US healthcare providers and research organizations."

"Good, and don't forget, the information from BioGenics that *I* provided to you allows that ability."

"Yes, we are grateful to you, Herr Bauer," Wu said. "Through these consumer sites, Americans and others pay for the privilege of handing over their personal genetic codes to us. It amazes me how readily people give their power away…their basic human code."

"My thoughts exactly, Wu," Bauer said with pride. "What are your next steps?"

"For those biotech companies that refuse to partner with us, we will simply hack into their systems. Unfortunately, many use the cybersecurity systems you created with impenetrable firewalls, Herr Bauer."

They laughed.

"That will not be an issue, Wu. When you are ready, I'll provide you the necessary means to enter through the back door. But, Mr. Wu, I want reassurances that all this genetic information will not be weaponized. I recognize that China could target vulnerabilities in specific individuals or people groups based on their genetic information. I do not want your government to take out world leaders or wide swaths of specific populations with genetically engineered pathogens."

"Herr Bauer, I assure you. I am a faithful member of The Fifteen. Only our members will have the final say on how this technology is used. But I believe China is an excellent testing ground. You have seen my country's 'guiding ideology,' yes? The use of DNA technology is publicly marketed to fight crime, but I'm sure you have connected the dots and understand it is also to control our society. Look at Hong Kong, for example."

"I chuckled when I read the *Xin Heiwulei*," Bauer said. "China's list of the five new undesirable categories: underground churchgoers, dissidents, leading commentators on the internet, members of the disadvantaged sector in society, and human rights attorneys. People predestined for elimination…I have a few attorneys I would like you to purge."

They laughed again.

Bauer turned serious. "I'm afraid the liberals have taken over much of the world, and our society has swung so far to the left that it will take generations to recover," he said. "We are forced to accept everything and everyone. They want us to take care of all facets of society: the sick, the handicapped, the elderly, and those with deviant behaviors. I look forward to a world of health and prosperity."

"I as well," Wu said. "Goodbye, Herr Bauer, I hope to hear a positive update on BioGenics and Dr. Christianson soon."

"Of course, Wu. And thank you for sending your operative. I understand she is stunning as well as strong."

* * *

Fog hung low over the city, and fresh snow left a four-inch blanket of fluff. Nick and Maggie walked through the Old Market Square on their way to lunch at the O Bulwa restaurant to celebrate the new year. The front desk clerk said that they served the best hamburger and fries in the city, something Maggie craved. The clerk told them to try the *frytki Belgijskie*, Belgian fries, twice-fried potatoes…her favorite.

They maneuvered around piles of snow the workers cleared off the square. As they came around the corner by Town Hall, a crowd had formed in front of O Bulwa, and Maggie groaned. "Not sure I can wait that long. I am eating for two, you know."

"Well, let's see how long the wait is. A big juicy burger sounds good right now," Nick said. When they got closer to the restaurant, the crowd's attention focused on the Town Hall towers instead of the eatery.

Curiosity got the better of their appetites, and Nick and Maggie joined the crowd, working their way to the front where a young man recited historical information about the Gothic building.

"Follow the three-story loggia to the attic walls. In 1675

lightning destroyed the main tower, but the town rebuilt the structure fifteen years later. A tornado again damaged it in 1725. When it was rebuilt, they added the eagle on top of the classical-style tower. It has a two-meter wingspan."

The young man looked at his watch.

"We have two minutes left, so I'll tell you the legends of the goats and bugle call. Shortly you will hear the bells strike noon, then the goats will appear above the clock to give us a show, and a trumpet will sound.

The first legend goes that a chef burnt the roasted deer he prepared for a military commander. He tried secretly replacing the deer with two goats he'd stolen from a nearby farmer. The goats escaped, ran up to the top of the tower, and head-butted each other. This drew attention to an undiscovered fire in the building. Both the hall and the cook survived. The commander ordered mechanical goats to be placed in the tower as a memorial.

The tour guide paused for comments, and when there were none, he continued, "The second story involves the bugle call. It is said that Bolko, the son of the tower's trumpeter, took care of a crow with a broken wing. Years later, an army invaded and scaled the Poznań walls when an enormous flock of crows attacked them and saved the city. The trumpet sounds to this day."

The gold minute hand of the clock snapped to vertical, and a loud clanking of a bell rang out. The doors above the clock opened as two mechanical goats appeared as the other eleven tolls chimed. A solemn trumpet call followed, and then the goats turned and butted heads repeatedly.

Nick looked at Maggie, smiled, and nodded toward the restaurant to beat the crowd.

People packed the O Bulwa, but they found a table near the front window.

"Well, that was about as much fun as watching paint dry," Nick whispered.

"I thought it was sweet," Maggie said, looking around and hoping no one had heard Nick criticize the local attraction. "I'm just glad we got a table."

When the waiter offered them menus, Nick said, "I think we already know what we want." He looked at Maggie, who nodded. "We'll both take your burger and Belgium fries."

"And I'll take a Coca-Cola," Maggie added. When Nick looked at her with surprise, she said, "Might as well go all in."

"I'll do the same," Nick said to the waiter.

They all laughed.

Nick looked out at the gloomy weather, then turned to Maggie. "I'm sorry about last night. I wasn't mad at you, just angry about the whole situation."

Maggie smiled and sighed. "Nick, I understand. But please, let's not have it tear us apart. If that happens, the devil wins."

"You any closer to your decision?"

Maggie shook her head. "I go over and over it in my mind and try to weigh all the pros and cons. I envision it from both sides, but the answer's not clear to me yet."

Nick gazed out the window over the square.

"Nick, are you listening?"

He continued to stare out the window and finally said, "Well, look who's here."

Maggie frantically searched the plaza. "Who?"

"You see the blond and that big ugly guy with the funny walk?"

She focused, then gasped, "It's Buck and Katy!"

* * *

"I cannot believe you guys are here. How in the world?" Nick said as they squeezed in two more chairs at their table.

"I had this hankering for a polish sausage." Buck laughed. "Besides, I wanted to get away to a tropical paradise," he said and motioned to the falling snow.

Katy grabbed Maggie's arm. "When we talked to you over the weekend, we knew we had to come. We found a flight yesterday, and here we are. You two can't fight this alone."

Maggie leaned over to Katy and hugged her tightly. "How are we ever going to repay you guys?" Her voice cracked with emotion.

"Well, catch us up," Buck said and put his hand on Nick's shoulder.

Nick opened his mouth to speak, but nothing came out as his own tears flowed. The pain in his heart stopped him from saying the words out loud.

Buck didn't force the issue and reached out to give him a bear hug.

The four grieved together.

Finally, Maggie found the words. "It's worse. Our little guy has more repeats than I do, and he will likely develop the disease early."

"How early?" Buck asked, red-faced.

Nick had seen the look before when the old Marine set his jaw for battle.

"Nine or ten," Nick said.

Katy covered her mouth, and Buck slowly shook his head and asked, "What does the doc say about all this?"

"Her first recommendation was to terminate…" Nick

couldn't say the rest. "…then proceed with Maggie's treatment."

"That's not happening," Maggie said defiantly.

"Since that is not an option," Nick continued, "the doctor urged us to treat both Maggie and the baby. We have to tell her first thing in the morning what we decided."

"Why can't they wait until after the baby is born?" Katy asked.

"They could, but Dr. Christianson worries that to continue the pregnancy without treatment is riskier," Maggie said. "The stress could escalate my symptoms. As the baby develops his systems right now, he needs the normal huntingtin protein to do that."

"The question comes down to this; do we mess with Maggie and the baby's DNA?" Nick said.

"Well, treating disease is biblical," Buck offered. "The Great Physician invites us to join him in healing bodies and preventing suffering."

"Right," Nick said. "Maggie and I have had this discussion. Should the person with diabetes go untreated because somehow that's God's will or design for that person? Do we withhold corrective surgery on a baby with a clubfoot because that is how it was born? No. We correct all sorts of things like vision or hearing or medical issues. How does that differ from treating someone with a genetic disease? Where do we draw that line?"

"Buck and I read up on gene therapy as much as we could to understand it," Katy said and looked at Maggie. "It does seem like the whole idea has both scientific and spiritual consequences."

Maggie nodded. "That's what we argued about. I'm not sure we humans should mess with God's handiwork."

Nick became more and more frustrated. He took a deep breath, let it out, and said, "But we can't paint the whole technology with broad strokes and call it all wrong. For example, the use of recombinant DNA brought the world insulin. Do we accept everything on the surface and not try to improve on it?"

"I can't get Dr. McCoy's statement out of my head," Maggie said. "'God is woven into our DNA.' What happens if we change it?"

"That is such a good point, Maggie," Buck said. "But what if our DNA has gotten corrupted somehow, by toxins in our environment, GMOs, electromagnetic energy, and the like… then is it okay to uncorrupt it with gene therapy?"

They all nodded, each with their own thoughts.

Nick started to speak but once again choked with tears. Finally, he got his words back and said, "This has shaken my faith to the core. How do I fit this into my belief…that God is good, that God doesn't make mistakes?"

Buck cleared his throat. "Let's get the answer to that question straight. God *is* good, and He doesn't make mistakes."

"All we've been able to do is pray for God to help us," Maggie said.

"Yes," Katy prayed, "Lord, help us."

CHAPTER 30

GREEN LIGHT

BioGenics resumed to full activity after the holiday break, and the employees returned in a chipper, rejuvenated mood, even Emy. She was glad to see the staff after the gloom of her holiday and happy to see the wheels of the biotech company whirl again.

As soon as she'd arrived, Emy's secretary greeted her with thanks for the end-of-the-year bonus.

"You earned it," Emy said, "and Happy New Year."

Her secretary unbuttoned her coat and started to shut Emy's office door when Emy reminded her, "The Harts have an appointment first thing. Also, please mark me out of the office for the next two days. I'm going to visit my daughters."

Two more reasons for Emy's good mood. Decisions that had weighed on her were falling away. Her sham marriage ended, and Keith had left. She'd given Bauer an affirmative verdict on his offer of a lifetime, and she could look forward to no financial problems for herself or the girls, and especially for BioGenics.

She neatly tucked away and compartmentalized the issues at hand and got back to work. It indeed was a new year.

She sat at her desk and sipped her coffee when voices came from the hallway outside her office. *The Harts must be here.* She stood as her secretary knocked on the door.

"Come in," Emy said.

She smiled at Maggie and Nick as they walked in, but was surprised to see another couple close behind. Like Maggie, the woman was short statured, but with cropped blond hair. The man towered over all of them with a square jaw, flattop haircut, and massive chest.

"I hope you don't mind, I brought my bodyguard." Nick grinned, taking his cue from Emy's astonishment of the man. "Dr. Christianson, these are our best friends, Buck and Katy. They surprised us yesterday…they came to give us moral support."

Emy shook Katy's then Buck's hand. His grip enveloped hers like a vice. Emy looked up at him and estimated his height at six-foot-four, but more fascinating were his radiant green eyes and a jagged scar down his left cheek.

"Buck is a highly decorated US Marine," Nick said.

Emy smiled politely at Buck. Like most Europeans, she held considerable conflicting views about the American military and its wars and aggression.

She invited them into her office and asked her secretary to find more chairs. "By the way," she addressed her secretary, "I haven't seen Izzi yet today. Could you ask her to join us when she comes in?"

After the secretary offered everyone coffee, and the guests were seated comfortably, Emy turned to Maggie. "How are you today?"

Maggie nodded tentatively. "Pretty tired, I guess. I'm not sure if it's the weight of the decision ahead of us or the effects of the Huntington's."

"Maggie, I apologize," Emy said. "I've forgotten to ask how your mother and brother are getting along."

"Mom is doing okay. Mostly having problems with concentration and memory. My brother, on the other hand…" She lowered her gaze. "His symptoms have progressed rapidly. It's difficult for him to walk now."

Emy waited to see if Maggie wanted to share more information.

Maggie took a deep breath and continued, "My brother's deterioration is part of the reason I've made the decision to go through with the procedure." She looked at Nick and her friends. "We talked with Joe yesterday, and he begged me to go ahead with the treatment to spare myself and the baby from what he is going through." Maggie looked at Nick and their friends for agreement. "The four of us debated the pros and cons through the night," Maggie continued. "To be honest, I'm still not sure I have peace about it. But I believe all things are possible with God. And Nick reminded me that sometimes… many times…God uses doctors to bring healing."

Emy smiled. She liked Maggie. *There was something different about her: was it profound faith or sincere naïveté?*

"He also reminded me last night," Maggie went on, "that if God didn't intervene supernaturally, and I went without treatment, our child would grow up without a mother." She reached for Nick's hand, and a tear rolled down her cheek. "Our child may have a rough road ahead, and I'll need to be there."

"We are all curious about how you will treat the baby," the blond woman said.

Emy had already forgotten her name. "This is an excellent question. I'm sure the Harts have told you how CRISPR/Cas9 works. Unfortunately, the mutation is unique between Maggie and the baby—the number of CAG repeats is different. Even though we want to cut out the same section, the messenger RNA that we design to recognize the area will be specific for Maggie's sequence. Therefore, we will have to produce a separate system for the baby. It's easier to wait until after the baby is delivered to give the treatment."

Emy looked at all four of them to make sure they'd tracked the information.

"But I still believe that to treat your baby now will give it the best chance to develop properly," Emy said. "We would wait a couple days after your treatment to make sure you do well, then treat the baby."

"How would you do that?" Nick asked.

Emy paused to consider her answer. She knew the procedure would be worthy of a prize-winning, reportable case study. But she didn't know if the baby would survive Maggie's treatment—and there was a high probability she would miscarry.

"We inject the virus carrying the CRISPR/Cas9 into the umbilical cord," Emy said.

"Has that ever been done?" Nick asked.

"No," Emy said bluntly. "But it's no different from an amniocentesis where we put a needle through the abdomen. I am confident that with the advanced technology in our hospital, we could easily accomplish the task."

"Easy to say, if you're not on the receiving end of the needle," Maggie quipped.

"We would heavily sedate you, Maggie. You'd be very comfortable," Emy assured her.

The Marine spoke next. "Frankly, I'm afraid that the cost of the procedure shocks me."

Emy looked at the man. *Americans are so direct. Maybe, more so, this Marine.* Looking at him, she noticed shiny prostheses revealed at the bottom of his pant legs. *A wounded warrior and perhaps the reason behind his brashness.* She smiled at him, then turned back to the Harts.

"Dr. and Mrs. Hart, I considered the cost over the weekend. I still want you to talk with BioGenics's financial advisor this morning because I instructed her to find all the resources possible to cover the cost of your treatment."

"Oh my gosh," Maggie said. "I'm stunned."

"Well, you've dedicated your lives to helping people. Maybe it's time that some of that goodwill is returned to you."

Her words made Maggie cry copious tears of joy.

Emy enjoyed the feeling of doing something noble, and after accepting Bauer's offer, she had the opportunity to provide such generosity. She'd given it much thought and wanted to provide the therapy free-of-charge. She admired the Hart's spirit, but mostly, she understood the treatment on a pregnant woman and fetus was ground-breaking science—a successful treatment that had the potential to bring her accolades from the academic world.

Emy walked to her desk and looked at the calendar. "Today is Wednesday. Would you please ask my secretary to give you an appointment for Monday? We should be prepared for the procedure by then. This is nothing like surgery, but I want you to stay NPO Sunday night—nothing to eat or drink after midnight, on the off chance you have a reaction to the infusion."

A knock at the office door interrupted their discussion.

"Oh, good, that should be Izzi. I want her to start on the production of the CRISPR today. Come in," Emy called.

Izzi's bleached hair appeared around the opened door, followed by her face.

Her appearance shocked Emy. "Izzi, what happened to you?"

Izzi's nose was bandaged, and her eyes were battered black and purple. She sheepishly walked into the room, looking down at her feet.

"Who did this to you?" Emy demanded.

She bobbed her head back and forth and shot a furtive glance at Dr. Hart.

"Uh, I had a little run-in…" Izzi began. "Dang bitch knows Kung Fu or some crazy martial arts. I'm afraid she got the best of me."

Emy's cheeks flushed with heat. "We'll discuss this later, but for now…you know Dr. and Mrs. Hart?"

"Yes," Izzi said and held out her hand. "Hi, Dr. Hart. Good to see you again." When Nick shook it, she winced and withdrew her hand gingerly.

Nick took her hand back and examined it. When he pushed on her fifth knuckle, she paled and tried to pull away.

"Izzi, I think you have a boxer's fracture. It probably needs to be reduced and pinned, if you don't want a deformed hand," Nick said.

Izzi looked at Emy.

"Dr. Hart, I'm afraid with all the advanced care we have at BioGenics, we tend to focus on obstetrics and gynecology," Emy said. "We don't have an orthopaedist here on staff and I hesitate to ask this of you, but would you consider treating Izzi's fracture? My facility is available to you in any way."

Nick looked at Izzi and smiled. "I'd be happy to. First, let's get an x-ray."

"Thank you, Dr. Hart. That's very kind of you. My secretary will lead you to the hospital, and my staff will accommodate you in the OR if necessary. I recognize you are highly qualified. I don't need to see your credentials; your reputation precedes you."

"It must be nice to have your own hospital," Nick said and laughed. "It's my pleasure to help, after all that you're doing for us. I need to give you a good hand for work, huh, Izzi."

The Harts, their friends, and Izzi made their way to the door when Maggie turned back to Emy.

"Do you think our baby will survive? Will he be okay?" she asked.

"Absolutely," Emy said.

In reality, she had no idea. This was research. A twinge of guilt crept up her spine for the lie.

* * *

After sending Maggie, Katy, and Buck back to the hotel to eat and rest, Nick took Izzi to the hospital, got x-rays of her hand, and arranged to pin the bone in the OR.

He looked at his reflection in the stainless-steel cabinet above the scrub sink. It felt so weird to put on scrubs again. The last time he'd entered the operating room was in Turkey and thought he might never return. That was a year and a half ago. He smiled at God's sense of humor. Here he stood in an unfamiliar hospital, in a distant land, with scrub techs and nurses who knew nothing about orthopaedics. Fortunately, he could pin a boxer's fracture with his eyes closed. He smiled at his reflection staring back at him with a surgical cap over his head and a mask over his face. *Home.*

He threw the scrub brush into the trash can and backed through the OR doors. The suite was more modern than the run-down county hospital in Memphis.

"You okay, Izzi?" Nick asked as the scrub tech helped him don his gown and gloves.

"Right on, Dr. Hart. Thank you for fixing me up."

The nurse had done a thorough job when she'd scrubbed Izzi's arm. Nick slipped the sterile drape over Izzi's hand, set it down on the table, and sat on a stool.

"You feel this?" Nick asked and pinched the skin over her broken knuckle. He'd already injected the area with lidocaine for a digital block.

"Feel what?" Izzi said.

"Good answer," Nick said.

He nodded to the x-ray tech to slide the fluoroscopy unit in position. Nick stepped on the pedal of the machine, and the bony structure of Izzi's hand came into focus on the nearby monitor. He flexed the little finger down and used it as a lever to reduce the fifth metatarsal head into place, causing a loud snap.

"I heard that." Izzi said. "How gnarly."

"Did you feel it?"

"Not a bit."

Under fluoroscopy, Nick used the drill to drive two crossed pins across the knuckle and into the metacarpal, which held the fracture in place. He flexed and extended the finger, satisfied with the position and stability.

"Okay, that looks good," Nick said to the nervous staff. He understood their wariness. After all, he was a foreign doctor invading their domain to do an unfamiliar procedure.

But the scrub tech nodded her approval of Nick's skill.

"That's it?" Izzi said.

"Yes, ma'am. That will be a thousand dollars, please," Nick joked. The role of the captain of the ship stroked his ego. "I'm going to put a small plastic splint over your hand so you can use the rest of your fingers. I'm told you have some very important work to do."

He took off the drape, washed her hand, and helped her sit up.

"You okay?" Nick examined her eyes.

"Yeah…just a little embarrassed that the china doll got the best of me."

"What happened?" he asked.

"I saw her go into the bathroom. I simply wanted to talk to her. Words turned into a push and shove and then an all-out scuffle. I managed to get in one good slug," she said, raising her fist with a laugh. "But then she put some sort of karate moves on me, and before I knew what happened, I was on the floor with a broken nose and bloodied face." She shook her hand. "Skank. Next time I won't be so careless."

CHAPTER 31

AUSCHWITZ

Emy had left Poznań on the train to Kraków, and at Oświęcim hailed a taxi for Auschwitz—not a simple journey. The cramped and dirty condition of the train frustrated her. In her own car, the 451 kilometers would have taken less time. In the future, with access to Herr Bauer's jet, the five-hour journey would take under an hour—much more convenient. *Maybe I could have my own airplane and pilots. It'd take minutes to get to the girls.* As if she'd just won the lottery, she had already started to spend the money.

The taxi driver pulled to the front of the camp. She bent to peer out the window at the infamous, ribbon-shaped sign above the entrance, ARBEIT MACHT FREI. She also searched for her guide with a red umbrella who'd promised to meet her at the gate. It had cost extra to hire a private tour, but since she only had an hour and a half between trains, it was the most efficient use of her time. She'd lied to the guide—she came to do research for a book on Mengele, not that he was her grandfather. She also asked him to see if he could find information on two Jewish prisoners, Yuri and Eva Frankel.

The guide told her to dress warmly for the cold and blustery day. Snow fell, and the frigid temperatures frosted the windows of the taxi. The dreadfulness of the camp overshadowed the dreariness of the gray sky and landscape.

A chill ran up her spine, not from the cold, but from knowing that her grandmother and great-aunt had arrived at the same time of year, in January. *Perhaps they came through this exact gate.*

Emy recognized her guide and paid the driver. She asked if he would wait and promised to pay him extra on return to the train station.

She pulled her wool hat over her head and zipped her down jacket to her neck as she walked to her guide. Her hands and feet tingled from the cold. *Maybe I should have skipped this and gone straight to the girls.*

The guide had described himself as moderately tall, thin, and mulatto. The young man in skinny jeans and a fluffy North Face jacket smiled and held out his hand as she approached him.

"Dr. Christianson?" he shook her hand. "I'm Daniel. I'm happy to be your guide today."

"Hi, Daniel. Please call me, Emy." She looked at her watch. "I have to be back at the train station in an hour and a half."

He looked disappointed but said, "Yes, with pleasure. You said you were interested in the 'Angel of Death,' the infamous Dr. Mengele, so I'll expedite the tour."

"Did you find out anything about the Frankel sisters?"

He shook his head. "The Nazis, besides being narcissistic psychopaths, were fastidious record keepers. They were highly organized, proficient, and orchestrated the camps. The Germans marked, recorded, and logged every prisoner. Unfortunately, when they abandoned the camp, they burned many of the records. May I ask your interest in the sisters? You told me they were twins."

Emy hesitated. "Yuri Frankel is my grandmother."

He nodded. "I am a history major at Jagiellonian University in Kraków. I could continue the search—we're always looking for projects."

"That's most kind, Daniel. Thank you. You have an unusual accent for a Pole."

"That is because I am actually Hungarian. I simply attend the University here in Poland."

Emy nodded and acknowledged his grasp of multiple languages.

"Now, please let us start where most prisoners began their nightmare known as Auschwitz," he said dramatically.

* * *

Daniel had secured a golf cart to travel through the fields of two-story brick buildings and between Auschwitz I, II, and Auschwitz-Birkenau camps. He pulled into an expansive rail yard and parked.

As they stood on a concrete pad, he said, "This is the selection ramp. I ask you to close your eyes and let me describe a day in 1944."

A stiff breeze blew frozen flakes against Emy's face as she followed his instructions.

"This day did not differ from the many that came before or followed," Daniel started. "Cold, hungry, and filthy from the days and possible weeks in cramped conditions on the freight cars, the people arrived, day and night, with nothing to eat or drink and covered with their own excrement. The train came to an abrupt stop. Putrid black smoke bellowed from nearby stacks. Screaming and yelling…whistles and snarling guard dogs filled the air. *'Raus, Raus, Raus!'* The guards shouted—beating or shooting anyone who did not quickly obey. 'Throw everything out. Line up immediately.' The Nazi officers, positioned in the front, yelled while men in striped suits did the dirty work to separate the men from the women in two long lines—hundreds of Jews and Gypsies forced to stand quietly or face immediate execution. Confusion and rumors swirled. Work guaranteed shelter and food."

Daniel let the scene settle in the air, while Emy's heart pounded in her chest.

"Dr. Mengele, dressed sharply in his SS uniform, enjoyed his job as chief doctor, often whistling or singing. He looked at each person. 'Left, right, left, left,' he'd say nonchalantly, either pointing or nodding in the appropriate direction. He sent old men and women, and children under the age of fourteen to the left where trucks waited nearby. An ambulance preceded the vehicles. Perhaps the rumors were true. The Germans would take care of the elderly, the children, and the sick. Occasionally Mengele stopped and walked through the crowd, *'Zwillinge, raus, Zwillinge, heraustreten!* Twins, out, twins, step forward!' None of the prisoners knew if it was better to go right or to the left with the awaiting trucks. Nothing made sense. Half-frozen, starved, and confused, the people were warned to do as instructed, and all would end well. Families often begged to stay together and go left with the elderly and children."

As Emy shivered beneath her down jacket, images of Yuri and Eva flashed through her mind.

"Open your eyes, Dr. Christianson, and let us follow the trucks."

They drove to the gas chambers and crematoriums. This time, Daniel didn't ask her to close her eyes.

"We now stand in front of one of eight gas chambers where the Nazis gassed thousands of people *every* day. They called this one 'the white house,' complete with a white picket fence to give the prisoners the illusion of comfort in their new surroundings. The guards forced them to undress and stand in bitter temperatures; the lucky ones died from exposure. The SS chased the rest into the bunkers with whips and ferocious dogs as steel doors slammed shut and sealed behind them. Although the ambulance gave the appearance that the Nazis would care for them, it actually transported a doctor to administer the Zyklon B canisters. Upon the doctor's order, they opened a vent on the roof, and the prescribed number of blue pellets of hydrogen cyanide poured down the shaft. Mixing with the air, the Zyklon B quickly turned to the deadly gas that choked and killed. Through a small observation window into the chamber, the doctor watched the process and recorded how long the mass death took…typically up to fifteen minutes for the last person to die. He then ordered the vents opened, and the deadly gas evacuated. He signed a form denoting a successful execution and demanded the removal of any gold teeth."

Daniel looked at Emy, whose eyes welled with tears.

He continued. "The *Sonderkommandos*, prisoners tapped for such a job, dragged the corpses out, cut off long hair, removed all jewelry and metal dental work. They carried the bodies to the crematorium furnaces. In each of the four crematoria, it took twenty-four hours to incinerate eight hundred bodies. Not sufficient to keep up with the demand, the Nazis dug mass graves to burn the rest, often using human fat to keep those fires burning. At the peak of the extermination, the prisoners built eight gas chambers and forty-six ovens that daily disposed of four thousand four hundred of their own people. The number disposed of in the burn pits is unknown."

Emy and her guide stood in silent reverence. She regretted her decision to tour this horrific place.

Finally, Daniel whispered, "Let us now follow the others."

* * *

Daniel took her back to Auschwitz I, and they walked to the front of one of the brick barracks.

"The people directed right during the selection were marched to the camp. Other prisoners guarded the new arrivals, took all their possessions, and forced them to strip bare for the showers. All head and body hair were crudely shaved to rid them of lice, then they were showered with a caustic mixture of lye or calcium chloride and cold water. The *Sonderkommandos* issued ill-fitted clothes, tattooed a number on the captives' left forearm, and carefully recorded their names and numbers. After they marched to their assigned barracks, the prisoners stood for hours in the cold as the block *kapo*, another selected prisoner position, executed roll call over and over. Then the people were escorted into their barracks, where often seven hundred prisoners crammed into a space designed for forty. Three wooden bunks stacked on top of each other held the people, sardined on straw. One stove at the end of the barracks provided the only heat against the brutal winter in Poland."

Daniel raised his hands to catch snowflakes on his gloves.

"Then they went to work…back-breaking labor, done in the cold, and under the ever-present threat of the gas chambers.

Those who became too weak on the single meal of watery soup were shot on the spot or selected out at roll call and never seen again. The members of the Third Reich became resourceful murderers. They looked for ways to effectively slaughter an entire population group while protecting the psychological health of the Nazi soldiers. They overcame technical problems to eliminate the sick or the *Untermenschen*, the subhuman to make room for the healthy."

Daniel checked his watch. "I'm afraid our time is almost over, and I understand you are interested in Dr. Mengele's medical work. There is so much more to see—the room of shoes…thousands upon thousands…other rooms with the personal belongings and piles of human hair. But, please let me escort you to Block 10, one of the most infamous medical blocks."

Emy followed him down the row of buildings, past the razor wire fence that had once been electrified.

Soon they arrived at the entrance of the nondescript building.

Emy's knees weakened. According to her grandmother's letter, Block 10 was where she had been taken with her sister.

Standing at the entrance and the stairs that Yuri had walked up to face the brutality of Mengele, Emy's own DNA cried out, echoing the horrors her grandmother had endured. This is where the rape occurred and the conception of her mother. Bella forming the ovum that became her. Her own DNA set in motion in this very spot. Emy's breath escaped, and her head spun.

Daniel reached for her arm. "You okay, Dr. Christianson? You want to sit down? It is overwhelming for all of us."

He had no idea.

He reached into a satchel underneath his heavy jacket, produced a bottle of water, and handed it to her.

"Here, let's rest for a moment."

"Daniel…I don't know how you talk about this over and over." She took a long drink of water. "My heart aches."

"Dr. Christianson, I am a Hungarian Jew, half-black man, who is gay." He let the words settle in the air. "Every time I give tours of what these monsters did, I feel it's a victory."

Emy nodded and took another drink.

"Before we go inside, I want to prepare you for the horrors of these medical blocks. Terrible, terrible experiments were done to the prisoners. Some for research to improve the care of German soldiers—such as head injury experiments, the freezing of prisoners and suitable ways to warm them back to life, exposure to malaria, typhus, tuberculosis, yellow fever, or hepatitis, and both seawater and high-altitude experiments. They broke the prisoners' legs and created wounds that they rubbed with feces to infect them. They experimented with the treatment of sulfonamide and other solutions to see if they could cure the gangrene. The Nazis performed additional research for the purpose of eugenics, typically revolving around the issue of sterilization with radiation or by an injection of caustic chemicals. The Nazi doctors became efficient killing machines and optimized their ability to inject phenol directly into patients' hearts as they waited for a medical exam."

Emy took another gulp of water, as Daniel continued.

"I understand, Dr. Christianson, that you're interested in Dr. Mengele's twin studies. Twins fascinated him because he believed that they held the key to genetic transmission. He

would typically use one twin as a control and experiment on
the other. He subjected one to injections with diseases, ampu-
tations, blood transfusions, and reproductive experiments that
included forced insemination and rape. He then examined
the other twin to see if the physical insults mysteriously trans-
ferred. When he finished with the experimentation, the set of
twins was most commonly euthanized, often by Mengele himself, dissected and shipped to his professor at the University of
Münster, Otmar von Verschuer. He and Mengele, both strong
eugenicists, believed that twins provided the perfect research
subjects."

Daniel looked at Emy, and his focus went from one of her
eyes to the other.

"He was especially interested in twins with two different
eye colors such as yourself. It is estimated that Mengele con-
ducted his shocking experiments on up to fifteen hundred sets
of twins, many of them children."

"Have you ever thought about how these doctors crossed
the line—from healers to murderers?" Emy asked.

Daniel nodded and looked away. Finally, he turned back.

"We discussed this 'slippery slope' in class. You must
understand that these travesties started way before the war.
Society determined what was best for the masses—what caste
of people became a burden to the health of the entire community, and which had value. After the first world war, Germany
fell under a tremendous financial burden. Combine that with
a stout dose of national pride and elitism, and you have the
genesis of eugenics. The medical community was brought in
early to contribute to the discussion of how to create healthier,

stronger people. And how to kill so many people…and then what to do with the bodies?" Daniel paused. "It's disgusting, I know."

Emy nodded.

"As World War II started, the young and vigorous died off in the fighting. Enormous financial pressures mounted, including a need for hospitals and facilities for the war effort. The Nazis emptied out psychiatric wards for this purpose. They also created 'Jew reservations' and gave their homes and belongings to families of the soldiers."

Daniel looked Emy in the eyes.

"But then came the problems of how to take care of the old, the sick…the children. The medical community grew in authority and influence. Many idolized Hitler and were drawn to the promise of success and rewards. They heeded the warning 'Do it, or we'll find someone who will.'"

Emy thought she might vomit.

"I think the hardest thing for me to swallow is that many of them truly believed that they advanced the practice of medicine. The physicians wanted to understand how they could enhance the genetic pool."

Bauer's voice echoed in Emy's mind. This iniquity had been passed down to him by his father. She needed a break from Daniel and wanted to find a bench inside Block 10.

"Can I go inside by myself?" Emy asked.

Daniel checked over his shoulders for other visitors, "Sure thing, but please don't touch anything. I could get in trouble."

Emy didn't hesitate and pushed open the steel door. The lights glowed, but frozen stale air hit her face. Emy felt flush from the surge of emotions, and she unzipped her coat and fanned reviving air under her jacket. Thankful for some privacy, she sat on a bench at the entry, confident she was not the first or the last who became overwhelmed with emotions. Judging by the displays and placards, it became clear that group tours passed through here.

She finished the last of the water, took a deep breath, and decided to look around before time ran out.

The heels of her snow boots clipped against the bare concrete floor as she walked down the abandoned hallway with doors on each side marked as examination rooms. Halfway down the hall, one door stood open but roped off. The museum outfitted the room as though the Nazi physicians still practiced there—an old steel exam table with stirrups, glass syringes, instruments, and other antique medical equipment set up on a side table. She looked over her shoulder to see if Daniel had followed her in and quickly bent under the rope and entered the room. She walked over to the exam table and put her hand on the cold steel. Closing her eyes, she pictured her grandmother lying here, naked. She'd read the report of what they did to twins—examining every inch of them, measuring and remeasuring every feature, down to their private parts. At eighteen, it must have been so scary for her grandmother. Anger rose up within Emy. How could these monsters do this? She imagined Ceci or Hanna lying here. Her knees buckled, and she almost fell. She too, teetered on the slippery slope that Daniel described. This generational curse…this evil had to be broken.

She steadied herself, ducked under the rope, and walked back into the hallway.

A placard caught her attention, and she read:

> "Dr. Mengele was a contradiction of a human being. One minute sending thousands to the gas chambers, the next playing with the Gypsy children. Often, he was said to bring them food and candy, sometimes little toys, and take them on brief outings. Whenever he appeared, they would greet him warmly with the cry, 'Onkel Mengele.' Days later, their kind 'uncle' drove the same children in his car to the gas chamber, speaking tenderly and reassuringly to them to the very end."

Emy focused on a picture underneath the words of a naked boy said to be seven. He looked more like a four- or five-year-old with his tiny body, emaciated and deformed—his ribs showed through, his cheeks and eye sockets sunken, his development retarded from starvation.

He looked like her son, Danek.

Emy collapsed and wept.

CHAPTER 32

CHIMERA

Nick and Maggie sat with Katy and enjoyed a hot breakfast in the dining room of the Brovaria.

"You want some more coffee?" Nick offered the ladies and held the thermos to each.

Both declined.

"The ol' man sleeping in this morning?" Nick asked Katy.

"No, he woke up early this morning and worked on a project." Katy took a bite of toast, "Some sort of surprise."

When everyone in the restaurant turned toward the entrance, Nick figured his imposing friend had walked in. Buck had that effect on people, and Nick turned to enjoy the show. Sure enough, the other diners gawked at Buck. He wore shorts and a T-shirt that read *Powered by Duracell* stretched over his powerful chest and biceps. But what really got their attention were his green and red prostheses. Buck smiled and nodded as he passed their tables.

"Nothing like a grand entrance, my friend," Nick said. "Only you could get away with shorts when it's freezing outside."

Buck grew two feet taller in front of their eyes. "What did you say to me, little man?" he said in a deep baritone voice. He produced a small remote from his pocket. "Had the guys make this for me and speed up the mechanics a bit." He pushed a button and shrank down to his normal height.

People at the surrounding tables murmured, and Buck turned and bowed. "Thank you, ladies and gentlemen. That trick provided by the good people of the US Army."

He smiled and joined his friends at the table. "I found a wonderful benefit of these babies when we flew here; I could shorten them and have all the legroom I needed." He laughed and rapped his knuckles against the metal.

He then spread out a handful of brochures on the table. "I've done a little research on what we could do for the next few days to get our minds off of things. The front desk helped me out. I thought we could go to Warsaw or Kraków and visit some war sites, but that might be depressing. The girls at the front desk suggested visiting the spa resorts up north along the Baltic Sea. They said they're famous."

Nick picked up the pamphlet from the Sofitel Grand Hotel in Sopot. "Wow, beautiful."

"It is a five-star resort with a wonderful spa and world-class dining," Buck added. "And look at these pictures," he opened the brochure. "It looks out over the Baltic Sea."

Maggie grabbed the pamphlet on the Ciekocinko Palace Hotel Resort and Wellness. "Oh my, look at this one. It looks like a French royal estate. I think I might like any place with *palace* in the title." She laughed. She opened the trifold. "Look at these rooms, they're magnificent."

It was the first time in weeks that Nick had seen life and excitement in her eyes. But it quickly disappeared as she set the brochure down.

"There is no way we can afford something like that," she said.

"That's what is amazing, Maggie," Buck said. "These kinds of places cost three or four hundred dollars a night in the States, but here they are under a hundred. I figure we could spa hop; massages, pedicures, manicures, facials…anything you girls want. Besides, the front desk said they'd have our rooms ready for us when we return on Sunday. We can rent a car right here at the hotel."

Maggie looked at Nick. He nodded enthusiastically.

"I don't know—" Maggie argued.

Nick reached across the table and gripped Buck's arm. "Let's do it. I think it's just what the doctor ordered."

* * *

Emy sat on a loveseat outside the dressing rooms in a boutique shop in downtown Kraków as her girls modeled clothes. It was a relief to get away from BioGenics, Keith, Herr Bauer, her visit of Auschwitz, and her gene pool. To sit here in her jeans and sweatshirt, she felt wonderfully casual and content—how life ought to be.

"You ladies doing okay?" the storekeeper came around the corner and asked.

"We're good, thank you," Emy said.

"You and your girls are so cute together. You might as well be sisters."

"Thank you. That's very sweet of you."

"Shout out if you need anything."

Emy heard the girls giggle from inside the dressing room. Such a relief from her tour yesterday—the tragic stories and the catharsis of disturbing emotions. She'd cried all the way to the train station. She worried the taxi driver thought she'd gone mad, but when he dropped her off, he admitted he had the same reaction from the camp.

Afterward, Emy was so distraught about her life that she considered stepping off the platform in front of the oncoming train. The thought of leaving the girls to deal with a life of psychological scars stopped her.

Now, thankful she'd pushed away the suicidal consideration, she basked in Hanna and Ceci's laughter. She'd miss out on so many things if she ended her life—times like today and eventually grandkids.

Emotions overwhelmed her when the girls came from the dressing rooms. They'd grown up—*such shapely figures*. Her mind flashed back to the days when they'd worn frilly outfits of pink and lace, and their eyes were full of life and promise.

"What do you think?" Hanna asked and modeled a tight pair of jeans, a royal blue blouse, and a black leather jacket. Ceci sported a short red dress over leggings and knee-high boots.

"Hanna said I look like a hooker," Ceci said.

"I think you both look beautiful," Emy said as tears welled up.

The girls sat down on either side of her on the loveseat.

"It's okay, Mom," Hanna said.

"Where in the world does time go? It seems like yesterday you guys ran around the house with your favorite dolls. I'm such a failure as a mother."

"Oh, Mom, you're not. We love you."

Emy put her face in her hands. "I was so busy building my empire that I forgot…" She wept. "Now, look at what I've done to our family."

"It's not your fault, Mom," Hanna said and threw her arms around her mother. "You are the best. We are so proud of you."

With tears in her eyes, she leaned back and looked at her daughters. "I am so thankful for you two."

"Look how you have provided for us," Ceci added. "We lack for nothing."

Emy nodded and finally said, "That's what I need to talk with you both about. Herr Bauer has made me…us, an offer hard to ignore. He has no other family in which to pass on his estate. We are his family; he has asked me to become his beneficiary."

"Holy crap," Hanna said. "What did you tell him?"

"For now, I said yes. But it means more work, more time away from you girls. But it is also a way to ensure you're set for life."

Ceci huffed. "We don't care about any of that. We'd rather have you more than whatever Herr Bauer could give us. Not that we don't appreciate what he has always done for us, but it sounds like we'd lose you in the process."

Hanna stared at her. "It sounds like there is more to the story, Mom."

Emy looked away. "Well…it's complicated. He has tied the offer to my work at BioGenics. He wants to expand our processes and research into areas I'm not sure I feel comfortable with."

"Like what?" Ceci asked.

"Using our knowledge of DNA for enhancement."

"You mean like changing who we are?" Ceci asked.

Emy bobbed her head from side to side. "Again, it's more complicated than that. I don't think we'd be changing people so much as..." She found it hard to continue.

"Mom, you have always worked to improve the health of your patients. That's why I want to go into medicine. But this—" Hanna stopped.

"Hanna, please speak your mind. I need that right now."

"In my genetics class, we had this contest. The professor called the project the Chimera," Hanna said.

"Chimera, the mythical Greek beast with all the different body parts?" Ceci asked.

Hanna nodded. "He wanted us to make up the perfect human. It was fun to imagine—like designing a superhero. Each group presented the perfect human and defended why they'd picked certain characteristics. The groups argued about each one. The winning team would receive dinner, bought by the others."

"Who won?" Emy asked.

"See, that's the weird part. None of us could decide on any of it. We found problems with every improvement. Our professor laughed and told us the other definition of a chimera: a thing that is hoped or wished for but is an illusion or impossible."

Emy nodded.

"Our class had a long discussion on this whole idea of enhancement. Where do you draw the line? Our professor suggested that an enhanced world is one in which we recognize all people possess an inherent value. Where we respect them, no matter what they look like or what their abilities are."

Emy smiled at Hanna as she continued. *Yes, Hanna has grown up.*

"Mom, I don't want to hurt your feelings, because this is your field. But Herr Bauer is asking too much," Hanna said. "If you treat a child as a product, are they discarded if they don't meet the standards or expectations of the parents? Is a child considered defective or less suitable if an undesirable trait is not improved? And what about the child's choice?"

"Hanna, these are all such good questions," Emy said and held her daughter's hand.

"Our professor argued that this is true racism—the thought that I'm superior to someone else…maybe they're poor, fat, a different color, or a different culture. Throughout history, there has always been an upper class that believed that they should decide for the commoner. The technology is ripe for abuse."

Emy knew these controversies but had locked them away.

"Mom, did you know that when the scientists manufacture the CRISPR/Cas9 molecule and they combine the two different strands of RNA to make the messenger RNA they call it a chimera?"

Emy smiled at Hanna. *Of course, I know. My team created the process and coined the term.*

"Our professor said that to the Greeks, the sight of a chimera was an omen for disaster."

CHAPTER 33

FINAL DECISION

Friday morning, Emy sat at the breakfast bar in her home, opened her laptop, and turned it on. Between her visit to Auschwitz and vacation time with the girls, the way forward came into clear focus. In good conscience, she could not steer BioGenics down the road of enhancement—often what medicine *can* do runs counter to what it *should* do. Thank the stars, the girls, especially Hanna, had become free thinkers. They explored their own belief systems, and like many millennials, were not afraid to speak their minds.

Emy opened her photos and enlarged the image she had taken of a picture in a display of a group of a hundred or more Hungarian Jewish women in Auschwitz. They faced the camera and lined up five abreast, but not one looked at the photographer. Their heads were shaved, and none wore a coat to protect them from the elements. Their filthy one-piece dresses hung off their emaciated frames like rags, and their braless breasts sagged with their shoulders, weighted down with defeated spirits. They stood in four inches of snow with wooden clogs for shoes. Had they just arrived? Did her grandfather select and march them to the gas chamber, or to work in the fields in freezing temperatures? There was not one guard in sight, as if they were unnecessary. Like animals beaten into submission, the women did not dare complain or step out of line. Were they afraid they'd all be severely disciplined, or their meager daily ration would be withdrawn?

Emy couldn't take her eyes off the photo. *How could these women even find the strength to stand?* They had been separated from their husbands, parents, and children. Forced to listen to the rumors that their family had become part of the black smoke that filled the air around them. *How did they find the courage to go on?*

Emy needed to discover this powerful inner strength.

She didn't believe that Bauer would remove her from BioGenics. She'd built it. She remained the brains behind the science and the discoveries, and her attorneys had written the contract clearly—without her, BioGenics did not exist.

She started to dial Herr Bauer's number but stopped. She realized that through the army of attorneys who Bauer employed, he could have hidden some loophole. Tying the company up in litigation would result in a slow death by attrition or starvation, much like the Hungarian women in the picture still on her computer screen.

Emy walked to the desk in the kitchen and pulled out a drawer. She rummaged around and found a flash drive that Ceci had left behind. It was a pink Hello Kitty silicon figure. The head came off, and the USB port jutted out from the body of the cartoon character. *This will have to do.*

She went back to the computer, sat down, and logged into the BioGenics's network. The high-tech security installed in the system ensured that the company had a pathway to lock down the entire computing structure in case of a breach.

No one, including her, ever imagined the breach would come from within. Once inside the IT administrator site, she typed several commands and hesitated before she hit enter. The instructions denied access for everyone until she entered the new codes the computer generated. The shutdown would not affect the hospital as it relied on a separate system. Still, the four floors of researchers would have their computers frozen, forcefully slamming the firewall doors closed on every aspect of their proprietary processes and research. She'd hoped it wasn't necessary, but she needed leverage over Bauer. If he reacted favorably, she could reenter the codes now stored on Hello Kitty. She had to laugh…billions of dollars of potential locked away on a flash drive that looked like a toy.

She hit enter, and an alert flashed across the BioGenics's administration page. Her phone rang almost immediately.

It was the head of security. "Hi, Bruno."

"Dr. Christianson, what is going on? I don't remember a test on the system today."

"I'm sorry I didn't warn you, Bruno…I uh…need to shut it down for a minute."

"I'm going to have a whole pack of angry scientists in my office shortly. The phones are already ringing off the hook. What do I tell them?"

"Tell them to please be patient. We should have the issue resolved soon."

She hung up, and before her courage evaporated, she dialed Herr Bauer's number.

"*Guten Tag*, Herr Bauer's residence. How may I assist you?"

"Hello, Kenny, it's Dr. Christianson. May I speak to Herr Bauer?"

"Certainly, Dr. Christianson. He is right here."

Heat rose up Emy's back and instantly turned to sweat, as Herr Bauer answered.

"Dr. Christianson." He sounded angry. She regretted that she hadn't planned out her dialogue.

"Herr Bauer, how are you?"

"Fine," he responded gruffly.

Obviously, in no mood for small talk. She would have lost her nerve if it wasn't for the women on her screen. "Herr Bauer, I have given much thought and consideration to your suggested direction of BioGenics. I hope you understand how grateful I am for all you have done for the girls and me personally and for the company, but I must respectfully ask you to reconsider your position. We should not expand our work into enhancement."

There was a long pause. Emy thought the call dropped and looked at the phone.

She heard Bauer sigh.

"And this is why you have shut down BioGenics's computer?"

"Herr Bauer, I believe there is still so much good we can do with the treatment of diseases that will bring financial success."

Still no answer.

"I'm afraid, Herr Bauer, I have already stepped across lines that I regret. I cannot go any further. I think we should use this powerful science for good, not evil."

"That is an overstatement," Bauer finally said. "I can't tell you how disappointed I am."

Heat flushed Emy's cheeks as he scolded her.

"Please, Herr Bauer, let us continue the good works that we started."

The line went dead.

CHAPTER 34

DARKNESS

Emy roused with a start. Her heart pounded, and she breathed hard, but once she got her bearings, she was relieved it had been a vivid nightmare. In her horrible dream, it was pitch-black, and a chimera chased her and the girls—this fire-breathing creature had the head of a lion, a goat's head protruding out its back, and the tail of a snake. The beast was almost upon them as her legs got heavier and heavier, and she told the girls to run from the danger, but they wouldn't listen.

Emy turned over and fluffed a pillow, trying to push the images away and control her breaths. *Thanks, Hanna, for putting that image in my mind.* The nasty nightmare had interrupted Emy's sound sleep; she'd slipped into a sweet slumber after she'd made the final verdict. Herr Bauer was unhappy about her decision, as were her scientists for having the computer system shut down for the entire day. But it was necessary because she had to wait to see what Bauer did next. Hopefully he would put the nonsense of enhancement behind them.

Emy rolled on her side and stuffed a pillow between her legs when she heard a muffled sound. She froze and perked her ears. The old house often creaked and popped in the winter—*that was probably it.* But as she lay there, she wondered if her subconscious had heard a sound and woke her. She rolled onto her back to listen.

When the decisive sound of the bottom step that led to the upper floor squeaked, her heart thumped in her chest, and she sat up.

Halfway up the stairs, another board often squawked when stepped on. She waited for the creak, but it never came.

She listened for another minute and heard nothing. She decided that she'd either imagined it or the house had shifted again. She lay her head back on the pillow. The low crime rate in Poznań was one reason they loved it here. Most cities in the US and other parts of Europe had twice the amount of crime. Home burglaries rarely occurred to where she often left the house unlocked for convenience.

Emy pictured Hanna and Ceci in the new outfits she'd bought them and snuggled under the covers.

She had almost fallen back to sleep when she heard a piece of furniture scraping across the wood floor downstairs. This time she sat up and turned on the bedside lamp. This was no dream. Someone was in the house.

She remembered the machete that Keith had put in the closet after she'd denied a gun purchase. Quietly she folded back the covers, crept to the closet, and retrieved it. She withdrew the blade from its leather sheath and frowned. *Great, like I really know how to use this thing.*

Perhaps Keith had come home and rummaged through his belongings. She hoped his girlfriend had kicked him out.

Emy stood frozen in the closet and listened.

She heard a noise again. This time, a drawer opened and closed. Why would a thief do that? It had to be Keith. She tiptoed to the window and separated the curtains. Sure enough. Keith's red Fiat Panda sat in the driveway. *That asshole.*

She moved forward through the bedroom, holding the machete, and cracked open the bedroom door. Lights flashed on in the kitchen.

"Keith?" she yelled.

She looked over the landing and approached the top of the stairs. Nothing.

"Keith?"

She took a step at a time but skipped the two noisy stairs.

"Keith, what are you doing here?" she yelled when she reached the bottom.

Emy turned to the kitchen.

She sensed movement from behind, but before she could turn, an arm went around her neck, and a rag covered her mouth.

As her body and mind went limp, her last thought was… *chloroform.*

* * *

In the fog of confusion, Emy thought she'd returned to the chimera night terror. She assumed she had her eyes closed. Forcing them wide, she realized they were already open, and total darkness enveloped her. Dank and moldy air stifled her breath. She shivered and wondered if she was naked or still in her pajamas. All she could surmise was that she sat in a chair with her hands tied behind her back.

She twisted her wrists, but only chafed the skin with rope burns.

"Hello?" she yelled. Her voice echoed. "Keith?"

The sweet chemical smell of chloroform lingered in the back of her throat. The lack of visual stimulation disoriented her.

It angered him when she'd kicked him out, but he was incapable of anything like this.

"Hello?" Anger and fear forced her to try and stand, but when she couldn't, she realized her ankles were tied to the chair legs. Only then did she comprehend that she was barefoot, and her feet hung numb and frozen. Her body tremored.

A mechanical device sounded somewhere in the distance, then a swoosh of air hit her eardrums as though she were in a tunnel. A single bright light appeared, hurting her eyes. The dark distorted her orientation and depth perception, and for a split second, she feared her chair sat in front of an oncoming train.

She squinted at the light and moved her head back and forth to peer around it. As it came closer, she understood a person wearing a halogen headlamp came toward her.

"Who are you? Keith, is that you?"

"Dr. Christianson, I take it you are uninjured."

"What? Who are you?" The female voice surprised Emy. "Why are you doing this to me?"

"My goal is to release you unharmed."

"What do you want?" Emy tried to stand again, but the ropes cut into her flesh. She screamed in agony. "Help me!" she yelled.

The woman laughed. "Dr. Christianson, I would advise you not to resist. You will only hurt our eardrums."

"Where am I?"

"You are only a short distance from your house. But no one can possibly hear you in this underground bunker."

Emy searched the space, given the limited light from the headlamp. The chair sat upon a concrete floor. To her right, she thought she saw a brick wall. Nothing else. *Close by my house is Fort VII.* Had they taken her to one of the many abandoned underground bunkers? If so, the woman was right. No one would hear her.

"Please, please, don't hurt me. I'll give you whatever you want."

"Herr Bauer will be pleased to hear that."

"Herr Bauer?" Emy startled and stared at the shadow behind the light.

"All you need to do is give me the codes, the program and password to access BioGenics's computers. Then we do away with all this nonsense."

"What? Is that what this is all about? Herr Bauer is behind this?" Emy's heart sank. Betrayal—the worst of insults. Her anger rose, and she screamed at the light. "Let me go! You will never get away with this."

"I'm afraid we already have. No one will find you here. You might as well give us the information and save yourself an icy night."

Emy fought to understand. *Think.* The woman's voice did not sound familiar at all. "Is it money you want? I will give you everything I have."

The woman did not speak.

"Whatever Herr Bauer is paying you, I will double it."

The woman laughed. "Dr. Christianson, both of us understand that is not possible. Now please do not resist. I have no interest in escalating this."

Would Bauer really do this to her? An image of Mengele in Auschwitz flashed into her mind. He smiled, ready to plunge a needle attached to a syringe of phenol into a prisoner's heart.

"I do not have the codes," Emy insisted. "Please, I have done nothing. We can work this out."

"You are correct, we can work this out. But first, you must give me the codes."

Emy tried to trigger her neurons to come up with a plan. "Uh…they're at my office. If you take me there, I will activate the system." If she could get into public domain, then she'd have the possibility of escaping. If she gave them the codes now, there was a significant chance no one would ever see her again. *Ceci…thank god she's not at home.*

"I'm afraid, Doctor, that will not happen. Now please tell me where I can find them so we can end this charade."

"I cannot do that from here!" Emy screamed.

"As you wish, Dr. Christianson. Please enjoy the rest of your evening."

"Please, please don't leave me here," Emy shouted as the woman turned and walked away. What sounded like a steel door opened and slammed behind her. Blackness returned and squeezed the breath out of Emy.

CHAPTER 35

DELIRIUM

The putrid smell of burning flesh and hair choked Emy's throat. She was wedged between the brick wall and electrified fence that buzzed with high voltage. The guards hollered, and frantic dogs closed in through the darkness. Searchlights feverishly arced around the compound. She tried cramming tighter into the crevice to avoid detection but could not move, her hands and feet frozen in the snow. Every muscle ached as if they would snap in two if she flexed them.

How did she escape? She didn't know. She'd fallen out of the long line of Hungarian Jews. As if the world had tilted, and she'd slid into this secret place. Screams from the other women made her shudder. The Nazis tortured them to give up her position.

She had done this to them. It was her fault for stepping out of line.

Gunshots.

Screams.

How could I have betrayed them?

Self-preservation.

The Nazi guards lingered around the corner of her secret place. The dogs snarled and snapped at the air.

Run, Emy, run.

They'd shoot her in the back, but that fate was better than torture.

Her hands opened and closed to reach for an invisible handle. She sat so near the electrified fence her hair sizzled and burned against it. She could not move.

They appeared.

An SS soldier flashed a light beam in her eyes as a German Shepherd pulled and lunged at its leash. White fangs snarled and snapped inches from her face. Hot breath and rabid saliva shot from its mouth.

She closed her eyes and tried to scream, but nothing came out of her throat.

Then silence.

Had they left her?

Had they not seen her?

She slowly opened her eyes to shiny black boots and above them to an immaculately dressed SS officer snapping a riding crop against his gloved hand. Emy knew he was wicked and trembled, even though he said nothing. He simply stood there and smiled. He whistled between the gap in his front teeth then extended a hand to help her.

She understood he gave her a chance to escape.

Emy stood. The leashed dog morphed into a chimera—its lion's head roared, the goat laughed, and its tail of a snake slithered and hissed.

Mengele smiled and pointed toward the exit.

Emy propelled her legs forward, but they grew stiff and heavy. Her feet slid and slipped in the snow. She glanced over her shoulder, and her captors stood in place. *Are they genuinely letting me go?*

Her lungs burned. Her heart pounded almost to the point of exploding.

Near to the gate, she allowed herself one more look behind. This time Mengele nodded, and the guard released the beast.

She pushed her legs and her feet harder and faster, but the more she struggled, the less she could move. Inherently, she knew the monster would not pass the gate. If she reached the exit, she would be safe.

Steps away now, the creature's thunderous footsteps came closer.

With every ounce of strength, she flung her frame across the finish line.

But as her arms and torso passed the invisible barrier, the beast's teeth bore down on her ankles—tearing at her flesh and pulling her back.

"Dr. Christianson?"

"Dr. Christianson, wake up."

Emy's mind rose from the depths of the night terror into the current one.

Her eyes tried to focus but blurred from exhaustion and hypothermia.

"What—"

Nothing made sense, like coming out of the fog of anesthesia.

"Where—"

A warm woolen blanket wrapped around her shoulders. Someone held a canteen to her lips. She sipped and then gagged on the water.

"Dr. Christianson, how was your night?"

Emy followed the voice. Confusion overtook her. Somewhere in her brain, she presumed she'd suffered a psychotic break. But then she realized she was still in the bunker, and the voice belonged to her captor. Something had changed. A small lantern cut through the intense darkness.

She touched her face. Her hands and feet moved freely. The blanket warmed her body. Still, she shivered. Then the shivering gave way to shaking.

She took another drink of water.

As in her nightmare, she stood and tried to run but collapsed onto the cold concrete.

"Dr. Christianson, that is not a good idea. You will simply hurt yourself."

For the first time, she focused on the woman.

Have I gone mad? The lantern illuminated the beautiful Chinese woman, Keith's girlfriend, who held out her hand to help Emy.

Reflexively, Emy took the hand, but tried to strike the woman with her fist. Instead, Emy received a hard thump to her sternum, which sent her tumbling and breathless into the chair.

"Please don't make this harder on yourself," the woman scolded.

"Why…why, are you doing this to me?" Emy asked breathlessly.

"I think you know why."

"Who are you?"

"That is not important. What is important is what you want me to tell Herr Bauer this morning."

"Tell Herr Bauer he is a monster…like his father."

* * *

Bauer sat at his desk eating a croissant slathered with apricot jam. He stared at his computer screen as a red message flashed: Access Denied.

Damn her.

He had to hand it to Emmanuelle—of the billions of euros he'd made in building security systems, she had stumped his engineers. They'd worked through the night to unlock the system with no success. It was her genius that prompted him to invest in her in the first place, but now it was that same intellect that baffled them. *How in the world did she accomplish the feat of locking down the entire system?* She had encrypted the encryption and created a fatal loop. Every time the engineers got close to resolving the codes, the artificial intelligence sensed the threat and altered them. The access program Emmanuelle developed was essentially alive, just out of reach. She used his very own AI against him.

His phone rang, and he answered it after the first ring.

"Yes," he growled.

"I'm afraid, Herr Bauer, that Dr. Christianson is stronger than we thought. She refuses to tell us where to find the program and how to access the system. We have searched her home and have her laptop that will be handed over to your engineers this afternoon."

"Then it's time to step things up." Bauer slammed his fist on the desk. "We must extract the information from her."

"I understand."

"Don't let her die. For now, we need her."

"Yes, I can take her to the edge. I will try not to push her over."

CHAPTER 36

TERROR

Emy jerked awake, her legs cramped from dehydration and hypothermia. *What time is it?* She couldn't tell if hours or days had passed. How long had it been since the woman was here? *No idea.* Darkness had swallowed her again. She lay on the concrete floor in a fetal position, wrapped in the blanket. At least the woman had left the blanket and a bottle of water. Emy tightened her grip on the blanket. She'd cocooned her body with one little air hole for her mouth. Her skull and hip ached from the concrete floor; one layer of wool was the only cushion.

There was not one photon of light—nothing filtered in around the frame of the exit.

She tried to take her mind to a different place. *How did the women in Auschwitz cope?* Day after day—they survived the cold, loneliness, hunger, fear, and the constant threat of death.

Her mind had unraveled in a small fraction of time, compared to the women's captivity. Her thoughts raced as if she were viewing a screening of her life—scenes from her childhood, her mother, her father—happy times, sorrowful times.

Her mind flashed through painful memories of adolescence, body image issues of a maturing girl, social pressures, and the constant battle against the feelings of not fitting in.

Growing up, her emotions had been a jumble of guilt, anger, and pain. A particular horrific memory as a young girl was when she started her period on a day she wore white pants.

Papa had provided a loving, comfortable life. The soothing smell of his pipe was the most potent sleeping pill. He'd tucked her in at night—read to her or made up a story, then patted her on the head. "You're a special girl, Emmanuelle," he'd say, and kiss her on the cheek.

If Papa read the letters, he'd known about her kinship to Mengele and probably the reason he'd discouraged her from pursuing a career in genetics. And if he'd told Mother, the emotional distance now made more sense.

Her mother never saw her to bed. She'd tuck in her brother, Lukas, but never her. Growing up, Emy had not understood why her mother was always aloof and angry with her and thought it was her fault. Perhaps, if she'd been more obedient or done better in school, her mother would have treated her nicer. Emy had tried but to no avail. The only attention she got from her mother was negative reinforcement. She didn't understand then, and now as an adult, her heart still couldn't comprehend. *How could a mother be so cruel?*

She'd been too proud to ask for help. Emy had avoided counseling, even after she'd had a meltdown from the pressures of her first year of medical school. The shameful affair with her professor and other sexual encounters had left her with regret. Her solution then and now was to pour herself into her work with more conviction.

Emy rolled to relieve the pressure on her shoulder and hip as her mind continued to sort through her life. She pictured Keith when they first met. He was everything she wasn't—carefree, reckless, impulsive, and most of all, passionate. *Could he be involved in this somehow?* Her mind stopped there and wouldn't go any further with that thought. It was too painful.

The girls. She wanted to think everything she'd done was for them. But she knew better, and the weight of her narcissism pressed down on her heart. She had craved fame and recognition—to finally be someone important. *God, was it all because of my mother?*

Bauer. She wanted to scream and kick her legs in a tantrum. *How could I have blindly trusted the man?* She knew why; she needed him to gain that fame and recognition. She had sold her soul to the devil, even before she'd known he was Mengele's son. Evil begets evil. *I guess the business world brings out true colors.* The greed and ruthlessness manifest.

Emy shivered and pulled the blanket tighter and wrestled with what she should do…*give in to his demands? Become my grandfather's reflection? Push the science onto thin ice?* She could tell Bauer where to find the Hello Kitty flash drive and the keys to the entire system. *Better yet, make them take me to it.* It could be her only chance of survival. Perhaps it was too late, and he would discard her. *I built everything he wanted, and now he's done with me. They haven't hurt me yet, but will they?*

Or was she willing to walk away from BioGenics? *My company.* The awards, the accolades. She was one of the greatest geneticists in the world. Her colleagues would think she'd gone crazy to walk away from it all. Eventually, the world, like Bauer, would disregard and discard her. She'd end up as a teacher in some no-name college.

Danek. The image of her little boy, a healthy, pink baby that had mutated to the horrific creature she had turned him into in her attempt to heal him. Bauer had pushed her. They started the trial too prematurely; they weren't ready. She'd let herself compromise for the sake of building her empire. *Please forgive me, my child.*

Emy's body started to tremble, then evolved into violent shaking from the torrent of emotions she had been processing. No wonder people buried their frustrations in booze and sex, and, yes, work. Guilty as charged.

What was that sound? She tried to force her body to quiet, but with no success. *Yes, there it was again.* Scratching.

"Help me!" she screamed.

She waited. "Please, help me!"

She waited again. "Is someone there?"

She listened. Nothing.

Terror eclipsed her memories. She had no idea how far back the bunker went. *Maybe it snakes all the way back into the hillside.* She turned and uncovered her face but couldn't see anything. Total darkness did strange things to her mind. Occasional flashes of light or movement jittered through her neurons, left over from sensory stimulation. She put her hand in front of her face, or that's what she thought because she couldn't see it. She felt along the floor. Maybe if she crawled. What if the woman came back? Was there something there to use against her? Could there be a back passage out of here?

She crept along on her hands and knees; the concrete sliced into her knees and palms. She stretched her arm out and then crawled forward a few feet. *Nothing.* She had a terrible sensation of falling and tried to stay grounded to the floor. She inched forward until the top of her head bumped into the brick wall.

Okay, now I'm getting somewhere. She pulled herself up to stand; her head spun with disorientation, but she edged along the wall. Two steps. Three more. She carefully moved forward, the brick gritty in her hands. She extended her foot and tapped with her toe. She hoped there wasn't a drop off and she'd fall.

Five more steps.

Her mind played tricks on her. *Was there light down there?* Then fear hit her, imagining glowing eyes staring back—the chimera waited for her to get close enough to pounce.

She gripped onto the wall and forced her mind back to reality. *Breathe.* This was a dumb idea. She realized she'd left the blanket and water bottle back behind. Where had she come from? Where was she? Everything was dark.

Emy reached further on the wall. Her hand landed on something soft and silky. But before she could withdraw her palm, some sensation scurried across her arm. She screamed and brushed it off, but another crawled up her neck and into her hair.

She screamed, shook, and ran her hands through her hair and over her shoulders and arms.

She swatted at another sensation on her leg. And then ran into the darkness.

She only got five steps when, in the disorientation of the blackness, she caught her toe on the cement and went down hard. She hit her chin and scraped her hands and knees.

Emy screamed, curled up into a ball and wept. Then she did something for the first time since she was a little girl with Papa before her goodnight kiss. She prayed.

CHAPTER 37

The first two nights of the spa adventure, Maggie and Nick and their friends stayed in plush hotels that overlooked the Baltic Sea. But the last night in the Ciekocinko Palace Hotel was Maggie's favorite by far—a French estate nestled into Poland's countryside. They followed winding roads through Kashubian forests and villages to arrive at the château. Hundred-year-old red oaks stood as guardians to the entrance of the expansive property. Horse barns and a carriage stable stood to one side of the estate—the grandeur of antiquity.

Once through the tall regal doors, the two couples were met with exceptional hospitality, as if they had arrived at the home of a long-lost friend—an extremely wealthy friend. The staff was eager to pamper the guests and treated them like royalty. The concierge greeted each by name and took them directly into the sitting room, warmed by a roaring fire, and offered them hot tea and pastries. He bowed and said, "Please relax and enjoy. Your rooms await, and we will take care of your luggage for you." Maggie and Katy sighed: it was pure luxury.

Each room of the hotel was filled with priceless antiques and treasures that included a grandfather clock, a Josef Köppl piano, bronzes, expensive-looking artwork, and a vintage Austrian gramophone playing a Glenn Miller record.

The concierge put Buck and Katy in an executive suite with a balcony that overlooked a tranquil horse farm. Nick and Maggie stayed in the tower suite with a spiral staircase that led to a master bedroom loft.

The four enjoyed an enchanting five-course candlelit dinner that lasted the entire evening.

In the morning, still full from the previous night's feast, both couples savored a light breakfast and enjoyed their coffee in the elegant library.

"I feel like a princess," Maggie said. "This is so romantic." She brought the cup to her mouth and stopped to admire the manicure that she and Katy had received the day before in the previous hotel. She raised her other hand to Nick and wiggled her fingers. "Darling, do you like my nails?" she said in her best British accent.

"Yes, we must prepare for the queen. Would you please send my chambermaid to dress me?" Katy chimed in.

"We may have spoiled you a little too much," Buck said.

"You men can go back to your humdrum lives." Maggie waved them off. "Katy and I are moving into our new estate."

They all laughed.

"I hope that the CRISPR treatment tomorrow removes some of that sass," Nick said.

Maggie understood that he meant it as a joke to keep things light in view of what lay ahead; nevertheless, her eyes watered. She caught her tears before they fell, dabbing her eyes with a hanky. "That is exactly what I'm afraid of," she said, "that this treatment is going to change how God made me."

Nick paled. "Maggie, I am so sorry. I wasn't thinking—"

"It's okay," Maggie cut him off. "I'm still trying to get used to the idea of altering my DNA. It's kind of scary."

Nick put his arm around her. "Please forgive me, I'm an idiot."

"That's the truest thing you've said all week," Buck said. They all laughed again. "I'd make him sleep out in the cold for that one."

"I think that's a brilliant idea." Maggie smiled, then turned serious. "Since we've been surrounded in affluent comfort, I've thought a lot about that exact thing."

"Comfort?" Katy asked.

"Yes…this weekend has been so wonderful, but it's not exactly real life. I think we all work so hard to find comfort, that we are not ever satisfied. I swear, the people who we've cared for in Guatemala had a fraction of this luxury and a hundred times more contentment. It's such a paradox. There is something about this sorrow that has shaken the core of my beliefs and grief. It's like the more I feel sorry for myself, the more I realize the collective misery that is out there in the world."

"I think it's okay for you to grieve," Katy said.

"I understand that and am so thankful I have friends to cry with," Maggie said. "Not that I think all comfort and pleasure is bad." Maggie gathered her thoughts. "I don't know, it's kind of hard to explain. After all, where would we be without electricity or modern medicine? But this whole thing has challenged me to go deeper into my faith." She turned to Nick. "Maybe I really do need a little attitude adjustment." Maggie laughed, then gave Nick a peck on the cheek to let him know all was forgiven. "Don't worry. I wouldn't make you sleep out in the cold."

A staff member stuck her head around the corner.

"The horse trainer called from the stables. Are you ready to see the horses now?" she asked. "The barns are heated, but you better bundle up to get there. It's pretty cold today."

They slipped on their coats and walked to the front entrance, where a heated SUV was parked to shuttle them the short distance to the stables.

The cobblestone drive wound to the front of a complex that would make the most prestigious of Kentucky horse farms envious. The brick stable with large wooden doors was topped with a clock tower. A carriage house was attached and converted into additional guest accommodations. On the other side was a massive indoor riding arena.

"Speaking of comfort," Maggie said as the head trainer greeted them at the door.

"Welcome, welcome," the well-built man said. He looked more like a Russian prizefighter than a horse trainer. "Please come in before you all freeze."

After introductions, he took their coats, hung them on hooks along the wall, and led them down the immaculate hallway to the stalls.

"Don't you love that smell?" Maggie asked.

"You mean the horse poop?" Buck laughed.

"Oh man, it smells like home: horses, hay, and yes, a little manure." She smiled.

"The concierge told me you and Mr. Hart are from Montana, America," the trainer said. "The home of cowboys and indians?"

"Yes, I'm the indian, and he's the cowboy," Maggie said and laughed, certain the man didn't understand how correct his assumption was.

"Forgive me for not calling you over sooner, I had a little problem with one of our stallions this morning." He rolled up the sleeve of his T-shirt and exposed a black and blue bite mark on his deltoid. "Not sure why he's so bent out of shape, but I turned my back on him and wham, he got me."

Nick pushed on the wound. "Doesn't look like he broke the skin. You'd better be careful," Nick said and added, "I took care of a farmer who led a mare in heat down the center aisle. His stud reached out of the stall, and the darn thing bit his shoulder so hard that it took a big chunk of his muscle off. I had to take him to surgery to fix it."

"You're a surgeon?" the man asked. "I should refer to you as Dr. Hart. Please forgive me. I will let the front desk know to put that on your information card."

"No," Nick protested. "Just call me Nick."

"Please come in." The trainer smiled. "It is my honor to introduce you to our horses."

He stopped in front of the first stall and opened the door. Inside was a small-statured mare with a blue dun coat and thick mane munching contently on a mouthful of hay.

"This is one of our Koniks," the trainer said. "The Konik is a surviving member of the Eastern European wild horse. They can be cantankerous, but this one is old and tame."

The horse raised and lowered her head as if she understood.

In the next ten stalls, huge curious heads of equines hung out the open windows above heavy wooden doors.

"This is our Sokolski team of draught horses. You must return in the summer, and I will give you a ride on our eight-horse-powered wagon. There is nothing like it."

He reached into a bag that hung on the wall and handed the humans all horse biscuits.

"This is what they are waiting for." He laughed.

Maggie held the treat out to the first horse, and it readily took it off her flat palm.

"Oh, aren't you handsome?" she cooed. The chestnut-colored horse with a long blond mane towered over her five-foot-one frame. It crunched happily on the treat and grunted with satisfaction. It stretched its neck and sniffed for another. Maggie couldn't resist.

Several enclosures down, a distressed pony kicked and thrashed in its stall. Its cry echoed throughout the barn. All the horses and humans looked toward the sound.

"He's the stud that bit me this morning," the trainer said. "Something has him all riled up."

"Sounds like he's in pain," Maggie said and trotted to the stall before the trainer could stop her.

"I wouldn't—" the trainer warned and tried to make his way between Maggie and the door to the stall.

But Maggie beat him to it and stood fearlessly in front of the half wooden entrance with the top bars closed. The trainer came to her side. "Please, Mrs. Hart, be careful. Especially in your condition," he indicated her pregnant belly.

The horse tossed his head back and forth and frothed at the mouth. He let out a series of high-pitched cries. The muscular, sorrel-colored horse pawed frantically at the air with black-socked front feet. His long black mane and tail swept side-to-side in high anxiety.

"He's beautiful. What breed is he?" Maggie asked and took hold of the bars.

"He is a *Wielkopolski*. They originated in Poznań, the town you stay in. He is a prized stud, so I am quite concerned about him."

Maggie studied the horse, looking for telltale signs of injury or other apparent issues—a swollen belly or lame foot. She saw nothing obvious.

"How long has he been like this?"

The trainer bobbed his head and said, "He has been quite agitated for three or four days now. He was getting more and more restless, so I locked him in here. You can see he is not happy about that."

"What is his name?" Maggie asked.

"*Odkupienie.* It means Redemption," the trainer said.

As Buck, Katy, and Nick approached the stall, the horse reared, and Maggie held out her hand for them to step back, out of sight of the horse. She turned back to the trainer. "No injury or sickness?"

"No, I checked him over pretty well a few days ago. Now, I can't get close to him." He pointed to his injured shoulder.

The horse pawed at the ground, and Maggie looked into his eyes. She saw past his rage, and what she saw ignited her own grief, and it flowed out in her native Blackfeet tongue.

The horse instantly stopped his frenzy, raised his head, and turned his ears forward. Maggie continued to whisper to the stallion until he took two steps forward to smell the air between him and her.

Slowly, she reached up and unlocked the bars to open the top half of the door. She glanced at the trainer, who was about to speak but stopped. Then she stood with her palms held up. The Blackfeet language rhythmically rolled off her tongue. The sound mesmerized the stallion, and he took two steps forward with flared nostrils. He exhaled a low guttural moan and stretched his neck. He sniffed so close to Maggie's face that his exhalations ruffled her hair.

"It's okay, boy."

The horse smelled her breath as she spoke. He snorted and lowered his head. She reached for his jowl, and first let the horse sniff both her palms. Then she gently stroked the sides of his face and mouth.

Tears rolled down Maggie's cheeks, as the horse nuzzled her face and let out a soft vibrating nicker. The horse held her stare and then dropped his head further so Maggie could scratch his ears and neck. His shoulder and chest muscles relaxed as she lovingly stroked him.

She leaned in to whisper into his ear. "It's okay. I understand. You're going to be okay." Tears flowed with her words.

The horse gently nosed and lipped her hair. Sighing deeply, he draped his head over her shoulder, and the two embraced. Maggie laid her head on the horse's neck and wept.

* * *

The wintry countryside flashed by as they drove their rental car back to Poznań. Maggie had explained to the trainer that Redemption was grieving. The trainer nodded, and with tears in his eyes, he told Maggie and the others that a week earlier, he'd had to euthanize an old mare that had gone lame. He didn't know how deeply it would affect the stallion and felt awful that he'd missed the signs. He promised to take the prized horse out to where he'd buried the mare to say his goodbyes.

Maggie told the others she'd seen it many times on the reservation, horses that grieved over the death of a pasture mate or owner. "Horses feel deeply," she'd explained.

Nick, who was driving, reached over and patted her knee. "You okay?"

She smiled and nodded. "I guess we both needed that."

"How did you know the horse was grieving?" Buck asked from the back seat.

"Maybe it's my Blackfeet blood." She laughed. "But honestly…I don't know how to explain it. It's like I simply knew—grief and suffering are universal languages. Something sacred."

They rode along in silence.

Finally, Maggie turned to her friends. "No one chooses to suffer, but there is something holy about it. We all go through suffering in one form or another, and somehow, it brings us closer to God. I suppose no one wants to talk about it, because it's impossible to understand. As I stood there with that beautiful animal, I could feel God's presence. It's as though the connection to the horse brought me back to a firm foundation…to my faith and trust that I can face any trial that comes my way…even this current one I am in."

CHAPTER 38

Emy lay somewhere between delirium and reality. The blackness of the bunker disoriented her and filled her mind with vivid dreams of an altered existence, as if she floated through the vastness of space and eternity. Hypothermia and dehydration changed the neurotransmitters in her brain, producing hallucinations. People from her past shuffled in and out of her mind for joyous and horrifying reunions. In one instance, she met her mother, Bella. *Is that really her?* She'd never seen a photo of Bella, but her mind had conjured an image. In another instance, Emy trudged through a snowy field beside her grandmother, Yuri, and Yuri's sister Eva. They were all cold and hungry. Monsters in Nazi uniforms chased and abused them with whips, the butts of their guns, and ferocious canines. They never arrived at their destination—only the marching and marching until their legs became stumps and stuck to the ground.

In moments of clarity, Emy considered trying to move to search for the blanket and water bottle. But in her panic, she didn't know which way to go. If she picked the wrong direction, she could end up back in spider webs and scurrying rats. All she was sure of was the hard, cold concrete floor against her body, so she stayed in place, freezing, hungry, thirsty, and lost in a sea of disorientation. As best as she could, she pulled her pajamas around her neck for protection from real and imagined assaults.

Her mind had separated, like the two halves of her brain, as she argued what she would do when the woman returned. The self-preservation side reasoned that she should relent and give them what they wanted. The stubborn side argued for telling them to go to hell.

Perhaps it was too late. What if they had found the flash drive? Would they leave her here to die? She was at death's door already, hypothermia pulling her into an icy grave. She'd stopped shivering—her body's defense against the cold had lost the battle. What was left of her physician's mind reasoned she was now in stage two of the insult—her blood shunted to the vital organs, her heart rate slow and irregular. Soon, her body would trick itself into thinking she was too hot. She'd rip off her one layer, only to send her into the third and final stage— labored breathing, heart failure, pulmonary edema, and finally, cardiac arrest.

Not the way she thought she would die. Her life had been too comfortable for that. True, her genome had revealed mutations, including the odds of succumbing to cancer that put her at higher risks. But her DNA could not have predicted betrayal and the immoral acts of others.

She would give Bauer what he wanted, perhaps salvage the relationship and live in warmth and comfort, sheltered by the man who was like a second father as she'd sit by the fireplace on his estate. Who cares about where the technology goes? It could lead to discoveries never thought possible. A new human race with enhanced IQs who could solve the most challenging puzzles known to mankind—living longer and healthier lives. That side of her brain justified the compromise. Bauer's voice seemed audible in the darkness: "If we don't do it, someone else will. You can control the narrative."

Control—isn't that what she'd always wanted? And the girls…this was her way to protect them. The argument seemed so clear now. Why had she endured this confinement? Emy's mind begged the woman to return.

But the other half of her brain continued to argue. *Are you sure you want to be the person who makes irrevocable changes to creation? You know the risk. Look at what happened to your own son. Advances in medicine always cost something, isn't that what Bauer always says? The perils are too high, the traps too deep.*

Her embattled mind reminded her of the prisoner doctors she'd read about while at Auschwitz—Jewish and Polish doctors who were captives of the Nazis. The video of Dr. L. played on a projector in her mind. The ninety-year-old survivor's voice was weak and raspy.

"I did what I needed to do to survive," she said. The woman never looked at the camera, her voice filled with regret and sorrow. "I truly wish my body would have died…my mind and spirit were dead already. I can only tell you what I remember as my mind has locked away many secrets." The woman took a drink from a crystal glass, her hands shaking. "I am both a Jew and a Pole. My family was gathered…my parents, my husband, and our two young children. At the selections, they called out for doctors. I was not going to respond, but my husband shouted and pointed to me. Dr. Mengele himself came over, and I told him I was indeed a physician. I did not want to go with the man, but he reassured me that if I did, my family would be cared for."

She tried to take another drink but could not make her trembling hands cooperate and set the glass back on the table.

"The Nazis deceived us in small increments. Each time we compromised our conscience a brick at a time. They enticed us with extra food and accommodations—quid pro quo. 'You do this for me, and your life and your family's life will improve.' They assigned us to the SS doctors and made us feel special, like we were somehow the elite in this despicable place." Her face grew sour. "They convinced us that we were there to take care of our own people—the saviors of our families and culture." She shook her head. "We deceived ourselves…one brick at a time."

The camera zoomed in to catch a tear rolling down her cheek.

"I was assigned to Block 10 and instructed to care for the women undergoing treatment. You see, one had to carry on as though life continued, but we all understood that with one misstep, we would fuel the ever-present fires. It was a constant moral dilemma. The SS doctors depended on us for the gas chamber selections from the patient population. They wanted to remove themselves from the task. I was asked to provide twenty names a day to make room for new patients. How could I choose?"

The woman stopped. The emotion was too heavy, but the interviewer coaxed her on.

"The Nazis gave us twenty sulfa tablets a week to treat infections. Do you treat one patient with a full course or twenty with a nod of reassurance? This was my daily dilemma. Maybe

I actually helped a handful of people. This is my only consolation."

The interviewer asked her about the most difficult task she performed.

The woman swallowed hard and hesitated to continue.

"Becoming pregnant in the camp was the greatest sin and an instant path to the gas chambers. We had to choose…the mother or the baby. It was a risk to our own lives as well. We would sneak them into Block 10 and give abortions or deliver the babies in the dark of the night."

"What happened to the babies you delivered?"

The woman held her forehead in her hand.

"They would have been brutally killed by the Nazis, anyway." She paused and forced the rest of the words out. "We thought we did the right thing as we pinched off their noses and mouths. And so, the Nazis succeeded in making murderers of even us."

"What happened to your own family after the selections?" the interviewer asked.

"I never saw them again. I believe that monster took my parents and children to the furnace. Perhaps, my husband survived in the work camp for a short time. I do not know."

Emy woke from this memory with a start. Whatever fluid was left in her body exited in tears and a cold sweat. The last few functioning neurons signaled her impending death.

"Forgive me," she whispered. To whom she did not know.

Suddenly a blinding light pierced the darkness.

Sounds.

A voice.

Pressure buzzed in her ears.

A presence was near that lifted and carried her.

Warmth.

"Dr. Christianson, what did you do? I thought you were some kind of genius."

That voice. Emy tried to focus her eyes and mind.

She floated.

Her skin burned.

A woolen blanket wrapped around her body. Warm coffee burned her lips and the roof of her mouth. But she gulped hard and gulped again. The hot beverage slid down her esophagus and spread warmth throughout her body like fire over dry grass.

"Herr Bauer would not be pleased if you had died. You must be more careful." The voice laughed.

Herr Bauer. Had he come to my rescue?

The fog over her mind lifted, and she grasped it was the Chinese woman that supported and gave her coffee. She wanted to pull away, but she was too starved and cold. As she warmed a degree, her traumatized body shook violently.

Her lips and voice cracked as she tried to speak.

Her captor anticipated her words. "Yes, Dr. Christianson. Are you ready to talk now? Please tell me where I can find the information to get into BioGenics's system."

BioGenics. Her company. It seemed a million miles away and so unimportant to her survival. But, she realized, they had not found the flash drive. Maybe there was still a chance.

"Please tell us, so we can end your suffering."

Emy tried to whisper.

"Tell me, doctor."

"Brick by brick," came from Emy's mouth.

"I don't understand. Tell me where it is. What do you want me to tell Herr Bauer?" She shook Emy's shoulders.

"Tell him to go to hell," she rasped.

"Then perhaps, this will change your mind." The woman spun her around to show another figure tied to the chair.

Emy's mind reeled. The unconscious young woman's head hung lifeless. A large open gash bled across her cheek.

She tried to force her body to move and escape the Chinese woman's grip.

"Ceci," she gasped and strained to go to her child.

"Now you could save both yourself and your daughter," the woman hissed.

"How dare you!"

"Now, what do you say, doctor?"

With her last ounce of strength, Emy pushed her captor back.

The woman stood. "If that's the way it is, I leave you with one blanket. You, doctor, get to decide who lives and who dies."

The woman walked to the door and slammed it behind her.

At that moment, Emy understood, she was a prisoner doctor.

CHAPTER 39

FRUSTRATION

Herr Bauer sat at the head of the table in the conference room at BioGenics and glowered at the men and women gathered around. It was highly unexpected and an inconvenient complication that Emmanuelle had locked down the entire system.

"No one can tell me how we can circumvent this issue?" he demanded.

The room fell dead silent. No one dared speak, nor even look at the man who'd screamed at them and called them imbeciles.

Bauer pulled his pipe and tobacco pouch from the inside pocket of his jacket. He methodically stuffed the bowl, put the pipe to his lips, and lit it. He looked around the room to see if anyone was brave enough to challenge him with the no-smoking policy.

Finally, his lead engineer spoke up. "Herr Bauer, every time I think I find an access point, the AI readjusts and shuts the system down again. I'm sorry. At least Dr. Christianson didn't put a limit on our attempts to crack the code," he added.

Bauer ignored the silver lining. He inhaled deeply and blew a large cloud of smoke defiantly into the room.

"What if we shut the system down completely and rebooted it?" he asked the group.

One of the female engineers bobbed her head from side to side. "We have discussed this," she said with an Indian accent. "We are concerned that we may lose all the data. It should only be considered as a last-ditch effort."

"You mean to tell me we've had access to the computer this entire time, and not one of you idiots thought to back up the data off-site?" Bauer slapped the tabletop. "Is there not a single hard copy of the research?"

The staff locked their eyes on the table in front of them.

"Damn it! Someone answer me!" He hit the table again, this time with his fist. They all jumped.

The engineers looked at their superior, who wiped sweat from his upper lip. "That is correct, Herr Bauer. We didn't think it necessary," his voice trailing off to a near whisper.

"Unfortunately, we found that having a backup or hard copy, as you say, would not be the entire answer," the Indian engineer bravely spoke up. "It seems that Dr. Christianson has some formulations stored elsewhere, or possibly in her head. She is no dummy."

"Unlike you fools," Bauer muttered under his breath. His emotions threatened to spring him from his chair and choke the woman. Instead, he drew a long puff of his tobacco.

"All this research is published, and the researchers reside within the building. Can't we reconstruct the data?"

The Indian woman shook her head. "Yes, that is true, Herr Bauer, however, our proprietary processes are protected in the computing system."

"Come on, people, fire up your brains, for which I pay a premium," his voice grew louder.

"We could talk to each individual department and re-searcher and reconstruct their past and current projects," one of the other engineers spoke up.

"That would take years," the lead engineer said.

"BioGenics has ongoing trials and patients to care for," Bauer said. "I understand a woman from the US is supposed to get treatment today. Months or even weeks are unacceptable."

Bauer finally turned to Dr. Chen Wangwei on his right, who'd been sitting quietly the entire time, his hands folded in front of him on the table. His face was emotionless, as if he sat at a poker table. Bauer already detested the Chinese scientist who was difficult to understand with his strong accent, manic speech, and cackling laugh. Wu, Bauer's friend from The Fifteen, had made the arrangements to hire Chen, who had been under house arrest in China for producing two live births from CRISPR treated embryos. Wu helped with his expatria-tion. Deep down, Bauer hoped that Emmanuelle would come to her senses, but Chen would have to lead for now.

"Dr. Chen, what do you think of this idea?" Bauer asked.

"Oh, no worry," Chen said and moved his hands as quickly as he spoke. "I do whatever you need and want."

Bauer sighed. He hated to deal with the Chinese, who were always over-promising and under-delivering.

"Has anyone talked to Dr. Christianson's assistant? Does she know anything?" Bauer turned back to the engineers.

"We have, and no, she knows nothing," the lead engineer said.

Dr. Christianson's secretary opened the conference room door and stuck her head inside. "Herr Bauer, your visitor is here. I put her in Dr. Christianson's office."

Bauer got up stiffly from his seat and took a few tentative steps. This inconvenience made his body and his mind ache.

He walked into Emmanuelle's office and slammed the door shut. An attractive Chinese woman stood by the window. Bauer knew who she was, even though it was the first time he'd met Ping Wusu in person. The rumors were true—she was a stunning specimen of a woman—a perfectly shaped figure, flowing black hair, glowing skin, and plump lips.

"Ms. Ping, I hope you bring good news today. I am surely in need of some."

"Herr Bauer, please call me Lilly." She smiled gracefully behind dark, mysterious eyes and reached her hand out to shake his. She had perfect English except for a slight British or New Zealand lilt. Perhaps her childhood tutor was not American.

"I can see why Emmanuelle's husband is enchanted with you."

Her china doll smile did not change. Bauer tried to read her eyes but couldn't tell if she wanted to seduce him or kill him. He knew from reports that either was possible. With all his power and control, he felt slightly intimidated by her.

"Does her husband suspect anything?"

She sniffed through her nose. "The man has no brain." She paused and added. "Well, a tiny brain that is not in his head." The corners of her mouth turned up.

"Please, won't you sit?" Bauer said and directed her to the sitting area.

"Herr Bauer, I just came from—"

He held up his hand to stop her. "The less I know, the better," he said, lowering his voice.

She nodded without emotion, then said, "I'm afraid our

persuasion of the doctor has not yet been successful. These things often take time."

Heat rose up Bauer's neck, and he swallowed angry words. He'd need a different tack to deal with Ms. Ping.

"How much more time?"

"Soon, I think. She asked to speak with you."

He held up his hand again. He did not want that involvement. That was what he hired others to do.

"We have her daughter with her now," Lilly said.

"Ceci or Hanna?" Bauer said with surprise. "I did not authorize for the girls to be involved in this," he shot back.

"Ceci." The woman did not blink and coldly added, "Herr Bauer, you told me to do whatever was needed."

* * *

The four sat in the waiting room at BioGenics. Maggie hadn't slept a wink, and her spirit was still unsettled even though she had decided to push on with the procedure. She prayed as she often did during hard times, "Your will, Father, not mine."

The strength and faith from her encounter with the stallion wavered this morning. If she had to wait much longer, she'd change her mind.

"Wasn't our appointment with Dr. Christianson at ten?" she asked Nick.

He nodded and looked at his watch again. "Yeah, this is atypical for her."

Many new people hustled past them this morning. They had been to BioGenics during the calm of the holidays, and maybe the frenetic pace of the employees was the company's norm. However, Dr. Christianson's secretary seemed unusually short in her hospitality and answered with, "Someone will be with you shortly." That was over an hour ago. They had not seen the doctor's assistant, Izzi, either. Hopefully, she was able to finish the CRISPR formulation for today, possibly the reason they waited.

Maggie sighed with frustration just as an attractive Chinese woman came from the doctor's office. *If CRISPR can make me look like that, I'm all for it.* Maggie smiled to herself. She admired the woman's athletic figure and her attractive ankle boots and wondered if she'd bought them in Poznań.

She looked at the woman and smiled, but the woman ignored her courtesy and walked past.

Maggie crossed her arms over her chest. Her frustration increased at the long wait. She knew that doctor's schedules were often at the mercy of unexpected emergencies and complicated patients, but the striking Chinese woman didn't seem like much of an emergency.

Now an Asian man came from a room down the hall and walked into Dr. Christianson's office. Maggie frowned at Nick. He reached over and interlocked his fingers into hers.

"Lord, help us," he recited their mantra.

"Yes, Lord, help us." She smiled back.

"I hate being on this side of medicine," Nick said. "Doctors and their families make the worst patients."

"Dr. and Mrs. Hart," the secretary finally spoke to them. "Please come in." She stood to open the office door.

Buck and Katy stayed in their chairs until Nick waved for them to follow.

As they entered the office, Maggie was surprised that Dr.

Christianson was not in the room. The elderly businessman they had seen before stood beside the desk, while the Chinese man sat behind it. She glanced at Nick, who looked equally confused.

"Where is Dr. Christianson?" Nick said with irritation.

The elderly man in the old-fashioned suit stepped forward. "Dr. and Mrs. Hart, please come in," he said warmly.

He shook Nick's hand and then Maggie's and invited them to sit in the two chairs in front of the desk. Then he noticed Buck and Katy and said, "Forgive me, we will get more chairs." He snapped his fingers at the secretary.

"That's okay, we don't mind standing," Buck said, furrowing his brow and crossing his arms, assuming the position of Maggie's bodyguard.

The elderly man sat on the corner of Emy's desk. "I'm afraid, Dr. and Mrs. Hart, you have caught us at an awkward time."

"Where is Dr. Christianson?" Nick asked again, with elevated agitation.

The man ignored his question and said, "Dr. Hart, I am James Bauer, and I own BioGenics."

Maggie glanced at Nick and saw his face flush.

"There has been an unfortunate incident—"

Maggie interrupted with a gasp. "Has Emy been in an accident?" she asked.

"No, no, nothing like that." The man smiled uneasily. "Dr. Christianson has, unfortunately, left the company for personal reasons. She's had some issues at home and has decided to take a leave of absence." His jowls waggled as he spoke.

"Mr…"

"Bauer," the man filled in.

"Mr. Bauer, this is highly unusual. What about my treatment?" Maggie asked.

"Please forgive us, Mrs. Hart. This has taken us all by surprise, and Dr. Christianson has left us…uh, flat-footed. Unfortunately, your treatment is not yet finished."

Maggie started to speak, but Bauer continued. "I want to introduce you to Dr. Chen Wangwei. Dr. Chen, like Dr. Christianson, is one of the world's leading geneticists. He has done remarkable work in China."

Maggie looked at the man behind the desk who said nothing and nodded slightly.

"You do the same work as Dr. Christianson?" Nick asked.

"Oh, yes, yes, yes," the man said manically. "We do exact same thing—"

"Please, give us a few more days to make this transition," Bauer cut him off. "Again, please accept my apology. I hope you will give us a chance to earn your trust. I will see to it that the secretary schedules another appointment for Wednesday, two days from now." He stood to indicate an end of their time and started toward the door.

Maggie and Nick also stood and followed him.

"Where is Izzi?" Nick asked.

"Izzi?" Bauer asked and looked over his shoulder at Chen.

"Emy's assistant," Nick said.

"Oh, ja, ja, of course," Bauer said. "Working, I'm sure."

The secretary gave Maggie an appointment card, and the four walked to the elevator in silence.

Once the doors closed, Buck said what Maggie thought. "Well, that was about as strange as it gets."

CHAPTER 40

ROTTEN

Nick looked at Maggie as she took another bite of the Polish *pierogies* at the Brovaria Café in their hotel. The dumplings stuffed with potato and onion, then sautéed in butter and garlic, were her favorite.

"Oh my gosh, I love these things," Maggie said and smiled back. "Truly pillows of heaven," she repeated the waiter's words when he described them.

Katy had ordered the same, but Nick and Buck had chosen steaks, fries, and beers. It wasn't Nick's typical lunch beverage, but he needed something to settle his nerves. He had ranted and cursed all the way back to the hotel until Maggie finally told him to stop. He'd raged from anger to fear and back again. The worst part was the unknown. Why was Emy missing in action? Who were these other people? And most importantly, what were they going to do for Maggie? No one at BioGenics had given them an answer except to go back to their hotel and wait.

Buck, who had been unusually quiet, asked Maggie, "You don't seem to be upset by this whole delay?"

She smiled. "No, I've had such an uneasiness about this gene-editing, but I understand I can't always run my life based on my emotions and feelings. That could be dangerous. But in my experience…even with difficult decisions or challenges, God gives peace. I waited for that and asked Him to either open or close the door. I think what we heard was the sound of a door slammed shut. This Bauer guy and the new doctor gave me the heebie-jeebies. I couldn't get out of there fast enough, and I'm sure not going to let them mess with my DNA."

Nick's frustration returned. "You can't go untreated, Maggie. Our baby…" Nick caught a cautionary glower from Buck and stopped before he said something regrettable. He sat in silence and let Maggie continue.

Finally, she said, "Look, I don't know why I…*we*, have been dealt this hand. I choose to put my trust in the One who made me. Not that I want to seem like some religious fanatic, but everyone has a choice—where to put their faith. My decision may change tomorrow, but today I'm living in peace that doing nothing is the best course for now."

"So, what do you want to do?" Nick asked, trying to cover his frustration.

"Let's go home."

Nick set down his fork, crossed his arms, and closed his eyes. He didn't want to fight in front of their friends. Not that they'd judge. Buck and Katy understood the stress and the weightiness of their decision. Neither had offered an opinion— they listened and loved, and most importantly, prayed. Nick opened his eyes and turned to Katy, "What do you think?"

She pursed her lips and nodded. "I try to put myself in your shoes," she finally said. "Honestly, I don't know if I have a good answer. Everyone has to come to this decision on their own." She dabbed her mouth with her napkin. "Maggie, you said something the other day that really struck me, 'trying to find peace within the midst of darkness.' I've prayed for that light to shine in this present darkness."

"Thanks, Katy, I need that. I believe that the Lord has all my days numbered. I constantly repeat one of my favorite Psalms over and over, 'Your eyes saw my unformed body; all the days ordained for me were written in your book before one of them came to be.'"

"That shines a bright light on the issue of our DNA, for sure," Buck said.

"I have to lash my faith to something and right now if I had to choose between the science of BioGenics or my heavenly Father…well—"

Maggie stopped mid-sentence, and Nick sensed someone walking toward their table, but his mind didn't register until she stood beside him.

Izzi's cheeks and ears were bright red from the cold. Frost covered her black leather jacket and snow clumped on her boots. Her usual effervescence was absent from her eyes.

"Izzi, you okay?" Nick asked and looked down at the splint over her hand.

"Hey, Dr. H, I'm sorry to come to your hotel, but…" she looked over her shoulder and lowered her voice. "Something is jacked up at work. Dr. C is MIA, and there are some crazy douchebags running around."

Maggie stood and hugged the girl. "Izzi, you look frightened. Please sit and let us get you something warm to drink," she said and pulled over an empty chair from the table next to them.

"I'm so sorry, Mrs. Hart, that I didn't finish your treatment for today." Her arms hung heavy at her sides. "The computers have been down since Friday morning…I've been totally buggered."

Maggie hugged her again. "You're half frozen, Izzi. Why are you so cold?"

"I rode my bike here. It was further than I usually go, but I didn't know where to turn." Her teeth chattered as tears rolled down her frosted cheeks, her normal hardened exterior shattered. "I don't trust anyone at BioGenics right now and didn't want to go to the police. I'm sorry, I don't know what to do."

Katy poured her a steaming cup of coffee from the urn on the table and offered her cream and sugar.

"You remember our friends, Katy and Buck?" Maggie asked.

Izzi nodded and cradled the cup in her hands, absorbing the heat.

"What are they telling you at BioGenics?" Nick asked.

"They called me into Dr. C's office and that creepo Bauer wanted to know how to get into the computer. I told them I had no clue. And now they tell me that some new doctor from China is taking over."

"And what about Dr. Christianson?" Nick asked.

Izzi checked over her shoulder again. "They told me she wanted some time off. I know people get fired, but Dr. C *is* BioGenics. I don't think she'd go willingly. She's been under a lot of stress, but we're pretty tight." She held up two crossed fingers. "I think she would have told me. I tried her cell like a kazillion times. First, it went straight to her voicemail, but now it's off." She shook her head.

"What kind of stress?" Maggie asked.

Izzi looked at Nick. He'd decided to not share with Maggie about the marital issues so she wouldn't worry.

"Emy's husband is apparently having an affair," Nick said.

Maggie shot him a glance but didn't pursue the subject as Izzi continued, "Then there is this whole family thing she's got going on."

"What's that?" Nick asked.

"I probably shouldn't say, but Dr. C found out recently that she was adopted and got some letters that rocked her world."

She offered no more clues and changed the subject.

"The weirdest part was I saw that sleaze, china doll at BioGenics this morning." Izzi held up her broken hand. "The whole thing has my head spinning. Nothing makes sense."

"That is strange," Nick added.

"I followed that skank out of the building. Crazy thing was that she drove Dr. C's husband's little red Fiat. When she drove off, I tried to follow her, but I only have my bike and didn't get very far."

Nick looked at Buck, who'd taken it all in. His hardened Marine affect showed.

"Something is rotten in Denmark…uh, Poznań," Buck said.

"You think we should go to the police?" Nick asked.

Buck tilted his head from side to side. "What would we report? It is possible, you know, Dr. Christianson is truly taking time off. Have you checked out her house?"

"I was gonna ride my bike there, but I decided to find you first."

"You know where she lives?" Buck asked.

"Oh yeah," Izzi said.

"I have an idea," Buck said. "Why don't Katy and Maggie enjoy the rest of the meal, while we," he pointed to Nick and Izzi, "take a quick trip to her house. If we find her huddled under a blanket with a good book, we can stop worrying."

CHAPTER 41

RANSACKED

Emy moaned at the hard kick to her back. The door to the bunker was opened, and light poured in. It was daytime, and Emy and Ceci had survived. In fact, Emy reasoned with more clarity than she'd had since the start of her captivity. What their captor had meant for evil may have saved her life. It gave her a reason to fight. Sharing body heat with her daughter, a new resolve grew in her belly. Emy and Ceci had finished the water, using only a small amount to cleanse her daughter's wound. It needed stitches, but at least the bleeding had stopped. They'd huddled under the blanket and made their escape plan. Emy's body was weak, so she'd be the sacrificial lamb. Ceci still had her strength. This was possibly their last chance to escape.

"You survived, Dr. Christianson. I am surprised," the Chinese woman said and held out a bottle of water.

Emy untangled herself from the blanket, sat up, and took the bottle. She opened it, took a long drink, and looked in her captor's eyes. They were dark, with neither emotion nor life.

"Why have you done this to us?" Emy asked with defiance. "Have you no conscience?"

A slight smile crossed the woman's face. "I am a mere pawn like yourself, Dr. Christianson. I only do what Herr Bauer has asked me to do. And he pays me well for it."

"What is your name?" Emy asked.

The woman shrugged slightly. "People call me Lilly."

"Such a gentle name for a terrible person," Emy fired back. "I know about you and my husband."

Lilly laughed. "I only used your husband to get to you. Please don't take it personally," she scoffed. "He is a stupid man. He knows nothing about this and doesn't care. He only thinks of one thing."

"What will happen to him?" Ceci said, uncovering herself from the blanket and standing up.

It forced the Chinese woman to take two steps back in a defensive stance.

"I have to pee," Ceci said and moved to the wall. As she pulled down her pants and squatted, the woman answered her question.

"Do you really care?"

"He is my father," Ceci snapped.

Emy rolled to her hands and knees, gagged and coughed. The woman glanced at Ceci, who stood at the far wall. As Lilly took a step forward, Emy collapsed on her side and clutched her chest.

"Help me," Emy gasped.

Lilly took another step. Emy wheezed in a breath and then held it.

It was enough.

Just as Lilly stepped within reach, Emy struck, digging her fingernails into Lilly's face with all her strength. Like a mountain lion locked on its prey, Emy dug them in deep and tore at the flesh.

Lilly screamed and pulled at Emy's hands. But before she could pull them off, Ceci was on top of her—arms wrapped around her neck and legs scissored about her waist.

The crimson-faced Lilly swung wildly to throw Ceci off. Emy got to her feet and charged her, clawing wildly at her face again.

But before Emy found a stronghold, Lilly's foot snapped forward and caught Emy in the jaw, sending her tumbling backward into a curtain of darkness that threatened to close over her consciousness. Emy hit the ground hard and couldn't catch her breath.

Lilly gain rearward momentum with Ceci on her back. Emy tried to scream to warn her daughter of the approaching wall. But it was too late, and they hit it with a sickening thud, loosening Ceci's grip enough that Lilly pivoted, sending Ceci over her shoulder and slamming her onto the ground.

"No! Please stop!" Emy screamed.

Lilly grabbed Ceci's body from behind and secured her arms around Ceci's neck, slowly squeezing the life out of her.

"We have come to the end of the road, Dr. Christianson," Lilly sneered. "Tell me now, or your daughter is dead."

"Please, please, no," Emy yelled.

Her plea only made Lilly tighten her grip. Ceci hung defenseless as her lips turned blue.

"Please." Emy tried to stand, but her legs wouldn't lift her.

"Now!" the woman screamed. "Tell me."

Ceci's breath gurgled.

"I'll tell you. Please stop," Emy cried. "I'll tell you."

Lilly's arms relaxed slightly—enough for Ceci to wheeze in a breath.

"The information you want is on a flash drive." Emy wept so hard that her words were barely understandable. "It is in my office."

"Where?" Lilly tightened her grip on Ceci.

"At BioGenics," Emy cried. "The flash drive is in the curio cabinet," she murmured, trying to catch her breath. "There is a jar next to a crossbow. You will find the codes to access the computer in there," she said, hoping she'd buy it. "Now, please, let my daughter go. You have what you want."

Lilly released Ceci, shoving her to the concrete, causing her head to bounce like a melon.

"I hope Dr. Christianson, for your sake and the sake of your daughter, you are telling me the truth. There will not be another chance. Some things are worse than death," Lilly said as she walked to the door and slammed it behind her.

Emy understood. They were already dead.

* * *

Fortunately, Nick had not yet returned the rental car, and following Izzi's directions, he drove them to Dr. Christianson's house. The front door was unlocked. Nick and Buck were uneasy about entering, but Izzi charged in. Once inside, they saw immediately that Emy was in trouble. Drawers had been opened, the contents spilled out, the furniture was out of place, and the cushions scattered. The house had been ransacked.

"You better take us to the closest police station, Izzi," Nick said.

"What do you think is going on?" Izzi asked. Her face paled, and her hands shook.

"I don't know, but this is bigger than all of us," Nick said and scrambled down the steps to the car, followed by the others.

Nick took the driver's seat and looked at Buck as he sat in the passenger seat beside him. Buck returned his worried look and raised an eyebrow. As a war-hardened Marine, Buck had keen insight and intuition that Nick often relied on, but Buck simply grimaced and said nothing as Izzi jumped into the back.

"Which way, Izzi?" Nick asked.

She pointed down Polska Street. "I guess we should go to the main station in town."

Nick backed out of the driveway and accelerated into the street.

They rode in silence until Buck pointed to the structure across the street. "What is that place?"

"That's the old Fort VII," Izzi said. "It's a historical site."

"Maggie and I visited the museum," Nick added. "It's an old fort that the Nazis took over. Half of it's been restored as a memorial—it's not a pleasant place."

Nick shook his head in disgust, remembering what they had seen there, but in his peripheral vision, Nick sensed Izzi's agitation. He looked in the rearview mirror to see her kneeling on the seat, staring out the back window.

"Izzi?" Nick asked.

"Holy crap," she said. "I think that was Dr. C's husband's car. It pulled out back there."

Nick hit the brakes, skidding slightly on the icy road. He turned into the next available street and was about to do a U-turn when a red Fiat zipped by behind them.

"That's the car," Izzi exclaimed. "But he's not driving. I think it's her...in the car...that Chinese woman."

Nick turned around and stopped. "Are you sure? I've seen a lot of red Fiats here in Poland."

"Yes...well, maybe. I don't know."

Nick glanced at Buck. "What do you think?"

Buck looked back at Izzi. "How certain are you?"

Izzi's face flushed. "Well, maybe sixty-forty."

"This is awfully close and convenient to Dr. Christianson's house. I say we take a quick look, then we better go to the police."

Nick pulled back onto Polska, and Izzi pointed to where she thought she saw the Fiat exit.

Nick's heart sank as they entered the main road into the old fort. He drove slowly down the lane. "Izzi, it could have been a tourist leaving." He sighed.

He slowed when Buck pointed to a set of tire tracks in the snow off the main road into an isolated pullout.

"Let's take a look," Buck said.

Nick turned into the pullout. Clearly, another car had been parked there.

They got out, and Buck examined the footprints.

"What is this place again?" he asked.

"Fort VII is an old Polish stronghold built in the late 1800s. In World War II, it was taken over by the Nazis and turned into a death camp," Izzi said, pointing to their left. "That whole side has been excavated and turned into a museum and historical site." She motioned to the right where the footprints left a trail. "This half is vacant."

"They built the fort into the landscape, lots of underground bunkers," Nick added.

"Maybe we should go get the police?" Izzi asked, her face full of fear.

Nick guessed Buck's answer but asked anyway, "What do you think?"

"Let's take a quick look," Buck said.

The path led through trees. "There are multiple footprints. We might encounter some resistance," Buck said. "Izzi, maybe you should wait in the car."

She shook her head, and they filed behind Buck. As they emerged from the trees, the trail came to a bridge over a moat-like structure. Then, on the other side, it went back into trees.

Izzi started to speak, but Buck whipped around, glared at her, and held up his fist. They followed the footprints in silence through an overgrown forest. Buck stopped them when they came to a clearing. He pulled them close and whispered, "I haven't seen any other tracks leading off the main path. It looks like the trail goes to some sort of brick bunker down there. I think I see a door. You guys wait here until I wave you down. I want to make sure we don't encounter any hostiles."

"Buck, please be careful," Nick said. His friend slowly made his way down the slippery slope, carefully holding onto branches to support himself. The man exuded courage; after losing both legs in battle, he still waded fearlessly into the unknown. There was no one else Nick would trust with his life.

The Marine crouched at the opening in the trees, scouted in all directions, then made his way to the brick wall with the entrance to an underground bunker.

Buck waved at Nick and Izzi to follow. When they reached Buck, he held his finger to his lips. All three stood in front of a rusty metal door.

"This has been here a long time," Buck whispered. "But *this* is new." He pointed to the silver padlock and then herded them away from the entrance to decide the next step.

"I don't know what to think," Buck said with his back to the door to shield his voice.

"You know, this could be a maintenance worker's storage unit," Nick warned. "I'd hate to see us behind bars for breaking into a historical site. Maybe we should go get the police."

"If there are combatants in there, we'll be sitting ducks. I sure miss my Heckler and Kock right about now."

Nick raised an eyebrow.

"It was the assault rifle I carried in Iraq—"

A loud crash behind them caused the men to jump.

CHAPTER 42

LUCID

The sound of the rock against the metal was loud enough to wake the dead. The two-handed stone that Izzi had heaved at the door fell to the ground. It had not smashed the lock, but it broke the rusted mechanism and left it hanging from the door.

She grimaced at the men as they stood in silence and listened for a reaction inside the bunker.

Nothing.

Nick had decided they'd trespassed into a storage area when a faint sound broke the stillness.

Buck stepped forward past Izzi and pulled open the door. Nick and Izzi followed him. The smell of mold and stale air slammed Nick's nostrils, along with another noxious odor… human excrement.

Nick dug into his pocket for his cell phone and clicked on its flashlight. Two sets of eyes glowed at them from the far reach of the bunker.

Izzi ran past the men. "Dr. Christianson. Is that you?"

Nick and Buck followed to find Izzi, who'd already wrapped her arms around the doctor. A young woman lay across the doctor's lap, moaning.

"Please help me," Emy sobbed. "My daughter, please help my daughter."

The doctor's face appeared sunken and red, her hair matted, and her eyes filled with fear.

Nick bent to examine the girl. Barely conscious, she had a gash through her cheek and bled from a scalp wound. Blood pooled on the doctor's legs. Nick set his phone on the ground, held the girl's head, and put pressure on the wound with his hand.

"Dr. Hart?" Emy sputtered, then sobbed aloud.

"Yes, we're here for you," Nick said. "We need to get you to medical care."

"And call the police," Buck added.

Emy looked at Buck and Izzi with confusion and then back at Nick. "How did you find us?"

"Dumb luck," Nick said.

"More like the grace of God," Buck said.

Emy's eyes filled with fear as she looked toward the bunker entrance. "Could you please get us out of here?"

* * *

Once they got Emy and her daughter to the car, Ceci became lucid. Still dazed from a concussion, she knew who she was but was confused about where or why. Nick had tied his scarf tight around her head to stop the bleeding and performed a quick neurological check—pupils equal, round, and reactive. With all the cranial nerves intact, an internal head bleed was less likely.

"You want me to take you to your hospital?" Nick said and then realized what a dumb question it was when Emy glowered at him. "Well, we've got to get your daughter sutured up."

Emy nodded. "But we need to leave now. They will be back when they find out I lied to them." She said, looking around furtively.

"Them?" Nick asked.

"I will tell you everything, but please…" she motioned to start the car.

"Then we should take you to the police," Buck said.

"No!" she yelled. "I'm sorry, no."

"But, Dr. C, look what these a-holes did to you and Ceci," Izzi said.

Emy nodded and sighed. "There will be a time for that, but not yet." Emy paused and touched Nick's shoulder. "Please, no police…yet. First, I have a crime to commit. I have to break into BioGenics."

Nick looked at her in the rearview mirror. The determination set in her face confirmed she was dead serious.

"Would you take me to my house first? I have medical supplies there for Ceci…and I have to pick up something."

"Only if we hurry. That will be the first place they look when they find you've escaped," Buck said.

Nick pulled onto the main road and sped to her house.

Still too weak to get out of the car, Emy described to Buck and Izzi what she needed.

The pair seemed to take forever, but in reality, it was only minutes. Nick had backed out of the driveway and turned the car around for a speedy exit. He kept a wary eye out for the red Fiat.

Izzi returned and jumped into the back with Emy and Ceci, clutching a briefcase-like nylon bag. Buck returned to the front passenger seat holding a small plastic figurine between his fingers.

Emy seemed relieved to see both. "Thank goodness."

Nick squealed the tires when the car hit the pavement and headed back down Polska Street. They had only driven a quarter of a mile when a red Fiat flew past, going the opposite direction. A Chinese woman piloted it.

"That your friend?" Buck asked.

"That's her," Izzi answered for Emy.

"You think she saw us?" Emy responded, her pupils dilated with fear.

"She'll know you're gone soon enough. Where do you want us to take you?" Nick said, looking at her in the rearview mirror.

"I have no idea," Emy cried.

* * *

Nick and Buck decided the best place for warmth, safety, food, and water was back at their hotel. The people after Emy would not have a reason to connect the dots to them. They could sneak the pair up the back stairway undetected.

Maggie and Katy went to the restaurant and retrieved two trays of food and hot cocoa. They encouraged Emy and her daughter to eat and drink before they answered one more question.

Emy's doctor bag contained lidocaine to numb Ceci's wounds, sterile saline to wash them out, and a variety of suture material. Nick asked Emy if she wanted to sew up her daughter's wounds, but she lifted her shaky hands and declined. Maggie donned a pair of sterile gloves to assist Nick.

The first few throws of the suture were a bit clumsy for Nick's rusty hands, but muscle memory took over, and he closed the wounds like the best of them. He'd started with the scalp wound, then worked on her face. He used the finest suture in the kit to give her an aesthetic closure.

Emy watched over his shoulder. "Very nice, Dr. Hart."

"Not quite like a plastic surgeon, but not bad for a clumsy bone doctor," he chuckled. "I'm almost done, Ceci. You okay?"

She nodded slowly.

He placed two more stitches, then cleaned both wounds with a sterile four-by-four. He spread a thin layer of Neosporin and covered her cheek with a sticky, transparent plastic dressing.

"Thank you," Emy said again and helped Ceci sit up. She'd paled from the blood loss and trauma, but youth worked in her favor, and she swore she was no longer dizzy.

Nick motioned to Emy for her to follow him into the adjoining room while Katy cared for Ceci.

"Can I get you anything else?" Maggie asked Emy.

"Perhaps some more water," she said as Buck held out a chair for her to sit and wrapped a blanket around her shoulders.

Emy's body shivered, and she looked at Izzi, "I imagine I owe you my life." She smiled and reached for her hand.

"Hey, Dr. C, no worries. I'm glad you're okay," Izzi said.

Emy looked at Nick and Buck. "Thank you, as well."

Buck waved her off, dug into his pocket, and produced the two-inch-high Hello Kitty. "This really holds the keys to your life's work?" He held it out to her.

Emy scoffed. "Yes, that's about it." She shook her head. "My life is in shambles otherwise." She rubbed her forehead. "I am thankful they didn't find it."

"It was right where you'd told me—on the shelf next to the breakfast bar. I'm sure they thought it was simply one of the girls' things. Unfortunately, your computer was missing."

"Yes, I figured that. But without this," she held up the flash drive, "it's not going to do them any good." She gave it back to Buck. "You mind holding onto it for now?"

Maggie handed Emy a glass of water, and she drank half of it.

"Amazing, what dehydration does to your brain." She took another drink. "I'm not sure where to start. You have done so much for me, I don't know if I should ask one more favor. I need to get back into BioGenics tonight."

"Why in the world would you do that?" Nick asked.

Emy stared into the water glass for a long time before answering. "Like you, Nick and Maggie, I have worked my whole life for good…to help people. I don't know when it started, but there were small compromises at first, then more until they seemed necessary—brick by brick." Tears ran down her cheeks. "But no more," she said with determination.

"Who are these people that did this to you?" Buck asked.

Emy looked Buck up and down. He had changed into shorts, and she focused on his prostheses. "Thank you, Mr…"

"Buck, call me Buck."

"Thank you, Buck, for carrying me out of the bunker. I now see what a feat that was for you."

She hesitated, probably deciding if she could trust them.

"Herr Bauer, James Bauer, is the majority stockholder of BioGenics and an extremely influential man. He is the one who has made my work possible. He has invested billions and wants to take the company in a direction I am no longer will-ing—I am done compromising."

"But why kidnap you?" Nick asked. "In the orthopaedic industry, CEOs are a dime a dozen. It's like a revolving door. Why not fire you?"

Emy nodded. "Please forgive me, Nick, but there is much more at stake here than the latest knee replacement. Gene ther-apy, gene modification, has the potential to change the world forever. Perhaps even more than the atomic bomb."

She looked up at them all.

"I don't mean to sound melodramatic, but I'm not strictly talking about the elimination of genetic diseases. I am talking about changing humankind."

"What do you mean?" Maggie asked.

"Maggie, changing one single gene like yours will one day be child's play. With the use of artificial intelligence, I am talking about the manipulation of multiple genes at once… enhancement of the entire human race."

Nick crossed his arms. "You're talking about eugenics."

Emy nodded.

"Seventy-five years ago, that is precisely what the Nazis were after," Nick said.

Emy sighed, and copious tears poured from her eyes. Finally, she said, "Still after."

Nick furrowed his eyebrows and waited for her to finish.

With her eyes brimming with tears, she looked at Nick. "Herr Bauer is Josef Mengele's son." She looked at her hand holding the water glass and whispered, "And I am Mengele's granddaughter."

CHAPTER 43

GOD'S IMAGE

Bauer examined the woman from head to toe. Angry scratches and gouges pockmarked her face as she stood erect in front of Dr. Christianson's desk. She'd explained how the doctor and her daughter attacked her, then lied to her about the location of the flash drive. In the short time she was gone, they had escaped.

Lilly was obviously not accustomed to failure, and as much as her reinforced veneer tried to hide it, her unblinking eyes betrayed her fiasco.

"The tracks indicate that someone broke the lock and took them away," Lilly said.

"Keith?" Bauer asked.

Lilly scoffed, giving the question no validity. "There were three people, I believe."

"Keith and friends?" Bauer asked again.

"Keith is clueless."

"Someone must have seen you drive back and forth," Bauer reasoned, his anger rising.

"Unlikely, Herr Bauer. I was quite careful."

"Not careful enough!" he yelled.

Lilly finally blinked.

Bauer leaned back in Emy's chair and drummed his fingers on the desk.

"And you went to her house?"

"Yes, absolutely," she said. "There was nothing."

"And you took all evidence from the bunker?"

"Exhaustively."

Bauer nodded, sat forward, and leaned on his elbows on the desktop. "I assume she will talk to the police. Although it will be her word against mine. In any case, I shall be out of the country. My airplane is on standby as we speak. You and Dr. Chen will stay."

Bauer noticed her eye twitch.

"Judging by your reaction, you object. I spoke with Mr. Wu, and this is our decision. You may call him if you like," Bauer said and pointed to the phone on the desk.

Lilly didn't move.

"Very well. You will continue to work to unlock the system and, above all else, keep Dr. Christianson out of the building. She could cause irreparable damage to the company if she somehow gains access. Do I make myself clear?"

"Yes," Lilly said sharply.

* * *

Emy's revelation was a nuclear bomb for Nick and Maggie, as well as for Buck and Katy. With Ceci asleep in the adjoining room, Katy had joined the others. They'd sat in silence as Emy told the story of her adoption and her ancestry, including Mengele and her Jewish mother and grandmother. Chills rose up Maggie's spine when Emy described her visit to Auschwitz, touring the camp and seeing pictures of the atrocities at ground zero and the depravities inflicted on human beings.

"That's why I need to get into BioGenics tonight," Emy concluded.

"But why?" Maggie asked. "Given what you've said, it's much too dangerous."

"I have to stop them," Emy insisted. "The research can't leave BioGenics."

"What do you mean?" Buck asked. "It belongs to you, and you are BioGenics."

"Not quite. Bauer owns the company. He can do whatever he wants with the research, and I believe he has plans to work with the Chinese." Emy looked him in the eyes. "Nothing good can come from that."

Buck pursed his lips and nodded in understanding.

"Some people in China have demonstrated a willingness to push past moral boundaries and ignore international recommendations," Emy said. "If they get a hold of BioGenics's proprietary processes, it will allow them to do things not yet possible in their own labs."

Maggie began to understand. "But what can you do about it?" she asked.

"I can prevent anyone from accessing the information. Right now, the data is locked in the computer on the third floor. I purposefully didn't share it on the cloud or other back-up platforms."

"Is there, like, an on-off switch?" Buck asked.

Emy smiled at him. He blushed, thinking it had been a dumb question. "Well, it's interesting you should ask. Herr Bauer's company provided the artificial intelligence and the computing system. I always had a concern about that, so I designed a 'virus'—a safeguard."

"So you're the only one with the on-off switch," Maggie said. "I think God's Spirit whispered to you."

Emy frowned. "I'm afraid, Maggie, I don't believe as you do."

Maggie smiled. "Just because you don't believe in God doesn't mean He doesn't believe in you. Darkness is not an entity in and of itself. It is only the absence of light. Your doubt is simply the absence of faith."

Emy nodded but looked unconvinced.

"How do you shut down the computer, then?" Buck pressed.

Emy pointed to the Hello Kitty flash-drive on the table. "That contains both the codes to reboot the system and the program to infect the computer, basically rendering the data useless."

"You'd destroy your life's work?" Nick asked. "You sure you want to do that?"

Emy's shoulders drooped, and she sighed. "I don't think there is another way. Do I give it to the Americans? I'm not sure they have been any better stewards of technology."

"What about Maggie's treatment?" Nick asked.

Emy turned to face Maggie. "Maggie, I'm sorry that you had to get mixed up in this," she said and hesitated. "I'm afraid this was one of the bricks...I wasn't candid with you. Our CRISPR technology, advanced as it is beyond anything else in the world, is still in its infancy stage." She looked at Nick. "I'm sure Dr. Hart, you understand the challenges of progress in medicine. Early trials are often disastrous."

Nick's face reddened. "Are you telling me that your technology is not as advanced as you reassured us?"

Emy bowed her head. "I think, Maggie, you should wait until after your baby is born for treatment. You would've been the first in the world to receive treatment while pregnant…and the baby, the first to receive treatment in utero." She looked at Maggie. "I was wrong to suggest you move forward with treatment. There are too many risks. I'm sorry."

Nick stood so abruptly, his chair fell over behind him. "You were about to experiment on my wife and baby!"

Maggie reached for his arm, but he pulled away, his hands becoming fists, and stepped toward the doctor. "We trusted you," he shouted. "Now you want our help?"

Emy started to cry.

"How could you do this to us?" Nick raged. "You are…" he stopped and turned away, going to the window.

Maggie was glad he didn't say what they all thought. No wonder she had never felt peace with their decision. "Thank you, Father," she whispered under her breath.

"I'm sorry, Maggie," Emy said, looking at her. "Please forgive me."

Maggie looked into her eyes—full of sincerity and sorrow—and she reached for Emy's hand.

Emy gripped her hand, and with a flood of emotion, she said. "My son, Danek, was born with cystic fibrosis. He participated in the early trials. He died not too long ago." She choked on the words and wept.

Maggie knelt and put her arms around Emy.

"I'm so sorry. I'm so, so sorry," Emy repeated over and over.

Maggie held her to let her grieve. She carried no bitterness toward Emy, only shared grief.

"I forgive you and thank God you are willing to do the right thing now," Maggie said, hugging her tighter.

Maggie turned to Nick. "We need to put a stop to this

generational curse. We have to help Emy break into BioGenics and crash the data before more people get hurt."

Nick nodded and returned to the others.

"Dr. Hart, please forgive me," Emy begged. "Please help me make this right."

Nick picked up his chair and sat back down.

"I think of some of the early disasters in joint replacement," he said. "Now a million are done every year in the US alone. I'll try not to be so judgmental."

"Truly, I only want the best for your family."

"I do believe that," Nick said, settling into his chair.

Maggie released her embrace, got to her feet, refilled the glass with water, and offered it to Emy.

Buck stood, patted Nick on the shoulder, and cleared his throat. "I think one of the problems with humans is that we are so short-sighted," he said. "Here's a problem," he held out his left hand, "and here's a solution," he held out his right. Buck brought his hands together with a loud clap. "We're too myopic to predict what our intervention does ten, twenty, or fifty years from now."

Nick nodded, "You're right, Buck. If we begin to change the genome for enhancement, there is absolutely no way to predict what that interference will look like in a hundred years. We may eradicate our species as we know it. What is good for today may be a disaster in the future. We might never be able to reverse the process."

Emy took a sip, dried her tears, and gathered her thoughts. "People are too tempted to try to improve our minds and bodies," Emy said. "Especially when there are billions and billions of dollars at stake."

"I suppose the world values people with certain skills, looks, or attributes," Buck said and pointed to Nick and Emy. "Who is more valuable to society, a doctor or a person with Down syndrome?" he added bluntly.

This silenced everyone in the room.

Maggie wrestled with the thought. *Is that statement true?* "Oof," she said. "I'm starting to see what's at stake. Are you saying that a short person, or a blind person, or someone who is disabled or has a disease like Huntington's is less valuable than someone with a higher IQ or physical superiority?"

"Well, look how much baseball and football players get paid," Buck said. "That says it all right there."

Again, they sat without speaking.

Maggie broke the silence. "So it comes down to what is the value of a human being? Is it their physical attributes? What they contribute to society? What they do for a living?" She stopped to gather her thoughts. "Or do people have worth simply because they are human? Are we truly created equal in the eyes of God?"

"I believe God sees us all equally as his children," Nick said. "But physically, I think being created equal is a myth. We are all given a set of strengths and challenges that are overlaid with our environment…our upbringing, surroundings, and our support systems. We are given different opportunities."

"Yes, but at the core of all things, we are each given an essence of life…an equal measure. Maybe that *is* our DNA," Maggie argued. "Does someone born into a royal house have more rights to live out that essence than a person born in war-torn Syria or the slums of Chicago? Or better yet…one born with a genetic syndrome?"

"I recently saw a news program about a family with a Down syndrome child," Buck said. "The interviewer asked if they would change that child if they could. The father got mad and said, 'At times it has been hard, but I would change nothing about our situation or my child.'"

"Perhaps, this is the real war...fear versus love," Maggie said. "One that humankind has faced from the beginning of time. Are we all equal in the sight of God?" she asked. "God created mankind in his own image," she quoted from Genesis, then added, "What is the inherent worth of a person?"

"I suppose if we let someone else decide, well...we are all destined for the gas chamber," Nick said. "Heck! I'd be sent there because of my battle with depression...my *mental illness*."

"Or the injuries to my legs," Buck added.

Everyone nodded without speaking. No one wanted to add to the long list of infirmities.

Finally, Emy spoke, "Where have you been all my life? I feel like fresh air is blowing in." She smiled. "I'm afraid I was blinded by the rewards."

"So, how do you get into BioGenics?" Buck asked, ready for action.

"It will be tricky...our security system is the most secure in the world," Emy said. "And dangerous. You have seen what Bauer is capable of."

"What about accessing the computer through the clinic or hospital?" Nick asked.

Emy shook her head. "Their computers are on different networks. I guess I didn't think this all the way through... remember, we are all short-sighted. I have to gain access through the computer in my office."

"Why don't we have the police escort you in?" Maggie asked.

"Theoretically, I am now a disgruntled ex-employee. If we get the police or attorneys involved, I'll never get in. I need to get in tonight. One of Bauer's engineers could eventually create a workaround if they haven't already."

"Then how do we get in?" Buck asked.

"We?" Emy asked.

"We're sure as hell not going to let you go by yourself."

"We'll need help from someone inside the building," Emy turned to Izzi, who balanced on two legs of her chair and chewed on a toothpick.

Izzi let her chair clunk onto all fours. "Hey, if the Marine is in, I am too."

CHAPTER 44

ASSAULT

Nick huddled with the team in the hotel room. After a private conversation with Maggie, he'd managed to relinquish his anger toward Dr. Christianson for potentially putting Maggie and the baby at risk, and they'd agreed helping her was the right thing to do.

Now, they were all together—Nick, Buck, Emy, Maggie, Katy, and Ceci. Everyone's input was valuable, including prayers for wisdom and guidance. Izzi had been dispatched to her lab at BioGenics before the research wing was shut down for the evening.

Nick looked at Buck and knew he was frustrated. Buck studied the Google images of the BioGenics's facility on his phone, zooming in and out for closer looks.

"I can't tell you how many assaults my teams have made on secure facilities," Buck said. "But we usually plan for weeks or months. I'm afraid the failure percentage in this operation is unsatisfactory."

"Are you saying you can't do it?" Emy asked.

"Hell no, ma'am. Just sayin' it's gonna be difficult."

Emy described the four-story building as a fortress: The E-shaped structure was designed for function and security. With thick stucco walls and little glass on the first floor, it looked impenetrable. Buck commented that with C4 explosives, the wall could be easily breached. They all understood that was not going to happen. Buck had waved off the chain link fence topped with razor wire that surrounded the facility as nothing more than a nuisance.

The one vulnerability of BioGenics's security was they designed it to protect from outside threats, not those from within. That's why they'd sent Izzi back to her lab. Although security swept the building and rooms each night, Izzi had confessed she'd hidden from them on many occasions to finish her work without interruption. Emy had supplied her with the security codes to shut down the alarm system, including the motion detectors outside. Once the system was off, Nick, Buck, and Emy could approach the building undetected. Fortunately, Izzi could access the system in her lab without having to enter Emy's office.

But they still faced tremendous obstacles: Emy had no idea if Bruno and his security team were on her side or not. Bauer now signed their paychecks, so she had to assume they'd stop all intruders. Waltzing in through the front doors was not an option.

"Just so you know, the security team carries weapons," Emy warned.

Buck nodded. "Then it is best not to encounter any of them, if possible. How many are inside the building?"

"We post one at each of the front doors, and others patrol each wing."

"So, six total?"

"Yes, but they may have tightened things up with me on

the loose," Emy said. "I typically enter the building at the side door, but security would most likely spot us."

Buck showed Emy the map of the building on his screen and said, "Is this your office?" Pointing to a corner on the fourth floor of the research arm.

Emy nodded.

"An assault team either has to go through, over or under," Buck said. "Give me a heli and rappelling ropes, and we'd be in and out before you could say Herr Bauer."

"I hate to tell you this, but when Izzi shuts off the alarm, it automatically notifies the head of security," Emy said.

"How much time between when Izzi shuts off the system to when he is notified."

"Immediately," Emy said.

"So much for the element of surprise." Buck looked at her. "Could you make this any more difficult? You have anything else you want to cheer us up with?"

"I'm sorry." Emy looked down. "I shouldn't have involved you in this."

"I'm afraid it's too late for that," Nick said.

Buck focused on the side door where Emy usually accessed the building. It required using the palm and retinal scanner. Since she'd disappeared, they'd more than likely updated the system to deny her entry. The same was true if the team attempted to pass through the hospital or clinic, where they were sure to encounter more guards.

"Could Izzi open this side door from the inside?" Buck asked.

Emy nodded. "Yes, but it would alert security."

Nick threw his hands up. He was about to call it quits—take Maggie and his baby home.

"When Izzi shuts down the alarm system, security will recognize something is up; they just won't know where," Emy added.

"Then we'll need a distraction," Buck said.

"How about a ruckus at the hospital," Nick suggested.

Buck nodded, then turned to Emy. "What happens if there is a disturbance in the hospital or in the Emergency Department?"

"Remember, we are a pediatric and women's hospital. The only thing that comes in through our Emergency Department is OB/GYN patients—mostly women in labor, and they don't raise much of a ruckus," Emy said.

"Except during delivery," Nick joked.

Emy smiled at him. "It's probably pretty tame compared to what you're used to in Memphis," she said. "I'm not sure I remember the need for a security response ever. They might not grasp what to do."

"That might be in our favor," Buck said. "What would happen with the security in the different sections of the building if there was an incident? Would they all respond?"

Emy frowned. "I don't know. We've never had the need. I suppose if the ruckus is a big enough event."

"What about a fire?" Buck asked.

Emy shot him a look of shock. "In the hospital...I don't think that's prudent. Besides, both the police and the fire departments would respond."

Buck put his hand to his chin. "Again, that's not a bad thing. It adds to the chaos."

"You can't start a fire in my hospital. We have patients, for God's sake!"

Buck grinned at her. "Not a fire, the illusion of one. What if we, let's say, have a pregnant woman show up to the ED with her concerned friend." Buck smiled at Maggie and Katy. "I'm sure there are bathrooms inside the ED."

"Of course," Emy said.

"You want us to start a fire in a bathroom?" Maggie's eyes widened.

"No, but a little smoke goes a long way." Buck thought for a moment. "You don't have any potassium nitrate, I suppose."

Emy frowned.

"Sugar and potassium nitrate make a wonderful smoke bomb." He raised his eyebrows. "You have a ping-pong table at home?"

"We have one in the basement for the girls."

"Okay, great. Ping-pong balls are nitrocellulose. You ignite them with a lighter and voilà, you have lots of smoke. A handful should set off the smoke detector." He turned to Katy as if she'd already volunteered. "To be safe, empty the trash can and light them in there."

"I'm not sure how I feel about getting the ladies involved," Nick said.

"I believe the risk to them is low…" Buck said, "a pregnant woman who doesn't feel well and her friend. The docs will check you out and send you home."

"Unless they stop to question us about the ping-pong balls stuffed in our pants," Maggie laughed, relieving the tension. "We're in," she added and looked at Katy, who eagerly nodded.

"Okay, but that still doesn't help us get into the building," Nick said. "Even if the fire trucks show up, we can't simply stroll into the research wing."

Buck ignored him, glued to his phone. Finally, he turned the screen back to Emy. "What are these separate glass buildings behind the main structure?" he asked.

"They're greenhouses. We recently built those for one of our new researchers."

"Please tell me there's underground access from the main structure."

Emy grinned for the first time all evening.

"Yes…yes, there is an underground walkway. But, because they are relatively new, I have no idea if all the doors are locked."

"Are the interior doors to the hallway on the alarm system?" Buck asked.

"I don't believe so," Emy said.

Buck looked at Nick. "We just found our way in."

Emy shook her head. "Unfortunately, I'm positive that these greenhouses are locked up tight—reinforced doors and shatter-proof glass. I signed off on the design myself."

"How tall are the walls of these greenhouses?" Buck asked.

Emy shook her head. "If I remember right, ten feet or a little higher."

Buck zoomed in on the roof of the glass structure and held it out to Nick. "We're going in through these climate control panels. We're going to need a bolt cutter, some rope, and a crowbar." He turned to Emy. "You don't happen to have a gun, do you?"

"I think we have the first three items at the house. No gun, though."

"I was kidding about that." Buck chuckled. "Best to be unarmed, I think. The worst that can happen to us is they charge us with breaking and entering."

"You all could go to jail," Maggie said, her eyes watering. "Or worse."

CHAPTER 45

BREAK-IN

Nick, Buck, and Emy sat in darkness in the rental car on a farm road along the large field behind BioGenics. They'd made a quick and careful stop at Emy's house and were relieved that no one was waiting for them. They'd secured all the supplies they needed, including a flashlight they'd use sparingly to avoid detection. They'd sent Maggie and Katy to the hospital in an Uber, with Ceci as a translator.

Izzi was to shut down the system at 0300. Katy and Maggie would set off the smoke bomb at 0315. Hopefully, giving Nick and the team enough time to get inside the building.

If successful in shutting down security, Izzi would ping Nick's phone. They'd discussed Izzi opening the door of the passageway, but decided it was too dangerous to have her move about and risk detection. If the door was locked from the inside, they would chance it only then.

Buck looked at his military-style watch with a luminescent dial. "Ten more minutes," he said.

Nick's phone vibrated, and he read the text. WE'RE IN! "Okay, the ladies are in the ED."

Emy had mapped out the route through the greenhouse roof and the underground walkway. Hopefully, the door was unlocked to the rear stairwell of the building. Then it was up four flights of stairs and approximately twenty paces down the hall to Emy's office, where she'd need ten minutes at the computer.

Emy promised Nick she would put Maggie and their baby's information on a separate flash drive in case they ever decided to get treatment. Someone in the states might pick up Maggie's case. With Emy's guidance, she'd advance the institution's knowledge by leaps and bounds and help Maggie in the process.

Now in the car, Buck glanced at Nick and then at Emy. "Look, if we're caught, no one should be a hero. Surrender and face the music. They have guns, we don't."

Buck looked at his watch again.

"We'll follow the road along the trees and position ourselves at the last one. We should be well outside the motion detector sensors. When Izzi gives us the word, we must sprint like hell to the fence. No telling how long it'll take them to reactivate the system. I hope they investigate before thinking about reactivating. There is a half-moon out tonight, enough to give us a hint of light, but watch your step."

They exited the car. The night had turned clear, and the stars shined brilliantly, but the icy air bit at Nick's face. There was no wind, and except for the clicking of the cooling car engine, the evening was dead quiet. Floodlights on top of BioGenics brightly illuminated twenty-five yards around the structure in all directions. There was nothing they could do about that and hoped no one looked out the windows.

The moon produced a surprising amount of light that made moving down the road less difficult, and as they got to the last tree, Nick and Emy huddled behind Buck, who grinned and nodded at them. Buck was in his element. Nick panted heavily, even though the physical exertion had only begun. This was way outside his comfort zone, and adrenaline flooded his body. It was hard for him to catch his breath.

Nick's phone vibrated Izzi's signal in his pocket. "Okay," he whispered.

Buck took off in a sprint with Nick and Emy close behind. Nick was amazed at how fast the big man moved on his prostheses. Emy slipped and fell to her knees. Nick circled back and grabbed her by the arm to help her up.

Nick's legs throbbed during the fifty-yard dash, but by the time they met Buck at the fence behind the greenhouse, he'd already cut several links with the bolt cutter. His powerful hands made them snap like twigs. Then he lifted each flap of the chain-link. They had planned out every detail—Emy first, then Nick, then Buck, each sprinting to the greenhouse.

The three leaned against the glass wall. Buck held up his fist to remain still. Except for the pounding of Nick's heart, there was not a sound—no alarms or shouting. Emy had mentioned that power fluctuations occasionally affected the security system, and there was a chance the security detail would suspect that first.

Emy looked at the eave of the building. "We need a ladder," she whispered.

Buck put his finger to his lips, and the familiar sound of hydraulics whirled in Buck's legs. Emy gasped, looked at Nick, and nodded with astonishment. Soon, Buck was within reach of the eave and waved for Nick to step up on his prosthetic knee. Buck helped him climb to his hip and crawl up his back to the roof.

Buck had warned that with any operation, there were always variables one couldn't predict. Nick encountered the first. The snow-covered glass roof was slippery. He kept sliding down and almost tumbled over the edge as Buck tried to support his footing. The vent panel was several inches out of reach. Nick was able to find a toehold and took a blind leap. If he failed, he would end up in a crumpled heap on the ground below.

At first, there was nothing to latch onto. But Nick's hands slid to the edge of the panel and caught the ledge with his fingertips. Before he could warn Emy to wait, she was on top of him, army-crawling up his body. His arms and fingers ached, begging to give way. But before they gave out, Emy put her hand around his wrist and pulled him up onto the panel.

Nick unwrapped the rope from around his shoulder, looped it around an exhaust duct, and threw Buck the remaining length. Buck hoisted himself up, hand-over-hand. If not for his light metal legs, the pipe would have broken.

Buck nodded to Nick and Emy. Then, unstrapping the crowbar from around his waist, he thrust it under the panel and pressed his entire weight onto the iron.

Nick frowned when nothing happened. He shifted to add his weight when there was a loud snap as the frozen door opened, and the panel lifted.

Buck grimaced and stopped to listen.

Nothing.

As he lifted the rest of the panel, another loud creak filled the silent night. He threw the end of the rope into the greenhouse and lowered himself, waving the others to follow.

"You're quite the bionic man," Emy whispered to Buck.

Buck ignored the comment. When he clicked on the flashlight, Nick caught the steely determination in his eyes.

"Oorah," Buck grunted the Marine cry and moved forward.

It was impossible to navigate the greenhouse without the light, even though it increased the danger of detection. Buck and Nick followed Emy to the door that led to the underground walkway. Fortunately, it was unlocked. They sighed with collective relief, quickly took the stairs down, ran through the hallway to the door at the far end, and to the entrance to BioGenics.

Buck stopped to let them catch their breath. "Remember, no heroes," he whispered.

He reached up to the handle of the door and pulled.

Nothing.

He looked at Nick, who pulled out his phone and texted Izzi.

THE DOOR IS LOCKED.

Izzi must have bounded down the stairs two at a time, as it was minutes later when they heard the lock click open.

Buck reached for the handle when they heard a male voice shout.

"Hey, what are you doing here?"

"Dude, you scared the crap out of me. Just going for a smoke."

"Who are you?" the voice demanded.

"I'm Izzi, I work on the fourth floor…one of the research students. Sorry to startle you. I was trying to get a project done tonight."

"The computers are down."

"Uh, yeah…bench work, you know."

"Come with me."

Buck looked at Nick and grimaced.

As they waited for the voices to disappear, Buck turned to them and whispered, "The worst they could do is fire her."

When the words left his mouth, they all jumped at the shrill wail of the fire alarm.

"Good girls." Buck smiled.

He cracked open the door and peered into the stairwell. Halogen lights flashed, and the ear-piercing alarm bit at Nick's eardrums.

Buck motioned with his head for them to follow as he entered. They got up two steps when a door slammed open, and voices came from a floor above them. Buck forced the trio back to the passageway door and closed it quickly behind them. The rush of footsteps and radio chatter came past the door.

"It sounds like they exited onto the first floor," Emy whispered.

Buck nodded but waited another minute before opening the door. He moved forward and up the stairs.

Nick wheezed as they made their way to the fourth floor.

Buck stopped at the door and put his ear to it. He looked back at Nick and Emy and shrugged, then pointed to the blaring fire alarm in the corner of the stairwell.

"My office is on the left," Emy yelled into Buck's ear.

Buck nodded and slowly turned the doorknob. He peered into the hallway, then moved quickly with Nick and Emy down to the corner office. Emy reached for the light switch, but Buck guided her hand away, turned on his flashlight, and pointed to her desk.

The flashing lights of police and fire trucks sped down the road outside the window, their sirens screeched over the building's alarm.

Of all they'd endured, the most significant unknown was at Emy's computer. Had anyone thought to change or erase her passcode? If they had, their efforts were all for naught.

Emy sat at her desk and powered up the computer. Unlike her Macintosh at home, the Windows-based network took several minutes to boot up. Adrenaline flooded Nick's body as Emy typed her twenty-digit number into the computer and hit enter.

Nick found he was holding his breath.

He patted Emy's shoulder when her home page came to life. She looked up at Nick and Buck and smiled.

Buck rolled his finger to give her the 'let's get on with it' sign. She'd told them that crashing the massive third-floor computer was similar to stopping a freight train. It was not done instantaneously. She'd placed multiple safeguards.

Nick handed her the one-terabyte flash drive from his pocket, reminding her to download Maggie and the baby's information first.

Emy slid it into a port alongside the computer screen and typed in commands. Files for their genomes and treatment protocols appeared, and Emy dragged and dropped them onto the drive. It only took a moment for the data to transfer. Emy hit eject, pulled the thumb drive out of the slot, and handed it to Nick.

"Thank you," he said.

Buck already had Hello Kitty out of his pocket and handed it to Emy. She did the same with this flash drive and started typing as Nick and Buck looked over her shoulder.

Nick's heart skipped a beat when the shrill of the alarm went silent, and the flashing lights stopped.

"Well, so much for that," Buck said. "Let your fingers fly, doctor."

Emy had told them that there were many layers she had to work through.

Buck looked at his watch. "Two minutes," he said, indicating how long they'd been in the office. They had no idea how much time they'd get.

"I hope Maggie and Katy are okay," Nick said.

Emy looked up at him.

"And Ceci," he added.

As he did, the door to the office banged open. They could make out the shadows of two individuals in the doorway.

Buck nudged Emy and rolled his finger for her to continue.

Emy turned back to the computer, and the office lights flicked on. A Chinese woman stood behind Izzi. Izzi's eyes blazed with fear.

"Dr. Christianson, please stop," the woman said and pushed a pistol at Izzi's temple.

Buck took two steps around the desk, holding out his hands, and moving toward the assailant.

The woman pulled Izzi to one side and fired a shot that missed Buck by a fraction of an inch.

"Hey! There's no need for that," Buck said and stopped in his tracks.

"Yes, no one needs to get hurt," she said with one hand clutching Izzi and the other the gun. "Doctor, please stop typing."

Buck stepped between the woman and Emy.

Nick expected the woman to take another shot at Buck, but instead, she dug the end of the gun into Izzi's head.

"Not one more keystroke," she screamed.

Izzi cried out in pain, and Emy lifted her hands in surrender. "Please, don't hurt her."

"Now walk away from the desk," she demanded.

Emy pushed back from the desk just as Izzi thrust an elbow into the woman's abdomen. The blow sent the woman staggering back, but at the same time, her gun exploded.

For an instant, the room was silent.

Izzi turned to them. She was holding her chest as blood poured from a wound.

Buck charged.

The woman regained her balance, aimed the gun, and pulled the trigger.

The gun jammed.

Buck leaped over Izzi's crumpled body and hit the woman with full force, sending her tumbling backward.

Nick grabbed Emy's arm and pulled her back to the computer. "Keep typing," he said and went to Izzi—her body lifeless as he felt for a carotid pulse.

Nothing.

He started chest compressions and watched the mortal combat between Buck and the woman.

Buck attacked like a bear, but the woman fought like a cobra. She stopped his charge with a front kick to the throat and finished him with a spinning roundhouse kick to the head.

"You son-of-a—" Nick said and sprang to his feet, but the woman came at him with a flying sidekick that sent him into the desk. His head hit hard.

Fighting unconsciousness, Nick forced himself to stand, expecting another blow. When he got to his feet, he saw that the woman had pulled a crossbow from the cabinet next to the door.

"Doctor, I command you, stop!" the woman yelled.

The computer keys continued to click behind Nick.

The crossbow in the woman's hand snapped, and there was a deadly thud.

Emy cried out. Nick turned to see her holding the shaft of the arrow, its point impaled under her left breast.

CHAPTER 46

BROKEN-HEARTED

Nick jumped to Emy's aid.

"Help me," she gasped.

"Emy, hang on, we'll get you help."

He leaned her chair back. The arrow had entered under her left breast, an inch off the sternum, aimed for the heart. Death or life depended on how deep it penetrated.

"Help me," she begged again.

For an instant, Nick had no idea what to do. He didn't know if there was such a thing as 911 in Poland. Fire trucks and paramedics could still be at the hospital. He glanced over his shoulder and half expected to see the Chinese woman reloading the weapon. Instead, he saw Buck staggering through the doorway.

"I've chased her off," Buck said, but gasped when he saw Emy.

"Stretcher, we need a stretcher!" Nick yelled.

Buck turned to leave when Nick shouted, "Wait. It'll take too much time to run down, notify the EMS and bring them back. Emy could be dead by then. Buck, we've got to get her downstairs."

There was significant danger in moving her. The arrow could push into her heart. Worse, if it had already pierced the heart, it could dislodge, and she'd bleed out in seconds.

Nick felt her carotid pulse; it was weak and irregular. She was murmuring and losing consciousness.

"Let's wheel her down in the chair," Buck said. "It's our only option."

Nick nodded.

They each held one of her shoulders, tilted the chair as far back as possible, and pushed her toward the door. Buck slowed as they passed Izzi's body. He looked at Nick.

Nick shook his head and motioned to continue.

The chair bounced awkwardly as they passed over the threshold. Nick expected to see the woman ready for them again, but she had disappeared.

Once they hit the tile floor, they picked up their pace.

Buck pushed the down button, and the elevator doors opened immediately.

They bumped across the gap, and Emy moaned.

Once on the elevator, their progress was painfully slow.

"Come on, come on," Nick pleaded.

On the first floor, the doors had barely opened when they pushed Emy through and wheeled her down the hallway as fast as possible without creating more trauma.

"Thank God," Nick said after he pushed against the safety bar of the door between the research wing and the clinic, and it opened.

Emy was correct that the doors between sections of the building unlocked with the threat of fire.

As they approached the hospital, Nick had to decide—straight to the ED or turn into the OR. Emy's chest needed to be opened immediately, the arrow removed, and the damage to her organs repaired.

As they pushed through the hospital door, Nick looked at Emy and felt for her pulse. It was thready at best. When he saw her neck veins distended, he knew she was in trouble. If she didn't bleed out, the pressure around her heart would compress the life out of it.

"She's in cardiac tamponade," Nick said. "Her pericardial sac is full of blood."

As they passed the automatic doors to the operating suites, they swung open, and a young woman in scrubs exited. Nick immediately recognized the scrub tech who'd helped him repair Izzi's hand the other day.

"We need some help here," Nick yelled. "Dr. Christianson has been shot."

"Oh my God," the woman gasped. Then yelled down the hall. "Code blue, code blue. I need some help."

A swarm of medical personnel poured into the hall from the first room.

"We've got to open her chest. She's bleeding out," Nick yelled.

"We were cleaning up from a C-Section," an older woman said. "Follow me."

Nick guessed she was the anesthesiologist.

They wheeled Emy into the second OR. Buck lifted her out of the chair and gently set her on the table. She didn't even moan—she had lost consciousness. If they didn't get her stabilized soon, she'd lose the battle.

The anesthesiologist immediately slapped on pads for the heart monitor, placed the pulse oximeter on Emy's finger, and started an IV.

The woman eyed Buck warily but handed him the IV bag. "Here, squeeze the bag to push fluids in," she said. Then she turned back to Emy and slipped an emergency King airway down her throat and started respirations. Emy still had a heart rhythm, but it was slow.

Like a well-oiled Formula-One pit crew, no one hesitated. Nick thanked God they all spoke adequate English.

"Which one of you is a surgeon?" Nick yelled to the rest of the staff.

A young woman who looked fresh out of residency sheepishly raised her hand.

"You ever crack a chest?" Nick asked.

"Never," she shot back.

Nick swore. "I need a basic surgical setup and the biggest retractors you use in OB."

The scrub tech handed him a pair of trauma shears, and Nick sliced Emy's shirt and bra off, cutting around the arrow.

"Rolled blankets. I need rolled blankets."

A nurse brought several in her arms, and Nick bolstered Emy on her side.

"Paint her chest with Betadine," he instructed the circulating nurse, "and gown and glove me," he told the scrub. "You, too," he nodded at the young surgeon.

Things moved at a rapid pace. They had to.

"She's coding," the anesthesiologist could not hide the fear in her voice.

Nick grabbed the scalpel off the Mayo stand. His hands shook as he sliced the skin under her breast and curved it up along Emy's rib cage. He'd done the procedure once as an intern under the watchful instruction of his chief resident—twenty-one years ago.

All these years later, Nick could still hear the voice of his chief. "Go, go, go!" he'd screamed in his ear. The young man under the knife had been in a motorcycle accident. He didn't survive—they rarely did.

There was no need to cauterize bleeders as Nick went through the subcutaneous tissue and the intercostal muscle between the fifth and sixth ribs. Emy had no blood pressure. When Nick entered the chest cavity, Emy's pink, fleshy lung expanded and collapsed rhythmically with the respirations from the anesthesiology machine.

The scrub tech handed him two large Langenbeck retractors. He placed them between Emy's ribs and nodded to the other surgeon. "Pull hard...watch the arrow."

Nick reached up and adjusted the surgical lights. The pericardial sac was blue and bulging.

"Metz," he said and held out his hand.

The scrub slapped the curved scissors into his palm.

With the first cut, the pressure in the sac released, and blood shot six feet out the chest covering the floor and Nick's shoes.

He didn't stop.

The scissors continued to slice until the hole was big enough to fit his hand.

Blindly, he reached into her chest, through the pericardium, and felt for the arrow. It had pierced the right ventricle of the heart. With the release of the pressure, the heart beat irregularly.

Nick barked out orders.

"Give her as much fluid as you can dump in. Preferably blood," he directed the anesthesiologist.

He looked back at the nurse, who stood horrified at the mess he'd made of her operating room. "Get me a Foley catheter, some 2-0 Prolene, and pledgets or Teflon strips if you have them." Nick realized that a delicate heart muscle repair was different than the fibrous hamstring. The pledgets or strips would give the suture something to anchor into.

The nurse didn't hesitate and returned quickly with his requested supplies.

With his hand in Emy's chest, he looked up at the scrub. "When I say so, I want you to pull the arrow all the way out."

"Now." He nodded at her.

The arrow came out with a sickening sucking sound.

"Asystole," the anesthesiologist barked in his ear.

Emy's heart had stopped. Nick stuck his other hand inside her chest cavity as well and looked up as if in prayer. He prayed, but he also felt for the anatomy.

"Okay, I have my finger in the hole and beginning cardiac massage now." He looked at the heart monitor. The manipulation of the cardium initiated aberrant beats on the screen.

"Hook the Foley to the syringe and hand me the end of it."

The tech did what she was told.

Nick added. "When I tell you, inflate it with five cc's of saline."

Blindly he passed the tip of the catheter into the heart, guessing at how deep it went. He figured it was better to over insert it and pull back than to tear the heart muscle.

He nodded to the tech and felt the catheter stiffen under his fingers. After she injected the saline, he gently pulled back and let the balloon plug the hole from inside out.

He pulled his hands out of Emy's chest. "Okay, let's readjust so I can see what I'm doing."

The scrub tech had asked for and received a Balfour abdominal self-retractor and handed it to Nick.

He nodded in approval and fashioned the blades under the ribs and cranked them apart. He redirected the Langenbecks through the pericardial sac. "Don't pull, just hold," he instructed the surgeon. "We want to avoid tearing the pericardium."

He reached up and redirected the lights.

Emy was lucky that the arrow had missed her coronary arteries.

The scrub held out the first suture with a preloaded pledget. Nick rolled the needle through the myocardium, careful to push back the Foley and not entrap the balloon in the stitch. He added another and then asked the scrub to deflate the Foley and pull it out. One more suture, and the hole was closed.

"Give me one milligram of epi and prepare for more if needed," he said and rhythmically squeezed Emy's heart. He glanced at the clock and thought she'd been in asystole for less than a few minutes.

"I suppose you don't have any internal cardiac paddles," he said to the tech, not expecting an affirmative.

She shook her head and handed him the syringe of epinephrine. "We can give you a two-million-euro robot, though," she said with sarcasm.

"I wouldn't even know what to do with that," he scoffed.

He pushed the needle through the heart muscle. "If any of you are praying types, now's an appropriate time."

He pushed the plunger of the syringe, "Come on, Emy... come back to us."

CHAPTER 47

AFTERMATH

Maggie sat on the stretcher in the Emergency Department with Katy and Ceci standing on either side of her. A pleasant Polish doctor strolled in, holding a chart. She spoke only a little English and nodded at Ceci to interpret.

"Mrs. Hart, I'm afraid this was quite an eventful night for us. I am sorry you've had to wait so long," she said through Ceci. "The good news is all your labs look fine, and your exam was normal. I think your abdominal pain is from something you ate or a travel bug. How are you feeling now after the nausea medication?"

Maggie nodded and said through Ceci, "Thank you, doctor, I feel much better." It wasn't a lie. By now, Nick and Buck should have accomplished everything and were hopefully on their way to the hotel. "What happened tonight?"

The doctor's face saddened as she looked down.

"Someone must have smoked in the restroom and caught the paper towels on fire. The firefighters said it was out by the time they got here." The doctor looked up.

Maggie studied her eyes. There was more, so she waited.

The doctor spoke slowly to Ceci to translate the events of the night for Maggie. The only words Maggie understood were Dr. Christianson, which she said over and over.

Ceci gasped and burst into tears.

Maggie sat up as Katy came around the bed and hugged Ceci.

Maggie looked from the doctor, who seemed in shock, then to Ceci, who was inconsolable.

"Ceci, please, tell us what is happening," Katy begged.

"My mother," Ceci said between sobs. "Someone shot her."

Maggie looked at the doctor, who said something in Polish.

Finally, Ceci managed to say, "They had no idea I was her daughter. She's in surgery. They don't expect her to survive."

* * *

Nick and Buck sat on the cold tile floor of the hallway outside of the recovery room. With Nick's elbows on his knees, he rested his face in his hands. Buck finished a prayer.

"Amen," Nick whispered.

Buck put his hand on Nick's shoulder.

"Dude, that has to have been the most amazing thing I've ever seen. You, my friend, are a master surgeon."

Nick huffed out his nose. "We'll see…we'll see."

"I've seen pictures of a human heart, but to sit there and watch you squeeze Emy's. I'll never forget that. And when you injected that medication, and it started to beat again…" The big man's chest quaked with emotion. "Talk about a miracle."

Nick nodded. The images were fresh in his mind. "Oh, that's a beautiful thing," he had said, watching the heart beat in her open chest after the third injection of epinephrine.

"You can actually mend a broken heart." Buck slapped him on the back.

Nick appreciated Buck's enthusiasm, but he knew Emy

was far from safe. He expected the nurse to burst through the doors at any moment to tell them that Emy had coded again.

In Nick's experience, the heart doesn't respond well to manipulation, so the anesthesiologist would need to carefully balance medications to fight the erratic heart rhythm and bolster her blood pressure with fluids and blood. Emy still had one foot on a banana peel and the other in the grave.

"Come on, Emy, fight," Nick said under his breath. It had been a year and a half since he stood as captain of the surgical table—the highs and lows had not changed.

Nick looked at Buck. "Izzi is still upstairs." He shook his head and swore. "Remind me again how we got into this mess."

"Brick by brick," Buck repeated Emy's words.

The automatic doors to the hallway opened.

Buck stood, but Nick's exhausted body was frozen to the tile. Surgical images clouded Nick's mind, so it almost didn't register when the people who entered included Maggie and Katy.

But it did when Katy raced in and jumped into Buck's arms, and Maggie knelt beside Nick and wrapped her arms around his neck. He looked up and choked back a flood of emotions when he saw Ceci.

He wanted to say something but was interrupted when the doors to the recovery room swung open, and the anesthesiologist appeared.

Everyone turned to her.

She focused on Nick and nodded. "I think I have her stabilized for now."

Ceci dissolved into tears. Katy scrambled from Buck's embrace to support her.

"Thank you," Nick said to the doctor. "Thank you."

She guffawed, "It is you, Dr. Hart, that we all must thank. You saved her life. I'm afraid we would have been helpless without you. You should be very proud."

"Can I see my mom?" Ceci cried.

The anesthesiologist looked surprised.

"This is Dr. Christianson's daughter, Ceci," Nick said to her.

"By all means," she said. "Please follow me."

As she led Ceci into the recovery room, Nick registered another woman in a business suit standing close by.

The woman thrust her hand toward him. "Dr. Hart, I am Detective Nowak—"

She started to add more but stepped back, distracted by the amount of blood on his pants and shoes.

Maggie explained. "Ms. Nowak came to talk with us in the Emergency Department. We have tried to tell her everything we know."

"Dr. Hart, you cannot leave until I can sort through this… uh, mess," the detective said, staring at the blood.

"Where is Izzi?" Katy asked.

Both Nick and Buck looked at her and slowly shook their heads.

CHAPTER 48

Two days later, Nick and Buck sat on one side of the hospital's conference table, and Maggie and Katy huddled with Ceci and Hanna on the other side. Hanna had traveled from the university the minute she'd heard about her mother.

Between the constant vigil over Emy and answering all the questions asked by the police, they were all exhausted. They'd spared no detail. Ceci had filled in the blanks of the kidnapping, and Hanna told what she knew of her mother's business dealings, including the mysterious Herr Bauer.

Detective Nowak sat at the head of the table and looked from person to person. She occasionally pursed her lips or nodded. The detective leaned back in her chair and sighed.

"We have cordoned off the research building," she said. "The coroner has the grad student's body, and we have the murder weapon…weapons." She sighed again. "We have started the forensics on them, of course. Unfortunately, we have not found the Chinese woman. Nor have I been able to reach this…" she looked at her notes, "James Bauer in Berlin."

She turned to Ceci and Hanna. "We have picked up your father for questioning."

Ceci whimpered, and Maggie and Katy wrapped their arms around her.

The detective rolled her hands on the table. "There is still much to unravel here. I will need your passports and ask that you remain in Poznań until we can get all the details sorted out. At this point, I have no reason to doubt your story. For all intents and purposes, until we can talk with Bauer, it looks like you and Dr. Christianson broke into her own company. I don't think there are laws against that."

Nick relaxed his shoulders.

Detective Nowak stood and extended her hand to Nick. He rose to meet it.

"I understand that you saved Dr. Christianson's life," she said. "Thank you. She is well known in our city."

Nick nodded and hoped the present tense was correct. Emy remained in critical condition.

"Do you mind if we go check on her?" he asked.

"No, please do," the detective said and opened the door behind them.

The group walked down the hallway to the elevator. The doctors had moved Emy to a small intensive care unit on the second floor with a dedicated hospitalist on staff. He'd handed over Emy's continued resuscitation to her.

They approached the desk and asked the staff to see Emy. A nurse beamed at Nick. "Please, Dr. Hart, follow me."

As they walked down the hall, Buck put his hand on Nick's shoulder and whispered in his ear. "The handsome American cowboy doctor's reputation precedes him."

Nick shot Buck a glare and frowned.

"Don't let it go to your head," Buck grinned.

When they entered the room, it was clear that Emy's situation was still dire. Several tubes extruded from her body—a measure of her critical state. She was intubated with a breathing tube, and a nasal-gastric catheter extended from her nose. There were multiple IVs with blood and medications that dripped, a Foley catheter inserted into her bladder, and a large chest tube protruded from her ribcage, under suction to re-expand the left lung.

The four let Ceci and Hanna have a moment with their mother and waited silently in the back of the room. The cacophony of ICU sounds instantly brought Nick back to his days spent on the trauma service: the rhythmic puffing of the respirator and the pulse of the heart monitor, the beeping of the IV infusion pumps, the gurgling of the patient's endotracheal tube, and the strong smell of antiseptic cleanser battling with the nosocomial bacteria. It was all universal.

When Ceci swayed, Maggie and Katy rushed to steady her. Nick and Buck joined them on the other side of Emy's bed.

They stood in silence and watched Emy's chest rise and fall. Each with their own thoughts and prayers.

Finally, Katy pulled out her phone. "I have a recording of Hebrew prayers of healing. Can I play it?"

The girls nodded.

Katy found the soundtrack and hit play.

The throaty, airy voice of a rabbi reading the healing Psalms, accompanied by soft piano music, filled the room.

Nick listened to the beautiful ancient language and recognized the occasional enunciation of the Hebrew, *Adonai*, my Lord.

They listened to the entire track, after which, Katy said, "Psalm 16."

"Preserve me, O Lord: for in thee I put my trust." Maggie paraphrased the first line of the scripture, then asked the girls, "You think your mother would mind if we prayed over her?"

Hanna nodded enthusiastically.

"Please," Ceci added.

All four took a turn praying out loud.

Nick finished with, "Father, we speak life into Emy. Death has no authority here."

* * *

Bauer mopped the sweat from his forehead with his handkerchief, then dialed the number on the payphone. He wiped the receiver before he put the device to his ear and mouth. How undignified, but he worried about using the telephone in the hotel. Once he heard about the disaster at BioGenics, he had turned off his cell phone and removed the battery. Now the authorities could not trace him.

The phone rang and rang. When there was no answer, Bauer slammed the receiver back in place and swore.

Kenny handed him a bottle of cold water, and Bauer rubbed it over his face. "This Brazilian sun is going to kill me."

Kenny extended an umbrella and cast shade over his boss.

Bauer stood, undecided what to do next. *Why isn't Wu answering?* Bauer had his pilots fly him directly to Brazil, where there was no extradition. In the beginning, it seemed a thrill to follow in his father's footsteps, escaping the authorities. But as sweat poured under his suit, he wondered if he'd made a mistake. *How much can they really pin on me, after all?*

He looked at Kenny, sweaty and pale, about to pass out from the heat.

Bauer nodded in the hotel's direction when the payphone rang.

He turned and picked up the receiver.

"Hello?"

No one answered.

"Hello?" he repeated.

"Herr Bauer," the caller sounded relieved. "I wondered who called me repeatedly. I'm sorry I did not recognize the number."

"Wu!" Bauer said, happy to hear a familiar voice.

"I am glad to hear you are safe," Wu said.

"Kenny and I are in Brazil. Your operative has made a mess of things. I did not expect things to go this far."

There was silence, and Bauer looked at the receiver.

"Ms. Ping is standing here with me, along with Dr. Chen," Wu finally said. "We extracted them out of Poland through Lithuania and flew them home from there."

Anger welled up in Bauer's mind, "Well, I'm relieved you are all comfortable," he snapped, wiping his sweaty brow. Then softened his tone. "Forgive me, Wu, the heat is frying my brain."

"Unfortunately, Herr Bauer, I think you should remain in place until we identify which direction the investigative storms are blowing."

Bauer squinted at the sun. Something had changed in Wu's tone.

CHAPTER 49

WITHIN THE MIDST
TWO WEEKS LATER

Nick and Maggie walked hand in hand into the police station in Poznań. The front desk officer recognized them from their multiple visits and escorted them to Detective Nowak's office.

"Dr. and Mrs. Hart, please come in," the detective said and stood. "Can I get you some water or coffee?"

They declined and sat in the chairs in front of her desk.

"You get the Hansons off to the airport, okay?" Nick asked cheerfully.

"Yes, and we finally got the Marine a *Polska Kielbasa Wędzona*. I had to explain to him repeatedly, however, that you can't go into a meat shop and ask for a Polish sausage. It's like going into a cheese shop in Switzerland and asking for Swiss cheese. The store owner would look at you with a confused look and indicate that *every* cheese in the cooler is Swiss." She laughed. "We sent them home with a bundle of sausage and helped them get through customs."

"Thank you." Nick smiled.

"Mr. Hanson is a unique person," she said. "He told me some of his military adventures and other tales about you." She raised an eyebrow.

"I swear, we try to stay out of trouble, but…" Nick left it at that.

"He is a brave man," the detective said.

Images of Buck flashed through Nick's mind—half blown to bits when they medevac'd him out of Iraq. Nick shook his head. "You have no idea."

"Oh, before I forget," she said, opening her top desk drawer. She pulled out their passports and handed them to Maggie. "When will you return to the US?"

"Nick and I will attend Izzi's service in a few days in Warsaw," Maggie said. "We leave two days after that."

"That is very kind of you," the detective said. "I have only spoken to her father, and he is broken-hearted. Losing his daughter was even more difficult for him because Izzi and her parents had been estranged. He had hoped to reconcile with her after the new year." She shook her head. "It goes to show that you should never let silly differences separate you from the people you love."

Nick agreed.

"How is Dr. Christianson today?" Nowak asked.

"Her chest tube comes out this afternoon," Nick said. "She's still weak but growing stronger every day."

The detective nodded. "We appreciate your cooperation in this difficult time," she said with sincerity. "The Polish government plans a takeover of BioGenics. I expect an official announcement as soon as today. We will continue to pursue charges against the Chinese woman and Mr. Bauer." She crossed her arms over her chest. "But justice may never be served. Working with the Chinese is *odwracać kota ogonem…* how do you say? Like turning the cat by its tail."

Confused, Nick looked at her.

The detective laughed. "Our Polish sayings rarely translate well. It means a task that is impossible," she explained. "But we will keep pushing through diplomatic channels. Mr. Bauer, on the other hand, is another problem. He has fled the country, and rumors indicate that he traveled to Brazil. Extradition is difficult from there, although we are working with the German government to freeze his assets. Because of his family ties, the Israelis have taken a keen interest in the situation and offered assistance."

"What will happen to Dr. Christianson?" Maggie asked.

"That is in part up to her and in part up to our government. We shall see." She shrugged and paused. "Do you have any other questions for me?"

Nick looked at Maggie, and they shook their heads.

Detective Nowak stood. "Then I pray blessings for you and your new baby," she said. "I am sorry that your visit to Poznań was not more pleasant."

"We think Poland is a beautiful country," Nick said.

"Your people are something special," Maggie echoed Nick's sentiments.

* * *

Bauer had looked forward to meeting with The Fifteen. It was one of the few reasons he was grateful he'd survived the sweltering heat of Brazil for the past two weeks. But, after the call from Wu's secretary that the meeting location had changed to Berlin, he was furious to the point of rage. So much so that Kenny left in a huff and had not yet returned.

"They did this to me on purpose," he continued to swear at no one. "To humiliate me."

He'd given up using the payphone and lifted the receiver from the nightstand, asking the hotel operator to ring the number again. She sounded irritated that he continued to interrupt her. The manager had the nerve to knock on Bauer's door that morning and inform him that his credit card was no longer valid. He needed to bring another form of payment, or they would require him to surrender his room.

Stupid people. This was a case in point for eugenics.

The phone rang in his ear after the operator connected the call, and it surprised Bauer when Wu picked up.

"Herr Bauer, it is good to hear from you," Wu said.

"What in the hell is going on, Wu?"

"We are about to surrender our phones and start the meeting."

"Why was the location switched to Berlin without consulting me?" Bauer said. His blood pressure elevated and throbbed in his ears. "I demand to know what you are up to."

"Herr Bauer, no need to worry, my friend. For now, The Fifteen thought it best to be prudent in our actions and associations. The recent incidents at BioGenics makes you…" he paused to choose his words carefully, "…a liability."

Bauer could hardly contain his rage. "*I* am The Fifteen."

"Perhaps, for now, we should change the name to The Fourteen," Wu's cackle burned Bauer's eardrums.

He swore at Wu in German and then said, "One of my engineers called. He thinks the data on the BioGenics's computer may have been compromised."

There was a long pause.

"I know nothing about that," Wu said.

The connection went dead.

* * *

Before they knocked, Nick and Maggie heard laughing from Emy's room. They pushed the door open, and Emy's girls sat beside her on the bed. All three looked bright with joy, and Hanna wiped orange Jell-O off her face.

"We're sorry to interrupt. Could we come in?" Nick asked.

"Oh, please do," Emy said. "You must rescue me from a food fight."

Nick and Maggie walked in and hugged the girls. They had grown close to them in the last two weeks—and found them such a delight. Hanna had asked Maggie about her missionary work as part of her exploration of faith, and with Emy's approval, Maggie had given her a Bible.

Nick hugged Ceci, then looked at her scalp and cheek where he'd removed the stitches a week ago. He smiled at her and nodded. "Keep using vitamin E oil on the scars. They will continue to fade."

Ceci hugged him tightly. "Thank you, Dr. Hart…for everything."

"You're welcome, Ceci. I'm glad you are all okay," he said and patted her affectionately on the head. Then he turned to Emy. "And how are you feeling today?"

"Not bad. Just ready to get rid of my leash here," she held up the line for the chest tube.

"All the systems working good?"

"Yes, *doctor*, I'm eating, peeing, and pooping," she said, feigning a salute and grinning.

The girls blushed at their mother's graphic description.

"Ladies, why don't you step out while I remove your mother's chest tube," Nick said.

"We're headed home anyway, Mom. We'll see you later," Hanna said. They kissed their mother on the cheek and excused themselves.

Emy pointed to some supplies on the shelf. "I asked the nurse to get your setup ready," she said and turned the volume down on the TV.

"You *are* eager to get that out," Nick said and picked up the medical pack.

"Oh, I almost forgot. I keep meaning to ask you what suture you used to repair my heart," Emy said.

"Hmm…I don't exactly remember. I think some cheap absorbable kind," he said over his shoulder as he slipped on a pair of gloves. "I hope they hold." He then glanced back over at her and smiled.

"Thanks a lot!" Emy teased back. "It's only a matter of time until they dissolve and give way."

"No, really, I used Prolene…and some pledgets. I felt good about the repair, good enough for a dumb bone doc." He laughed and turned back to the supplies. But the image of the hole he sutured in Emy's heart haunted him. He could see it clear as day when he closed his eyes. It was an excellent repair, but for some reason, he kept imagining it bursting open. If that happened, Emy would die immediately. He shrugged; it was probably his own anxiety, and he realized that he did not miss the constant second-guessing that most surgeons battled. *The art of medicine is not perfect.*

Nick gathered the supplies and placed them on the table next to Emy.

"I'm going to lay you down," Nick said and pushed the power button on the bed. "You may remember from your training that this shouldn't hurt, it's just uncomfortable."

"Yes, says the doctor yanking on the tube," Emy said and laughed.

Maggie walked to the opposite side of the bed and held Emy's hand.

Nick used Betadine and cleaned the area around the tube that stuck out from between her ribs. *The practice of medicine takes practice.* When he was a medical student, a resident had helped him remove his first chest tube. "Pull it forcefully and swiftly. If you don't hit the wall next to the bed with a splash of blood, you didn't do it right," the resident had joked. Nick had followed the resident's instructions: he carefully removed the stitch that anchored the tube in place and then yanked it hard and fast. When the patient cried out in pain, both he and the resident discovered that two stitches had been placed. The tube had come out with a chunk of skin attached to the missed suture. After that, Nick always double-checked for more than one stitch.

Since he had secured the chest tube in place, he was confident he'd placed two stitches. But out of habit, he double-checked for a third, anyway.

He cut both. "Take a deep breath in and hold it," Nick instructed, then pulled hard. The tube came out with ease. He used the sutures still in the skin to quickly tie and pull the wound closed and placed a sterile dressing over the top.

"Okay, you can breathe again." He squeezed Emy's arm. "How was that?"

She tilted her head back and forth. "Painless...for you, I think."

"We can let you go home tomorrow after a chest x-ray to make sure that lung is still inflated."

Emy nodded as he raised the head of her bed.

"You feel strong enough to go to Izzi's funeral with us?" Maggie asked.

A cloud of sadness covered Emy's face, and tears filled her eyes. "Poor Izzi," she said. "Every time I think of her, I'm so overcome with grief…and gratitude…I…" She looked at Maggie. "Yes, absolutely, if you don't mind taking me. I don't want to miss it."

Maggie hugged Emy's neck.

"I am so glad you and the girls are here. I don't know what I would do without you all," Emy said through her tears.

"What about the girls' father?" Nick asked.

Emy shook her head. "Keith has visited a few times…like a dog with his tail between his legs. The girls urge me to give him another chance. I don't know yet."

"We will pray for you, Emy," Maggie said.

Emy reached for Maggie's cheek. "I'm afraid my words fail me. I am sorry…I hope you will forgive me. I feel like I've forsaken you."

Maggie smiled and held her hand. "But I know that God has not. For now, He is where I'm putting my trust."

"How are you feeling?" Emy asked.

"I think some rest in my own bed will do me good."

"How about you, Emy?" Nick asked after putting away the supplies. "What are you going to do?"

Deep sorrow and tears filled her eyes.

When she said nothing, Nick probed. "What is it, Emy?"

"I haven't said anything until now, as I am still unsure," she paused. "The night we broke into BioGenics, I could only unlock the main computer." She looked up at Nick. "I was unable to crash it. I didn't have time. All the data was vulnerable."

Nick felt weak in his knees. *Oh, my God. What if all this was for nothing?*

"The computer is completely locked down now," Emy said. "The government demanded that nothing else be done at this point until they finish their investigation. I talked with Bruno, the head of my security."

She looked away.

"Unfortunately, he could not tell me if the information on the computer was compromised." She shook her head. "We may never know."

Nick started to speak when a news alert flashed on the TV with a tag line that read "BioGenics." He reached over, turned up the volume, and looked at Emy.

She focused her attention on the screen. "They say the president of Poland is about to speak. I will try to translate for you."

A nice-looking, middle-aged man in a dark suit stepped to the podium.

"My fellow Poles," Emy translated, "the people of Poland are resilient; we understand that all too well. We are leaders in the fields of science, medicine, and technology. We should be proud of the advancements and world-renowned discoveries by our people. No one in the world has experienced the destruction and persecution that we have endured. Nor have they witnessed such rebirth and redemption."

Emy took a sip of water and tried to keep up as the man paused and stared into the camera.

"But it is with great sadness that I inform you of a great evil from the past that has tried to seep into our country once again. BioGenics, a company held in high regard, has betrayed our trust."

Nick looked at Emy, who was still able to continue even as her face contorted in pain.

"Rumors of unauthorized abortions, human experimentations, and modern-day eugenics have been relayed to my office." He shook his head. "Images and events we will never forget. Nor will we allow…" he raised his voice. "We will not let this these abominations happen again."

The president paused for applause.

"BioGenics will continue to work for the good of our country and the benefit of society in battling some of the most devastating diseases that affect women and children. Our government has taken control over BioGenics and has placed a highly qualified scientist at the helm. We will continue our work for the good of humanity. But I also sound the alarm for global oversight of genetic manipulation. In one of our own towns, Miejsce Odrzańskie, not a single male has been born in almost a decade. This manipulation of God's work must stop. I will present my resolution to the United Nations at the next meeting."

Nick examined Emy's face; it was sad, but not shocked. She listened for a moment more without translating and then turned down the volume. "He is now talking about immigration." She looked at Maggie and then to Nick. "The officials had told me about this. I agreed to fully cooperate. I'm acquainted with the doctor they put in charge. She is a good person." Emy nodded. "I promised to work closely with her."

"Is it true—the story of the town in Poland that is only birthing baby girls?" Maggie asked.

"Yes, but unrelated. BioGenics had nothing to do with that. It is probably a coincidence."

"Emy, what is your greatest fear in all this?" Nick asked.

"Once we started using supercomputers and artificial intelligence to analyze DNA sequencing, it gave us many great advances, but it also gave me great anxiety. As the AI capabilities improve, it allows the computer to make changes to the DNA as *it* sees fit."

"Yeah, combine artificial intelligence and gene therapy… what could go wrong?" Nick scoffed.

"Exactly," Emy said. She reached for a manila envelope on her over-bed table. It was marked, *Immanuel*.

"I've told you most of my story, but I want to share this with you and Maggie, so you understand the entire picture," she said, handing it to Nick.

Nick opened it and took three letters from inside. He sat and read the translated notes sequentially, first from her adopted father, birth mother, then her grandmother. After finishing each letter, he handed them to Maggie.

He waited until she finished the last one.

Emy looked from Maggie to Nick. "And now you know who I really am," her voice cracked.

They sat in silence, processing the information.

Finally, Maggie reached for her hand. "It seems like you have some searching to do."

"Yes. Perhaps you will pray for me." Tears dripped onto her chest.

"Emy, don't let this define you," Maggie said. "Let the One who created you do that. You are a child of God."

* * *

Four days later, Nick and Maggie took a taxi to the airport. Maggie looked out the window at the sifting snow falling on a beautiful winter day. She decided she'd miss the gracious Polish people. She'd learned so much about strength in the face of adversity.

As the landscape passed by, her heart filled with a flurry of longing, homesickness, and sorrow. Izzi's funeral had been small and somber—only her father attended, along with a handful of girlfriends. Her mother had wholly disowned Izzi for her lifestyle.

Maggie glanced at Nick and he smiled back.

"You okay? What are you thinking?" he asked.

"I don't know." Maggie sighed deeply. "I think a better world is one in which people recognize that everyone possesses a priceless value." She paused to gather her thoughts. "I worry that gene manipulation could lead to discrimination toward those who lack certain qualities, and privilege to people with enhanced traits valued by society. Changing the basic DNA code risks losing what makes us specifically human—compassion, and the honoring of the humanity of our fellow human beings—compelling us when we see someone hungry, sick, or oppressed."

Nick squeezed her arm.

Maggie shook her head and sighed. "It's hard to go home with all our questions unanswered. For now, I'm thankful I didn't undergo the gene therapy."

Nick looked out the window. She could sense his discouragement.

She found his hand and interlaced her fingers with his. "That doesn't mean we don't keep contending for my health and the baby's…and believing."

"And if God doesn't give us a miracle?" Nick asked.

Maggie watched the Polish countryside flash by, then turned back to Nick. "Then we keep on fighting and believing…and we do it together."

TABERNACLE
SIX MONTHS LATER

Emy contemplated the passing trees, awash in autumnal brilliance, from the back seat of the taxi. It was her first time in Budapest. Once inside the city, the driver routed them along the River Danube and pointed out the ornate Hungarian Parliament Building across the waterway. With multiple spires and a red dome, it was impossible to miss.

She smiled at Daniel, the tour guide from her visit to Auschwitz last year, who sat next to her in the back seat. He had been kind enough to accompany her and help translate from Hungarian to Polish.

"Thank you for coming with me, Daniel," Emy said.

"My pleasure, Dr. Christianson. Besides, this is an outstanding senior project," he said. "I should be thanking you."

Her heart beat with excitement—not for the visit to Hungary, but for who she came to meet.

Since the government takeover of BioGenics six months earlier, her life had become topsy-turvy. Between testifying before the parliament, continued cooperation with the police, and working hand-in-hand with the new medical director of BioGenics, she had plenty on her plate.

As suspected, there was no trace of the Chinese woman, and China had stopped cooperating. Emy suspected that the woman had accessed her computer when Nick was saving her life in the operating room. How much information she'd downloaded may never be known. Emy decided if China swept all gold medals at the 2036 Olympics, she'd have the answer—they'd used her expertise to enhance their future athletes.

Polish intelligence officers continued to pursue the issue, but the secretive Sleeping Giant would never acknowledge stealing trade secrets or admit to technology espionage. Yes, the authorities believed, even though the Chinese woman worked for Bauer, she was, in fact, a double agent.

Brazilian authorities located Bauer; he'd hung himself in a rundown apartment. Kenny had fled. Emy wasn't sure why the news of Bauer's death was bittersweet to her; perhaps because he was the end of her family line, corrupt as he was. Interestingly enough, the Israelis remained silent on the issue.

Emy tongued the back of her incisors and the closed gap between her front teeth. She'd given herself this gift, one of the few selfish things she'd done in a while. She hated the constant reminder of that part of her past and wanted to end that chapter. Although her life and work were busy, she saw the girls more than ever before.

When Daniel called out of the blue a few weeks ago, she was shocked.

He practically screamed with excitement, "I finally found her, Dr. Christianson," he'd said. "I found Eva Frankel, your grandmother's sister. She is alive and lives in Budapest."

Emy turned her attention to Daniel. He looked back at her and smiled.

"How are you doing?" he asked.

Emy nodded, then said, "How does she seem?"

"Eva? Old…but she is excited to meet you."

"She's ninety-two?" Emy asked. "Does she have any children?"

"Eva and your grandmother were born in 1927. She told me she could never have children of her own…" he paused, "as a result of what they did to her in Auschwitz."

Emy looked out her window as the buildings flashed by. She had so many questions for her great aunt. She didn't know where to start.

She turned back to Daniel. "Does she speak English?"

"Strictly a few words. A little more German—mostly Hungarian. Her accent is quite strong. I hope I can interpret well for you both."

"How do you say great aunt in Hungarian, again?"

"*Nagynénje*. But I'm sure you could call her auntie, *Nénike*. Nee-nee-ka," Daniel said phonetically.

"Was it okay with her that we are visiting on Rosh Hashanah?"

"She was most excited about that," Daniel said and smiled as the taxi pulled to the curb at an old apartment building.

Emy paid the driver, and they exited, walked up the short set of steps, and rang the doorbell. Emy didn't know what to expect, but a short, frail woman answered. She looked nothing like the picture Emy had of her grandmother, Yuri. A walker supported the stooped woman at the door. Her short gray hair had replaced the blond locks. Her skin was wrinkled and freckled with age spots, but the one thing that Emy recognized immediately was her eyes—the right, an icy blue, and the left, a hazel brown.

Her great aunt must have noticed the same in Emy and gasped with such delight, she almost fell backward. Then, catching her balance on the walker, she alternated between fanning her face, speaking strings of excited Hungarian, and crying tears of joy.

Daniel turned to Emy, not able to keep up with Eva's excitement, and simply said, "She is glad to see you."

Eva let go of the walker and threw herself into Emy's arms, weeping, hugging, and reaching up to stroke her face. Finally, she took a small step back but kept hold of Emy's arms. She spoke in quick Hungarian that Daniel translated: "I ask God why He has allowed me to live so long when all my other family is gone. Today, I understand the reason. It's you! I am so thankful." Eva hugged her around the waist again, then invited them into the apartment.

They entered a sitting room, and Eva sat next to Emy on a love seat and held her hands.

Then, as though she'd forgotten her manners, she excused herself and grabbed a plate of apple slices and honey off the table and offered them to Daniel and Emy. "Please, you must dip the apple in the honey and eat it for a sweet new year." She demonstrated for them. "I think this will be the best year yet."

"*Nénike,* I did not grow up Jewish," Emy said timidly.

Her great aunt smiled at her and reached out for her hands again. She surprised Emy when she said in broken English, "You *are* a Jew."

Eva looked at Daniel to translate: "Today, God is inscribing each person's fate for the coming year into the Book of Life. We will spend the week in prayer and repentance of our sins. Next week on Yom Kippur, He seals the book closed." She slapped her hands together. "I am glad you are here, so you will see what it means to be Jewish."

Emy smiled. Her heart was fuller than she could remember. "Thank you, *Nénike.*"

Tears flowed down Eva's face. "It is like I sit again with my dear sister, Yuri." She reached out to touch Emy's cheek. "My dear child, you are the spitting image of her. We used to sit on this very couch and laugh together."

"This is your childhood home?" Emy asked through Daniel.

"Yes, I returned here five years after the war. They took your mother, Bella, away after your grandmother died…sweet little Bella." Sorrow darkened her face. "I never heard what happened to her. But now I know she bore a beautiful daughter." Her smile returned.

Eva reached to the coffee table in front of them and pulled a shoebox onto her lap. "We have so much to talk about, but I have some gifts for you." She opened the lid. "I hope you stay for a week to look through many pictures," she said, revealing the contents of the box. "I have more, and there is so much I want you to know about your family. But first, I want you to have this. On this blessed day of Rosh Hashanah, the Jewish new year, my father, your great grandfather, would wear this *tallit.*"

Daniel stopped her for help with the word. "Prayer shawl," he told Emy and pointed to the striped fringed fabric.

"He would sound the *shofar* and allow me and Yuri to try to blow it." Eva laughed through tears.

She paused to collect her words.

"Father was wearing this when the SS came." She pointed out a bloodstain on one end of the shawl and looked Emy in the eyes to see if she understood.

"*Nénike*, I don't know how you all endured what you went through."

Eva reached for her hand again. "You must remember, after the war, we were mostly concerned about survival and reuniting with what family we had left…we no longer wanted to be victims."

"And you?" Emy asked through Daniel.

"I decided to prove them all wrong…that my life had value."

* * *

Six months had never flown by so fast for Nick. He didn't say that to Maggie, especially the last few weeks when she reached the stage where she could hardly get off the couch without help. Thank God, it was the pregnancy and not the Huntington's. Perhaps all the growth hormones that flowed through her system had kept her healthy, but it surprised all her doctors. Still, Nick worried that the disease had advanced every time Maggie didn't feel well or even got a leg cramp. He gave thanks, it hadn't progressed.

"Hold my hand!" Maggie screamed. "Don't touch me!" she said in the next breath. She grunted loudly and then panted.

"That was a good one, Maggie," Dr. McCoy said as he stood between her legs that rested in stirrups.

Maggie nodded. Sweat dripped down her face and neck, and Nick thought twice before trying to wipe at it with the cold washcloth. McCoy attended, and the nurses buzzed with activity, but this was something Maggie had to do on her own. She was in the zone, and her attention laser-focused. Maggie was brave, but if this was every woman's experience in labor, Nick had a new respect for the stronger sex.

McCoy reached into her birth canal and hooked the amniotic sac. A gush of fluid flowed out and splashed on the floor. He looked up at the monitor that loudly signaled both the baby and Maggie's heart rate.

"You're doing great," the doctor said calmly.

Nick wished the same was true for him. He helplessly watched her howl in pain. He'd never been so nervous in his life, knowing full well all the perils of delivery.

"Awwww," Maggie cried. "Here comes another one." Her abdomen contracted into a rock-hard ball.

"Okay, Maggie, I'm going to ask you to push with the next one."

She nodded and breathed with short gasps.

The next contraction came almost instantaneously.

"Bear down, Maggie, like we practiced."

Maggie took in a deep breath and pushed down hard; her face turned bright red.

McCoy and the nurses encouraged her. "You're a champ, Maggie, you're doing great." Then McCoy reached for supplies off the Mayo stand and said, "Try not to push for a moment."

Nick looked down between her legs and saw the baby's head protruding from the birth canal. The doctor quickly suctioned the baby's mouth and nose.

The contraction monitor crescendoed in a high-pitched squawk.

"I gotta push…" Maggie bore down.

In an instant, McCoy caught the baby in his hands and lifted it onto Maggie's chest.

The room erupted in cheers and activity as the nurse cleaned the baby's face, and McCoy clamped the cord.

He handed Nick a pair of Metz scissors. "Nick, you want to do the honors?"

Nick cut between the clamps.

McCoy held out a crying little human to him.

"Dr. Hart, would you like to hold your son?"

Nick reached out and tucked the tiny pink body close to his chest. It was as if space and time came together in an instant with the child—hopes, dreams, love…it all came into sharp focus.

Baby Hart was perfect—the dwelling place of God.

CALL TO ACTION

I can't tell you how much it means to me to hear from my readers. The best way to do this is if you would sign up on my website: AuthorTimothyBrowne.com

(I promise not to bombard you with tons of newsletters or communications!) For a thank you, I would like to give you a free eBook copy of Maya Hope. Just click the button that says, START MAYA HOPE NOW to get your free book and to sign up. I look forward in connecting with you!

Also, I hope you enjoyed reading The Gene, Book 4 in the Dr. Nicklaus Hart medical thriller series. I would appreciate you leaving a review with Amazon, BookBub and Goodreads (You can simply copy and paste into each one).

These reviews are so very important to my career as a full-time writer. Your honest reviews truly make a difference and so easy to do. Just go to the respective website:

- Amazon
- Barnes & Noble
- Goodreads
- BookBub

Thank you!

THE DR. NICKLAUS HART SERIES

MAYA HOPE

A doctor stumbling through life. A North Korean bio-terrorist plot. The two collide in an unforgettable tale.

Dr. Nicklaus Hart, a gifted trauma surgeon, searches for meaning in his life. His self-reliant spirit is broken with the death of his missionary best friend, found sacrificed at the base of a Maya Temple. Going to Guatemala to fill the shoes of his friend at the mission hospital, he discovers God's redemption and peace in the smiles of the children he cares for. But his own life is in danger as he and his team stumble onto a deadly North Korean plot.

THE TREE OF LIFE

A massive earthquake hits Eastern Turkey, the ancient area of Mesopotamia, unveiling hidden secrets and opening an epic battle between good and evil.

Dr. Nicklaus Hart has lost his moral compass. As an orthopedic surgeon in a busy trauma practice, the cares of the world overshadow what Nick knows is true about himself. With his life unraveling, he falls into his old patterns of stress relief but knows they are a poisonous cure. Nick is shaken from his moral slumber when a massive earthquake strikes Eastern Turkey, and he makes the snap decision to respond. Thrown into the chaos and devastation, Nick must face his internal struggle head-on.

THE RUSTED SCALPEL

A pharmaceutical company promises you hope and happiness in a pill. Would you take it if it cost your relationship with God?

Dr. Nicklaus Hart returns from responding to a massive earthquake that rocked the Middle East, allowing an ISIS terror cell to enter the ancient area of Mesopotamia. Captured, tortured and blinded by the hands of the radical terrorists, Nick arrives home a broken man. He has lost everything he holds dear—his sight, independence, profession and most of all, hope. But at the bottom of the pit, God sends him a lifeline and restores his physical and spiritual vision.

THE GENE

Following their marriage, Dr. Nicklaus Hart and Maggie Russell enjoy the splendor and passion of a honeymoon in Hawaii. They learn that their union has brought new life, but the overflowing joy of Maggie's pregnancy and their romantic getaway is interrupted by the shocking news of a genetic disorder discovered in Maggie's family lineage—that both Maggie and the baby carry the mutated gene for the horrific Huntington's disease.

Nick and Maggie travel to Poland, where the top geneticist, Emmanuelle Christianson, has founded and operates BioGenics whose mission statement is: Advancing the Human Genome. Their journey reveals more than the fight for knowledge, it uncovers a simmering evil left over from World War II. One that puts their lives in danger.

AUTHOR'S NOTE

After finishing, *The Gene*, the fourth book in the Dr. Nicklaus Hart Series, I have been able to look back at this body of work. The heart of my prose remains the same: to entertain and educate—fueled with imagination, inspired by history, and grounded in truth. I explored the mystery of North Korea and the threat of bioterrorism in *Maya Hope*, the complexities of the middle East and the history of Mesopotamia in *The Tree of Life*, the controversies of Big Pharma and our health in *The Rusted Scalpel*, and now examine the history of eugenics and the pitfalls of gene-therapy in *The Gene*.

Writing *The Gene* has taken significant research: exploration of Poland, investigation of the Nazi doctors and their horrendous medical experiments, the history of eugenics around the world, and of course, the science of genetics. The work has been satisfying, edifying, and many times, heartbreaking.

And that brings me to a warning: The theme of *The Gene* is harsh, especially when examining lessons from the past. This book details fictionalized, but historically accurate accounts of Auschwitz and other horrors of World War II. The book also contains images of graphic violence and medical scenes that some of my sensitive readers may find disturbing. However, I hope that through the fictional story the reader will gain understanding and wisdom, as Solomon in his Proverbs encourages us all to fight for.

Gene-therapy, gene-manipulation, is no longer science-fiction. It is a reality of today and we must, as a society, have educated and honest deliberations about the technology and the ramifications—including the scientific and spiritual implications.

To me, I wrestle with the question, "If I had a child with one of these awful genetic diseases, such as cystic fibrosis or Huntington's disease, would I allow manipulation of my child's DNA?" The answer for me is a resounding "YES" (especially if the technology continues to advance and the risks are lowered.) What parent wouldn't fight for their child to prevent them from succumbing to a horrific existence? But the technology can and will move past this into human enhancement. This is the slippery slope into eugenics. Some important questions remain: Who chooses the human traits that are desirable? Who enforces the policies?

And to make matters worse, we have already seen parents so motivated to see their children succeed they will pay millions of dollars to fudge college enrollment and testing. Then, layer in the money and greed of the "gene industry" and we are setting ourselves up to produce two classes of humans, those who can afford enhancement and those who cannot.

As humans, we have a poor track record in focusing on the here-and-now problem and not foreseeing future issues. Knowing what we know now, would we all be so excited over plastic bags and bottles that now are choking our oceans? Another failure comes to mind here in Montana. Invasive fish had overrun a beautiful mountain lake. A decision was made that seemed legitimate; poison the lake—kill all the fish—and then simply repopulate the lake with beautiful rainbow trout.

Great idea, right? Except, all the invasive fish, sensing the poison, simply swam upstream to avoid it. When the poison dissipated, they came back to the lake and took it over in an even greater measure.

The people who I discuss gene-therapy with, including my Beta readers, have all thanked me for opening their eyes to the realities, possibilities, and pitfalls of gene-therapy. They tell me they've had rousing dinner table debates with their families. So, this is my hope: Read *The Gene*, share it with your family and friends, and then talk about the issues. This is how we as a society will come to wisdom and understanding.

In writing *The Gene*, I consciously battled to keep an open mind. As a scientist, I am fascinated at the possibilities, as a physician I want to first do no harm. I found myself in head-spinning conflict. As an orthopaedic surgeon, I treat broken bones or congenital abnormalities such as clubfeet, but do I deny treatment for someone suffering with a genetic mutation? The conflict also involves spiritual aspects: Do we let the patient with diabetes go untreated because that is some-how God's design for that person? How does that differ for someone with a genetic disease? Do we not continue to push the technology forward? It was, after all, work in genetics that gave us insulin by introducing pieces of DNA into bacteria that produce the medicine.

We cannot paint gene-therapy with broad strokes and deem it all good or all evil. But we must come to the discussion table armed with knowledge. All the while, keeping in mind, we must learn the lessons from the past! **We must demand a call for global oversight of gene-therapy.**

Lastly, thank you for reading *The Gene*. I'm afraid I leave you with a difficult riddle.

Lord, help us!

May your eyes be open to the truth… *Timothy*

Please visit www.AuthorTimothyBrowne.com

and sign up to receive updates
and information on upcoming books by Tim.

RESOURCES

Even though The Gene is a fictional story, I could not write about eugenics and World War II without using true stories from the brave survivors of Auschwitz and the appalling speeches and history of the villains of that time. We cannot forget. We must not forget. I am thankful to the authors and researchers who came before me and indirectly contributed to this work of fiction.

Specifically:

Robert Jay Lifton: *The Nazi Doctors*,
    Basic Books 2017

Web Archive:
https://web.archive.org/web/20120212053624/http:/
www.holocaust-history.org/himmler-poznan/speech-
text.shtml

US Holocaust Memorial Museum:
http://www.holocaust-history.org/himmler-poznan/
speech-text.shtml

Vivien Spitz: *Doctors from Hell*, First Sentient
Publication 2005

Peter Sichrovsky: *Born Guilty*, Basic Book 1988

Francis S. Collins: *The Language of God*,
    Simon & Schuster 2006

Writings of Father Richard Rohr

Internationaler Militärgerichtshof Nürnberg
(IMT) (1989). Der Nürnberger Prozess gegen
die Hauptkriegsverbrecher (in German). Band
29: Urkunden und anderes Beweismaterial.
Nachdruck München: Delphin Verlag.

The International Huntington Association:
    https://huntington-disease.org

Huntington's Disease Society of America:
    https://hdsa.org